MW01254920

SHADOW AND THORN

KENLEY DAVIDSON

PAGE NINE PRESS

Published by: Page Nine Press
Editing by: Janie Dullard at Lector's Books
Cover Design, Layout, & Formatting by: Page Nine Media

http://KenleyDavidson.com

For Janie. May you someday be willing to forgive my terrible spelling.

"You are very ungrateful," said the Beast in a terrible voice. "I have saved your life by receiving you into my castle, and, in return, you steal my roses, which I value beyond any thing in the universe, but you shall die for it."

"LA BELLE ET LA BÊTE"

Jeanne-Marie Leprince de Beaumont, ***Le Magasin des enfants***

◦∾◦

PROLOGUE

*D*arkness was her world. Darkness and silence.

There was nothing and no one to break the silence, for she was alone, and when she was alone, she had neither ears nor voice.

So deep was the darkness, that she had begun to wonder if there had ever been anything else.

From time to time a whisper would find her from outside her formless cocoon, but the whispers could neither break her nor free her, so she slipped further and further into the void, further and further from memory and thought and caring.

At last, she slept, and she forgot that sleep was another word for danger. Even if she had remembered, the memory would have done her no good, for she fell ever deeper into oblivion—so deep that, had she been alive, she might have been said to be dying.

It was the light that woke her. Called to her.

Such a strange, gentle light. Soft, and barely even aware of itself.

She rose through the darkness, barely able even to perceive the light, or to remember why it mattered, but it was important. Before she was even fully awake, it caught her in a snare of fascination and hunger and she could not look away.

It was beautiful. Quick and lithe, graceful and fanciful, a delicate tracery of lavender on the unseen winds of thought. She remembered this. Or something very like it.

She stirred. Or tried. But everything was heavy and slow, and even her thoughts did not obey her as they should. Had she fallen so far?

An irritation began to trouble her, the closer she came to consciousness. Something was not as it should be. She cast about, looking for her bounds, testing the limits of her awareness, and found a crack. A tiny shard of wrongness.

Increasingly roused, she arrowed towards it, faltering now and again, but determined. She had a purpose, and she must not fail. When she found the shard, she circled, pressed and peered into the dark, until the light brightened, and she remembered.

She remembered what the light was for! What *she* was for!

Light was life, and life was safety. Light was precious, and she must have it for her own.

Reaching out with all the awakening tendrils of her being, she seized it, wrapped those delicate strands of lavender in the unbreakable bounds of herself and exulted, for now she would live.

She almost did not hear the screams, for she was waking faster now, and the wrongness needed to be dealt with. Something had pierced her defenses and it could not be allowed to stay.

Her entire being trembled. The very air bowed to her summons, and with a surge of power and rage, the wrongness was purged, her boundaries were restored, and all could again be at peace.

Except she could still hear the screaming.

She searched, but the wrongness was gone. Her awareness was secure.

She turned inward, and found something she had not anticipated.

The delicate motes of lavender, the lovely and mesmerizing tracery of light was part of her now. And so were the screams.

CHAPTER 1

"*C*an't you make him shut up?"

Alexei Nar Trevelyan cast a startled glance at the man who had spoken and felt his lip begin to curl.

It wasn't that he disagreed with the sentiment. He'd been considering the same question for the past five days, ever since their party of three left Evenleigh by way of the King's Road to the north.

But it was the first time his bitter, angry cousin had spoken since the start of their journey and Alexei had no intention of encouraging him. Not to mention he'd be damned before he let Porfiry know that they agreed about something.

Even if that something happened to be Malichai Cherting, the third member of their party, who was currently warbling his way through yet another pathetic ballad of tragic heroism in a resonant baritone that could probably be heard from one side of Andar to the other. If it was anything like the last forty-seven of its kind, the song probably featured twenty-four epic verses and a tear-jerking refrain.

Alexei looked back over his shoulder and marveled once more at the sight of King Hollin's chosen emissary. Malichai had been solemnly entrusted with the safety of the king's Erathi guests and with protecting Andari interests once their party crossed the border. Now flushed and exuberant, the leather-clad warrior rode unheeding down the center of the road, head thrown back and arms flung wide as he bellowed the final words of the fourth verse. At least Alexei thought it was the fourth. He could have missed one or two while envisioning his next conversation with the Andari king, who had never once mentioned that his chosen ambassador was of a musical inclination.

"Five days!" Porfiry hissed. "If he keeps this up, I'll have no choice but to throw myself off this horse and pray that it kills me!"

Alexei'd refused to allow his face to show his feelings. Instead, he reined his mount sharply and dropped back to ride next to the Andari, who paused his song and smiled—the peaceful smile of a satisfied man with nothing more to want in life.

Malichai Cherting was very possibly the biggest man Alexei had ever met. He was at least a head taller than Alexei himself, and twice as wide. His hair and beard were both long and brown, with only a few strands of gray, though Alexei would have sworn the other man was a good bit older than he. One would need far more than forty-two years to accumulate such a vast knowledge of the worst romantic ballads known to the world.

"I would take it as a personal favor if you would sing the rest of this song as loudly as possible," Alexei said, with a courteous nod. "Full court version, if you know it."

"It would be my pleasure," Malichai answered, his expression deeply serious, almost reverent. "It's a great pity you cannot experience the intended harmonies. The last seventeen verses represent some of the most beautiful and moving work from the early foundations of Andari epic poetry."

"I look forward to hearing it."

Alexei admitted to himself that those who knew him best—which was not to say well—might have been surprised to discover how petty he could be. The thought did not disturb him as much as it probably should have. He had earned his revenge, petty and otherwise.

"Perhaps after the final verse we might find a place to camp?" he continued. Petty he might be, but not dangerously insane. Seventeen more verses was as far as he was prepared to go for retribution's sake.

Malichai nodded and burst into song once more, while patting the neck of his remarkably impassive mount with spiked leather gauntlets. The enormous piebald mare, who stood several hands taller than Alexei's own horse and had hooves the size of Alexei's head, seemed well used to her master's eccentricities. Or perhaps she approved, considering that she wore her mane in braids and answered to the name of Loraleen.

With the tiniest of smiles, Alexei urged his horse into a trot and returned to the side of his cousin, who shot him a murderous glare from under lowered eyelids before returning to the stoic silence that had marked their journey to that point.

A pale, hunched man who appeared some ten years Alexei's senior, Porfiry was actually three months younger. He was several inches shorter and a great deal lighter, but, despite their differences, despite the bitter set to Porfiry's pale, thin lips, the two of them had once known each other well. Other than Alexei's brother Andrei, they were likely the last two left of a once large, tight-knit family.

Though Alexei had admitted long ago that he had probably not known Porfiry as well as he once thought. His cousin's bony wrists were tied together in front of him and lashed to the saddle for a reason. For so many reasons.

There were few left now in the world who remembered Erath as it had been before the Caelani invasion. So few who could share Alexei's memories, his anger, or his grief, thanks to the actions of the wretched excuse for

7

a man riding next to him—a traitor being forcibly returned to his home-land to begin making restitution for his unspeakable crimes. If Porfiry felt any anger or grief, it would be for himself rather than the people he had betrayed so entirely that Alexei was the only one left to bring him to justice.

The queen should have been the one to mete out punishment and restore her people, but the queen was dead. Had been dead for twenty-six years. Her brother and heir, a lazy, congenial man of great talent and little application, had perished, childless, some twenty years past as a slave in Caelan. Which left Alexei—eldest offspring of the fourteenth generation of the House of Nar—to take up the Stone Scepter and protect what remained of his kingdom.

Not that he would ever be fool enough to let anyone call him a king. There was no longer an Erath to be king of. But, for a brief moment, Alexei considered accepting the responsibility of the position, if only for the purpose of declaring war on Andar.

Because Malichai had only just started in on the sixth verse. If there were truly fifteen more remaining, Alexei would have no choice but to initiate hostilities with King Hollin over the blatant insult to their diplo-matic relations represented by his emissary's musical proclivities.

Looking for a distraction, Alexei patted the front of his shirt, checking to see if his talisman was still secure around his neck. Reassured by its rough edges, he held out a hand in front of him and focused. He had not called on his gift since he last left Andar, and wasn't sure it would respond yet. They might not be close enough to the border.

"Suffering from the pangs of self-doubt, cousin?" Porfiry muttered snidely, eyeing him sidelong with an expression of satisfaction. "Won-dering if everyone will still stand in awe of your mighty works?"

"I only hope to find someone still standing," was his measured reply. "I don't care if they remember my works or not. My gift means nothing to me if our people have been destroyed."

But that was not as true as it should have been. He did care about his magic. He cared very much indeed.

It had been so many years since he'd truly used it. Alexei had spent more than half his life in Andar, where magic simply did not exist. During his visit to Caelan, the vast eastern empire where magic was both acknowledged and reviled, he had been able to feel his gift once more, and to use it in small ways, but it was not the same. He, like all Erathi, had always been tied to his land. The wonders his people had wrought there would have staggered the imagination of outsiders had they been able to perceive them, but once away from the blood and bones of their home, even the strongest Erathi could do little more than parlor tricks in comparison.

"Can you feel it?" he asked suddenly, unable to help himself. "Does it still sing to you?"

Porfiry did not answer. He seemed to curl back in on himself, and resumed the stubborn silence he had clung to for the last five days. It was just as well. Even if Porfiry were the last Erathi left alive, Alexei could never bring himself to share his memories, or his insecurities, with the man who had betrayed everything he ever knew.

And it could be that Porfiry simply didn't have any magic to feel. Alexei had seen little of Porfiry since they were boys together, so he had no way to estimate his skills. He knew the younger man to be marginally competent with small blades, considering that Porfiry had been responsible for the injuries that left Alexei's face permanently scarred. But magically? When they were young, Porfiry had been shunned by some of their people for his lack of power. If he had any gift at all, he had never shared it openly, and it was understood that his magic was too weak to be of use, even amongst a creative and peaceful people.

But now that he was an adult, who knew what Porfiry's gift could have matured into? There was a chance he might possess magic that could aid him in an escape attempt, and Alexei would do almost anything to prevent such an attempt from succeeding.

Almost. His Andari friends had suggested that Alexei capitalize on his knowledge of Caelani mage slavery and use silver to neutralize Porfiry's magic before it became an issue. But he'd be damned before he resorted to the ugly and inhumane practices of the empire that had destroyed his kingdom and dragged his people away in chains. He would never stoop so low—not even for the man who had cost him an eye—though he would probably sleep with his remaining eye open until they reached their destination. Especially once they reached the edge of Erath, wherever that proved to be.

The border between Erath and Andar had long been a matter of contention in the field of cartography. Most maps placed it somewhere in the middle of the Vorsh mountain range, but its precise location seemed to wander about by miles in either direction, much like most would-be visitors to the isolated kingdom of Alexei's birth. Travelers inevitably lost their way between the foothills and the peaks, and would end up back in one of the tiny mountain communities of Andar, wondering why they'd come.

At least, that had been the case when Alexei was a boy. The magical barrier that made it possible, the powerful protection once enjoyed by his peaceful people, was no more. Now, the only way to know where the border lay was the growing sense of his magic unfurling deep within him, calling him home.

Alexei's horse shifted under him without warning and stopped to stare, ears forward, into the trees off the side of the road nearest Porfiry. Alexei had deliberately given his cousin the slowest, least excitable animal he could find that was still sound and capable of travel, so it was little surprise that the aging gelding had not responded as Alexei's mount had. The pack horse tied behind Porfiry merely shook his head to dislodge flies and looked bored.

Beckoning Malichai forward, Alexei was about to ride closer to investigate when a cloaked form stepped out of the trees and approached at a sedate walk.

Loraleen, clearly far more agile than her appearance suggested, arrived only a moment later at a dead run and came to a sliding stop by Alexei's side. Malichai placed a hand on his staff and eyed the newcomer with suspicion.

"Good evening."

The low-pitched voice that issued from the lowered hood caused Alexei to look sharply at its owner. It was clearly a woman's voice, and, by its accent, an Erathi one, though they were still a full two days from the general vicinity of the border.

Alexei folded his hands over the pommel of his saddle and suppressed the urge to hide his own face. The scars that marked and twisted its right side were not going anywhere, and he may as well prepare himself for the probable reactions of strangers.

"I have been waiting for your party for several days," the woman continued, speaking Andari with ease and fluency, despite her accent. "Might I travel with you the rest of the way?"

Malichai shifted the bow on his back.

Alexei spoke up before the warrior had a chance to issue any unnecessary threats. "Will you not remove your hood, madam, that we might know whom we are addressing? I swear to you, we pose no threat unless you mean us harm."

Malichai shot him a strange look, for Alexei had spoken Erathi.

The woman reached up and lowered her hood. It was evening, and shadows had begun to fall, but Alexei could see well enough to note keen, watchful dark eyes and blonde hair mixed abundantly with silver. Though she still appeared fit and moved with the sure grace of youth, the hands that grasped her hood had begun to show the lines of time and care. And when her cloak fell back with the motion, it revealed both a simple traveling dress and a trio of sheathed daggers belted at her waist.

"The House of Elanon greets the House of Nar," she said formally in

11

Erathi, forcing Alexei to conceal considerable shock. How could she know his house?

"The House of Nar is pleased to receive Elanon," he responded as tradition demanded, though he nearly stumbled over the simple words. "What might Elanon be doing so far from her home? And why does she wait for us by the road?"

"Silvay Elanon Oridian. I wait because I have Seen that you are returning home. Because the Stone Scepter has languished long enough. And because I once swore my life to the House of Nar."

She was a seer. Alexei's heart lifted at the simple reminder of truths he had once taken for granted. She had known he would come. And she had once served his family.

"Tell me, Silvay, have we ever met before?" His heart pounded at his own question. If she said yes, how would it feel to waken a dormant connection with someone—anyone—besides his despicable cousin? To speak with another soul who remembered Athven Nar as she appeared before she fell, her turrets and towers glowing with magic instead of fire?

But a twinge of fear accompanied the excitement. What if Silvay was one of the few who could recall Alexei as he had once been, before bitterness and scars, both emotional and physical, drove him to hide from the world?

"I do not know, Son of Nar."

"Alexei Nar Trevelyan," he answered, giving his full name to another soul for the first time in twenty-six years.

"I do not remember you for certain, Trevelyan," the woman answered, her eyes seeming to shimmer for a moment. "But I was only a minor member of the household. A maid, to one of Her Majesty's ladies."

Alexei concealed the feeling of relief. "And you have been living here, in Andar?" Could it be that there were more refugees than he had imagined? In all his years of service to a wealthy Andari family, he had never met another Erathi besides his brother. He had assumed the vast majority to be dead or taken prisoner.

"At times," she acknowledged. "I have crossed the border frequently in secret. Those few of us who survived together waited many years for it to be safe to return."

"Then you know of others?" Alexei wondered at his own eagerness to know. Even if there were others, he did not yet have the ability to save them, or restore what they had lost.

"There were five who escaped with me," Silvay answered slowly, fingering the hilt of one of her daggers. "Only three who survived. The other two…"

She stopped when Malichai drew his bow from behind his back, nocked an arrow, and leveled it at her chest. Alexei realized abruptly that his bear-like companion would not have understood a word of their conversation.

"No!" he commanded in Andari, hoping to gain Malichai's attention before the warrior committed himself to an action they would all regret. "She is a friend. One of my people. She means us no harm."

"The one does not equal the other," Malichai rumbled, not lowering his bow. "I do not trust a stranger in the woods merely because she happens to speak my language."

"No, but neither are you forced to rejoice every time you meet someone who speaks your tongue because your land has been destroyed by treachery and war," Alexei answered flatly. "I don't care if you trust her. She has requested to join us for the remainder of our journey and I have decided to accept."

"As you wish, then." The bow returned to Malichai's back. "I can shoot two nearly as fast as one if need be."

"Have you a horse?" Alexei inquired of Silvay. "We can talk more as we ride."

She smiled and a dimple appeared briefly on her cheek. "I have a mule," she said.

∼

After Silvay returned leading a glossy brown mule, they resumed their journey, though Malichai chose silence over his former melodic generosity. Alexei was grateful, as it permitted him to converse with Silvay without being required to shout. They spoke of her companions in exile, and of Athven Nar as they remembered her. Porfiry gave no sign that he heard or cared, until eventually Silvay noted his silence and turned to look at him.

"Tell me why this joyous homecoming includes a prisoner. And one that I feel as though I remember."

"The Betrayer," Alexei answered simply.

"Who has he betrayed?" she asked curiously.

Alexei dragged his mount to a full stop, shocked beyond words.

"How could you not know?" he exclaimed. "He betrayed us all. He is the one who stole the Rose and destroyed the barrier. The one who allowed the Caelani army to cross the border and destroy everything in their path. That betrayer."

Silvay stopped beside him, her face pale in the gathering dark. "Then it was not simply an accident? We thought the enchantment failed. That it grew weak with age. We never dreamed..." She broke off and looked at Porfiry again. "I may be a seer, but we do not See everything. You are sure?"

"I have never been more sure." Alexei bit off the words harshly. "He boasted of it as Athven prepared for a final stand. As we looked out and saw the smoke rise across Erath and felt the pain of her destruction, he laughed."

Alexei spurred his horse forward as though he could escape the memory, and Silvay followed.

"But he is Nar," Silvay said when she caught up to him. She said it as though it were fact rather than conjecture, so perhaps she truly did remember him.

"Yes."

"You know you cannot shed Nar blood. Not once we cross."

"I didn't bring him to make him bleed," Alexei answered shortly. "He is going to tell me how to find the Rose."

Silvay jerked in surprise, her gaze darting to Porfiry and back again. "You mean… it is still there? The barrier can be restored?"

"He claims to recall where it is hidden. But he will say no more until we reach the border. After that I fully expect he will give me a cryptic clue and then refuse to say another word until we reach Athven Nar. But I will find it."

She fell silent as they rode on a few more paces, then glanced at Alexei, concern written on her features. "I cannot help but share your hopes, now that I have heard your story, but you should know what has been happening. I often seek out news from those few who dare the mountain roads, and… It has been almost thirty years, Trevelyan. And Athven has had no one to protect her. I very much doubt if she is even…"

"The truth, Silvay."

"There have been rumors," she said slowly, "circling through other lands ever since the shield fell and the towers burned. After all our years of secrets and silence, the world assumed we had something valuable to hide. And when they learned that the way was open, they came. They descended on the ruins and they trampled and they looted, and even though they found nothing, some of them stayed."

"And Athven? What have you heard of her?" Alexei could not keep the pain and the fear from his voice. He would not give up on the Rose, no matter what she said, but this mattered too much to feign indifference.

"Athven stands. At least her walls did when last I heard. But treasure hunters do not give up easily. When they found no trace of any valuable secrets elsewhere, they turned to Athven herself, looking for some trace of what they believed us to be hiding. They have not yet been able to breach the walls, but, even if by some miracle Athven herself is not gone, she cannot last forever. Not without someone to stand beside her."

Alexei glanced at her face, which had returned to serenity despite his revelation and the ill news she had to impart. He feared she had come to entirely the wrong conclusion. "I am not a king, Silvay. That is not why I've come. I would restore the Rose and its protection to whatever may be left of my people and see the Betrayer punished, but I do not aspire to the Stone Scepter. If that is why you waited, why you have chosen to join us, you will be disappointed."

She shrugged. "A seer's gift is a tricky one," she allowed. "As I have said, we do not See everything. Not even all the important things. But I have Seen you—all of you—enough times to trust that my place is here. Whatever future that may bring to pass."

"As you will." Alexei knew enough of seers to reject any notion of dissuading her. And he was not yet ready to lose the gift of her conversation. She shared his memories, even if she could not share his guilt, and he would accept her companionship for as long as she chose to offer it.

They stopped for the night in the shadow of tall narrow rocks that jutted out of the earth at an angle to create a leaning cliff face. Alexei and Malichai went about their predetermined tasks, Alexei seeing to the horses and Porfiry, while Malichai erected tents and gathered fuel. When it came time to eat, Silvay joined them and watched with some trepidation as Malichai added seasonings to the pot simmering over the flames.

"I have my own provisions, so I will not need to impose upon your hospitality," she said politely.

Malichai frowned severely at her offer. "Do you doubt my culinary abilities? Because I am a man or because I wear too much leather? Is it the boots? The beard?"

Silvay eyed him, from his iron-tipped boots to the elbow-length brown hair he had braided to keep out of his way while cooking. "You do have a certain, er, warlike appearance that does not often occur in conjunction with such skills," she allowed.

"Nonsense," Alexei broke in before Malichai had a chance to become belligerent. "Malichai happens to be one of the finest cooks I have ever known." Despite the singing, Alexei could admit the man had at least one useful skill.

"When a man has to eat his own cooking every day of the year, he either becomes an artist or he ceases to truly live," Malichai explained expansively. "I choose to eat like a king, and I have spent many years perfecting the largely unexplored art of eating well on extended campaigns. And I have never"—he scowled behind his beard—"heard any complaint from those who have shared my fire."

"Then I will apologize for my prejudices and beg for a bowl," Silvay answered gracefully, seating herself on the ground and smiling at the burly warrior.

Between the beard and the shadows it was difficult to tell, but Alexei could have sworn the man blushed.

"Now," Silvay went on, glancing across the fire to where Porfiry hunched over his knees, both wrists and ankles bound. "I would know more of the Betrayer. Who is he? What does he say of those days? I cannot twist my mind around the question of how and why anyone could have done such a thing."

"He is Porfiry. My cousin," Alexei replied shortly. "We grew up together with all of my other Nar cousins, haunting the halls and the shadows of Athven Nar. And I do not ask him why. Whether it was for money or vengeance, I don't need to know."

17

"Don't need to know?" Silvay answered gently. "Or don't want to know?"

"Does it matter?" Alexei asked, with a hint of anger. He might have been overjoyed to have the opportunity to speak his own language, but that didn't mean he wished her to invade his private grief, or his private doubts. "When he stole the Rose, he destroyed our home and betrayed our people. My family is all but gone because he chose himself over everything else. That is enough." He could sense Porfiry watching them, but would not give him the satisfaction of noticing. He didn't care what Porfiry thought. He didn't care what Porfiry wanted. All that mattered was the Rose.

Silence fell, but for the crackle of the fire and the scrape of Malichai's spoon in the steaming pot.

Suddenly unable to remain still, Alexei jumped to his feet. "I'm going for a walk." He didn't wait to find out if they would try to stop him, but stood and strode away from the circle of light, into the darkness that would hide his shaking hands. Hands that had almost moved to his scars, the painful and ever-present reminder of what else Porfiry had destroyed only a year ago.

Alexei had never considered himself vain. He had been described as stern rather than handsome, and the gray in his dark hair had never particularly disturbed him. With his lean, wiry build and forgettable looks, he could easily disappear into any crowd, which suited him perfectly. Until his cousin nearly killed him, leaving him with scars no one could ignore or overlook. Now he found that he occasionally resented his cousin as much for the destruction of his face as he did for the destruction of Erath, and the realization filled him with shame.

As did his own choices for the past twenty-six years. He told himself he hid because there was no other way. What could he have done, without the Rose? His homeland had been overrun, his people were dead or in chains, and he was helpless to change their fate without its power. But was he genuinely being honest with himself? Or had he remained in hiding so he never had to face the reality of his cowardice?

The waning moon shed enough light to see where he stepped, but it might hide predators, so Alexei was cautious enough to stop before he strayed too far from the fire. He leaned back against a rock that was cool and solid against his shoulders and looked up. The stars winked dimly, laughing at his fears and his insecurities.

There was no room for such weaknesses now. He had found Porfiry and all of his excuses were gone. His own reasons for staying or going didn't matter. What mattered was that there was a chance—a chance to find the Rose, which meant a chance for whatever was left of his people, whether Athven lived or no. The new leader of Caelan had promised to free the Erathi slaves from their silver collars. They would be coming home, looking for refuge, and he had to make sure they would find it. There was no time for personal grievances, or wallowing in his regrets. Not when so many had suffered and died.

And yet, Alexei still could not share in that pain as deeply as he ought. A part of his heart seemed numb, uncaring, uninterested in anything but bitterness and revenge.

Perhaps when he set foot on Erathi soil once more, he would find it easier to feel as he should. It had been so long, even his own happy child-hood almost didn't seem real. He couldn't remember much more than glimpses of those days spent playing with his cousins, exploring the farthest corners of Athven Nar, serving as a page to his much older cousin, the queen, and learning his gift.

Alexei stared at his hands in the pale, cold light. They looked as they ever did— marred by the scars of his early trade, yet still strong and compe-tent—except lately they seemed to shake and curl themselves into fists as often as not. It was not weakness, or even age, he knew. After forty-two years, he hoped he was wise enough to admit—even if only to himself—the true depths of his fear.

When Alexei was ten, one of Beatra's uncles had announced to the court that Alexei was probably the greatest enchanter to be born in several generations. Almost as great as the enchanters of old. Enchanters like Nar himself. Creator of the Rose.

That moment had sustained him for years. It had given him the energy to hope that he could do something for their people; even enticed him to believe that he would someday create a work of great significance. But that dream was gone and now he was afraid. Afraid to find out just how much he lost when Porfiry attacked him on that dark night in Caelan.

The twisted, silvery lines that marred the right side of his face rarely bothered him, except when people stared. It was the sightless white wreck of his eye that troubled him most, and not because of its appearance, as frightening as that was.

Part of an enchanter's art was the ability to "see" the interaction between magic and the physical. To create objects and imbue them with power required immense concentration and the ability to perceive several realities at once. What if he could no longer see the delicate balance between the work of his hands and the working of his magic? What if his imbalanced sight meant he could no longer be an enchanter? What if he had lost the chance to use his gift to help him save his people?

And what if none of it mattered because there was not enough left of Erath to save?

Alexei pushed off the rock and began to walk again, back towards the fire, before Malichai decided to come looking. He had no doubt the man would consider it his duty to save his companion from whatever might be lurking in the dark, should he fail to reappear in a timely manner. Just as Alexei's brother would have done, and had done, so many times in their lives.

He wished Andrei could have been convinced to return with him. Andrei had always been the more settled of the two of them, more at ease with himself and his gifts. He had also found peace many years ago, working with horses, content to let the magical part of his ability with animals lie dormant. Andrei had even given up his talisman to the young woman who was now princess of Andar, when she needed courage in a dark moment of her life. And the younger Trevelyan had never cared much for politics, or the inner workings of even such a simple court as their aunt's.

Beatra Nar had been one of their strongest sovereigns in terms of natural magical ability, but she had never cared much for pomp. She rewarded her retainers for their abilities and their dedication and showed little regard for wealth or ostentation. Unmarried at forty, she'd designated her younger brother to be her heir, and insisted that the horde of Nar cousins be properly trained to benefit their people with their gifts.

And she'd had such great hopes for Alexei. The queen would be deeply disappointed in him, were she alive to see what he'd made of his life. She would no doubt deem him a coward for doubting his gifts, and a traitor for remaining in hiding until it might be too late. Too late for him, too late for Athven, too late for Erath.

Silvay was only the beginning. Once he crossed the border, he would have to face others who might want very much to know why the House of Nar had abandoned them. And he would have to give an answer, even if it brought him nothing but grief and shame.

It was a quiet party that set off next morning, into the bright sun of a late summer day. The road was climbing noticeably, and now and then between the trees they could catch a glimpse of the mountains they intended to cross. The way should be easy this time of year, at least in terms of weather. The snows were several months off and the rains well past.

Once they approached the border, however, there would likely be a new threat. Andari roads were kept clear of brigands who might see their party as a target, but there was no law now in Erath. It had doubtless become something of a haven for those whose lawlessness had driven them from their own lands in search of a place they could exist without fear of apprehension.

If Alexei and his companions were able to find the Rose and restore it to its rightful place, brigands would no longer be a problem. Until then, however, Alexei would need to consider the safety of returning refugees. Or rather, he would need to hand the problem to whomever would be the new sovereign. Even had he been willing to take up the Stone Scepter, the Erathi might prefer not to follow the House of Nar. And if Athven Nar no longer held any power, they could just as well remove all but the Rose to another seat, much as it pained Alexei to think of it.

Less painful, he suspected, than being asked to attempt the job himself.

The sound of the earth moving behind him signaled the approach of Loraleen at a ground-shaking trot. Malichai drew even and pulled his mare to a walk.

"Up ahead," he murmured in a low voice. "Someone walking. Be wary."

Alexei glanced up, but whatever Malichai had seen was still out of range of his vision. He had not thought his eyesight as bad as that.

"Silvay." He looked back over his shoulder. "Can you see them?"

She shaded her eyes with her hand. "Oh, I expect it's only Wilder."

Alexei and Malichai turned in unison to regard her quizzically.

"The next member of our party," she explained. "He was due to join us shortly."

"When were you planning to inform us?" Alexei didn't care if she knew he was irritated. He'd forgotten how difficult it could be to spend time around seers. They so often forgot the difference between their visions and reality, and assumed everyone knew the same things they did. And sometimes, they simply enjoyed being annoyingly mysterious.

"When we found him, of course." Silvay did not look overly concerned.

"And what do you mean by 'next'?" Malichai inquired.

"Did I say next?" she echoed. "Oh dear. Must be my age. I'm sure I meant other."

There was no moving her from her statement, so Alexei dropped the matter as they drew even with the figure of a small boy who was trudging determinedly down the margin of the road. He wore cheap, poorly made clothing, boots with holes in the toes, and a floppy brown hat that seemed to be growing along with his floppy brown hair. Alexei was reminded strongly of a stray puppy.

"Hallo," the boy greeted them cheerfully, in Andari.

"Wilder," Silvay said with a nod.

"You're a seer." He acknowledged this as though it were both common and expected, then glanced around her at Porfiry. "I can't tell much about him, just that he's angry." Next he looked up at Alexei and Malichai. "You'd be the king," he told Alexei, without any sign that he had said anything astonishing, "and you"—he tilted his head to gaze up at Malichai—"haven't really got an aura at all. Are you Andari?"

Malichai glanced at Alexei and burst into full-throated laughter. "And here I was thinking His Majesty had sent me for simple guard duty. I'll have to thank him after I return. He's gone and given me my very own epic ballad!" He slapped his thigh with one studded leather gauntlet, unquench-able enthusiasm shining in his eyes. "We have a king in exile, a quest for treasure, a band of friends on a journey, and here's me with no one to record it."

"Shut up." Alexei regarded the boy wearily. A prescient, if he was any judge. They could read auras and were generally aware of needs beyond any idea of words. It would explain why he was traveling alone, miles from anywhere.

"Where are you going, Wilder? Is that your real name?"

"Oh, it's my name," the boy said. "I needed to be here, so I came."

"Won't your parents miss you?" Alexei lifted a hand to rub absently at his scars. They rarely pained him, but it had become a habit, especially when he was feeling self-conscious.

"Haven't got any. A farmer took me in a few years back after my mum died."

"And won't this farmer wonder where you've gone?"

"Nah." The boy dismissed the possibility with an airy wave. "I told him I needed to be somewhere and that I probably wouldn't be back."

Alexei closed his eyes to contemplate the probable reaction of the nameless farmer. Had he assumed the boy was mad? Been thankful to be rid of a burden? Did it matter? "I suppose you want to come with us."

"It's what I'm to do." The boy shrugged. "Can't say why. Don't know. Just know I'm to be here and that you'll need me."

Alexei gritted his teeth and wondered whether the universe was getting its revenge for his years of hiding from his responsibilities. "Very well, Wilder. I expect you'd only follow us if we said no. You can ride with Silvay, since she was so eager to collect you."

Silvay smiled serenely and offered the boy her hand. "Up with you then. Pleased to have you, Wilder. You can tell me more of yourself as we ride."

"Oh, not much to tell." His lack of a story did not seem to distress Wilder very much. In truth, nothing did. Neither Alexei's scars nor Malichai's size. "My mum and I have lived around here ever since I was born. Close enough to the border that Mum could teach me about my magic and all. She knew things like me. Always knew when we needed to move so we wouldn't be found out."

Alexei kept half an ear on their conversation as Silvay drew the child out and listened patiently to his tale of refugees making their way as best they could—moving from job to job, hiding in barns, sleeping in the forest, trying to stay close enough to their borders that they did not lose their sense of self and purpose.

Was it so hard, then, for most Erathi to walk away from their magic? Alexei remembered feeling a strange sense of relief along with the loss when his magic had been smothered for the first time by the silver that ran through Andar's veins. He had told himself it was better to forget, better to forsake his heritage entirely than to endure the agony of waiting for an opportunity, or a reason, to return.

But that was only half of the truth. If he was honest with himself, his relief had more to do with guilt than practicality. How could he return, after his failure? How could he go back and face the ruin that was Athven Nar unless he had a way to make it right?

So he had let himself pretend it was for the best. If Porfiry had not crossed his path, he might have spent the rest of his life as a simple horseman, content for his magic and his guilt to lie dormant together. But when Porfiry appeared out of his past, Alexei had seen his chance to redeem himself. To return the traitor to Erath and achieve justice for his people.

Yet even as he let himself dwindle into forgetfulness, hiding from the terrifying burden Beatra had bequeathed him, looking only for a chance at revenge, it seemed the last remnants of his people had been waiting too. Waiting for an opportunity. Waiting for hope. Had they been waiting for *him*?

～

The road continued to climb over the next few days, and the footing grew somewhat worse. The nights were cool, almost cold, and the trees grew shorter and more sparse. They were getting close. Alexei could feel his gift awakening within him, stretching out tendrils, testing the surroundings. He noticed Malichai checking his weapons one afternoon and asked if he expected trouble.

"Borders are always trouble, no matter where they lie," the Andari answered. "And here more than most, I'll wager. King Hollin protects these lands with his word and his laws, but the moment we can reasonably be assumed to have crossed, we're on our own. There are no rules but what a man, or a woman, make for themselves." He eyed the length of his iron-bound staff before reattaching it to his saddle. "I can't say I mislike the chance to make my own rules."

Silvay cast back the edge of her cloak and adjusted the belt that held her sheathed daggers. "And I can't say I'm looking forward to enjoying the hospitality of brigands."

"If you have seen something, now would be a good time to share with your companions," Alexei told her dryly. "I don't mind being surprised by small, grubby boys, but if I find that you knew beforehand of an attack and chose to let us chance our fate, I could find it in me to be annoyed."

"Oh, do you mean me?" Wilder looked at him, wide-eyed with surprise.

"Do you see any other small boys in need of baths?" Alexei asked, trying to smile to let the boy know he was not upset. Though with the pull of his scars, he might simply scare the child instead.

"I don't see *any*, at all," Wilder replied firmly.

"Then perhaps we ought to find you a nice quiet pond," Alexei retorted, but before he could finish his thought, a shout rang out some hundred-odd paces ahead, where the road came to the top of a rise.

Six horsemen had appeared out of nowhere and ranged themselves across the path, sword hilts visible over their shoulders. Their uniform was that of the average mercenary: mismatched, patched clothing under cobbled-together bits of armor. Their leader even appeared to have an eye patch.

Alexei sighed and pulled his horse to a stop. "Well, they're certainly going about the business properly, aren't they?"

"I'd say they could use a bit more local color," Malichai responded thoughtfully. "Perhaps a war hawk, perched on that one's shoulder. A wolf, snarling at their feet. Braided hair, dyed red with the blood of their enemies."

"Oh, do be serious," Silvay reprimanded them sharply. "A day like this demands a necklace of skulls, at the very least."

Alexei glanced over and was surprised to see a slight smile on her lips. Wilder was peering out from behind her with what appeared to be bloodthirsty glee. "You all do realize we are horribly outnumbered," he mentioned casually. "We're close to the border, certainly, but not close enough for defensive magic."

Porfiry began muttering nervously, but Alexei ignored him, even if he agreed with the sentiment. He was feeling a trifle nervous himself. He didn't want to scare the boy, but they were unlikely to get out of this confrontation without a fight.

"Perhaps they're simply guarding the road," Silvay suggested. "Making sure no one has any nefarious intentions."

"Shall we ask them?" Malichai grinned. He pulled his bow from his back and laid it across his lap.

They were saved the trouble of deciding. The man with the eye patch spurred his horse towards them, sword in hand, though his leisurely canter indicated that he did not intend to run them through. At least not quite yet. He pulled his horse to a sliding stop just before there would have been an actual collision.

The brigand was about as hairy and unwashed as Alexei had expected, though his armor, seen up close, was decent enough. His good eye raked their little group and he grinned, clearly having seen something he liked.

"Welcome," he rasped, "to the free territory of Grissom. I'm Grissom. It's sixty-weight of silver to pass, though I'm adding another twenty for the sheer size of that one." He gestured to Malichai, who leaned on his pommel and looked entirely at his ease. Loraleen flicked an ear and cocked one hind leg.

"How very... unexpected," Alexei replied, raising an eyebrow at the name. "According to my maps, we are still well within the borders of Andar."

"Well now"—the man spat on the ground—"His Fine Majesty isn't here, is he? And I am, and there are six of us, and none of us are women or children or prisoners." He smiled again, baring yellow teeth that looked as though they'd begun life in the mouth of a small horse.

"Be that as it may"—Alexei shrugged in apparent helplessness—"sixty-weight of silver, even without the tax on unreasonable size, is entirely beyond our means. As I'm sure you must have realized."

"If you won't pay, we'll be happy to take it. I'm sure there are enough valuables on you lot to make it worth our while. Can sell the horses, and probably the woman too."

Alexei's grip on the reins turned to iron.

"No." His tone should have frozen the man where he sat.

"No?"

"No slaving. Not here. Not ever."

"We weren't planning to ask."

The man lifted his reins, preparing to turn back to his men. Only the slightest shift in his other hand betrayed his intention to signal them, but it was as far as he got. Malichai nocked an arrow and shot him through the heart before Alexei even realized he'd moved.

The brigand's face went slack with disbelief as he slid gracelessly from his saddle and fell in a lifeless heap under his horse's hooves. The horse blew nervously and sidled away, jerking at the rein still caught in the dead man's grasp.

"He wasn't inviting us for tea," Malichai said, in response to the looks on his companion's faces.

"I hadn't supposed he was," Alexei responded, still in shock at how quickly his bear-like companion had moved. "I simply hadn't realized how fast you are."

"No one does." Malichai appeared quite comfortable with Alexei's dismay. "I think it must be the beard. Now, in a moment, his friends are going to come looking for revenge." Almost the instant he spoke, the five remaining horsemen spurred forward as one.

"Plan?" Alexei barked.

"Back up," Malichai bellowed over his shoulder as he urged Loraleen forward. "I'll try not to splash any blood on you."

Placid as she might have looked, Loraleen hit her stride with a vengeance after only a few steps. Three arrows later, only two men remained on their horses to clash with the bellowing form of Malichai, who had cast aside his bow and drawn his staff.

And then, somehow, it was over. The last two men lay groaning on the ground and Malichai was trotting back towards them, pausing only to hook his bow from the ground using the end of his staff.

"Wasn't even a proper fight," he complained when he reached them, stowing his weapons and smoothing the windblown strands of his beard. "Those men had no idea how to work as a unit. That bounder ought to be ashamed." He glared at the very much dead leader of the gang.

"I..." Alexei had no idea what one said after such a one-sided contest. "Thank you?"

"I'd say it was my pleasure, but that was a bit embarrassing. Perhaps we should ride on. There may be more of them." He sounded pleased by the possibility.

"Ah, Malichai..." How did one phrase this? "Why exactly did King Hollin choose you for this mission?"

"To protect you, of course." The big man shrugged as though this were simple. "And to report back about conditions on the other side of the border."

"And you weren't needed elsewhere?"

"Well..." Malichai at least had the grace to look embarrassed. "It suited me to leave the Evenleigh area for a time. May have gotten in a spot of trouble while I was waiting for a task. Fighting in taverns. Bit of a brawl with a few of the Thalassan ambassador's guards... that sort of thing."

"I see." Alexei rode on in silence as they crested the hill and continued down into a shallow mountain valley. He did see. He just didn't want to.

He *was* in an accursed epic, just as Malichai predicted. All they needed now was a healer and a priest. Possibly a dog. And he wasn't even going to pretend to be surprised when at least one of the three showed up around the next bend.

CHAPTER 2

othing. After all her painstaking work with the lock, the room at the peak of the north tower proved to be as empty as all of the unlocked ones below. Empty of all but echoes, and shadows that lay where they shouldn't. By now, Zara barely even noticed errant shadows. They were as much a part of her day-to-day existence as the silence and the stone.

It had probably been a beautiful room once. Even the stones of the floor were so smoothly fitted, they appeared to have been hewn by magic. Zara could imagine retreating here, far above the bustle of life, with a cozy couch, loads of cushions, and a pile of histories taller than her head. Someone had used this room, and she didn't think it had been a prison. There was too much light. Too much whimsy in the slope of the ceiling.

Removing her protective gloves, Zara ran a wistful finger across one of the diamond panes of the casement. Dirt came away on her finger, leaving a tiny streak of clean glass where she could place her eye and peer out at the world far below if she wanted to.

She didn't. Perhaps the room's former inhabitant had enjoyed the view, but Zara had seen it all before. Why bother looking at a world you couldn't get to no matter how hard you tried? She might not be locked in a tower, but she was a prisoner all the same.

Pulling her gloves back on, Zara swept her long white braid over her shoulder and left. She closed the door behind her because... well, it was what one did, even if no one was there to tell her to close doors. And because when one was utterly alone in an ancient, drafty castle that was probably haunted, one closed doors. It didn't make it much better, but there was no one to judge her, so Zara did as she pleased.

Her torch flickered fitfully in the brass fixture outside the door, illuminating the first steps of the seemingly endless spiral of stairs that awaited her. Back down. Another useless tower to cross off her list. Another cold, cheerless evening with no sound but the crackle of the fire and her own breathing. The cat, as far as she knew, had never made a sound.

How many days had it been now? By her scratches on the kitchen wall, she thought about three months had passed since her father and the others had left her to her fate.

They had learned how close they were to the castle through a chance meeting with another band of treasure hunters in a tavern three days' ride to the east. She had heard of it before, of course, and the retreating hunters had repeated what had consistently been rumored among their kind—that no one had ever been able to enter the castle, so it was probably filled with loot should anyone manage to get inside.

It was enough for her father. Geb and Finch were chafing for a payday, so the four of them had travelled to the castle to try their luck. Zara had tried to find out more about its past, but she had no access to books or records and the people, Erathi or not, seemed strangely close-mouthed about the abandoned seat of a long-dead queen. It bothered Zara, but there was no stopping the men when they had a goal in mind.

Once they arrived in the valley, they had prepared for a protracted hunt, hoping to chance upon some hidden ingress. Much to their surprise —and Zara's dismay—the great door at the front of the castle swung open with an experimental push.

Had everyone lied about not being able to get in? And if not, why was it open now? She'd been curious, of course, but wary. She'd heard enough tales of Erathi sorcerers to wonder whether there might actually be some truth to them. After all, there had to be a reason why Erath had remained so isolated and mysterious for hundreds of years.

But her father claimed not to believe in magic, so they entered the great hall and camped there for about three days, exploring a little farther each day. On the third night, about sunset, a wind arose out of nowhere, spinning through the hall, bringing a host of shadows and a blast of wintry cold. Suddenly her feet had seemed swallowed up by the stone, and a roaring sound surrounded them, blending with the echoes of her own terrified screams. It felt like standing alone in the center of a whirlpool, at least until the great doors slammed shut and locked themselves behind Geb and Finch. Her father had fled even faster.

The castle itself did not terrify her as much as it probably should have, with its wind and shadows and whatever ghosts still lingered in its halls. She had experienced no further incidents since the men's departure, and even if she had, Zara had been exploring buried tombs, abandoned temples and mysterious caverns since she was ten years old. There was little to frighten her in something so simple as wind, no matter where it might have come from. The locked doors and the silence, though... That was another matter.

So she made as much noise as she could without feeling silly as she began her descent from the tower. The stairs wrapped around the outside of the wall, probably to protect the space on the inside from cold during the winter months. Zara had found access to a few of the tower rooms, but there was definitely a space where no doors were evident. She'd been half hoping to find a trapdoor in the room at the top, but the floor had been disappointingly solid.

A task for another day. It was a mercy, really, the sheer size of the place. There seemed to be no end to the rooms and halls she could explore. No end, as long as she did not attempt any of the outer doors. Disabling locks of all kinds had been her specialty since she was very young, but there were no actual locks to defeat—only wood and stone that had simply refused to budge once her father and Geb and Finch were on the outside.

At the bottom of the tower, Zara took a right-hand turn down a long hallway carpeted in faded blue, though the carpet was the only evidence of habitation to be seen. The recesses that might have held torches or candles were empty, and the walls featured evenly spaced patches of slightly discolored stone, where she assumed paintings or tapestries had once hung.

It was curious, the barren emptiness, especially when one considered the tales told of this place. Erath had frequently featured as the subject of legends, lying unexplored by outsiders for centuries until its destruction some thirty years ago. But even after the land itself lay open and empty, ripe for the plucking, the castle had proven impregnable.

All across Erath, abandoned houses crumbled into ruin, though even the earliest looters had turned up little of value. The terrain was too wooded for much farming, and the passes difficult to reach. No one wanted to settle it, so it became a refuge for raiders and lawless bands of predators who needed a place to hide from the laws of other lands.

And as the years turned and people came and went, the castle at the heart of the desolate kingdom kept its secrets.

Zara wished it had gone on keeping them. She could imagine few secrets less thrilling than a cold, empty castle, especially one that stank of magic. Doors did not lock and unlock themselves and wind did not simply appear out of nowhere. Her father might disregard such things as stories to frighten children, but he also believed if he drank enough his hair would never fall out. Or so he claimed. Zara had learned at a very young age not to take her father's assertions too seriously.

At the end of the hall, she turned left, and then right, through an iron-bound oaken door that opened onto a grand balcony. The sweeping stair-case at the center led down into a vast entryway, where even the echo of her footsteps seemed ashamed of trespassing.

Zara stomped harder out of sheer annoyance. If she could have scraped dirt off her boots and left it on the enormous rose mosaic in the center of the floor, she probably would have. The castle had clearly been impressive once, and had it been filled with light and color and voices it might have been a pleasant place to live. But as a prison and very possibly her tomb, it left rather a lot to be desired.

Out of every place she'd explored, the grand entryway left her feeling the smallest and most alone, so she hurried across it and passed under an archway on the other side. The passage beyond had a low, arched ceiling that made it feel like a tunnel, but it was better than the soaring emptiness of the entry. At the other end of the tunnel were what Zara had deter-mined were probably servants' quarters and kitchens.

She had appropriated the smallest of the kitchen fireplaces for her use, and kept the fire there going at all times. She never lit any of the others. It meant that she was cold any time she stepped out of that corner, but there was no sense in being greedy. Though the stack of wood in the scullery was large, and should last for several years at the rate she was going through it, she had no idea when her imprisonment was likely to end. As long as she kept the kitchen warm, she was unlikely to freeze.

Food was eventually going to be problematic, but not yet. She tried not to consider too hard the fact that in a castle so empty it didn't even have cobwebs—a castle that had proven impenetrable for thirty years—there had been a stack of wood, a generous supply of grain, and enough root vegeta-bles and jerked meat to meet her needs. Such things kept well, but they were still perishable fare, and ought to have already succumbed to mold or simply shriveled into dust.

The water, too, that flowed from the kitchen pump was clear and unspoiled.

But Zara simply ate and drank and asked no questions, because, really, what choice did she have? What choice had the wretched castle given her? If the food and drink was enchanted and turned her into a monster to haunt the place for the next hundred years, what could she do about it?

Dinner that night, as every night, was stew that had simmered over the fire while Zara was exploring. The meat was tough and stringy and the broth was thin, but Zara had eaten worse. Frequently. Itinerant treasure hunters did not generally eat well, and considering that she was a better cook than any of the men, it was probably a wonder none of them were dead.

As she did every night, Zara ate her way down to the bottom of her bowl and left the last few bites. Then she set the bowl off to the side, pulled off her boots, and waited.

And just as it did every night, the cat meandered in before more than a few minutes had passed.

It was a female, mottled gray, with numerous scars and part of an ear missing. Nevertheless, she possessed a certain dignity that Zara could not help but admire. She would enter on silent paws, then sit beside the bowl Zara had left. After a minute or two of an unblinking, green-eyed stare, the cat would finish the stew and lick the bowl. Then she would stretch and wash her front paws and wander over to rub herself against Zara's legs. She never purred or permitted Zara to pick her up, but Zara treasured each and every gray hair that adhered itself to her patched leggings. It felt like proof that the cat was real and that she had not yet gone crazy from the silence and the solitude.

And because the silence was thick and the shadows close, while the cat shared her kitchen, Zara talked. She felt like an idiot, but she talked, sometimes about what she had done that day, sometimes about the past. The cat never seemed to notice, except for the occasional flick of an ear, but Zara didn't care.

She wished the cat would stay, and sleep beside the fire, but it never did. After her evening ritual, after Zara had talked on for a time, the cat would leave as soundlessly as she had come, and Zara would be alone once more to fortify herself against the cold, endless night with bitter, useless longings.

Sometimes she wasn't even certain what she was longing for. Something else. Something other. Certainly something other than an enchanted castle. It wasn't that she had spent her entire life feeling discontent. She couldn't even imagine living like any of the other girls she'd known—tied to one place and confined by expectations. But to have someone besides herself that she could talk to, someone who might care what she had to say or what she was feeling—that, to Zara, might be considered a greater treasure than any she had yet found.

Dezarae her father had named her. Desire of his heart. His one true treasure. But in truth, the only treasure he seemed to care about most of the time was the kind that glittered. The kind that could be sold. Her mother had learned that truth sooner than Zara and drifted away from her family both in dreams and in drink by the time Zara was six. After her mother died four years later, Zara had travelled with her father, and for the first few years, she had loved it. The thrill of travel, of danger, and of discovering the unknown had been a heady experience for a young girl with a taste for adventure. She was, in many ways, every bit the treasure hunter her father was, and sometimes better. But by the time she was twenty, she yearned for more. For friends. For a home. For some place to rest after their adventures. And every year, her father would promise her that they would one day have a home. That she would have a dowry and he would find her a husband and she would not have to travel with him anymore.

This last bit had never seemed very appealing. If she married, her husband would expect her to wear dresses and cook and have babies. She would never again experience the joy of awakening to an unfamiliar horizon, or pitting her skills against an unexplored labyrinth. For her, the true treasure was not the objects they carried away, it was the getting there—the journey into history that so few would ever have a chance to experience.

But. A home? That she would have given much for. And it was the one thing she knew she would never have. Not as the itinerant daughter of a perpetually impoverished treasure hunter who was all charm and promises and no substance. He would plan and spin visions of the future out of nothing, and when he was finished, nothing was exactly what she would have. And at thirty years old, she was unlikely to have many chances to be anything else. Adventuring was all she knew how to do.

Before she slept, Zara firmly put aside thoughts of the outside. She could not bear to wonder whether her father was trying to find her or looking for another way in. Because the moment she let herself think about whether or not he was trying to get to her, she had to consider the possibility that he wasn't. That he had given up and left her behind. That no one would ever find her and she would die, alone, in this echoing pile of stone.

And on that cheery thought, Zara fell asleep.

Next morning, after dining on cold mush and the dried up carcass of an apple, Zara donned her leather vest and her tool belt, banked the fire, and set off on the day's exploring. She didn't really know what she was looking for. Rumor proclaimed that the castle must be home to astonishing treasures, given the strength of its enchanted protections, but considering that in the past three months she had found quite literally nothing of value, Zara was ready to consider the rumors little more than drunken exaggeration.

But if she didn't do something she might lose both hope and what was left of her mind, so she kept on. There was a crude map of places she'd already searched, drawn in charcoal on the wall in the kitchen, next to her tally of the days she'd been trapped. Thus far, most of her adventuring had been in the upward direction, as she hadn't felt quite ready to find out what lay below ground. But, given that she had discovered nothing but stairs, she couldn't imagine there was much more to fear below. Shadows had never hurt her yet, and she doubted there was anything worse to avoid.

After she returned to the grand entry, Zara paused to consider what she knew of the castle's construction. From the outside, the castle had been built on a low rise in the center of a valley. The ground sloped gradually away from its flanks, revealing a rocky foundation beneath the ruins of the castle gardens. If there was anything beneath the castle, it must have been tunneled out of solid rock, and probably would have been built beneath the most stable, most inaccessible part of the structure—the center.

On one of her first days trapped in the castle, Zara had found a small, insignificant-looking door in the back of what she'd assumed to be a closet. When she picked the relatively simple lock, there was nothing but a narrow set of stairs, leading down into darkness. At the time, she'd slammed the door and relocked it, because even when one was unafraid of the dark, there was something horrible about the idea that if anything *was* down there, it could come up out of the depths any time it felt like it.

Of course, if anything really was down there—and still alive—a locked door was unlikely to stop it, but by now she'd regained enough of her professional dignity to pretend it didn't scare her. Much.

The door was still there, and still locked. She shouldn't be relieved by such a thing, but she was, and her relief no longer even surprised her. Considering what else the castle had done, it could probably make a door disappear if it wanted.

The lock was as she remembered it, and the stairs were just as dark, but this time she held her torch a little higher and started down, after using one of her tools to prop the door open. It occurred to her, not for the first time during this ordeal, that if she encountered anything hostile, she had no way to defend herself. She had never carried a weapon and would have little idea what to do with it if she had.

On their crew, she had been the solver of locks and puzzles, good with numbers and finding hidden things. If anything needed slaying, one of the men took care of it. Despite his distaste for work, her father was passably skilled with a sword, and though he had never attempted to train his daughter, neither had she ever cared to learn. On this occasion however, Zara suspected that she might have felt better with something wickedly sharp to hide behind.

The stairs curved as they went down, much as she'd expected. After three spirals, they let out into a hall that was narrow, but did not appear designed to be inhospitable. There were hooks on the wall, probably for lanterns, and the floors were of smoothly joined stone with a pattern in different colors. The stone glittered in the light of her torch, tiny flecks of some shiny mineral reflecting the fire back at her.

Zara decided to go right. If she was not mistaken, that direction should take her back under the entry hall, under the heart of the castle. Though when she thought about it that way, it seemed a little ominous.

As she walked she let her fingers trail across the wall, feeling how smoothly the stones had been finished, sensing a care that was unusual for a part of a building that would rarely, if ever, have been in the public eye. People had walked here, once. People who belonged, who knew the purpose of these halls and who had a purpose there themselves. The thought made her feel even more alone, so she shoved it away and watched for irregularities in the floor or walls.

The corridor came to an abrupt end at another nondescript door, but this one, like the main doors into the castle, had no lock and no handle. It was simply closed, and if it was anything like the main doors, it would refuse to budge. Zara gave it a halfhearted push and was rewarded by an easy swing inward, as though the hinges had been oiled only yesterday.

A jolt of excitement darted through her stomach as she peered into the dark space beyond and, for the first time, saw something that piqued her interest.

The room was perhaps eight to ten strides across and perfectly round. The floor, she noted as she held the torch closer, was not of plain, rough stone, but of highly polished marble in shades of gold, pink, gray, black, and what she thought might be a pale green. Each piece was fitted so seamlessly that even Zara's father might have agreed it had to have been done by magic. And as she walked further in, it became clear that the colors made a picture. There was some kind of pattern in it, that she could probably understand easily if she could see it all at once. She looked around the walls for a way to get up higher, and then noticed a pedestal in the exact center of the room.

Heart pounding, Zara moved closer. After a few moments, she realized she was trying to walk without making a sound and stopped to roll her eyes. Moving more normally, she stepped up to the base of the pedestal. It was empty, of course, but there was writing on it. Traced in gold, the letters curled lovingly around the column and shone brilliantly in the light of her torch. The pedestal had to have been intended for some important purpose. Some object must have rested on it. There was a slight indentation in the top, irregular in shape, but whatever had once lived there was obviously long gone.

Stifling disappointment, Zara turned to the rest of the room. There did not appear to be any other doors. Nor were there any niches in the walls. Realizing with a wry twist of her lips that she could be desecrating an important cultural artifact, she managed to pull herself up on the pedestal and crouch on top to get a better look at the floor. What she saw took her breath away.

It was a picture. She could see clearly enough from her new vantage point, and though she couldn't be certain, she thought from the maps she had seen that it was meant to represent the whole of Erath. Mountains, forests, rivers, and valleys were laid out at her feet, centering on the pedestal on which she stood.

The castle. The pedestal was meant to be the castle. Whatever had been given the place of honor at the top of the pedestal had probably been something her treasure-loving father would have sold his soul to possess. For that matter, Zara could feel her own heart constrict at the knowledge that she was standing in the place of an object that had clearly been deeply meaningful to the people who had once lived there. Sacred, even.

It had never been the treasure that drove her, though she enjoyed being paid as much as the next person. It was the knowledge. The thrill of uncovering secrets that had been lost for hundreds of years. Of holding a piece of the past, a piece of someone else's life in her hands. Of wondering where it had been and what it had seen.

This entire edifice, if tales were any judge, had seen something so horrible that it had destroyed an entire people. But there were no stains to bear witness, no destruction to tell what might have become of the people of Erath. From the outside, several of the towers had appeared blackened and pitted, but she had not had time to investigate before she'd been trapped within. The inside of the towers seemed unscathed.

It was as though the people had simply faded away and disappeared.

They hadn't, she knew. No one knew much, but it was generally understood that invaders had conquered the country and carried its peaceful populace away in chains. But why? And how had a country that had existed in splendid and impenetrable isolation for hundreds of years been so suddenly overrun?

It was a mystery, and Zara could feel it wrap itself around her heart and beg for an answer. All of her instincts were shouting that this room she was in held a clue, but unless she could magically learn to read the writing, it would likely remain beyond her ability to decipher.

Zara was about to jump down from the pedestal when something darted through the open door.

She tripped. Terror spiked up her legs, into her stomach and she fell hard, onto her shoulder. At the resulting shock of pain, she dropped the torch and it rolled away towards the wall, its light barely flickering.

Jerking upright, Zara scrabbled backwards, putting her back to the pedestal, her single breath a harsh gasp in the deathly silence. She patted her vest until she found one of her tools, a miniature pry bar, and held it in one shaking hand.

There was still no sound. Whatever had come in, it was waiting. Zara shut her eyes tightly and tried not to think about what it might be. She tried not to breathe. Tried to stop her heart from leaping out of her mouth. But all of her attempted control was for naught when something landed on her stomach.

She screamed. Experienced treasure hunter, mature adult that she was, she screamed and tried to scramble away but the pedestal was behind her and her eyes flew open in spite of her best intentions.

The gray cat sat on her stomach and regarded her with an expression of... amusement? Yes. There was no mistake. The cat was laughing at her. Except that cats didn't laugh.

"You." Zara breathed out the word with all the malice she could muster. "You smug little bastard!" The cat tilted its head to one side, eyes wide and unblinking. "I hate you. You almost killed me." Still, the cat seemed unrepentant. "You should know that humans are fragile and easily frightened. Some of us. I'm usually not. But you need to learn to make a noise so that my heart doesn't stop next time you come in a room."

The cat patted her chest with one velvety paw, lay down, curled up in a ball and began to purr.

Zara stared.

Something was not quite right. Either she was going crazy—always a possibility—or...

"Are you even a real cat?"

The thing on her chest lifted its head and looked her in the eye. Then it sat up and began washing its paws.

Zara shook her head in disgust. "Off." She pushed it to the ground. "You might act innocent, but I don't believe you. I don't want to not believe you, but you haven't left me much choice, not when you act like you understand what I say. And I don't know how long I can stand being here, in this weird room, under this creepy castle, with something that may or may not be a cat. Because if you aren't a cat..."

She let that thought echo off the walls.

The cat turned and walked away.

Zara rose to her feet, each motion firm and deliberate. For a moment she felt lightheaded with the echoes of her terror, but it passed and she walked across the room to retrieve her torch. When she held it up and looked around, the cat was standing by the door, watching her.

"Oh no. I am not following something cat-shaped anywhere. You tell me what you are and I'll think about it." Dimly, Zara listened to herself and wondered whether the shock had actually unhinged her. How could something be cat-shaped? How did she expect a cat to tell her anything? Really, the cat had just followed her. She had overreacted to the cat's friendly overtures. And it most definitely had not been laughing.

When the cat merely continued to look at her, Zara snorted and walked over to the door. She was leaving. Someday, maybe she would find the nerve to come back down here, but it wouldn't be soon. Setting her shoulder to the door, she expected it to swing as it had before. It held fast. She shoved, harder, but the door didn't even shudder.

Suppressing a swell of panic, Zara whirled to look at the cat, but it was ignoring her now, washing its paws again.

"Do you know, I'm thinking right now about how much I regret feeding you," Zara announced, proud that her voice shook only a little. "To think, when I was a child, I always wanted a cat, but my father would never let me have one because we had nowhere to keep it."

The cat paused, then continued washing.

"I would threaten you, but I would feel silly threatening a cat, even if I'm convinced you're not a cat and there's no one else here to see me act like a fool. Are you planning to keep me here till I die?"

The cat startled visibly and its tail began to twitch.

"Oh no, of course you're not. If you made a habit of trapping people down here there would be bones, scraps of clothing, desperate messages scratched into the walls."

The tail twitched harder.

Zara sighed and leaned back against the unmoving door. "What do you want from me?"

The cat appeared satisfied. It stood, whereupon the door swung open and Zara fell directly onto her butt.

She did not immediately get up again. She stared at the cat, and the cat returned her gaze solemnly.

"What are you?" Zara whispered, her eyes wide, her fear beginning to tighten her chest and clench at her stomach.

The cat approached, and pressed one paw gently against the back of her hand where it rested on the floor.

Zara gave up. There was really no sense in remaining sane, when succumbing to the pressure of her fear and uncertainty would permit her to place her trust in a cat that could lock and unlock doors. Such a creature seemed like a worthwhile ally for an erstwhile treasure hunter.

"Well then. I'm Zara. And I'm going to call you Shadow, because I'll be able to not care so much how creepy you are if you have a normal name." She could have sworn the cat scowled. "And if you don't like the name, you're going to have to tell me something else to call you, and since you apparently can't talk..."

Her mind was officially gone. She was congratulating herself for a victory over a not-cat because it couldn't talk. Shoving all remaining thoughts to the back of her head where they grumbled and whined at her for ignoring them, Zara followed the cat down the passage and smiled into the shadows. Exploring an abandoned castle with an enchanted cat might be her last adventure, but it might also be her greatest. And if she ever saw her father again, she was going to have a thing or two to say to him about believing in magic.

CHAPTER 3

$\mathcal{A}$ lexei paused inside the doorway of the ramshackle tavern and wondered how he'd allowed himself to be talked into this. Yes, he wanted news and gossip. Yes, this was the only public establishment in the run-down little place that called itself a town. In reality, it was no more than a makeshift camp for the miserable and the displaced. Plus there was the dirt... and the smell! He was convinced someone had died weeks ago and simply been shoved under one of the tables.

It caused an almost physical pain to see his kingdom like this. Ever since they'd crossed into Erath, the tale had been the same. Homes abandoned. Fences fallen into disrepair. Towns overrun by the lawless who cared nothing for one another or for the land off which they lived.

This tavern's clientele was uniformly unshaven and unwashed, except for the lone woman, who was guilty of only one out of two but looked as capable of violence as the rest of them. The tavern keeper, or at least the fellow serving drinks, was a tiny, rotund man with a drooping mustache, surprised eyebrows, and the saddest expression Alexei had ever seen. He poured and passed and wiped without once meeting the eyes of his customers, though Alexei couldn't blame him once he'd had a look around. Attracting notice in that crowd might be a swift way to die.

But it meant that Alexei had to push his way through that same crowd to catch the tavern keeper's attention. He jostled and shoved and tried not to do so more enthusiastically than necessary, but no one so much as blinked, at his rudeness or his scars. He caught one or two sideways glances, but whether it was because of his face or because he was relatively clean, Alexei chose not to speculate.

"What'll you have then?" The tavern keeper, despite his already diminutive size, ducked his head nervously and waited for an order without looking up at Alexei. He spoke Andari, like the rest of the crowd, but his accent...

"I don't suppose you have any cithren?" Alexei asked quietly.

"I have ale and soup. Out of bread. You want anything else, you make it." The man paused. Looked up, blinking. "Did you say cithren?"

Considering there had been no one to make any in nearly thirty years, Alexei doubted this pathetic excuse for a tavern would stock Erathi liquor. But it was as good a way as any to ask the question.

"I did. I would also be interested in news, if you have any."

"For you?" The tavern keeper darted a glance to each side. "Come." He turned and threaded his way through the crowd like a man of half his bulk. "Dru?" A man with a thatch of curly hair popped up from behind the bar like a child's toy. "You're serving. And don't drop any more soup, or it'll be *you* scrubbing the blood out of the floors this time."

Alexei followed his host through a crooked doorway and up a set of stairs that he wasn't sure would hold his weight, ending in a tiny apartment that was miraculously and scrupulously clean, unlike the floor below.

"I can't keep it up," his host said in quiet Erathi, "not with that lot, and not a one of them cares. They'd eat and drink just the same if I fed them swill served in a chamber pot." The keeper seemed ashamed, but pointed Alexei toward the room's single chair. "Sit, and I'll get you a drink."

"I don't need a drink," Alexei reassured him. "I took you for a man of Erath, but I needed to know if I could trust you."

"You can't trust anyone," the man answered, pulling a dusty bottle from the back of a shelf. "Not even those who share your language."

"It's gotten so bad, then?"

"Gotten?" the man echoed. His eyebrows gained an extra degree or two of surprise. "Where have you been for the last twenty-six years? Can't have been here."

"Traveling," Alexei responded shortly. It sounded better than hiding.

His companion leveled him with a look that suggested he knew rather more than Alexei was telling. "Well, for those of us who never left, it's been as many years of sliding deeper into poverty and hopelessness and disgrace. But we stay, because... well, where would we go?" He shrugged as he pulled at the cork. "No one else would have us, not willingly, and even if they would, who would give up half of their soul to leave?"

Alexei winced. "What is your name?"

The man appeared not to hear. He produced a pair of mismatched glasses from somewhere and poured a tiny amount of the dusty bottle's contents into each glass. As the golden liquid fell sparkling into the bottom of each glass, tiny sparks of light rose into the air and burst.

"You mean... you actually have it?"

Cithren wasn't just liquor. It was distilled using sunlight and magic and aged in the heart of an oak. No one but a single Erathi family knew how to make it, and Alexei had assumed those with the skill had perished. Considering the look of the bottle, perhaps they had.

"Last bottle," Alexei's companion said wistfully, patting his stomach and shaking his head. He handed one glass to Alexei. "Can't imagine drinking it with anyone who didn't know what it is. Don't know if there will ever be more."

The two men lifted their drinks.

"To Nar," Alexei muttered, out of habit, and then he drank. The bright, clean sensation of cithren against his tongue made Alexei's eyes burn with more than just magic. A brief, golden light shone from each man's face as they finished drinking and set down the glasses.

"What can you tell me of the state of things?" Alexei asked quietly. "As you guessed, I have been away since..." He shrugged.

"Doubt there's much I can tell you beyond the general rumors." The bald man settled his hands over his belly and sighed. "There's no law, as such, and folks do pretty much as they please. After the conquerors left, those of us who remained—and that wasn't many, mind you—came out of hiding and found that we'd been left with nothing. Crops burned. Houses destroyed. We tried to rebuild, but we hadn't enough people to build again *and* defend ourselves from the vultures. Every time we tried, it was taken from us. And many had lost hope. Why rebuild when everyone you knew was gone? When half your family was taken or dead?"

Alexei felt as though the shorter man had stabbed him. For years he had wondered how many of his people could possibly have remained in Erath. The news—that the few who stayed had not only survived but continued to suffer—settled into his bones, and he shut his eyes as the last flare of warmth from the cithren was swallowed up by the depth of his guilt. He should have come sooner.

"You'll find small pockets of us here and there, but we don't advertise what we are. Rumors say we were a race of evil sorcerers who got what we deserved. Not every man who's entered our borders is a bastard, but most are, and we've no desire to end up burnt or hanged for our imagined crimes."

"I've heard tales of treasure hunters."

"Aye." The man frowned and stroked his mustache. "The ones that aren't mercenaries or brigands looking to escape the law come here looking to loot what remains, little as it is. They expected evil sorcerers would leave their ill-gotten gains behind, I'll wager. 'Tis no more than they deserve to wind up poorer than when they came."

"What of Athven Nar?" Alexei tried not to let the man hear how much it mattered to him, but he needn't have bothered.

"Oh, and I heard your blessing. What do you know of Nar, then?" The man's eyes were keen when he fixed them on Alexei's face. "All of that line are dead, so much as we know. There's a seer, a few towns over, who mumbles now and again about a return, but we try to keep him quiet."

"I'm not a return of anything." Alexei couldn't stand the thought of anyone counting on him for something he couldn't control, couldn't possibly deliver. He was not a king. He would never be a king, no matter what Beatra wanted. "But I intend to help what's left of our people, if there is any way to do so." He did not think it was safe to say any more. Why give the man hope that would only fall to ashes in the end?

"Then I wish you well, for what it's worth." The tavern keeper pushed to his feet, as if signaling that the interview was over. "I've heard little of Athven Nar. Most stories say she still stands, and the doors are sealed, but there was a pair of men came through here... oh, a month or more ago." He shrugged. "They claimed to have been inside, but were driven off by a horde of undead warriors."

Alexei snorted. "Athven was strong enough, but undead warriors were never one of her preferences."

"And you'd know, would you? How old were you when the shield fell?"

Alexei had the uneasy feeling that he'd said more than he should. "Old enough," was all he answered.

"Well, then, if you know that much, you know Athven has her own ways. Can't say I ever knew her myself, but my grandfer did some of the gardening there. Said she took her strength from those who cared for her, and that she cared for them, in whatever ways she could."

"But she's been alone too long. There is no way she could have survived it." Alexei stared down at his folded hands.

"Well, as to that, I've heard from others that there are lights and noises

51

from inside. That perhaps she's haunted. Some say by a ghost, some say by the queen."

"Do you believe them?"

The little man smiled for the first time. "I believe that Athven will stand until another is found to stand with her. Whether a ghost or something more substantial. Beatra Nar would not have left us undefended forever."

Alexei winced. His cousin had been formidable, but no one could reach beyond the grave. He stood and bowed to his host. "I thank you, for the drink and for the news. Health to you, and to your family."

They descended the stairs again, and stepped quite suddenly into the middle of a spectacular brawl. Chairs, ale, and soup were flying, along with blades, accompanied by growls, grunts and screams.

Alexei's companion wilted beside him. "This always happens. Dru spills the soup, they fight. And I can't patch them up afterwards because they'd probably try to kill me even as they bled to death on my floor."

"Do you have a back door?" Alexei asked, not willing to risk adding to his scars by setting foot in the room.

"Yes." The man turned around and led him through a dingy kitchen to a sagging door in the rear of the building.

"Then I'll bid you farewell," Alexei said, "and better fortune until perhaps we meet again."

He set off into the night, but was brought up short by a shout from behind him.

The man was standing behind the tavern, hastily untying his apron. He picked up a leather satchel off the ground, wrapped a scarf around his neck, clapped a hat on his head and ran after Alexei as quickly as his rotund form would allow.

"I don't care who you are," he said. "You're going somewhere other than here. My name is Gulver. That's all really. My family was never big enough for a house, and I'm the last of them anyway, so I'm coming with you. I'm done scrubbing blood off the floor and I want to see Athven Nar."

"What makes you think I'm going to Athven Nar?"

"Aren't you?" Gulver asked innocently. "Even crazy seers aren't always wrong, and neither am I. Someday one of those men, or women, in there is going to take exception to my face and it'll be my blood on the floor and no one to care. I'd rather have an adventure, even if I don't live to see the end of it."

Alexei closed his eyes and counted to five. When he opened them the man was still there.

"Tell me, Gulver... what is your gift?"

Gulver beamed, his mustache bristling with pride. "Why, I'm a healer. Haven't had much chance to practice in twenty years, not since the burnings started, but I used to be known through three towns for my touch with injuries of the mind. Good with fevers and infections too!"

"Of course you are."

Malichai was never going to let him live this down.

Gulver may have seemed dour on first acquaintance, but once he arrived at the camp, there was simply no standing in the way of his evident relief at being amongst fellow Erathi. He greeted Silvay and Wilder like long-lost family and cast periodic dark looks at Porfiry after the Betrayer's presence was explained. Despite an initial expression of nervous alarm at meeting Malichai, the healer soon relaxed enough to swap tales with the Andari, whether of cooking for large numbers of people or dealing with the vagaries of the intoxicated.

Malichai, for his part, gracefully refrained from saying anything to Alexei, if one discounted the wink and guffaw that burst out of him upon learning the newcomer's identity.

And Alexei was grateful enough for Malichai's skill set that he probably wouldn't have complained in any case. They were now a party of six, counting Porfiry, and Malichai was still the only one of them with any reasonable grasp of weapons or tactics. Four times, they'd been accosted on the road, and four times, they'd all come off without a single scratch. Such luck couldn't be expected to last forever, Alexei knew, no matter how skilled Malichai was. Eventually, they would run into someone with more to lose. Someone like treasure hunters who might see them as interlopers.

If their luck—and the weather—held, he hoped to reach Athven inside of the next three days. There would be plenty of surprises then, and there was one thing he wanted to get out of the way first. He was going to have to talk to his cousin.

Porfiry sat on the edge of camp, hands and feet bound as they usually were when he was not on a horse. His wrists rested on his knees, and his head was bent over them, his mouth moving silently as he rocked back and forth.

"You're going to have to talk to me eventually," Alexei told him, crouching close by and striving to sound neutral.

Porfiry continued to mutter.

"You know I can't kill you, no matter how much I would like to. You are technically my blood, and the only family I have left, other than my brother, who will never leave Andar." Alexei looked at his cousin and swallowed the bile that always rose at the sight of his face. He had dreamed of his revenge for so many years, but revenge would have to wait. "We share memories, you and I, and even if we remember those times differently, I have to believe that there is some part of you that regrets what happened. A part that is as devastated as I when you see what's become of our homeland. Our people."

Porfiry looked up from his knees and laughed. "Poor fool. You don't understand. You can't. You couldn't even see it with two eyes, and now you only have one."

Alexei swallowed the impulse to grab his cousin and shake him till he screamed. "Then why don't you tell me? If I am so blind, tell me what happened. Tell me how this could have been different."

Porfiry's head swiveled strangely on his scrawny neck. He licked his lips and blinked into the firelight. "You've made me no promises. Given me no reason to trust. I won't give up my revenge for nothing."

"What revenge?" Alexei's hands curled into fists with the effort of holding back his anger. He longed to snarl and spit and twist that chicken neck between his fingers until it snapped. His memories of Porfiry were so deeply stained with blood and smoke and betrayal that it hurt, deep in his bones, to pretend he could forgive. He never could. Never would. But for the Rose, for Wilder and Silvay and Gulver, he would pretend.

"Nothing for free, Cousin." Porfiry leered at him, as though daring Alexei to react. "Not a word. The leeches have had their pint of me and they are not my masters anymore."

"You're going to have to be less cryptic, *Cousin*," Alexei said, his lips a thin, taut line. "I have no idea who the leeches are or why you might want revenge. Our people did nothing to you. You lived your life in a palace, with everything given freely. What could possibly have given you the desire to destroy everything you had ever known?"

"Poor, perfect Alexei!" Porfiry snarled, his amusement vanished. "Of course you wouldn't know. You never had to work. Your precious masters never pushed you beyond endurance to wring every last drop of talent from your pathetic hide."

"You think I didn't work for my gift?" Alexei barked, enraged by the accusation. "I worked. I tried. And sometimes I failed. My hands are still scarred from the hours in the workshops, learning to craft every possible material. I burned myself with backlash more times than I could count, trying to learn more and more complex enchantments. Don't tell me I never had to work for what I learned."

"Poor, poor Trevelyan. See how hard his life is. See how he immolates himself for his people. Let us all bow down before his selfless sacrifice."

"Don't pretend this is about me," Alexei said softly. He reminded himself that Porfiry had always had a talent for provocation and swallowed his anger, though with difficulty. "We were never adversaries, you and I."

"The great Alexei never even noticed me. How would he know who my adversaries were?"

"Perhaps you had enemies, Porfiry, but I was not one of them."

"A man like you has no need for enemies," Porfiry spat. "But we all have to find our strength somewhere."

Alexei picked up a rock and rubbed it between his fingers while he took deep, calming breaths and considered what he might say next. How could he convince his perfidious cousin to give him the information he needed? What could he possibly offer a man who cared so little for life and decency that he would betray his home and his people?

"What do you want?" he asked at last.

"I already have what I want," Porfiry whispered. "I have the look on their faces when they realized what I'd done. When they finally grasped that despite all of their power, all of their pride, they could do nothing to stop what was coming. They said I was weak. That I was useless. But by the end they knew they were wrong."

And there it was—the why that Alexei had spent so much effort convincing himself he didn't want to know. He couldn't tell whether it made him feel better or worse to find out that his cousin had betrayed them all not for money, or for power, but to prove something to his doubters. To show them that he didn't need great magic to be strong. The end was the same, and Alexei could not possibly despise the man more than he already did.

"Whatever you're thinking, whatever you're planning, you'll never find it without me." Porfiry's eyes glittered as they bored into Alexei's. "You could turn Athven Nar into a heap of stone and sort through it piece by piece and still never find it."

"What makes you think I'll need to?" Alexei asked softly. "Did you never think that Athven herself might take a hand in her own salvation? When Beatra was alive, she spoke of Athven like a friend. It is very possible that she is still aware and already knows where it is, and all she is waiting for is someone to tell."

Porfiry's face grew still. He swallowed.

"And if that is the case," Alexei went on, "I truly will not need you. And though I cannot shed Nar blood, there are those who would not hesitate. King Hollin was not pleased to be forced to give you up and I believe there is a charge of treason awaiting you should I task Malichai with returning you to the tender care of Andar."

He stood and brushed off his hands. "Think on it. Decide how you want this to end. I will find it, and I will restore it. Whether you choose to be a part of that is up to you."

Whether Porfiry believed him was really going to be the question. Because as confident as he'd tried to sound, Alexei doubted that Athven could do as he suggested. If she could, she would have done so before the invaders reached her walls. And if she was somehow still aware after all this time unbonded and alone... Alexei would have had no excuse for staying away so long. He could have returned at any time, instead of waiting, telling himself that the Rose was lost and Athven could not help them.

Despite his guilt, he hoped he was wrong. He hoped there was enough left of Athven to aid them in their search. If it was true that the treasure hunters had not yet gained entry, that was a good sign. Perhaps, if she had survived Beatra's death, she had found a way to lie dormant. But if that was so, she might not even be aware enough to let *him* in. They could be stuck waiting until Athven fell deeply enough into hibernation to lower her guard.

But whether Athven was alive or dead, awake or in hibernation, he still needed Porfiry. His cousin had probably not been exaggerating when he said they could tear the castle down and never find the Rose. They could search, but their hope would be slim indeed without guidance. Porfiry was simply going to have to tell him where to find it.

And if he refused? If he made demands? What was Alexei willing to do in exchange for the information? How far was he willing to pervert justice to restore the shield, expiate his guilt and give his people hope? Could he let Porfiry walk away, unpunished and unrepentant?

And did he even have the right to make such a decision?

~

The next three days were painful ones for Alexei. Each passing hour brought them closer to a truth he wasn't sure he wanted to learn, and his anxiety mounted. What if he was too late? What if Athven was gone, someone else had stolen the Rose and there was no hope at all for them to succeed?

In addition to anxiety, every passing moment brought with it another memory. As they pushed deeper into the heart of Erath, Alexei began to recognize the land and could feel how much it had changed.

On that first day, they forded the Dralten River. The bridge had been destroyed, but the river still ran shallow and clear over a bed of rose-colored stone. No one knew why so many of the stones had tumbled down from the mountains so perfectly smooth and round, but the Dralten had long been the source of Erathi hearthstones, and nearly every dwelling had boasted several of the glowing spheres during the cold winter months.

The following day saw them pass by the foot of Bone Cairn, a towering heap of rocks so long and smooth and oddly shaped that generations of Erathi children had decided it was the final resting place of a giant. Alexei and his cousin Yala had once climbed all the way to the top to find out if there was a skull and found only the deeply carven marks left by generations of other adventurous souls, no doubt wondering the same thing.

Their path even lingered for some distance on the eaves of Vrendel Wood, the only sanctuary in the known world for wyvern, indrik, and artenu, rare and magical creatures that Alexei hoped had somehow found a way to survive. Sightings had been relatively uncommon, even for Erathi who knew how to look for them, so it was probable they had avoided notice. If they hadn't, Gulver would likely have heard wild tales of hunters being carried off by winged reptiles, stalked by vengeful horned equines, or even devoured by giant bears made of smoke and fire.

But nowhere—not in the rivers, the plains or the woods—could Alexei feel the connection that used to run deep in his bones, the hum of the land's own magic in harmony with his. There were no golden threads lurking just outside of conscious thought, linking person to person, joining the present with the past. The music of that dance, the intricate tapestry of relationship between the land and her people, was silent, and the echoing emptiness of it left a hollow ache in Alexei's chest.

How could this be Erath? How could this dead and desolate place be his beloved homeland? The only proof that he was home coiled deep in his chest—he still had his magic, and it still drew strength from the land. His power had grown as they traveled, till he felt nearly as strong as he ever had, but with that power came a sense of terrible isolation. In Andar, he had isolated himself by choice. Now he had to feel and be reminded of just how alone he really was.

It was almost worse when he realized he was beginning to sense the others in his party, just in tenuous snatches of unheard sound, unseen color —the tiniest whispers into a silence that had once been a symphony. Silvay was a narrow ribbon of blue, a mellow tone that made everything around it sound more full and vibrant. Gulver was a deep river of earthen brown, shot with veins of gold, a clear chime that punctuated each moment like a shaft of sunlight. Wilder was pure silver, easy to miss, like a single note being played in a crowd, but filling in the spaces with a brilliant sweetness of purpose.

But three could never fill the space left by thousands of missing voices.

By night, around the fire, Silvay spun stories of the past to a rapt audience. Gulver looked wistful, Wilder fascinated, and Malichai frankly disbelieving as she recalled the former days of Erath, when gifts were valued and the people flourished.

"Here's what I don't understand," Malichai said one night, at a lull in the conversation. "If you lot could do all these things—control wood, water and stone, enchant your fields and your homes, bid animals obey and call the weather to heel—why did you never leave your land? Why in so many centuries did no one know of this? And how was there no one of you who thought to turn his skills to conquer others?"

Silvay laughed. "We are no saints, Malichai. There have been plenty of us, over the centuries, who wished to turn our thoughts to war, or to expansion, or simply to taking advantage of his or her fellows." She tilted her head briefly in Porfiry's direction. "But here's the plain truth of it—our land binds us together. We take the best part of our strength from the land, and from our bonds with each other. When we leave Erath, or when we choose to use our strength against it, we become little more than mundane folks, unable to feel or use the full measure of the gift we once had."

A rasping voice echoed out of the darkness behind her. "Or we wait. And we plan. And we find a way to use the poison of our ancestors to throw down their pious ideals and make something different for ourselves." Porfiry's bitterness seemed a stark note of discord in the harmony of their little group.

"What did he do?" whispered Wilder. "Why is he like this? I can barely see him at all and it's so... unhappy. I don't like to look."

Silvay glanced at Alexei, and he nodded. The boy, and Malichai as well, had a right to know the story.

"Near thirty years ago," she began, "we were a peaceful and prosperous land. And a good part of our peace and prosperity was due to the work of a man named Nar, who lived, oh, many hundreds of years past. He was one of the greatest enchanters Erath has ever known, and his deepest fear was that one day, Erath would be destroyed by those who wanted what we had but did not bear the gift that would let them see why we had it.

"We were a part of our land, and it was a part of us, and to preserve that, Nar poured his life into a great enchantment, a talisman so complex and powerful that no enchanter since has been able to fully grasp how it was made. The Rose of Erath is a piece of baryte crystal, as large as a man's head, and it holds within it the song of our magic. The whole symphony of Erathi love for our homeland resonates through its petals, and it was placed deep within the heart of Athven Nar herself. As thorns protect a rose, so Athven protected the talisman, which in turn protected our people. It drew on each and every living thing within our borders to create a shield, a barrier of magic that denied entry to anyone with duplicity and malice towards our people in their heart."

She paused to drink and sighed a little as she swallowed. "As you can imagine, this sort of intent is ever difficult to discern. And the enchantment was not guided by a human hand, so it judged for itself, and as a result, nearly everyone was kept out. Word of our land and our magic was rarely ever heard outside our borders, and those who carried it were either too young or considered too inebriated to be believed. Until one day, when a man of Erath acted in hatred and stole the Rose, removing it from the heart of Athven Nar and breaking the enchantment that kept us safe from discovery."

"And then the soldiers came," Wilder said in a small voice.

"Yes," Silvay answered simply. "When the barrier fell, we learned that an army waited just outside. They both coveted and despised our magic, and it did not take long for them to exploit our vulnerability. Our people were overrun by those who dealt in weapons and war, and all who survived were enslaved in hatred and prejudice."

"But you're going to fix it." Wilder fastened his eyes on Alexei. "I've seen the crown in your aura—that's why we're here. That's why he's here." He gestured to Porfiry. "To find the Rose and make it so we're safe again."

Alexei wished he could tell the boy that it was so. That they were going to make everything all right again. But nothing would ever be all right again, no matter what his aura claimed. And if they could not find the Rose, if Porfiry clung to his revenge till his dying breath, there would be nothing any of them could do.

Even if they found it, a voice within him whispered, nothing would bring back what had been lost. The innocence of their culture had been destroyed and Alexei could not fix that. He could not bring back thousands of dead, could not restore slaves to their families or wipe away memories of horror.

"We are going to try," he said instead, smiling sadly. "And we are not going to give up, not while we have any reason to hope."

"Just say the word then if you want yon beggar's toes held to the fire," Malichai announced cheerfully. "Not that I'm a man that enjoys such things, but I'm willing to make an exception for black-hearted villains who deserve to hang from their own guts till their eyes pop out and they scream for someone to run them through with a red-hot poker because it might end their suffering." He winked at Wilder, who was staring at him with wide-eyed dismay.

"Noted, my bloodthirsty friend," Alexei said dryly. He knew Malichai quite well enough by now to realize that the comment was for Porfiry's benefit. The giant warrior would never cook something he couldn't eat and would only kill a man in a fair fight.

But Wilder, without an aura to read, had no way of knowing this.

"Wilder, before you decide to be frightened of our resident berserker, you might ask him about his three greatest fears."

Wilder looked back at Malichai.

"That's easy," Malichai said promptly. "Losing a fight to fewer than three men, breaking my bow, or losing my Loraleen. Oh, and that someday I will meet a beautiful woman I adore, and she won't like my cooking. That's four, but it wouldn't have been fair to leave any of them out."

"Now," Alexei continued, not really caring whether Porfiry was listening or not, "does that sound to you like a man who would engage in gruesome torture?"

Wilder grinned. "No," he whispered, jerking a grimy thumb in Porfiry's direction, "but *he* doesn't know that!"

Alexei laughed along with the others, but his heart wasn't in it. They were getting so close. Perhaps tomorrow, the towers would be in view. And he didn't know if he would be able to bear it.

CHAPTER 4

*Z*ara gave the tiny door a halfhearted push as she passed, and, as expected, it didn't budge. Shadow shot a disgusted look over her shoulder, and Zara scowled back.

"You can't expect me to stop trying," she insisted. "Not until you tell me why you've trapped me here. And I know it's you, so don't try to deny it."

The cat walked on, down the narrow corridor that ran along the outside wall of the castle. Every other door in the castle, Zara had been able to unlock or had simply found open. But any door to the outside? Might as well have been an illusion.

She had followed the cat over most of the castle by now, waiting patiently as her four-footed companion sniffed in corners and rubbed against walls, with no indication of what, if anything, they were looking for. As they searched, Zara memorized as much of the castle's layout as she could, and amused herself by imagining it as it might have been.

There would have been furniture, of course, and rugs everywhere—deep, thick rugs in bright colors to warm the cold stone. There would have been art and music and conversation. Laughter and tears and shouting.

Night and day, fire and shadow. It would have been warm. And there would have been food. Mounds of delicious, freshly cooked food.

She tried not to think about food, not often, but the fare had long since grown difficult to choke down. Shadow still shared Zara's dinner, but these days the cat was getting more than half of what she prepared. It was a wonder the creature wasn't growing fat.

The cat had begun to spend more time in the kitchen, ever since the incident in the pedestal room, as Zara had named it. And Zara was grateful for the company, even if she did occasionally wonder whether she should be. Harboring fond thoughts of her jailer was probably in poor taste, no matter what shape the jailer wore.

When she finally reached the end of the outer passage, Shadow hissed quietly and trotted back towards the entry hall. It renewed Zara's impression that the cat was looking for something—something she needed Zara to help her find. But unless Shadow could find a way to tell her what it was, Zara had no idea how to help.

"You know, I'd be happy to come to some sort of agreement, if you like," she said casually. "I feel like you need me for something, and that's why you've trapped me here." The cat ignored her. "I'd be delighted to help. I'm good at finding things." Shadow shot her a dirty look, as if she was, indeed, aware of Zara's profession. Zara felt embarrassed until she remembered she was talking to a cat. "And I don't want to stay here forever. I'm sure it's a lovely castle, but I need more than myself for company." She hastened to add: "More people, that is. I'm grateful not to be entirely alone, but talking to animals is generally not considered normal. Besides, my father may be worried about me." She doubted that was true, but Shadow didn't know it. "And I won't last forever on a diet of jerked beef stew." That much was definitely true.

Shadow stalked on ahead, lashing her tail.

"Let's make a deal. You tell me what you need, and I'll help you. All you have to do is unlock the doors after it's over and I get to go free. I promise I won't leave until after I find what you're looking for."

The cat turned to glare at her, eyes narrowed, tail still lashing. Shadow was clearly thinking deep, feline thoughts.

"Can you draw me a picture? Help me understand what you're thinking? Even if you can't draw with paws, you seem smart enough to find some way to tell me."

Shadow stalked off again, head held high, so Zara rolled her eyes and followed. She refused to feel guilty. Cats were clearly far too easily offended.

Offended or not, that night Shadow did not leave the kitchen after dinner. Even when Zara drew off her boots and lay down on her blankets in front of the fire, the cat remained, basking in the warmth.

"I'm willing to share," Zara offered, pointing to one side of her bed. "If you'd prefer this to the hard floor."

Shadow rose and stretched carefully, looked around, washed her paws for a moment, then sauntered closer, trying to look uninterested.

"Hah!" Zara grinned at her companion. "You might not actually be a cat, but most of the time you certainly act like one."

The creature did not stoop to bestow her notice on such a comment, only sat, carefully, on the edge of the blanket.

Zara grinned. "Good night, Shadow. Pleasant dreams. If you have them." The last thing she remembered seeing was Shadow's eyes, gleaming in the dark as they reflected the wavering glow of the coals.

Zara blinked and looked around, wondering at the brightness of the light. There were windows, high above, and they were clean, allowing her to catch glimpses of blue sky and an occasional white cloud. She lowered her gaze. The walls around her seemed familiar, but changed. They were stone, but there were tapestries to soften their harsh gray surfaces. Every corner of the room held something green and growing, and the floor was covered in a deep blue rug.

Looking down at herself, Zara observed without much surprise that she was seated, and wearing a dress that matched her surroundings. The elaborate embroidery on her white bodice was a dark purple, and she could feel soft silken trousers beneath her pale lavender skirt. Her hands were even clean and unscarred, which was her first clue that she was dreaming.

She looked up again and saw a woman sitting across from her, in a chair that could only be described as a throne. Though perhaps it was more the occupant than the chair that gave that impression.

The woman was utterly unfamiliar, and yet Zara knew her, in the uncanny way of dreams. The stranger's expression was remote, but her green eyes were fixed unwaveringly on Zara's face, suggesting watchfulness. Her age was indeterminate, somewhat older than Zara's own thirty years, but she wore an air of unquestionable command along with her night-blue dress. Her thick gray hair was braided and wrapped around her head like a crown, and there was a short staff in her hand— a gold-banded length of polished stone that glittered in the sunlight.

"Where am I?" Zara wondered aloud, her gaze darting around the room to see if they were alone.

"In your own head, child," the woman said. "Where else would we be?"

"In yours?" Zara suggested flippantly. She didn't like the sound of the other woman's dismissal. "I've certainly never used mine to picture myself in such a ridiculous costume." She thought about it some more

and lifted a hand to her neck, her face and her hair. Sure enough, she was wearing some sort of necklace and her normally braided white hair was piled in an elaborately curled mass atop her head. A bracelet of deep purple gems glittered against her wrist.

"You would not last long in my head, as you put it," the other woman retorted dryly. "I wasn't certain I had enough strength to establish even this tenuous hold on yours."

"What are you doing to me?" Zara demanded, leaning forward in her dream chair with a flash of anger.

"What you asked," the woman replied coolly. "You wanted to find a way to talk."

Zara stared at her. This was a dream, of course.

"And before you deny my existence, you should know that your cooking tastes terrible. I wouldn't eat it if I didn't need to establish a connection between us."

"You might look like a woman," Zara returned, "but you still act like a cat."

The woman smiled. "I am glad to see you are taking this well. There are very few who could have accepted me for what I am, in such a short time. And my time was running out, so I had little choice. But you are strong and I have hope that you will be able to help me after all."

"Yes," Zara answered, "but I'm clearly insane. Utterly and completely bonkers. I've been following a cat around this castle for days and now I'm dreaming about talking to her."

"This is not truly a dream," the woman stated calmly. "It might more properly be called a vision, though you do not have the talent for a true vision so I was forced to improvise."

"Very well." Zara leaned back and folded her arms, noticing as she did so the softness of the chairback behind her shoulders. "I'm willing to believe you, but not because you say so. I simply don't dream about silk and velvet, and I don't wear jewelry. What would you like to discuss?"

"Your purpose here, of course." The woman acted as if Zara were quite dim for asking. "I have kept you here for a reason, as you have already grown to suspect. I need your help—your hands—to find something that is lost to me."

"Why does a cat need possessions?" Zara asked curiously.

"You know very well that I am not a cat, as you have mentioned several times in my hearing," the woman retorted.

"Then what are you?" Even in the dream, Zara's heart pounded as she awaited the answer to her question.

"I do not know if I can explain it to you, mundane as you are." The woman frowned. She seemed to have a distaste for being thwarted, whether by her own limitations or by Zara's.

And what did she mean mundane? That Zara was not a sorcerer, as the Erathi had been? She could only be thankful for that!

"I am what you might call... an avatar." The woman who was Shadow seemed to settle on the word reluctantly. "A representation of something large and powerful that cannot exist fully on the physical plane."

"Like... a goddess?" Zara asked, wide-eyed.

"Not exactly." The woman hissed a laugh, a very cat-like sound. "I am..." She gestured at the walls around them. "I am myself. I am the life in the stones and the shape of the magic that wrought them. I am the many years of dedication and sacrifice that have been poured into this place. I am the love of the land and the hope of the future, the tapestry of ties from person to person and from thousands of souls to their hearth and soil."

Zara's mouth opened and closed. She might not know anything about magic, but that seemed like a lot of power. "Then what could you possibly want with me?" she whispered.

"I do not know what I can do with you," the woman said with a sigh that seemed to settle into the stones of the floor. "I had not antici-

pated that I could be awakened by one with so little power as you have."

"So little?" Zara echoed with a laugh. "Let us be honest with one another and say none. I know nothing of magic."

"Oh, you have some." The woman waved a hand, dismissing Zara's protest. "Not much, and nothing that you would ever have been aware of had you not come here and slept on my stones for so many days. But it was sufficient for me to appear to you in a physical form, and to gain enough strength from you to share this vision."

"You're using me?" Zara asked, not at all pleased by this revelation. "For my magic? Will you get stronger and stronger until I wither away altogether?"

"Don't be dramatic," the woman replied, lifting the back of her hand to her mouth briefly, then lowering it with a start.

Zara stifled a laugh. She would have sworn the woman had forgotten she did not have paws to lick.

"Those who have lived here have always taken strength from me, as I have taken strength from them. We grow stronger and deeper together. My people defend me as I defend them. Each has something the other needs, and I would not be so foolish as to destroy my only hope of remaining awake and aware."

So, the woman—no, the castle—needed her. She needed Zara, a treasure hunter who had invaded the walls of a sentient fortress with the intent to steal her riches and sell them for profit.

"You know what I am," Zara stated boldly, lifting her chin and looking into the green eyes of the avatar across from her. She wondered how her father might have responded to a conversation where the castle he had intended to rob was staring back at him. "And surely you know why I came here. Why would you trust me? Why choose me for this?"

"Well, you can stop imagining it was for any sterling qualities," the

woman returned tartly. "I know you are a treasure hunter. That you steal from the dead and profit from their sorrow."

Zara cringed. She didn't think she could explain how very little she profited. How very little she wanted to.

"But," the woman went on, "your people were the first to breach my walls since my last caretaker died. She was a worthy guardian, and I had a great reserve of strength at the last, enough to sustain me through the shock of her death and preserve me as I waited for her successor. But too many years passed. I became too weak to keep out those who wished to take these halls for themselves, and I was desperate. I was barely aware enough to realize that you had a tiny spark of magic, enough to form a connection so that I could rouse myself and drive the others out." She was looking over Zara's shoulder, her eyes unfocused as if remembering. "It took some time to gain enough from your presence that I could appear to you in any form. Maintaining a physical avatar—even one so small and simple as a cat—is costly, but it was necessary for you to accept me. Once you acknowledged me, trusted me, I began strengthening the bond between us so that we could progress faster. But it may all be for naught."

"What do you mean?" Zara was still attempting to absorb the idea that she was a living, breathing energy source for a magical castle.

"I cannot find it." The woman's eyes snapped open and in them was something like fear. "We have been through every room, every hall, every cellar, and it is not there. I can feel it, but somehow it is still beyond my reach."

"What is? Maybe if you describe it I can help."

A breath hissed between the woman's lips and her eyes narrowed a trifle. "I am not a fool, treasure hunter. We might be forced by this bond to cooperate, but I will not put myself in your hands and risk a thousand years of sacrifice being destroyed in an instant of mercenary greed."

71

Zara felt angry, ashamed and defensive all at once. "I do not steal!" she burst out hotly. *"I would never take from any person by force, let alone someone in need."*

"And how do you know, little treasure hunter, what it is you do when you take? How do you know what bonds have been broken, what seals have been turned to dust? Had I not bonded with you, you might have gone on believing me nothing but an empty heap of stone and never known what complex magic there is in memory and sacrifice."

"No," Zara admitted, "I likely would not have known. But for all that, you truly are a heap of stone. You are deep and enormous and powerful, so you cannot understand what it is to be weak and limited and without options. I do what I must so that I can eat and drink and sleep in a place where I will not freeze during the winter. I will not apologize for surviving, any more than you will, though you stole my freedom from me when you imprisoned me here."

The avatar appeared startled. "I have given far more than I have taken," she insisted. "Our bond is not merely one of taking, as I explained."

"No, you really have not explained," Zara answered. "Whatever bond you speak of, it was made without my permission. And I have no idea how to use it, or what good it might do me. I do not want to stay here forever, silent and alone, simply because you need a source of energy."

Fingers tapped the arm of the throne-like chair as the woman considered. "Very well," she said abruptly. "You have helped me to realize what I must do." She smiled, which, being a very cat-like smile, did not reassure Zara in the slightest. "We will make a bargain, as you requested."

"And do I have the right to refuse?" Zara asked.

The woman stared at her and brought the stone rod to rest on her silk-clad knee. "Yes," she said finally, though it was an uncertain yes.

"Yes, I will grant you that right, but if you refuse I fear that I cannot ever unlock these doors. You must understand—had I been aware enough to realize what I was doing, I would never have bonded you against your will, and yet, there is no changing it now. If you were to leave me here alone, I would die and there would be no bringing me back."

Zara grew still and her mouth fell open slightly as she realized what the avatar was saying. "You would imprison me here forever to save your own life?"

"As you said," the woman agreed, "we do what we must to survive. But if you agree to my bargain, perhaps a different ending would be possible."

Zara hated being forced into things. She especially hated when it was guilt that forced her hand. But she couldn't walk away and leave a living creature to its death, no matter how much she hated what the castle had done to her, deliberately or no. "All right." She nodded reluctantly. "I will hear your bargain." She would hear it, but she wasn't going to give this cat/woman/castle the idea that she was in control. Zara might be the penniless daughter of a feckless treasure hunter, but she would not be anyone's pawn. "But first," she added, "before I make some sort of agreement with the avatar of a haunted castle, shouldn't I get to know your name? You do have one, don't you?"

"Of course I have a name, silly child. But a name is a thing of power. It gives shape and meaning and is not to be given or taken lightly."

Zara scoffed silently. Her own name meant less than nothing. "I suppose you know mine already, but you may call me Zara," she said flippantly.

"That is not your name," the avatar said slyly. "It is what you call yourself, but it is not your name."

Zara stared at her.

"But I will give you mine, all the same," the woman went on. "And I will expect you to treat my name with respect, as you may be the last person to ever hear it."

The thought sent a chill down Zara's spine.

"In the language of this place, I am Athven. And in former days, when I was not alone, those who cared for me called me Athven Nar. And now. About our bargain..."

≈

Zara woke herself with a harsh cry, sweating and gasping for breath. Her eyes flew open to see only her dim and shadowy kitchen. And a cat, watching her carefully from her seat close to the few remaining coals.

"You furry little bastard!" Zara snarled, leaping out of her blankets and grabbing for the cat with both hands. The animal darted away. "That was no bargain! That was a curse!" She dashed at the cat again, but was too fuddled by dreams and sleep and nearly stumbled.

The cat hissed, looking angry this time, and the hair on her back stood up.

Zara hissed back.

Until the stones under her feet began to shift. Her eyes and her arms flew wide and she staggered, nearly losing her balance.

When the floor stopped moving, she stood tall and glared, refusing to acknowledge her terror at the realization of exactly who she shared her fire with. And what the creature could do if she chose. "Very well," she said coolly. "You've proven you can be a bully. I hope you're proud of how strong you are. But I remember what you said. You need me, just as much as I need you. If you pull your own roof down on my head you'd be a far bigger fool than I. And let me be clear." She folded her arms and narrowed her eyes. "You don't get to push me around and you don't get to mess with my head. I am not your toy and I am not your plaything. I might have to live up to this bargain, but I will do it my way. And if you don't like it, you can be stuck as a one-eared cat until I drop dead of old age."

With a sharp nod to punctuate her words, Zara turned her back on the cat and marched back to the fire. It spoiled her dignified retreat just a trifle when she tripped on her own blankets, but she didn't check to see if the cat was laughing. She had a fire to build up. More tasteless stew to make. And a lot of angry muttering to do. The fact that she'd had no choice did not make her feel any better about the bargain she'd made.

She wasn't sure whether she should be more upset about the terms of the agreement, or about the fact that she might never have the chance to live up to it. That, she supposed, would depend on the future.

She'd heard of cursed princesses, be-spelled princes, and enchanted kingdoms. They simply had to find the right hero to break the curse so that everyone could live happily ever after. The only stories about cursed treasure hunters, however, ended badly. If this was a story, she, Zara, was the villain. But she didn't feel like a villain. She felt lost and alone and she wanted to go home, except she didn't have a home. All she had was a nameless longing for somewhere to belong and someone to belong to. Someone who cared more for her than for the glitter of gold and gems. And now, thanks to a magical talking cat, that possibility was further away than it had ever been before.

CHAPTER 5

hey entered the valley around midday, and the worst of the
tension in Alexei's chest eased somewhat. She still stood.
Even after all the stories, he had not quite believed it until he could see her
for himself. That last day, the day he fled, had been so dark, with so much
chaos and violence, he had wondered for many years whether Athven
might have crumbled under the onslaught.

She had her scars, just as he did, visible even from a distance. The
stones of the northmost tower were dark, and chunks were missing from
several of the turrets. But her walls appeared sound, and, best of all, there
was no smoke rising from the valley floor. Perhaps his fears of needing to
fight their way in would prove unfounded.

Wilder cheered when he saw the towers, almost falling off his perch
behind Malichai's saddle in his enthusiasm. Silvay and Gulver were both
silent, and Alexei caught Silvay wiping a surreptitious tear. Gulver made
no secret of his emotion, and allowed the tears to roll down his face
unchecked.

But Alexei felt nothing. Not relief, not joy, not pain. None of what he'd
expected. His eyes remained dry, and his memories lay quiet, locked behind

some unseen, unfelt wall. Everything drew back—the sights, the sounds, the smells—behind some distant curtain that deadened his senses and allowed him to note only the immediate.

They would ride to the center of the valley and camp. He would take stock of the surroundings. Strategies rolled through his mind, possible entrances, probable pitfalls.

They rode by the remains of the stone arch that marked the descent of the road into the valley of Athven. It had been destroyed, no doubt during the invasion, and heaps of piled stones lay to either side of the way, overgrown with vines and surrounded by grass. A hawk soared overhead, and a bird cried out harshly from a nearby tree. The sun was warm on their shoulders and the horses' hooves were louder than they should have been.

Alexei still felt nothing.

"It's normal, you know," Silvay said quietly, almost in his ear.

"What?" He wanted to lash out, but kept his tone coolly civil.

"The numbness."

"Then why are you and Gulver not affected? Why are you able to weep when I cannot?" It didn't seem fair. Why could he not cry for what had been lost?

"We have so much less to feel than you," she said, patience and sympathy in every line of her face. "When memories run that deep and dark, we find ways to keep them from rising."

"Will I be numb forever?" He fought to sound calm, rather than desperate, but Silvay heard his plea.

"Only until it's safe to mourn."

That might be never. And all Alexei could feel about it was a sort of guilty gratitude. He could not stomach the idea of his cousin rejoicing in his pain. He would never let Porfiry see him weep.

But he also would not look at his cousin's face. He didn't want to know what feelings might be visible there, be they triumph or dismay. He couldn't bear the sight of either.

They drew up at last beneath the shadow of Athven's imposing heights. Where the castle had once been flanked by cultivated gardens and artfully tended wilderness, it was now overgrown and wild, and parts had clearly been flattened by the camps of hopeful invaders. Trees had been cut down to make crude shelters, and fire rings had been built from the remains of crumbled fountains and toppled statuary.

Nothing stirred, within or without the castle walls, except for their own party going about the business of making camp, pretending it was just another end to another day on the road. Alexei knew that they were all watching him. All except for Porfiry, who sat straight and defiant, rather than his usual hunched and bitter posture.

Silence reigned until they had eaten and the shadows had fully fallen over their camp.

"We'll approach tomorrow," Alexei announced suddenly. "By daylight. I don't know what we may find, or whether we'll be able to enter, but there is little value now in being over-hasty. If anyone else was here to hinder us, that might be different, but I believe the valley to be abandoned."

He did not tell them of the dread that was growing with each passing moment. If Athven was still aware, she had given no sign of it. Perhaps he had barely dared hope, but his disappointment told him he had not quite given up the idea that she might still live. But if that was the case, he should have felt her by now. The fact that his magic had sounded no chime of recognition suggested that she was at least dormant. Which meant that her walls may already have been breached. The Rose might already have been found.

He glanced at Porfiry and wished he hadn't. After so many days of pinched silence, his cousin's face bore the ghost of a smile.

"We will, however, set a watch. Everyone but Wilder will take a turn."

"Why not me?" Wilder protested. "I'll never be able to sleep and I promise I would do a good job."

"Because you still haven't had a bath," Alexei said, lacking the energy or inclination to explain the truth. He hadn't the heart to tell the boy he didn't trust him to stay awake. "If someone wished to attack our camp, they would assume you were not a very good watchman because you haven't bothered to wash." Perhaps that was not the best argument to make to a child, but he hadn't known very many children.

"I know I'm not a very good watchman," Wilder insisted earnestly, "but I'm an excellent watchwoman."

Everyone turned to look at him—her—at once. Malichai's mouth hung open.

"Watchwoman?" Alexei repeated slowly.

Silvay dissolved into laughter. "So much for the amazing powers of seers," she said cheerfully. "I can't believe I didn't see that."

"I *told* you I wasn't a grubby little boy, but you didn't listen," Wilder said defensively. "And if you let me watch, I promise I would be wide awake. No one can sneak up on me and I can be very loud if anyone tries to attack."

"I have no doubt in your ability to be loud," Alexei assured her, smiling faintly, "but you're still not watching. Keep the watchman—or watchwoman—company if you must. Quietly."

Wilder frowned, but Alexei didn't give her a chance to protest. "I will be first. Malichai, you will be last, and Silvay and Gulver can fight for whichever shift they prefer."

"Second," Silvay chimed cheerfully, and Gulver agreed.

"I am accustomed to being awake at all hours, so it makes little difference to me." He rubbed his hands together over the fire. "And I may be too excited to sleep."

Once everyone else had retreated to their blankets, Alexei withdrew to the remains of a garden wall and seated himself carefully, in case it collapsed beneath him. He rubbed his arms to dispel a chill and felt older than the stones themselves. His scars twinged but he ignored them. Closing his eyes, he reached out with his magic instead of his senses.

He could feel the remains of broken enchantments. The wall on which he sat fluttered with torn bits of magic that had once protected the life of the garden. The earth beneath the stones still sparked with tiny flashes of the power that had sustained and nurtured it. But as soon as he stretched his abilities and inched closer to the walls of Athven herself, all traces of magic died out. There was a void, an empty place in the earth, and then a barrier, beyond which he could not feel.

It was as if something was deliberately shutting him out, but he could find no thread of awareness to suggest that she knew he was there, or even that she was awake. It might be a hopeful sign. If she had gone completely dormant, she may have found a way to shut everyone else out as well, and he might yet be able to wake her. But if she was not dormant—if she was truly dead—perhaps the barrier he felt was nothing more than the void formed where life had been utterly snuffed out.

As his watch wore on, Alexei extended his reach to look for any evidence that the valley sheltered more lives than their own. He found nothing but forest and elusive creatures who shied away from the gentle brush of his power. There was a brief glow of something larger, but it did not feel human and was gone almost as fast as it registered. Probably an indrik testing the possibilities of a life outside the bounds of Vrendel Wood. By the time Alexei retreated back into himself, he was exhausted and ready for sleep. He had not extended himself so far since he was young, and the small enchantments he had been able to work in Caelan had not come even close to testing the depths of his abilities. The phantom ache of skills long left unused was an almost pleasant distraction from the empty void of his heart.

He fell asleep moments after awakening Silvay, and did not stir until dawn touched the topmost tower.

~

Or rather, he did not awaken until he heard Wilder shouting.

"He's gone! The Betrayer is gone!"

Alexei jerked to wakefulness and threw off his blankets, fear clawing at his throat and stealing his breath. But no. Malichai had been on watch. He was the most reliable watchman they had. Porfiry could not have disappeared from under his nose.

And yet, when he looked across the remains of their fire to where Malichai and Porfiry would have been, there was nothing but the gently snoring form of Malichai stretched out on the bare, hard ground.

"Wake up!" Wilder was shouting in Malichai's ear, to no avail. The giant man snored on, and Alexei felt a terrible chill, a premonition that something far worse than fatigue may have befallen him.

A quick touch of his magic confirmed it. The sleep was not natural, but neither did it bear the imprint of Athven. Nor of any of his companions. He checked Gulver to be sure, as a healer would be well able to produce a magical sleep, but Gulver was as panicked as everyone else. Nor was the magic holding Malichai the brown and gold that marked Gulver's gift. It was... other. Bright as a morning, stunning as a sunrise, seductive as a fire in the dead of a winter night. It was gilded light, shot through with veins of crimson that flowed like blood and sparkled like rubies, colors that symbolized power and influence.

Alexei tore through it with barely a thought. Malichai snorted and blinked and sat up, perplexed by the circle of faces staring down at him.

Then he turned a deeply humiliated red. "Never," he said hoarsely. "Never in all my life have I failed on a watch. I swear to you, I have not betrayed you. I was awake." He slumped down, a miserable, defeated mountain.

"I know," Alexei said, surprising them all. "Tell me what you remember of your watch."

81

"There was nothing to remember," the larger man insisted. "It was quiet and still. Not so much as a rabbit or a fox. The prisoner was sleeping, and I began to think over the third verse of my epic..." He flushed again. "The rhymes weren't quite right, and I wanted to get them down before it was time to write another verse."

Alexei nodded. "I am not criticizing your choices. I merely want your memories."

"I... I was searching for a rhyme for tower. Or possibly pinnacle. Though I doubt there's any rhyme for that one. And..." He scratched his head. "I think the rest is dreaming. There was a man, but he wasn't one of us. I knew him, but I couldn't remember why."

"Tell me about him." Alexei's demand came out harsher than he meant it to. Unpleasant memories had begun to cast their shadow across the present.

"He had to be a dream. He was tall, and fair, and well spoken. Courteous too, and so familiar. He asked me about my work. About each of us. He wished us fair weather and fair luck. And then he said..." Malichai's voice hitched and wobbled. "He said the prisoner was his. That we'd done good service by bringing him this far, but that the need for our help was done. He untied him and led him away. And... I didn't stop him. I didn't even try." He broke down into sobs, tears rolling into his beard and soaking through to his chin.

"Be at peace, my friend." Alexei dropped to one knee and placed a hand on the weeping giant's shoulder. "You did not fail. You were defeated by dishonorable tactics."

He stood, his hands clenched so tightly that he feared his knuckles might bleed of their own accord. His shoulders shook and his teeth ground together.

"Pack up," he said. "And lead the horses. We're going in."

"But..." Wilder was instantly shushed by Silvay.

"Please fetch Halla," she urged, pointing at her mule, and Wilder went, though with much grumbling. "You know something," Silvay murmured in a low voice, looking pointedly at Alexei.

He jerked a nod. "I know that our chances were small at the start of this journey. I also know that they may have now been destroyed utterly. Unless we can find a way in."

"Who took him? Who would have known?"

"Don't ask me that," Alexei whispered. "I do not have the luxury of rage."

He was still shaking. Wilder returned leading Halla, and Alexei's own horse. Gulver had fetched Loraleen, and was now engaged in comforting Malichai, while surreptitiously using his own gift to sweep away the lingering effects of the stranger's magic.

Once Malichai was on his feet, they moved as one towards the walls of Athven Nar. They had no ally now but haste. If Porfiry found an entrance before them, he could once again steal what they had come so far to find, and all of their hopes would crumble to dust and ash. If they could only keep him out, there might still be a chance.

~

Zara gripped the ledge by her fingertips and pulled herself up till her chin touched the edge, then lowered her body again. At least it was simple enough to keep herself fit in a sprawling, deserted castle. She'd already run to the top of the eastern tower and back down again, and performed her stretches standing on the balustrade of the grand staircase. Once she'd even done flips down the long hall of the upstairs gallery, but mostly because it seemed to annoy the cat.

She was filthy and sweaty and her hair was escaping her braid, but it was better than being idle, waiting for something to happen.

Shadow had seemed agitated the night before and left the kitchen in the middle of the night. They still could not communicate, so Zara would probably never know what had set the animal off, but whatever it was had continued to distract her.

Letting go of the ledge, Zara dropped lightly to her feet and jogged off in the direction of the entry hall, where she had last seen the cat sitting in the middle of the floor watching the creep of moonlight give way to the gray of dawn. Perhaps while Shadow was feeling distracted she should take advantage of their new relationship to ask for things she needed. It might not be within the scope of Athven's abilities, but if there was the slightest chance of a bath, Zara would probably beg on her knees. No, not quite. But close.

She was almost to the hall when a subterranean roar split the air and seemed to cleave her head in two. The walls trembled and the floor grew momentarily soft, throwing her to her knees, but it was over almost as soon as it had begun.

Zara rose on trembling legs and walked carefully through the arch into the entry hall. In the center of the vast space, Shadow sat, ears pricked, staring intently at the door.

"Was that you?" Zara asked. "Couldn't you at least warn me before you do that sort of thing? It is possible for humans to die of fright, you know."

The cat was silent. And then, against all probability, defying all expectation, Zara heard something knocking on the main doors.

A thrill raced from her chest to her fingertips. Her father! He had come back!

"Athven, please don't hurt them!" she cried, but the cat ignored her, and continued to stare purposefully at the door.

Zara moved to stand squarely in front of her. "If it's my father, please let him in!" she begged. "I want to see him! He will want to know if I'm all right."

The cat shifted her gaze briefly to meet Zara's and the meaning in them was unmistakable. Denial. Scorn. Amusement.

It was not her father.

Zara suppressed an overwhelming surge of disappointment. "Do you know who it is? What they want?"

The cat seemed less certain this time.

"Well, are you going to keep them out or let them in?" Zara asked coolly. She would not be afraid, even if the visitors proved unfriendly. Athven needed her, and seemed well able to keep her safe, even if whoever was out there wished her ill. "Do I get a chance to live up to my end of our bargain or not?"

The cat did not indicate one way or another, but suddenly Zara felt very odd. Her hair began to crackle and stand on end, and sparks leapt from her fingertips into the air. Just as it had the day her father was torn away from her, a wind rose up and whirled its way through the hall, and when the next knock sounded, it echoed through the castle like a roll of thunder.

The sound faded. The wind died. And the door swung open on silent hinges.

~

It opened. The door opened and Alexei almost sobbed his relief. Athven was not gone. She was not dead. There was hope! When he laid his hand on the planks and pushed, the door had seemed frozen, but he could feel something small—no more than a whisper—that teased at the back of his mind and buzzed softly under his fingers. So he knocked. It probably looked ridiculous to his companions. They stood on the wide stone terrace at the front of an abandoned castle, and he was knocking.

But Athven heard him. And when the door opened he closed his eyes and drew a breath, soaking in courage for that step over the threshold into the past. Out of the light, into the shadows and the echoes and the memories. He took a step, and then three more. He felt the smooth stone under his boots. Heard the hiss of his breath reflected off the ceiling floating far above his head.

"Didn't your mother ever teach you to close the door behind you?"

Alexei's eyes flew open. His surroundings assailed him—the emptiness, the chill, and the darkness. And in the center of the great hall, in the middle of the rose mosaic where Beatra Nar, last queen of Erath, would have stood to greet visitors, was a woman.

And she was most decidedly not the ghost of his cousin. Queen Beatra had been short, sturdy and comfortable, with a wide, homely face and an air of uncompromising command.

This woman was tall and lean, clad in well-fitted but worn leather. Her skin was the color of oak leaves in the fall, her eyes were light, and her hair hung over her shoulder in a thick white braid. Despite the color, she was not old. Past her youth, perhaps, but younger than Alexei by more than a few years.

She had spoken in Andari, and yet she was looking at him as though he were the intruder. Her chin tilted up in a proud challenge and she stood like a warrior, though she bore no visible weapons.

Alexei stifled a cry of mingled shock, frustration and apprehension. After everything, after all his hopes and disappointments, the castle wasn't nearly as empty as he had hoped, and the discovery felt like a betrayal. Athven remained, but she may have been admitting others all along. He might very well be too late to find what he had come for, and he could no longer count on the castle as an ally.

"She certainly taught me better than to enter someone else's home without permission," Alexei heard himself answer. "You are not of Erath. What right do you have to trespass?"

The woman looked down towards her feet, where Alexei finally noticed a small, scarred gray cat.

"All these years," the woman said, "and this is what you decide to let in? Do you want my help or not? Because this is ridiculous."

She turned back to Alexei. "I was here first?" she said, and shrugged.

"What are you? An accursed treasure hunter?" he accused. What other reason could a foreigner have to be sneaking around in an abandoned castle? He itched to throw her from his home and lock the door forever on her and her kind. "If you think I will let you destroy or steal one particle of my people's past, you are mistaken."

"Can we come in?" Wilder's head appeared in the doorway and Alexei heard a gasp when she saw the inside. "Will the castle hurt us if we come in?"

The woman strode towards the door and rolled her eyes. "No, the castle won't hurt you. She can be peevish on occasion, but she's not destructive. Please, don't feel like you have to stand outside. There's not exactly a shortage of room in here."

Wilder came first, her head craned impossibly far back as she stepped over the threshold and stared into the distant shadows of the hall's towering ceiling. Silvay entered after her, but hovered uncertainly in the doorway.

"What of the mounts? Do you trust them to stay or should we bring them in?"

The second of the two doors swung wide, revealing Malichai, his bow held at the ready as he peered inside, eyes wide against the gloom. "Turn them loose," he suggested. "My Loraleen will look after them, and she'll never stray far from me."

Alexei had not intended to allow the horses to set a single hoof inside Athven, but he shut his mouth on the retort. He was busy enough glaring at the interloper as Gulver, Silvay and Malichai retrieved their bags and their saddles and stacked them in a heap on the floor. When the horses had been released, with a quick whisper from Malichai in Loraleen's ear, the party was finally able to step fully inside and shut the doors behind them.

In the midst of the process, the gray cat approached Alexei and twined herself about his ankles in a curiously watchful way. He all but ignored her until she reared up, planted her paws on his leg and dug in her claws.

"Ow..." He swallowed an undignified yelp and looked down, into a pair of uncanny green eyes that studied him intently. He heard a chuckle.

"She takes some getting used to," the strange woman said. "But I doubt you lot will be as surprised as I was. Allow me to offer you the hospitality of the house, such as it is."

"Many thanks." Malichai beamed at her and bowed deeply. "My name is Malichai Cherting, and I am a warrior of Andar. Whom might I have the honor of addressing?"

When she laughed, the sound was low and musical. "You are a very courteous warrior," she told him, bowing in her turn. "More courteous than others of your party. I am Zara. Of nowhere in particular. I am a guest in this fine but empty establishment."

"You cannot be a guest unless invited," Alexei broke in, "which you most certainly were not. I might stop short of throwing you back on the road alone, but you can give up the idea that you will be permitted to continue to roam at will."

"And I am Silvay, and this is Wilder." Silvay pushed past Alexei to offer a hand in greeting to the stranger, who took it with a surprised smile. "And Wilder is a she."

Wilder ducked her head and grinned.

"We are thankful to be sleeping indoors tonight," Silvay added, "whatever shape those doors may take."

"Well, you may change your mind when you discover the many unusual characteristics of these particular doors," Zara replied dryly. "It's taken me some months to come to terms with them myself."

"You've been here for months?" Alexei echoed, stunned.

"Oh, some three or four I expect," she answered, shrugging nonchalantly.

"And have you not yet determined to your satisfaction that there is nothing here to steal?" he barked harshly.

"Believe me, Erathi," the woman snapped, her temper finally rising to meet his challenge, "had I been given a choice I would not have been here to welcome you."

"There's your choice!" Alexei pointed at the door. "If you are so anxious to leave, I can't imagine why you are still standing here."

She sighed, crossed her arms, and sauntered past him. "This is your fault," she muttered, looking down at the cat, who still lingered at Alexei's heels. "When his poor head explodes, I am not going to clean it up."

Why did she continue to address comments to the cat?

Casting a pointed glance over her shoulder, the woman stepped up to the left door, leaned her full weight against it and pushed. Nothing happened.

Malichai's face scrunched up with confusion and he walked over to join her. He set his shoulder to the right door and heaved until his face flushed darkly beneath his beard.

"It's not her, Trevelyan. It doesn't even tremble." The warrior began to look troubled. "Are we trapped, then?"

Alexei shifted his weight and unclenched his hands slowly. It didn't make sense. Why would Athven let them in, only to ignore them afterwards? He reached out with his gift and felt for the stir and spark of magic in the stones. At first they seemed quiescent, but gradually he was able to discern the same faint hum he had observed from outside the door. He stretched farther, noting the signatures of Silvay, Wilder and Gulver, and then encountered another. No, two more. One the merest wisp of lavender, almost no more than a fragrance, a memory of beauty and longing. And the other... Alexei's eyes flew open and his magic slammed back into his body so hard that he jerked.

"What," he asked, his voice shaking as he pointed at the source of his disquiet, "is that?"

Zara laughed. "Oh, you mean Shadow? Well, in my land, we would call it a cat. But I don't know the Erathi word."

"Whatever else it might be, it is most certainly not a cat," he insisted.

"Well, I'm sure if she wants you to know what she is, she'll find a way to tell you." Zara shrugged as though the matter was of supreme indifference to her, but Alexei heard the truth behind her avoidance.

"You know," he said flatly, stalking over to stand in front of her, arms folded with indignation. Now that he stood so close, he could sense that she was the source of that wisp of lavender. "You know what she is. And you are not as mundane as you pretend to be. Where are you really from? And what do you want?"

She was tall enough to look him directly in the eye, and she did so, the pale, icy blue of her gaze flaring with anger. "You have been impossibly rude since you stepped through that door, so I have no urge to share any personal details with you. I already told you what I want. I want to leave. And if anyone else calls me mundane, I will lock the lot of you out of the kitchens and leave you to fend for yourselves."

~

Zara strode away, seething with anger, humiliation, and a tiny undercurrent of fear. She'd wanted not to be alone. She hadn't anticipated the possibility that whoever joined her exile might resent her very existence.

They'd all been speaking Andari, but she guessed from their proprietary attitude that more than one of the new arrivals were Erathi. Particularly the one who'd been so irritated by everything and everyone. The one who hadn't bothered to introduce himself.

He'd appeared frightening at first. About her height, with dark brown hair gone slightly gray and a confident, self-contained bearing, he'd clearly come out the worse in a confrontation at some point in the past. Scars marred the right side of his face, from his hairline to below his collar. They were old, but pulled and twisted the skin into a grim parody of the alert and regal appearance of the left side. Even his right eye appeared to have gone white.

Interesting, she thought, that he didn't bother with an eye patch, but wore his scars proudly. He might even have been handsome, before, but his arrogant and dismissive manners made it difficult for her to care.

"Wait, please!"

Zara turned to see the woman named Silvay hastening after her. She paused for the older woman to catch up.

"How can I help you?" she asked, polite but distant.

"Accept my apologies, and I hope you will ignore Alexei," Silvay answered, with a rueful smile. "He's..." She shrugged helplessly. "He's had a difficult thirty years."

Zara's brows shot up. "Unlike the rest of you? He seems old enough to have figured out how to control his temper." So his name was Alexei. Not that she intended to use it.

"In general, he is the most controlled man I have ever met," Silvay answered, surprising her. "Possibly to his detriment. But again, I do apologize. It has been a most trying morning."

Zara waited pointedly, but Silvay shook her head.

"No, not something that is mine to share. Perhaps in time he will tell you himself. But, as we are here, perhaps you can tell me more of what brought you to Athven Nar? And what we can expect from our, ah... stay?"

Zara barked a laugh. "If you would know what to expect, you should ask her." She pointed towards the ceiling. "I am as much a prisoner here as you. I came with..." Zara cast a sideways glance at Silvay, but the older woman did not appear to be judging her. She thought it might be safe to ask what she'd been longing to know since the moment they invaded her solitude.

"Did you by any chance meet any others, while you were finding your way here? A party of three men, perhaps? One would have been older, with gray hair and a beard. Two younger, dark." She could not bring herself to admit that one of those men had been her father.

Silvay looked regretful. "We did not. Alexei confirmed there was no one else in the valley. No one except possibly one man, who does not match that description. Your friends?"

"My companions, at least." Zara tried to sound flippant, but it hurt too much. They had not stayed. Her father had simply left her, trapped and alone in a strange land. She wasn't sure she should blame him, but she did.

"As your friend Alexei supposed, we are treasure hunters. We understood the castle was abandoned and thought to try our luck, despite rumors that no one could get inside."

"The rumors were wrong?"

"Not exactly." Zara didn't know how much of the truth the other woman might be able to accept. "We were allowed in, but then my... the men were forced out. I cannot quite explain how. I have been unable to escape since then."

"Athven," Silvay said quietly.

Zara's mouth fell open. "You know, then? You know what Athven is?"

"Not entirely," Silvay responded with a smile. "I know of her, and have heard many tales. But your story indicates that she is awake and aware of you and chose to keep you for a reason, just as she chose to allow us entry for a reason."

Zara could feel herself turning red. She didn't think she had the courage to explain what she knew of Athven's reasons. It was still too humiliating to contemplate, so she changed the subject.

"You'll be pleased to know that there is wood and sufficient food supplies to last for a time," she announced. "Apparently we were expected. I have been keeping to the kitchen to preserve fuel, but your party may find it cramped and hesitate to share the space with an intruder."

"Don't you mean a prisoner?" Silvay asked wryly. She laughed at Zara's expression. "I do not resent you, my dear. This adventure has many twists and turns yet to come, and I will be glad to share them with you. Besides, if Athven approves of you, then we are more the guests here than you are, wouldn't you say?"

Zara found herself smiling reluctantly, then a little more naturally as she felt relief sink into her bones. Perhaps it would not be as bad as she feared. As least she was not alone any longer, and a few of her new companions might even prove to be friends. She could worry about how to handle the antagonistic ones later.

Running feet sounded behind them as they continued on towards the kitchen.

"Wait for me!" the girl named Wilder called as she raced towards them down the passage. "I want to see everything! And I'm hungry." She caught up and took Silvay's hand as they walked. "You know, I've never seen a building with an aura before," she confided artlessly.

Silvay glanced at Zara a little nervously, so she smiled back to show she was not dismayed. "You'd be surprised," she assured them both, "how little will bother you after three months in an enchanted castle."

"Oh!" Wilder exclaimed, staring intently at Zara. "You have them too!"

"Have what?" she asked, her palms beginning to sweat under the intensity of the girl's gaze.

"Thorns," Wilder explained. "Like Athven. And a crown, I think. Just like Alexei."

Zara swallowed hard. Roses and thorns? A crown? What kind of child was this?

"You have music too, but it's sad," the girl announced. "I think it's lonely."

"Ah, Wilder," Silvay interrupted, "would you go and tell Malichai that he will be needed shortly in the kitchens? We are all going to want breakfast soon."

Wilder sighed in disappointment, but turned and scampered back the way they had come.

"I'm sorry," Silvay said gently. "She's just a child, and I think she forgets how disconcerting her prescience can be for those who aren't accustomed."

"Prescience?" Zara managed to squeak the word between frozen lips. Apparently she was still more easily surprised than she'd anticipated.

"Yes. I don't know what you might have heard, but we of Erath have different gifts. Ways of using our magic. Wilder sees auras and can sense needs, though not always clearly, as she is young and untrained. Auras," she added, "are generally believed to be a representation of a person's deepest self, but what she told you can be interpreted in many different ways, and I would ask you not to let it upset you."

"No," Zara managed to say. "What about you?"

Silvay looked somehow apologetic. "I am a seer," she confessed. "I occasionally have dreams or visions about what is to come, but they are rarely clear or easily interpreted."

"Did you know about me already?" Zara asked quickly. "Did you know I would be here? Or whether I will be able to leave?"

"It's not so easy, I'm afraid," Silvay told her. "I knew things would not be straightforward, but I had no direct knowledge of your presence. And I cannot speak at all to your future. Those things must work themselves out in time."

She did not say she hadn't seen it, just that she couldn't talk about it.

"And you are all Erathi but one?" Zara asked, not yet ready to admit why she felt the need to ask.

"Yes," Silvay answered, seeming more at ease now that they were no longer discussing her talents. "Malichai, as he mentioned, is from Andar. Gulver has lived here all his life, while Alexei, Wilder and I have remained in exile."

Zara's heart sank a little. Malichai had at least treated her with courtesy. The third man had said nothing at all, but he was also quite a bit older, unless she was mistaken. The resulting conclusion was making her faintly nauseated.

"Fortunately," Silvay went on, "Malichai is also an excellent cook. If you will permit him, I'm sure he'll be happy to take over the job of preparing meals for everyone."

Temporarily diverted, Zara couldn't help but express her skepticism. "The large one? With the weapons? He cooks?"

"Very well actually," Silvay answered with a chuckle. "Oh, I was skeptical myself at first, but I promise you'll be astounded at what he can come up with out of practically nothing."

"I'll probably be willing to kiss his boots, no matter what he chooses to make," Zara declared. "I'm an indifferent cook and I've been existing on jerked beef stew for the last three months."

"Then tonight, we will ask him to prepare a feast! As glorious a meal as he can conceive, to celebrate our arrival."

Zara laughed, but it was hollow and without much enthusiasm. When they learned what she knew, they wouldn't feel much like celebrating. And when she did what she had to, she would be lucky if they didn't toss her into the stew with the jerked beef. Though there was always the possibility they would laugh in her face instead.

It was depressing to realize that she couldn't decide which one would be worse.

When they finally stepped inside the kitchen, Zara stopped and looked around blankly. She'd gone the wrong way. Hadn't she? This was not the same room she'd left earlier that morning.

But no. There were her blankets. Her pack. The gently flaring coals of her fire.

Otherwise, the room was as different as it was possible for a room to be. In the center of the kitchen was now an enormous trestle table with sturdy benches pushed underneath. Pots and pans of every size and description hung from a rack overhead. Utensils sprouted up like flowers out of clay jars in the center of the table, and the walls were hung with dried herbs.

Zara's teeth clenched tightly on her scream of frustration. Had this been here the whole time? Had the damned cat been hiding it from her on purpose?

"Why, this is lovely!" Silvay exclaimed. "And so well preserved too. I would have slept here as well, had it been me."

"Yes," Zara answered between her teeth. "But you should know that as of this morning, none of this was here."

Silvay's brows went up, but she didn't seem terribly surprised. "Athven must be growing stronger. Perhaps she was only waiting for people to care for, and what was hidden will come to light now that there is more life in the castle."

Behind them, Zara heard the tread of feet and then a gasp of pure, unadulterated joy.

"I must be dreaming." The bearded Malichai had just entered the kitchen. "I think I may actually weep, if you all will forgive me. To be able to cook properly after weeks on the road will be a pleasure!"

"You may not feel so joyful," Zara told him, "when you see what there is to cook."

"Oh, never fear," he reassured her with a broad smile. "I can make a feast from very little. Only direct me to the pantries and I will have something delicious for you all long before my companions"—he jerked his head back in the direction of the hall—"have finished their reminiscing."

Zara found herself smiling at his enthusiasm. "I will show you," she agreed, "but don't say I didn't warn you."

She had just finished pointing out the wood and the stores of food when a strange feeling assailed her. It was faint at first, as if something was tugging at her spine, pulling her first one way, and then another. Her head began to spin and her eyesight went fuzzy.

"Are you all right?" Malichai was watching her with concern.

"I think so," she gasped, leaning against the wall for support. "Just a dizzy spell. Probably from too much of my own cooking." She stepped out of the pantries and felt another tug, back towards the entry hall. With a muttered curse, she headed that direction as quickly as her poor balance would allow, staggering across the kitchen as a fresh wave of dizziness hit her. In addition to the darkness creeping into the edges of her vision, there was a sensation like part of her was being stretched unbearably, a tearing, almost-separation that seemed to have nothing to do with her physical body.

When the pain shot through her chest, Zara fell to her knees, but pushed upward and tried again to walk. She thought about shouting for help, but didn't know if anyone would hear her. If only she could find where the feeling was coming from. Was it Athven? Were they under attack?

She took a final step into the entry hall and stumbled again. Her sight was almost completely gone, but when she squinted against the pain, in the direction the unseen force had been pulling her, she could make out the motionless figure of Alexei. He stood in the center of the floor, his eyes closed and his arms outstretched, and when his fingers clenched, the pain and darkness squeezed her so tightly that she screamed.

CHAPTER 6

*A*lexei planted his feet atop the rose mosaic and reached out for Athven once more. She was there. He could feel her growing ever more aware now that there was life within her walls. But there was still something wrong. He couldn't connect, couldn't seem to get her attention. Almost as if she were deliberately ignoring him.

He pressed harder, grasping at the murmur of her power and pulling it gently towards himself, hoping to awaken whatever lay dormant, whatever would not allow her to speak.

"Stop!" The anguished cry came from the far side of the hall, opposite the entry door. The woman, Zara, staggered in and fell to her knees, holding her head, tears streaming down her face. "Please, whatever you're doing, stop. I can't bear it anymore."

Stunned, Alexei released the strands of magic and dropped his arms, feeling the blood drain from his face as he did so. The woman collapsed to the floor an instant later. He and Gulver reached her at the same time, the other man placing his scarf between her head and the cold stone floor.

"She's in shock," Gulver murmured, as he felt for her pulse and peered into her eyes. Then he took her hand and dove in with his healing gift instead. A moment later, his jaw fell.

"Alexei," he said, appearing to be in shock himself, "she's..."

Her eyes fluttered open. Uncertain. Embarrassed. She looked at Alexei and despite her brown skin he could see her flush.

"What was that?" she whispered. "What were you doing?"

"I..." What could his attempts to awaken Athven have had to do with her? Why should he even try to explain?

Just then, the gray cat pushed its way past him to sit on the woman's chest and stare into her eyes.

Zara looked back defiantly. "Yes, I'm all right, no thanks to you," she muttered after a few moments. "Talk to him." Her hand lifted weakly to point at Alexei. "I didn't have anything to do with this."

The cat turned vibrant green eyes on Alexei once again, and this time, he fell all the way into them.

∽

He still stood in the Grand Hall, but it was the Grand Hall he remembered, rather than the cold, empty cavern of the present. There was light and color, and the rose mosaic glowed with life. Standing in the center of it now was an achingly familiar woman with gray hair, holding the Stone Scepter.

"Your Majesty!" He knelt before he remembered that Beatra Nar was dead. Whoever this was, it was not his cousin.

"Stand up," she snapped. "And stop meddling. If you kill the girl, you'll never get what you want, so I suggest you take better care of her."

"Athven," he whispered. "You are alive! But what has the girl to do with you? She is not Erathi. She barely has any magic."

"She was here!" The crack of the woman's voice left no doubt of her anger. "I was nearly past reviving when she arrived. Enduring Beatra's *death took much of my strength, but I survived and waited for a new guardian, as I have always done. But it was too long! I had never waited more than a handful of days before. I almost didn't have the strength to sense Zara's magic, and when I seized it I was not even aware enough to know what I had done."*

"You..." Alexei almost couldn't say the words. "You bonded... with her?"

"It was that or die!"

"I'm sorry," he whispered, knowing she spoke the truth, but devastated to his soul.

"You left me," the woman said softly. "All of you. I waited and waited and you did not come. I had no choice. Not if I wanted to live."

"Then I have failed you," Alexei said, still on his knees. "Nar has failed you and your anger is entirely justified."

"Perhaps," the woman answered. "But that is of little matter now. What matters is the Rose."

"Yes." Alexei came to his feet. His pain and shame were as nothing next to that. "You know where it is?"

"No." The woman who looked like his cousin had her same expression of frustration—the tightly furrowed brow, the flare of nostrils. "We have looked for it, Zara and I, but cannot find it. I can feel that it's near, but my senses are still dull."

"We will find it," Alexei promised her. He swallowed a surge of fear. "Perhaps you did not feel him, but I brought the Betrayer. I had hoped he would lead me to it, but he escaped."

"Yes, I felt him," Athven admitted. "But faintly. He has not yet retrieved what he stole."

"Then we have a chance."

Athven drew herself up. "If you work together, you have a chance."

Alexei growled under his breath in spite of himself. "How can I work *together with one who came here to rob you? To take the spoils of our people's destruction?"*

"You brought the Betrayer here, and you can ask that?" Athven responded dryly. "If I can work with her, so can you. You can do it because it is needed. Because I am bonded with her, and there is no changing that now. Because you are Nar and you will do what you must to help your people. It is your birthright. Your gift and your doom."

"Very well." Alexei bowed. "I will do what I can. But why will you not unlock the doors? Why hold us prisoner here?"

"I have my reasons," she said, and for the first time, she seemed somewhat evasive. "And if I were to open the doors, it would be as easy for others to enter as it would be for you to leave. Trust that I will do what is necessary to protect you and focus on the task at hand."

Alexei felt a strange surge of disquiet, but dismissed it. Athven was right. She had always protected his people. He could trust her, even if he didn't understand. "Then we will search. And I will not fail you again."

"You will," Athven retorted. "You are human and weak, and all of you fail in the end. But whatever you do, do not harm the girl. Whether you approve of her or not, she is mine."

Alexei inclined his head. The pain and betrayal still seethed within him, but there was no choice to be made. Athven still needed him. His people needed him. For that, he would do as Athven asked. He would not like it, but he would do it.

∼

He blinked into sudden darkness. After the brightness of the vision, the shadows of the hall seemed deeper and darker, but for the bright green of the eyes staring into his.

At least now he knew why the woman kept talking to the cat.

"I am sorry," he said again, bowing his head to the avatar of his childhood home. He hoped it would hide the devastation in his eyes. "I should have come sooner. But I will do what I can to help you while I am here."

The cat seemed satisfied and jumped to the ground before stalking off.

"Can someone please tell me what happened?" Zara asked.

Alexei pushed back all of his anger, all of his frustration, all of his disappointment and tried to think of her as simply another one of his companions, rather than a treasure-hunting opportunist who had stolen the only thing his family had left. The only thing *he* had left.

"My name is Alexei. When I was younger I used to live here." He didn't think it necessary to tell all of his secrets. If Athven wanted her to know, she would no doubt inform her new caretaker of his identity. "I have come back to see if Athven could be restored and I was attempting to communicate with her. It had not occurred to me that she would already have bonded with..." He stumbled over choosing a word and Zara's face turned bleak.

"With a worthless thief?" she asked, sitting up and flexing her fingers carefully. "With a foreigner? With a magic-less nobody?"

"Athven is yours now," Alexei answered, taking care to keep emotion from coloring his tone. "You clearly have some magic. And as caretaker of Athven Nar, you are responsible for the future of the Erathi people. She is our home and our hope. She is what binds us together. You are neither worthless nor a nobody, but rather carry an enormous responsibility."

Zara leapt to her feet, jaw clenched. "Wrong, Erathi. I am not responsible for you, your people, or your future. I am a prisoner here by no choice of my own. Your precious Athven didn't ask me before she forced this bond on me, and I have no intention of staying here simply because you have some misguided ideas about my responsibilities." Her hands turned to fists before gradually unclenching. "If you're so concerned with the future, you can be responsible for it. Instead of muttering and glaring at me, you'd be better served working on freeing me from this bond. Then I will leave you in peace and stop polluting the air with my foreign presence."

Alexei was trapped between anger at her dismissal and worry at her lack of understanding. Athven had admitted to bonding with Zara without permission, which was a grievous offense had it been done purposefully. But he believed Athven when she said it had not been intentional. She had been too near dissolution to understand what she was doing. And therefore too far gone to explain what the bond meant. If Athven had never explained the true nature of their relationship to Zara, the treasure hunter could still jeopardize everything.

"Perhaps you don't understand," he began, but she cut him off.

"No, I don't understand," she snapped. "And clearly neither do you. I don't want your wretched home. I want my own! I want to be free! I want to not be stuck here with people who despise me. I want to find my friends and never see this place again. But thanks to your magic castle, none of us get a choice in this. So don't talk to me about understanding, Erathi. You understand nothing!" On that note, she turned and stalked away.

Gulver sighed deeply. "Don't be too hard on her," he said softly.

"Why does everyone keep defending her?" Alexei protested. "All I asked was for her to cooperate with us. As she said, none of us have a choice here, but if she had not been trespassing where she did not belong, this could have been avoided. We don't have time to soothe her lacerated sensibilities."

Gulver eyed him sideways. "There is always time. And I don't think you'd like yourself if you were willing to sacrifice a person, any person, even for a goal as noble as ours."

Alexei winced. Gulver was right. He hoped he would never be that kind of man. And yet, to have come so far, only to be balked by an uncooperative thief...

"And she's afraid," Gulver added, not looking Alexei in the eye.

"Of what?"

"Of you."

~

Zara did not put in an appearance the rest of the day. Where she went, Alexei wasn't sure, but the rest of them ate and then began to explore the castle. Alexei explained to his companions what they were looking for and tried to recall enough of the Rose's signature to help them find it, but he doubted it would be enough. Without Athven herself to aid him, it would be a near impossible task.

He even ventured as far as the Rose Chamber, but not because he expected to find anything there. Part of him needed to see it, to know that it was still intact, still waiting should they succeed in finding the Rose before Porfiry did.

And while he was there, alone with the silence, he opened himself to everything he had been hiding, from himself and everyone else. He tried to feel the loss and emptiness and aloneness of realizing how completely his people had been devastated. Of finally understanding how far they would have to go if the Erathi were ever to be anything but a deeply hidden race of refugees, dependent on others for their safety. He considered the shame of having deserted them, and of having lost the birthright of his family.

But he was still numb. Except for the guilt, he still felt nothing.

He might blame Zara, might resent her for a theft she had not actually intended, but he knew the true fault was his. If he had not hidden for so many years, hidden from who he was and what he knew, he would have returned sooner. But he'd wanted absolution for himself. Wanted to return triumphant, and after several years of failing to find Porfiry, he'd let his shame outweigh his duty.

In addition to his guilt, Alexei discovered he was able to feel one other emotion—fear. Zara was not the only one who was afraid. But the man Alexei feared, the man Malichai had described, was a tall, golden-haired, fair-spoken stranger...

There were certainly many men who might fit that description. Many men who might have cause to want what Porfiry had stolen. But there was only one who might know where and when Porfiry would be in Erath; only one who would know exactly what Porfiry had to offer. Only one man who also had the gift of persuasion and would not scruple to use it against someone like Malichai, who had no defenses of his own.

Rowan Tremontaine. Former prince of Andar. Porfiry's employer. A man who had tried to kill his own father and been responsible for the death of the ruler of Caelan. He was ruthless, intelligent, and ambitious, and would have no difficulty determining a way to turn the Rose to his own advantage if he could get his hands on it.

He could never be allowed to possess it.

For a moment, Alexei wished that one of his Andari friends had been able to accompany him. Quinn, or Kyril, or even Brenna. They knew Rowan well and would have understood Alexei's disquiet at his presence. He feared he would not be able to explain what he knew to his current companions without sounding fanciful or paranoid.

Alexei placed a hand on the pedestal and ran his fingers lightly across the smooth stone, remembering the queen who had stood just so, touching the crystal and following the paths of its power to the edges of her kingdom. It had somehow allowed her to sense whether all was well inside their borders, and Alexei had often wondered what it might feel like.

Beatra Nar had not been an enchanter, like him, but a gardener. Her gift had been for things that grew from the earth, and, during her reign, Athven had been overrun by plants and trees of every description. Alexei remembered a pot or two in every corner, plants that sometimes flowered even in winter, and vines that would grow and grow until firmly brought to heel by a nudge from his aunt's magic. It had been so vibrant. Thriving. Full of life.

As it might never be again. Because he had been too late. If he had only... But that was pointless now. For so many years he had not wanted the responsibility. Hadn't wanted to bear the burden his aunt had placed on him—restoring Athven, reclaiming his homeland and rescuing his people. And now that he was here, now that Athven was lost to him, it felt as though he'd lost something vital to himself. He had not realized until it was gone just how much the Nar heritage meant to him. How much a part of his identity it was.

But he could still find the Rose. He could do that much to fulfill his debt, and afterwards, he could leave. Help his people in other ways. He didn't think he could bear to see Athven restored by a thief, no matter how beautiful she was.

Now where had that thought come from? For a moment he felt like a traitor, but it was true, and there was no point in denying it. Zara, treasure hunter or not, was an undeniably beautiful woman. He guessed her heritage to be Frenish, considering her dark skin and white hair, but wherever she was from, she likely had never lacked men's interest. She was also strong, to have survived alone as long as she had, and resilient, to have withstood the revelation that she had been taken captive by a being utterly beyond her ability to grasp.

All of these things he could admit, dispassionately, and yet loathe what she represented. Almost as deeply as he loathed himself. It was not going to be easy to follow Athven's wishes.

～

Dinner that evening was almost festive, considering the worries that dogged their movements. How much time did they have? When would Porfiry return?

But there were three fires in the kitchen and Malichai had outdone himself with the preparation of a feast, though perhaps it would not have seemed as grand had they not been so many days on the road. Even Zara slunk in quietly just before they sat down and was greeted enthusiastically by everyone but him.

"Well, this is the coziest meal we've had yet," Malichai announced as he served them all on wooden plates he had dug up from somewhere. "And we can celebrate the addition of another member to our party. Though I haven't yet decided what role you're to play, Mistress Zara."

When Zara shot him a confused look across the table, Silvay clarified: "Malichai is a lover of epic poetry. He has been preparing his own composition based on our adventures, and I believe he is planning to immortalize you in verse alongside the rest of us."

"I can't say I ever anticipated such an honor." Zara seemed neither distressed nor pleased by the announcement. "And how is your poem proceeding so far?"

"Sadly, I have only five verses to date," Malichai confessed. "Our battles have not lived up to my expectations for inclusion in even so simple a composition as a ballad. I have primarily been engaged in describing the addition of various members to our company, and our first sight of the castle."

"You should most certainly include the cat, as well," Zara told him with an innocent expression, and Alexei almost choked on his stew.

Gulver shot him a look of concern. "Perhaps we could all use a drink," he suggested.

"Alas, there is no ale to be found, but the water is surprisingly good." Malichai excused himself to fetch them all some water.

After he had poured a measure for everyone, Wilder piped up with a question. "What are we going to do now? Where did Porfiry go? And why can't we get out? Will we be stuck here forever?"

"Who is Porfiry?" Zara asked.

Everyone looked at each other in silence for a few moments.

"He is the betrayer of Erath," Alexei finally answered. "We brought him with us as a prisoner, but he escaped. As to what we are going to do now," he added, "we are going to continue to search. I do not believe Porfiry was lying when he told me the Rose was still here at Athven. The faster we find it, the less likely Porfiry will return and find it first. He may not be able to enter, but then again, he is Nar. Athven may let him in if she remembers him."

Zara shot him a quick, unreadable glance. She probably didn't know what the Rose was, but he wasn't quite ready to tell her.

"As to where he went," Alexei continued, "I do not pretend to know, but I believe I may know who took him."

"I have remembered," Malichai rumbled, shame written on his face. "And I can't imagine how I did not recognize him at the time."

"You did not recognize your prince because he did not wish it," Alexei reassured him. "Whether it seems possible or not, Rowan Tremontaine is a powerful mage. He twisted your mind and your memory and you had no chance of withstanding it."

In as few words as possible, Alexei described his knowledge of the Andari prince and his understanding of what Rowan might be capable of. "He will want the Rose for himself, though I do not believe he cares at all about Athven. Even if he knows what she is, his ambitions are bigger than one castle, or even one country."

"Do you genuinely believe the Rose could be used in such a way?" Silvay asked. "It is tuned to this place. Even more so than we are. If this Andari prince were to remove it from our borders, or even remove it from Athven herself, would it work as it does here?"

"I cannot say," Alexei told her, "but he will know even less. Porfiry will have described it to him as best he understands it, which is not well. And he may have even exaggerated what it can do, in order to increase his own worth in the eyes of his employer. Which is another point that gives me hope." He set down his spoon and rested his elbows on the table. "Porfiry will wait as long as possible before he gives up the one thing of value he possesses. Hopefully it will give us more time."

"And what if he finds it first?" Wilder asked in a small voice. "What will happen to us?"

Alexei smiled sadly. He wished he could reassure the girl, but he couldn't bring himself to lie. "I don't know, Wilder. I hope it will not come to that. If it does, I believe we could make a home for some time here at Athven. Even without the Rose, she is powerful, and could shelter many of the Erathi who remain, if we could find a way to convince her it would be safe to open her doors again. It will depend on her, and what she chooses to do."

Zara was taking a sip of her water and began to cough at his last statement. When she had cleared her throat, she set down her cup, very slowly and carefully. "There is a way." She stared at the table as she spoke.

"A way what?" Alexei asked, as courteously as he was able.

"A way to convince Athven to open the doors."

Alexei took hold of his temper and leaned back, away from the table, crossing his arms to keep from giving any hint of his anger. "Earlier you implied we were trapped. Even Athven indicated that she has locked the doors for a reason. What has changed? Has Athven been speaking to you?"

She hesitated, then shook her head. "Not today," was her cryptic reply.

"Then why did you lie?" Alexei jumped to his feet, his hands still on the table. For that matter, why had Athven not simply told him? "Why didn't you say something sooner? Why deceive us into thinking we had no options?"

"Because I didn't like the option you had," she snapped. She was still staring at the table.

"And how is it yours to decide whether you like it or not?" He didn't understand how one person could find so many different ways to frustrate him. "Tell us!"

Her silence stretched until he began to think she might never speak, but at last she burst out with two simple words: "Marry me."

A hush fell around the table. Malichai stopped with his spoon halfway to his mouth.

"What?" Alexei could hear the flat disbelief in his own voice. He couldn't possibly have heard right. He'd known she was plainspoken, but this was beyond absurd.

"Marry me," she repeated, embarrassment staining her cheeks and desperation coloring her voice. "You wanted to know how to get out, and that is the only way."

Alexei's anger flared up before he could stop it. "So. It was you and not Athven who imprisoned us here. What did you tell her? How did you convince her to agree to a plan that uses our need to manipulate us? Did you learn who I am and decide to force me into allying myself with you?" A disdainful laugh escaped him. "I am not so eager to reclaim my birthright that I would be willing to sell my name and my heritage. How could you think I would ever purchase my own home at the cost of my honor, or buy your cooperation at the cost of a crown?"

She flinched at his words, but what had she expected? And why had she lied and told them that she didn't want to stay when she had planned this all along? Had she hoped to play on his sympathies?

He had no sympathy left, and if he had, he would never waste it on her. "We are not all honorless thieves. I would never shame the House of Nar so deeply as to bind myself to an enemy and a usurper. Not even for this."

Her face frozen, Zara pushed back from the table. "Thank you," she said to Malichai. "The food was delicious." And then she disappeared.

CHAPTER 7

Zara's dignity got her out of the kitchen, but it failed her after about three more steps. She ran, blinded by tears and humiliation, to the point of the castle that was farthest from anyone who might see or hear her misery—the north tower.

The door was still unlocked as she had left it, but that was the only thing that was the same. Much like the kitchen, it seemed to have blossomed in the space of a day.

It had been someone's room. Some long-dead person had lived there, slept there, worked and dreamed and possibly even grown up within those walls. There was a bed, with a blue coverlet that felt soft from too many washings. A table and a chair stood near the casement window, and a wardrobe filled the opposite corner. Aside from the bedclothes, there were no personal belongings, but perhaps those, too, would reappear with time. The whole castle might eventually be filled with deeply personal reminders that this had been someone's home. Many someones' home.

But it would never be hers. Alexei had made that horribly, humiliatingly clear.

Her father had abandoned her to the mercies of Athven, and she had believed it hurt—to know that the one person who claimed to love her had cared so little that he hadn't stayed, hadn't even tried to conquer his fear. But this was somehow worse. Now she had not only lost the illusion that her father cared about her, she had lost even the possibility that she might someday have the home she had always dreamed of. She would very likely remain trapped in someone else's home forever, and they would go on hating her for it. Blaming her for Athven's ridiculous plan.

There was no point in trying to convince them it was all a misunderstanding when they already believed her to be a liar. It was Athven they trusted, and Athven, inscrutable creature that she was, might not choose to tell them the truth.

If she was going to face them again, she would have to pull herself together, and never let them know how badly they had hurt her. How badly *he* had hurt her. The others had had nothing to do with it, though she assumed they felt similarly. Even if they didn't, she did not intend for anyone to see her pain. Tomorrow, she would be strong and do whatever needed to be done. For tonight, she had too many tears.

Without removing her boots, she curled up on the soft, blue coverlet and cried, thankful for the multitude of stairs that kept anyone from hearing her sobs.

∼

"You've gone and made your task that much harder," the voice said. "And mine. Have you no patience at all?"

"Shut up," Zara said wearily, sitting up in the bed and observing her silken nightgown with a dispassionate eye. "This was your idea, and I wasn't going to lie to them. They deserved to know there's a way out. It isn't my fault he didn't like what I told him. And it's definitely not my fault he didn't give me a chance to explain."

"Explain what?" Athven asked, arms folded as she gazed out the window.

"That it wasn't my condition and I don't want his castle or his kingdom. If he had agreed, you could transfer the bond to him and I could leave."

"Hmm," Athven said.

"But now it's going to be worse because he despises me. He'll never listen, because he assumes I'm lying. Why can't you just tell him yourself?"

"Because nothing is that simple, child," the avatar chided her. "A bond with another reasoning being is complex, as is Alexei's past. If I tell him outright what I need of him, he might say yes out of guilt or duty, or even because he distrusts you, but any of those reasons would pollute our bond from the start. My bond with you has proven weak, not only because your magic is small, but because our connection was made without your full and heart-felt consent. I cannot begin to rebuild without a true partner who is willing to freely commit their life and their power to my cause."

"He's here, isn't he?" Zara objected. "Doesn't that mean that he's committed enough?"

Athven's expression grew remote. "You must believe me when I say that it is not."

"Then what do you expect me to do now?"

"You will have to prove that you can be trusted. Prove that he has nothing to fear from you."

"That he has nothing to fear from me?" Zara snorted at the thought. "He is cold and distant and dismissive and you want me to help him be less afraid of me?"

"I did not say this is entirely your fault," Athven said sternly. "The son of Nar has much to answer for, but he has a different road to walk and different demons to face."

"I will not grovel," Zara said firmly. "I won't become less than I am to make him happy."

Athven's brow raised a trifle. "I did not ask it of you. It is your strength that has been my greatest ally since we were bonded. Not your physical strength, though that is considerable, nor your magic, but your strength of purpose."

"What strength of purpose?" Zara asked bitterly. "I'm a thief. I have no home, no family, no idea what I'm going to do or even what I want to do."

"You do know what you want," Athven returned. "And you know what you are not willing to do to get it. That is far more than most people have."

"I think it's a bit silly to claim strength of purpose merely because I would never betray someone I love for treasure," Zara said dryly. "You don't proclaim someone a hero simply because they are less horrible than everyone else."

The avatar laughed. "I can see that this conversation is unlikely to get us anywhere. But I stand by what I have said. You are strong. Your life has not been easy, but it has not defeated you. You may be a treasure hunter, but I have come to agree that you are not a thief. You strive for rightness and yearn for beauty, even in places where it seems impossible, and I am pleased to call you my guardian. Even if you have no idea how to talk to men."

"I have no idea how to talk to anyone," Zara retorted. "And after a few more months here I might lose the ability to talk entirely from lack of practice."

"Don't be melodramatic," Athven said sternly. "You have begun very well with three out of five companions. Now you simply need to win over the others."

"Then I hope you are reconciled to a long wait," Zara said with a sigh. "Alexei is not going to forgive me anytime soon."

"He must," Athven replied simply. "There is no time for a quarrel. The two of you must work together to find the Rose."

"Then why are you telling me? I'm not the one starting arguments."

"I have already told him," the woman admitted. "It might take him a little longer to realize that I am right. So I am asking you to be the one to set aside your quarrel. To forgive his misunderstanding for the good of you both."

"I have spent my whole life being the one to forgive!" Zara argued angrily. "It is always my part to set my feelings aside and put someone else's happiness first. I am always the one who waits. The one who makes room for the tender egos of others. Why, Athven? Why would you ask this of me? Why must I give and give again?"

Athven suddenly looked tired. "Because you are here and no one else is. Because we deal with the situation we have, rather than the one we wish we had. And because we can none of us forgive on another's behalf. If you can find it in you to move past this, I believe that someday he will understand."

∼

Zara woke, her retort still on her lips, but Athven was gone, and the room was dark, except for the moonlight streaming in through the window. She thought about going back down. She considered the warm fire and her blankets. And then she considered the company.

She removed her boots, tucked herself under the blue coverlet and went back to sleep.

∼

She was awakened by the very last thing she would have expected—a knock on the door. It was gentle, almost tentative, and she was so alarmed at being found that she almost didn't answer.

By the third knock, however, it became clear that whoever it was, they weren't giving up.

"I'm coming," she called, and muttered to herself about early risers all the way to the door.

It was ...

"I'm sorry," she told him, "I don't remember your name."

It was the short, stout man with the nervous-looking mustache. In fact, he appeared rather nervous all over, except for his eyes, which just looked like a disappointed puppy's. "It's Gulver," he said. "And I was wondering if you would join us downstairs, Miss Zara."

"It's just Zara," she informed him. "And why should I? No one wants me, and I'd like to think I'm not foolish enough to keep turning up where I'm not wanted."

"But you're needed."

She saw the pleading look in his eyes and groaned. How had he known just what to say? She sat back on the bed to pull her boots on.

"Gulver," she asked suddenly, "why are you here?"

"Because Silvay asked me to find you," he said earnestly, before adding, "and because I followed the cat."

"No, I mean why are you here. In this place. Right now. Why did you come?"

"Oh." He walked into the room and sat down tentatively in the chair under the window, rocking a bit to test whether it would hold his weight. It was probably a wise precaution when using furniture that kept disappearing and appearing again.

"There are too many stairs for a man my age," he began with a smile, which made him seem a little less nervous than before. "I used to keep a tavern, you know. It was a terrible place. You'd have hated it. I hated it.

The floor was always dirty, and the people were always fighting. But I didn't know what else to do. My people have been hiding from the world for years. When they find out who we are and what we can do, they are not always kind. I've seen..." He swallowed and ducked his head. "Terrible things, Miss Zara. So I kept my head down and tried to make a living. Until Alexei came." His expression became rather embarrassed. "You should know, he is not as bad as he seems. He carries so many sorrows, plus the weight of his people's future, and finding you here..."

"Crushed his soul and disappointed all his hopes?" Zara allowed her sarcasm free rein.

"It is not an excuse, I know. When he came to my tavern, he was so grim and distant, so determined to pretend he didn't care, but all I could see was that here was a man who could help us. Who might be able to give hope to those of us who are left. We have had none for so many years, I couldn't help but follow him here, to see if I was wrong."

"And now?"

"I don't know," Gulver said, his mustache drooping. "I know he still wants to make things right, but... I think he's lost. And I know that unless we find the Rose, there is very little we can do. That is why we need you."

"I can't find it," Zara protested. "I've been trying. For days. But I can't feel it and even Athven can't help me."

"Please just come and talk," Gulver pleaded. "We have to try."

Against her better judgment, Zara followed him down the tower and back to the kitchens, where two fires roared and Malichai presided over an enormous pot of something that smelled delicious.

When he saw her, Malichai put down his spoon, crossed the kitchen in five or six enormous strides and actually hugged her before she could react.

"We were all wondering whether you might have frozen last night, off somewhere in this cold, drafty place," he scolded, smiling despite the censure in his tone. "Come and sit and have some breakfast."

A little stunned, Zara rubbed her ribs carefully and glanced around at the others before moving towards the table. Wilder waved from where she sprawled before the fire, drawing on the floor with a piece of charcoal. Silvay gestured to the place next to her, and Gulver sat down across from them, beaming at her as if to prove that she was not entirely unwelcome. Alexei sat at the head of the table and did not look at Zara at all.

After Zara took her place, Silvay reached out and squeezed her hand. "I am very sorry," she said softly, though she didn't look at all surprised. Perhaps seers never did. "You are welcome here, you know."

"No, I don't know," Zara replied. "But thank you for saying so. Now what would you all like to discuss?"

She could feel her face burn as Alexei lifted his head to look at her, and though he wore no particular expression of disgust or censure, she was convinced his one-eyed gaze went straight through her and found her wanting.

Not surprising really. She'd been forever without a bath, and hadn't bothered to re-braid her hair in days. And those were probably the least of her transgressions in his eyes.

"Tell us what you know about the Rose," he demanded.

"Say please," she shot back. She hadn't really thought about it, the words just slipped out.

"Please."

Zara raised a cynical brow. So he did know how to control his temper.

"Not much," she conceded. "You've mentioned it numerous times and I've gathered it is used in defense of the castle. Probably a magical item, and small, considering that it has been hidden. The traitor you brought with you was responsible for stealing and hiding it and you are worried that he may find it before you do."

"Accurate enough," Alexei allowed. "It is against my better judgment to share this with you, but we can no longer afford caution. Our need is great and our time is short so I am choosing to trust that Athven herself can prevent catastrophe if you prove untrustworthy."

"I'm overwhelmed by your compliments," Zara replied, showing all her teeth in a fake smile.

"You should be. They're probably kinder than you deserve."

"I'm sure no one will ever accuse you of the heinous crime of kindness."

Malichai's booming laugh startled them all. "This is as good as a play," he observed happily, as he set a full bowl in front of each of them. "And Miss Zara, I've finally realized who you are, so verse seven will be completed soon."

"Well, I won't be the swooning maiden waiting to be rescued, so you can just take it back now if that's what you think," she informed him.

"Why not?" Alexei asked, eyes on his bowl, his expression studiously bland. "You did swoon, after all. And you were waiting for someone to rescue you."

"Seems to me I'm not the one here who needs rescuing."

Alexei's mouth had already opened on another retort when a low rumble filtered up through the stones, just before the floor began to shift under them. Wilder yelled and dashed for Silvay, who pulled them both into a crouch beside the table. Malichai growled and stared at the ceiling, while Gulver went white and hunched into himself.

Zara and Alexei did not move, but locked eyes until the rumbling and swaying stopped.

"I don't know if you've realized this yet, but your enchanted castle is really nothing but a giant bully," Zara announced into the ensuing silence. "I don't know why you would think I have even the smallest desire to stay here. The minute that door opens, I am leaving and never coming back."

~

It hit Alexei finally that when he had said she didn't understand, it was a gross understatement. And a bit of an injustice. How *could* she understand? She might have a wisp of magic, but no one had ever told her what to expect. What her bond with Athven truly meant.

Yes, she had intruded in a place she didn't belong, and that fault was hers alone, but he could not continue to judge her for what she didn't know. He needed to make her see. It wasn't going to go well, he was certain. He'd believed she had to have known the truth when she proposed marriage the night before, but perhaps he had misjudged that as well. The proposal simply didn't make any sense the more he thought about it.

Now she was standing, as though she meant to leave again. He needed to convince her to stop running away whenever they had a disagreement.

"Please," he said, as courteously as he could manage. "Sit. Eat. I think..." The words were hard to force out. "I may have been too hasty in my statements before. Further explanation might resolve at least a portion of the tension between us."

Her blue eyes widened. She glanced at his companions. "Is this a trick?" she demanded, as Silvay retook her seat.

"I think not, and I concur with Alexei," Silvay said pleasantly. "We are allies, after all. We should at least try to work out our differences whenever possible."

"Then I will listen," Zara allowed, "but that doesn't mean I will agree."

"Believe me, no one expects it of you," Alexei returned dryly. When she shot him a glare, the corner of his mouth twitched. It had almost been a smile.

"When you talk of leaving," he began, "I am afraid you don't grasp the nature of the bond you and Athven share. It isn't simply you being bound to her as a servant, to do her bidding. It is a two-way bond, giving and taking, and you share as much with her as she shares with you. I believe it is a weak bond, considering the limitations of your magic, and the fact that neither of you knew what you were doing, but given that Athven has been able to sustain an avatar and restore some of what she has held in stasis all these years, it is a true bond as well."

"Yes," Zara agreed impatiently. "She told me that much. She said if I left, she would die. That it is our bond that makes it possible for her to do what she does. Like rattle the floor and scare us half to death." She shot a glare at the ceiling.

"Then..." Alexei was stunned by this revelation. "If you know, how can you still threaten to leave? You would sentence her to death!"

"I realize you think I'm a monster," Zara snapped, "but can you accept that I may not be quite as bad as you imagine? I would not leave until I transfer the bond to another. That's why..." She fell silent and blushed furiously. "That's why I said what I did last night. Athven told me it was the only way. That if I married, the bond could be transferred and I could be free. But I had to marry someone with magic. An Erathi. Or it wouldn't work."

Alexei stared at her, momentarily shocked speechless. She had to be lying. Had to be trying to convince him to marry her by whatever means possible. If she didn't know his heritage, if she didn't think he could make her a queen, why would she have proposed to tie herself to a hideously scarred stranger who didn't even like her? Surely a treasure hunter would never purposefully leave behind the greatest treasure of them all.

She couldn't be telling the truth. Because that would mean...

"She's telling the truth."

Alexei looked blankly at Wilder. Who was looking back with a solemn expression far beyond her years.

"I know you don't want to believe her, but she's not lying. Auras change when people lie. Hers stayed the same. She still has thorns, and—"

"Thank you, Wilder." Silvay interrupted the girl with a beaming smile.

Alexei shot her a glance of deep suspicion. Thorns were hardly surprising for a person as prickly as Zara, but the girl had been about to say something more—something Silvay already knew and didn't want her to reveal. Which probably meant it was important. Not as important, however, as what he had just learned about Athven.

She could lie. He had never considered it possible, but if Zara was telling the truth, Athven had lied to her. Probably more than once. The avatar may have simply used misleading language, but either way, it had to have been deliberate, and the realization made Alexei feel like a worm. Or worse. Zara had been manipulated by a creature far older and more experienced than she, and Alexei had been grossly unfair.

He would not—could not—like her. She was still a thief. One who had, inadvertently perhaps, stolen far more than she would ever know. But, he could almost admit that it might not be entirely her fault. Perhaps if he remembered that, he could bury his anger deeply enough to work with her until this was resolved.

"I am... sorry," he said at length, and every head in the kitchen turned to look at him. "Yes," he confirmed, trying not to grimace, "you heard me correctly. I am sorry. I thought..." He didn't quite have the nerve to admit what he'd thought.

"You thought I was a mercenary who saw a chance at a bigger prize and went for it," Zara said flatly. "You thought I wanted to marry you because it would give me some sort of position. A name, to pull me up from the disgrace of my heritage and my profession."

"Yes."

"And what do you think now?"

Her blue eyes met his, cool and level.

"I think you were lied to."

She did not flinch. "What's the worst of it?"

"Your bond... Your bond with Athven might be described as similar to that of marriage, at least for an Erathi. When we marry..." He paused. Looked for an easier way to say it. "You say that you know the connection goes both ways, but it is not only Athven who would die if you left Erath."

He saw her absorb this and blanch.

"When Athven spoke of transferring the bond, if that is the word she used, she misled you. The bond can be expanded, to include another, but the process does not technically require marriage. And whether the bond is between two or three, your own connection with Athven cannot be broken without resulting in death. If Athven is strong enough, she will survive, but you..."

He could see her begin to tremble. Her eyes went wide, but no tears fell.

"And when you say the marriage bond is the same..." The firmness of her voice belied the anguish on her face.

"Yes," Alexei said softly. "The bond between Athven and her guardians is usually an intimate one. She is able to speak to them mind to mind, and anyone added to your bond would be able to do so as well. The relationship would not be one you would care to share with a stranger. But if you were to marry that person, in the Erathi sense, the two of you would be bound to each other as tightly as you and Athven are now. You could not be separated for long, and not by very far. It is a lifelong partnership that cannot be dissolved, and partners are known to follow one another into death."

As difficult as it was to admit, Alexei found that he admired Zara's courage in that moment. She sat alone in a room full of strangers, and she may have blinked back tears as she absorbed what he had to say, but she did not break. Her breath hitched, but only for a moment, and when her eyes finally cleared, Alexei could read nothing—not fear, not anger, not hatred.

"I see," she said slowly. "Then perhaps you will acquit me of whatever crimes you believe I have committed, considering how dearly I will be paying for them." She straightened in her seat and lifted her chin. "And now we'd better set about finding this rose, hadn't we?"

"Yes." It wasn't over. The pain would come later, but for now, Alexei had enough tact to leave behind the subject of bonds and forever. "We have searched, but I am hoping your relationship with Athven may give you an advantage. The item we are looking for is a piece of pink baryte crystal, somewhat larger than a man's head. It might appear flower-like, but it is solid and in its natural form."

"I can assure you right off that I haven't seen it," Zara told them. "Until you came, there was nothing here but the stones and the kitchen stores, and what few items I brought with me. It wasn't until yesterday that other things began to appear. I suppose it's possible the Rose has appeared somewhere as well."

Alexei shook his head. "The things that are appearing are original furnishings, objects that I believe Athven has held in a sort of magical stasis while she awaited our return. They were merely hidden from sight. The Rose was concealed before Athven's retreat. I doubt that it is simply lying about somewhere to be seen."

"Athven has been looking for something for some time," Zara noted. "She has not been willing to tell me what it is, and even with my help she has not been able to find it. She says she can feel it, but cannot reach it. I don't know what that means, but I can't imagine we'll be able to do better. It must be out of her reach somehow. How sure are you that it is still in the castle?"

"As sure as I can be," Alexei insisted. "My... the Betrayer told us he hid it here. He was bragging of his cleverness at the time, and, considering my memories of those days, I believed him. It would have amused him to hide it under our noses and laugh as he waited for our destruction."

"All right." Zara placed her elbows on the table and rested her chin on her hands. "All we have to do is think like a sadistic bastard and make a list of all the places such a person might think to hide something valuable. Alexei? Clearly you're the one who should advise us how to move forward."

Her blue eyes challenged him to make what he would of her words. Even Wilder stopped breathing to look at him. Waiting to see what he would do.

He could choose to be angry at the insinuation. Or he could remember that she was hurting and faced with an exile that would never end. Could he offer acceptance without her misunderstanding him? "Yes, of course." He smiled faintly. "Isn't it lucky that I'm here to help?"

"Well, I know I feel like the luckiest girl alive," Zara said, with more than a hint of bitterness. "Who wouldn't want to be me right now?"

"Who indeed," Alexei whispered, and hoped that no one could hear him.

~

They split up to search. Silvay went with Wilder, Gulver with Malichai, and Alexei insisted that Zara stay with him. She protested that Athven didn't talk to her directly, and anyway, the cat hadn't been seen all day, but he wanted her near, just in case Athven decided she had something to say. If she did, he certainly had something to say back to her.

Being alone with Zara did not particularly trouble him, though it was undeniably awkward, and he could see how she might feel nervous about the situation. Or even frightened. For the second time since their arrival, he thought of his damaged face, but this time he wondered if it upset her. He doubted it. Very little seemed to upset her, but he couldn't quite suppress the desire to know. Though he would die before he asked.

"Where did you and Athven search?" He kept his tone vaguely polite as they stood together in the entry hall, listening to the footsteps of the others fade into the distance.

"Where did we not?" she answered tartly. "I don't know enough of this castle to tell you, but I assume Athven is self-aware enough to know when we'd been everywhere."

"Then where did she seem to feel the Rose most strongly? Or did she say?"

"Come on then," Zara turned on her heel and led him towards the back stairs. "I'll show you, not that it will do any good."

She led him north, to a lower level, where a long, narrow room butted up against the pantries on one end, and the north tower on the other. "We spent quite some time here, and also in the outer passage along the wall on the main level. Of course"—she shot him a grimace—"it didn't look like this then."

Along the length of what had probably been a bare room the first time she saw it were strewn tables of various sizes and heights. Some had chairs or stools placed in their orbit, but others had none. Carpets covered parts of the floor, and the walls were haphazardly bedecked with diagrams and paintings of complex designs.

"No," Alexei told her softly, "but it looked like this when I was here last."

It was the workroom, or so they called it. The place where the gifted would come to dream, plan, discuss and design. So many ideas had been born there. Bad ones, as well as good. Alexei almost laughed aloud when he saw a particularly unusual drawing hanging from the wall. One of his fellow enchanters had dreamed of a flying machine, and even designed a frame for it, but he'd never been able to convince any of his fellows to jump off one of the towers with the contraption strapped to their shoulders. Even magic had its limits.

He saw Zara watching him, her shoulders tense. "This is one of the spaces where we used to work," he explained. "Anyone who lived here could come and discuss their magic with others. We would consult with those who shared our gifts, or plan together how we might combine different gifts to accomplish something new."

"Then that burn mark on the wall could have happened before the invasion?" she asked, unable to mask the sarcasm in the question.

"Yes, actually." Alexei was so deep in memories, he actually smiled. "One of my cousins was experimenting with hearthstones." He glanced at Zara, who was clearly confused. "They are enchanted to give heat and light.

Most households use them instead of fires. Though"—he shrugged—"we still build fireplaces to put them in."

"Then why aren't there any here?"

"There are. But their enchantment would have run dry. Now that so much is being restored, perhaps I can find a few unused stones and we will not be forced to breathe smoke any longer."

He was silent, remembering, when Zara interrupted his thoughts.

"You say that so casually! Like it is nothing to make a rock that can take the place of a fire."

He regarded her thoughtfully. Perhaps even living in an enchanted castle had not quite prepared her for the reality of Erath as it had been. "It was a small thing, once. One of the first tasks enchanters learn to do as children."

"What else did you learn to do?"

She was trying to sound nonchalant, but her question was not without bite. He remembered Gulver saying that Zara was afraid of him. Was he making it worse, admitting to what he could do? Or would it help to know the full extent of the truth?

He pulled out two of the chairs and sat, beckoning for her to do the same. She did, but gingerly, as though she expected the chair to fall out from under her.

"It won't collapse, you know."

She ducked her head and leaned her elbows on her knees.

"Though that's another thing that probably happened many times in this very room. We might have been powerful, but that did not make us any less fond of pranks."

"Like collapsing chairs?"

"Yes." He grinned. "And rain showers indoors, and candles that flickered constantly, and silencing one's footsteps to make sneaking simpler. Among other, much more devious notions."

"How old were you?" She immediately looked as though she wished she hadn't asked.

"I was sixteen when Erath fell. Old enough to have spent a good ten years developing my gift."

"That seems young. Do Erathi make their children work instead of play?"

Alexei's lips twisted, pulling at the scar on his cheek. "Even at six, learning my gift was better than play. Though I certainly did enough of that early on. Growing up with forty-seven cousins is a boisterous affair, and even in a place as big as this, you soon learn you cannot escape entirely. You either learn to live with them or they trample you."

He could feel Zara's eyes on him, but he didn't want to see what was in them. Envy or pity would be equally unbearable at that moment.

"He was one of your cousins, wasn't he? Porfiry?"

How in all the hells could she have known? "Yes."

"Do you know what happened? Why he betrayed you?"

Did he want to tell her? He barely understood it himself. "Porfiry was born either ungifted, or with a slight enough gift that it was never fully identified. It is rare, among our people, but it does happen. We Erathi are not without our weaknesses, and in some families, the child is shunned or rejected."

"But Porfiry lived here. With you and forty-six other cousins."

"His parents sent him here, alone. Many of us lived at Athven with our families. My own parents travelled the kingdom so much, I rarely saw them, but they visited when they were able." His lips twisted with the memory. They had loved him, he knew, but he had spent so little time with them, he rarely even missed them.

"Porfiry's family sent him away. It seemed unfair that they rejected him for what he could not help, but we children always considered him one of us. We included him as best we could, but most of us had lessons, and he did not. We had plans for the future, dreams of what we would do one day. Porfiry, I believe, was left aimless and it ate at his soul."

"Did no one try to give him a task?" This time he heard the compassion in her voice and it stung him.

"It was attempted, on many occasions, and therein lies his complaint—that he was driven to do that which he could not, and then rejected again when he failed."

"So this was his revenge. What he could not possess, he destroyed."

"Or so he would have us believe. I do not claim to know his mind, cousin or no."

Zara was silent, and all they could hear for a few moments was the sound of their own breath and the whisper of a light wind brushing along the stones outside the wall.

"Being cast aside by a parent is not a small wound." Zara's gaze rested on the floor and her words were soft. "That is a great deal of pain for one person to bear."

"Pain he willfully inflicted on thousands of others," Alexei reminded her coldly, rising to his feet. "Instead of learning from their actions, he chose to hate."

"If you've never known what love looks like, what choice do you have?" Zara's voice was low and compelling and Alexei couldn't bring himself to listen. She knew nothing. She had never met Porfiry; had never heard the poison that dripped from his tongue or seen the hatred lurking in his eyes.

"Enough. We are wasting time."

He stalked away to look more closely at the walls, but he felt Zara's eyes on his back and, for the first time, knew a twinge of guilt over his treatment of her. She was more than he had given her credit for, and, for a moment, he had almost enjoyed her company. It was Porfiry who deserved his ire, so why did he continue to lash out at Zara, when he knew he needed her help?

But why would she defend the Betrayer? Unless she felt some connection with his story... But that was not something Alexei was willing to contemplate. He might have made his peace with Zara's situation, but he refused to listen to her make excuses for the man who had been responsible for so much death and destruction. There was too much to be done. Too many lives hung in the balance, and if Alexei could not manage to feel pain on behalf of his people, how could he feel compassion for the one who betrayed them?

In truth, he wasn't even sure he was capable of compassion anymore. Not for Zara, and certainly not for Porfiry. If that was what Athven wanted from him, she might find herself waiting for another thirty years.

CHAPTER 8

Zara stared at her companion's back and wished it would burst into flame. After all, he'd said she had magic. If Erathi children had managed to set things on fire, why not her? To her disappointment, even the most concentrated glare she could muster produced nothing—not even a wisp of smoke.

Alexei might not have been the first man she'd wished would burst into flame, but he was certainly the most annoying. And the most confusing. One moment he exuded patience, calm, and steadfast purpose. The next he was angry and dismissive.

She was willing to allow that she had gotten far more than she expected out of her questions. He had actually answered one. And for a brief time, she thought they had almost established a tentative... well, not friendship. Perhaps respect? Probably not that either. He had made it perfectly clear that he could never respect a thief. But at least they had seemed on the verge of not being enemies.

But then she had made the mistake of admitting to some sort of empathy for the rejected Porfiry and all that ground had been lost. She'd been trailing him around the lower floors of the castle ever since, responding to his terse questions with one-word answers, hoping someone else would show up to dispel the tension.

Of course, they didn't. Privately, she resolved to turn Shadow into a cat-skin vest the next time she saw her.

As if on cue, the shabby gray cat meandered around a corner ahead of them.

"You," Zara spat, eyes narrowed, "are a liar. You'd better have something intelligent to say for yourself. Or be here to help us. Otherwise, I might borrow one of Silvay's knives and find something decorative to do with your hide."

"Do you really want her to bring the roof down on our heads?" Alexei asked, sounding exasperated.

"Don't let her fool you," Zara answered shortly. "She's not going to jeopardize her existence by actually harming us, or herself. She's just trying to intimidate us into doing what she wants, with no regard for whether it's in our best interests."

"Whether or not I understand or agree with her methods, Athven's motives have always been above reproach. She cannot help but have the well-being of Erath at heart," Alexei insisted.

"That's what scares me," Zara shot back. "She might care for her kingdom, but she sees us puny individual mortals as means to that end. The only way to be sure she will preserve us is to make ourselves indispensable to her future."

"I disagree." Alexei folded his arms firmly. "Athven has never shown anything less than concern for the well-being of her people. She has guarded us well for centuries. Perhaps you simply don't understand what she hopes to accomplish."

"She hopes to make us do her royal bidding!"

"Well, whatever the case, you have nothing to fear, as you are already indispensable to her future," Alexei retorted. "Though perhaps you think the rest of us ought to be trembling in fear."

"Oh, yes, you should be trembling before the power of my ability to persuade her to do absolutely nothing!"

"You know, I'm beginning to think Gulver was mistaken," Alexei observed.

"About what?" she snapped, wondering at the abrupt change of subject.

"He said you were afraid of me. I believe he may have been hallucinating."

Zara stared at him, open-mouthed. Gulver had said that? When had she let him see her fear? "Of course I'm not afraid of you." She said the words almost automatically.

"Because I can understand if you are. My face is not exactly reassuring."

"I'm not afraid of your scars," she replied, before she could think better of it.

"You're not?" He turned to look at her, almost curiously.

"What makes you think anyone would care about your face?" She didn't even attempt to hid her scorn. "Contrary to your expectations, it just isn't that interesting."

He seemed to absorb that information slowly. "Then what are you afraid of?"

"I didn't say I was."

"Then you're saying Gulver was wrong?"

Zara turned away before he could see an answer on her face. "Don't you have anything more important to think about right now?" She wasn't afraid of the way he looked, but she'd be damned before she told him what she truly feared.

The cat strolled between them, lay down on the stones and began to look from Zara to Alexei, then back again. When neither of them responded, she sat up and began to wash herself.

Zara drew herself up and glared. "Well, I won't do it, so you can just stop." She had no idea how she knew what the cat wanted, but she did. Their bond must be getting stronger.

"Won't do what?"

Zara clamped her lips shut.

"Zara, what does Athven want you to do?"

She looked up at him, eyes wide and mouth slightly open. It was the first time he'd spoken her name. And, wonder of wonders, it had not sounded like a curse. But that didn't mean she was going to meekly do as she was told.

"Well, I'm not going to do it and I'm not going to tell you, so what does it matter?"

"Athven may be trying to help us. It may not make any sense to you right now, but perhaps it's for the best. Tell me what she wants."

"She still wants you to marry me, you imbecile!" Zara yelled. "Were you not listening when I made it clear that it wasn't *my* idea? I don't even like you! But she thinks it's brilliant! She's made of rocks! She doesn't understand that humans have hearts and are not toys for her amusement. Or that it's possible for us to die of humiliation!"

She turned on her heel and started to walk away, seething with anger, unsure whether it was more at him for forcing her to say it, or at her own mouth for not staying decently shut. Or at Athven. For being dastardly and manipulative.

"Wait."

Zara didn't want to wait. She didn't want his anger, his pity, or his rejection. But she could only run so far, and he'd probably just send Gulver to find her again, so she stopped, though she couldn't look him in the eye.

"Yes, initially I did think it was your idea. But you explained that and I understood that you were misled. I am sorry, I should have realized that Athven might not be so easily convinced."

Had he... Was that an apology? Zara wasn't quite ready to trust it.

"She is anxious," Alexei continued calmly, as though speaking of the weather, "and is trying to establish some sort of security. She may be attempting to persuade us to see things her way, but I believe we can find another solution that will satisfy her. She would not force either of us to do something against our will."

Zara looked back over her shoulder in spite of herself. Alexei appeared both serious and earnest, and he didn't seem to be mocking her. He might be rejecting her, but it wasn't as if she wanted him to accept her proposal now that she knew the consequences. He had even apologized. And at least he wasn't calling her names this time.

Shadow was sitting up and looking at Alexei, her tail lashing impatiently.

"I think," Zara said, a tiny smile tugging at the corner of her mouth, "that you've annoyed her."

"Then I hope you're right."

"About what?"

"That she is wise enough not to destroy us in a fit of pique."

"She isn't going to stop," Zara warned him. "For whatever reason, she still believes that a wedding would solve all of her problems."

"Well, in some respects, perhaps it would," Alexei admitted. "From her perspective, a marriage represents the foundation of a new future. The possibility of a new generation to aid her in protecting our people. But as her particular choice is in all other respects unconscionable, that is the least of our concerns."

Zara sighed and threw up her hands when Alexei wasn't looking. At least he'd managed not to insult her for a few minutes. It was an improvement. Maybe by the time this was over, he would manage a whole day.

"But why is she in such a hurry?" she wondered aloud. "Aside from providing more power, she has given no other reasons. You would think she would prefer her guardians to actually like each other. And what's another year or two after waiting this long?"

Alexei apparently did not intend to answer her questions. "We should resume searching. As soon as we've finished this area, perhaps we should meet up with the others and see what they've found."

Zara added Athven's "reasons" to the growing list of things that Alexei was unwilling—or unable—to talk about. Perhaps he'd decided he'd rather be quiet and mysterious than angry and insulting. If only she could be sure the change wouldn't prove equally as frustrating.

~

They combed the castle for the rest of the morning, which turned into afternoon, and then to evening. One day turned into two, and then ten, until Alexei stopped counting. The search slowed more everyday to accommodate the appearance of an increasing number of Athven's original furnishings, which provided an even greater array of possible hiding places to choose from.

Alexei remembered uncomfortably his cousin's statement that they could tear Athven down and search the stones and still never find the Rose. He had thought this to be exaggeration, but what if Porfiry had been telling the truth? Never mind the possibility that the castle had secrets even he didn't know. He needed to talk to Athven directly, but it seemed clear that her bond with Zara was too weak to sustain such a conversation. And while Athven clearly had the ability to speak to him, she seemed reluctant to do so. Perhaps it used too much of her strength.

After yet another day of fruitless searching, the party gathered in the entry hall to discuss their findings. Silvay had explored the rooms where her former mistress had resided, and Wilder reported that the bannister was not very useful for sliding. Gulver had found a collection of healing talismans, and though their magic had dissipated, he was exclaiming enthusiastically about the artistry of their design. And Malichai was worried about Loraleen.

"I never thought we'd be trapped here this long," he confided anxiously, "and she's not the sort to run off, but I'm afraid she'll think I've forgotten her." A tear made its way down his face and disappeared beneath his beard.

"She's the only love of my life, you know. Saved me more times than I can count. I'd never leave her, but I don't know if she believes that."

Alexei was not terribly concerned with the welfare of the animals. They were generally more sensible than people gave them credit for. There was water and grass, and horses could do well enough without the shelter of a stable. But he heard an intake of breath from Zara and felt her stiffen where she stood, a few paces from his shoulder.

Malichai's words had upset her.

"She's not alone, Malichai," Zara said softly. Upset or not, her first instinct seemed to be to comfort the distraught. "She has companions, enough to eat, and she has her freedom. And I think she knows you'll come for her when you can."

"I'm sure you're right." The bearded man swiped a hairy arm across his face.

Malichai had echoed some of Alexei's own frustration. He had never anticipated being trapped. Though it had its advantages—no one else could enter—it had far more drawbacks. What if the Rose was hidden somewhere on the outside? Somewhere Porfiry could just walk up and take it without them ever knowing?

Would Athven still not simply open the doors and let them come and go as needed? She continued to be evasive about her reasons, which struck Alexei anew as disquieting. Had she been hoping from the first to encourage a union between him and Zara? They had definitely established that a marriage was impossible, so why not set them free?

"Zara."

She turned to look at him warily. Even after their days of shared searching, she seemed ill-at-ease in his presence, though she'd established an apparent rapport with each of his other companions.

"How does Athven speak to you? Can you ask her questions and understand her answers?"

She looked uncomfortable. "So far, she's only been able to speak to me in dreams. But lately, when Shadow is in the room, I feel like I know what she's thinking. There aren't really any words. Just a feeling." She held up her hands to indicate confusion. "I don't think I can describe it. And it isn't two-way communication. If she knows what I'm thinking, she doesn't ever acknowledge it."

"Do you think she—Shadow—understands us when we speak?"

"Yes." Zara didn't even hesitate. "But that doesn't mean she'll answer."

It was worth trying. Considering the vision he'd had when Zara collapsed, perhaps she would relent and speak with him again.

"Athven." He crouched down and directed his gaze to where the gray cat was twining her way around Wilder's feet, probably trying to look harmless. "Please. I know you can hear me. I have so many questions, but even if you choose not to answer them, I'm asking you to let us out. Open the doors. Trust us to return. We are not going to abandon you. But we would feel less like prisoners if we were allowed to come and go."

Shadow rolled over onto her back and batted at the edge of Silvay's cloak.

"She's laughing at us," Zara muttered.

"I'm not going to marry Zara," Alexei said sternly, feeling a little silly for addressing such a remark to a cat. "No matter how long you keep us here. It would be a mistake, and would accomplish nothing other than making two people miserable. There must be another way to solve the problems we are facing."

The cat's tail twitched, but she continued to stare at Silvay.

"Alexei, you could perhaps have stated that more diplomatically," Silvay protested.

"What?" Startled by her remonstration, he rose and dusted off his hands. "You mean about Zara? Neither of us is willing to marry the other, so why should I not be straightforward about it? I cannot imagine a pair worse suited to a partnership."

There was a choked-off laugh behind him. Zara was trying to look innocent and failing. "Oh dear," she said in mock sorrow. "You're in for it now."

He raised an eyebrow.

"That's the second time you've disrespected your precious Athven," she announced in a sing-song voice. "She's going to get you for that. Whatever happened to 'all-knowing' and 'has our best interests at heart'?"

His brow lowered, but before he could respond, there was a heart-stopping crash. As one, the six of them whirled to find that the great iron-bound doors at the front of the hall stood wide and gaping. The pale light of evening streamed in, and for a moment, no one spoke.

They all turned to look at Shadow, who was staring at the wall with all the hauteur that is the birthright of cats, plus a healthy helping of disgust. Or maybe that was just her face.

"Thank you," Alexei said, feeling a little shocked. Had it really been that simple? All this time, had they merely needed to ask?

"Malichai, I believe you can go and look for Loraleen. Although you might want to wait for morning. There could be other travelers who arrived after us, and I would rather not invite anyone else in until we know their motives for being here."

He glanced at Zara, who was gazing past him, her eyes wide and frozen. In a single flash of intuition, he saw her intention on her face, but didn't have time to move or speak.

"Father," Zara whispered. Before anyone had a chance to ask what she meant, she bolted out the open door and was gone.

They watched her go, open mouthed, until Alexei broke the stunned silence.

"Malichai, stay!" he said sharply. The bearded man had clearly been about to race out the door after her. "You must defend the castle until Zara returns. We will look for Loraleen later, I swear it, but I beg you to keep Athven safe."

It was a stern task, but Malichai was a warrior, and he knew what was needed. His mouth hardened to a firm line and he ran from the hall, presumably to retrieve his weapons.

"Wilder, you stay with Malichai. Gulver as well. You will be needed if anyone attempts to gain entry and there is a fight. Silvay, would you come with me?"

The older woman nodded briskly, but her sadness was unmistakable. Like him, she knew the potential consequences of what Zara had done. Like him, she had been close enough to hear what Zara whispered as she fled.

Father. She had never spoken of her father. Why would she run out into the night to find him?

Alexei took only the time necessary to find his cloak and then stepped out into the deepening chill of evening. "Silvay, do you know her signature well enough to seek it?"

"I do," she said, "but I will only sense it if I am close."

"Do you feel safe enough to split up?" he asked. "We will cover more ground, faster."

"I have travelled alone many times," she reminded him. "And I am strong enough to know when others are near, so there is little danger."

"Even if we have not found her, we should return when the moon peaks. I don't know when Athven might decide she is tired of waiting for us to return."

Silvay bit her lip. "Why did she do that? After refusing to let us leave?" She was not talking about Zara.

"To prove a point," Alexei answered bitterly. "She knew something I didn't. Knew, or guessed, what Zara would do, given the chance."

"Zara told me..." Silvay hesitated.

"Silvay, I swear I will respect your confidence, but if you know anything that will help us, please tell me."

"Zara came with companions," Silvay confessed. "One of the ones she described was an older man, with gray hair. She didn't say it was her father, but I had the sense she was hiding something. She asked whether we had seen them, and I told her there was no one else in the valley. I could tell that it hurt her."

Abandonment. Zara had reacted strongly when he spoke of Porfiry's parents giving him up. She had reacted again when Malichai worried that Loraleen might think he had abandoned her.

Father, she had whispered. Had she believed he might still be out there somewhere, waiting for her?

A terrible feeling of regret clenched at his heart, matched by the stirrings of anger. Zara had indeed been abandoned. There was no one in the valley. No one waiting for her, no one hoping against hope that she would be released. And Athven had already known.

She was able to feel the presence of anyone within the valley, and should have simply told Zara the truth—that her father was nowhere nearby. But she had not, so she must have wanted this situation to unfold exactly as it had.

She had wanted Zara to bolt, in the mistaken belief that her father could never have simply walked away. Athven knew her bondmate well enough to be confident that she would not leave the valley and risk the consequences. And Athven must have guessed that Alexei would go after the runaway, because he wouldn't trust her to return of her own free will.

And yet, if Athven still wanted them to marry, why would she give Zara the opportunity to drive another wedge between them? Was this about control? To prove that she knew best? Or was it merely the clumsy efforts of a would-be matchmaker to bring two people together?

"I never thought I would say it, but Zara may have been right," Alexei told Silvay in a low voice. "This leads me to believe that Athven, in spite of all her power, does not truly understand the people she depends on. And she suffers from neither scruples nor compassion."

"A dangerous combination," Silvay noted.

"When we find Zara..." He did not say "if." He could not accept anything less than "when."

"Yes," Silvay answered with a sigh. "We have assumed too much. We will have a lot of apologizing to do."

"That's very kind of you," Alexei told her, smiling crookedly, "but I don't think you meant 'we.'"

Silvay smiled back. "Perhaps not. But a little extra apology never hurt anyone."

~

Sending Silvay to circle to the north, Alexei took the road, guessing that Zara's search for her father would follow the most obvious route. That she was strong, he knew, and from what he had just seen, probably fast as well. He would not be able to catch her simply by running. He would have to wait for her to tire, and hope that she would remember the consequences for her flight before she strayed outside the valley.

If not... He would not think about it. He couldn't bring himself to consider such a possibility. But even as he shoved the idea away, it was not Athven's image that lingered, but Zara's. The thought of her lying lifeless on the ground troubled him, though he could not understand why. He regretted their misunderstandings, and owed her a debt, but she wasn't even a friend. Was it simply that he could not bear the idea that Athven could have so callously sent someone to their death?

As darkness grew, with no trace of the ethereal lavender threads that made up Zara's magic, his apprehension grew with it. How far had she gone? What signs would she be looking for? Any search for human habitation was as likely as not to bring her into contact with someone they would both rather she avoid. And if Rowan was lurking...

Again, Alexei's mind shied away from the possibility.

He stopped for a moment to push outward with his senses, extending his magic farther, reaching for the edges of the valley. His magic was strong enough, but he was out of practice. He hadn't realized how stiff those inner senses had become with lack of use. Now that they were more limber, he should consider enchanting again. Not basic items, though if he could find some hearthstones he would certainly put them to good use. No, he needed to try more complex workings, to find out if it was still possible. And if not...

A scream splintered the night. Not the terrified scream of a woman afraid for her life, but the enraged scream of battle being joined.

Definitely Zara. She probably wouldn't have the sense to be afraid of anything she might find in that valley. As he plunged off the road into the trees and raced through the underbrush in the direction of the sound, Alexei almost laughed. He wondered whether he ought to be more worried for her, or for whatever she had encountered?

But when he stumbled into a clearing, all thoughts of levity vanished. It was Zara, indeed. She was sprawled on her side near the edge of the trees, thin moonlight reflecting off the white of her hair. Her head was up, but she wasn't moving. And what she faced was no lurking mercenary or predatory mountain cat. Only a few paces from her boots, the enormous form of an artenu flickered and swirled, the smoky form of its body lit by an eerie internal glow.

An unearthly snarl rumbled from its throat, and its eyes flared. Suddenly, Alexei realized how Zara must have stumbled across it. She had been looking for smoke. Searching for the cookfire of anyone who might have been encamped in the wood near Athven. And her keen senses had led her straight into the path of one of the giant bear-shaped creatures who lurked in the deep woods of Erath. They were made of smoke and fire and magic and the smell of their haunts could easily be mistaken for burning wood.

Usually, they did not leave Vrendel, but this one had, and Zara would have no idea what she was facing. Named demons by those outsiders who encountered them, artenu were indeed dangerous, but preferred to stay far away from humans. When surprised, they were downright deadly, even if you knew their weaknesses. They didn't have many.

Luckily enough, just as his brother's affinity was for horses, Alexei's was for fire. Most enchanters had an affinity for one element or another, but the most powerful talismans were shaped by fire, and Alexei had been one of the most powerful enchanters in his generation.

Grasping the stone pendant hidden beneath his shirt, he reached for the fire in the bear-shaped creature's eyes and tugged. It would have been better had his affinity been for water, to balance the fire, but he would work with what he had.

The beast grunted and turned away from Zara, sensing a new threat. Its mouth opened and flames leapt from its throat when it roared, while the smoke of its form swirled and danced in an unseen wind.

"Don't move," Alexei said, keeping his voice placid as a lake in summer. "It is very like a real bear in some ways. If you stay still and breathe slowly, it will shift its attention to me." He did not voice his fear that the creature might be too much for him. He could not risk her deciding that he wasn't to be trusted, or that he would do better with her help. She was not weak, but only magic could deter the artenu.

She listened. As the fiery gaze swung back and forth between them, she lowered her head, slowly, until it rested on her bent arm, and went utterly still. When the artenu's attention shifted fully to him, Alexei reached deeper into his talisman and unleashed power he'd almost forgotten he had.

Flames leapt from his outstretched hand. Without the enchantment in his talisman, without the power slumbering in the earth beneath him, he could never have done it, but the latent power of the land surged to life and overflowed with something that felt like relief. The flames grew higher, outlined both hands, his arms, and then spread to his torso. Holding the artenu's gaze, Alexei took a step towards it, and as he did so, the shape of the fire stretched and grew until it mirrored the beast it faced.

He had grown weak. Holding the shape almost brought him to his knees and sweat poured down his neck, but he took another step, and another. With a fierce joy he realized he did not need to see the form he had created with his magic. He could feel it, like a separate sense he had never used because he had never needed it. The bear took shape in his mind and when he called for more, it roared and the flames flared so brightly they nearly went white.

The artenu did not charge. It shook its head and roared back, but it looked more bewildered than anything. And when the flames roared again, the creature gave in to its confusion, turned, and ran from the clearing, leaving only the smell of smoke and charred footprints behind.

Alexei let go the flames and fell to his knees, exhausted and exhilarated at the same time. Until he realized that Zara was still not moving.

Pushing himself up, forcing himself to walk, he reached her side before falling again. The moonlight was dim, and did not show any injuries, until he placed a tentative hand on her shoulder and rolled her onto her back. Her eyes were tightly shut, but she made a hoarse sound of pain and held her left arm close to her chest.

It was burned. Something was clutched in her hand—a stick, he thought—but it was charred, and the flesh around it was blistered and blackened from what must have been an all-too-close encounter with the flames of the artenu. Zara must have attempted to defend herself with the only weapon she could find.

"I..." Her voice cracked and she groaned before trying again. "I almost had it." The ghost of a smile twisted her lips. "I thought I smelled a campfire. I didn't know..." She began to cough, a harsh sound that ended in a whimper of pain. "I'm sorry. I had to find him. I had to know."

"Shhh." Whatever anger he might have harbored had been burned clean by the flames. They had survived, and that was enough. "You can tell me later. We need to get you back to Gulver."

"What..." she coughed again. "Gulver? Isn't he a... a tavern keeper?"

"Gulver can help you." He laid a hand on her good arm and tried to prevent her from sitting up. "No, don't go anywhere yet. Rest, until you're sure you're able to move without injuring yourself."

Her eyes opened and he could feel her watching him.

"Why aren't you yelling at me?"

"Why would I yell at you?"

"Don't be an ass, Alexei."

He chuckled, for the moment glad to be alive, glad she was alive to call him whatever she chose. But she deserved an explanation.

"We were both manipulated, Zara. You were right about Athven all along. I shouldn't have assumed that I knew her. She knew what would happen when she opened the doors, and she did it anyway, whether to show me she knew best, or to throw us together. Either way, I have learned something important and I'm grateful."

Zara sat up then, with a low, pained sound as her injured arm moved. "You've got to take me back," she muttered hoarsely. "I think I've finally lost my mind."

"Well, don't get used to it. I'm sure we'll be fighting again before we get very far."

She snorted, and winced when the motion jarred her arm.

Rising wearily to his feet, Alexei offered her his hand. She hesitated, but only for a moment before accepting his help. Her hand was strong and callused in his, but cold and trembling with the aftermath of her ordeal. He gripped it gently until she was steady enough to stand on her own.

"Before we go, Zara, you should know that your father is not here. Not in the valley. I would have felt him, or Athven would."

Her head bent. "I know," she whispered. "Athven would never tell me one way or another, but I knew. I just... I had to be sure."

Alexei felt an irresistible impulse to comfort her as she had comforted Malichai. "I'm sure he waited. I'm sure he tried to find you."

She made a sound that was trying to be a laugh, but ended up more of a sob. "You don't know him like I do." She scrubbed at her face with the back of her good hand. "He had to be terrified, and he's never been good with anything frightening or stressful. Why do you think I was always the first one in? It was my job to check for danger, not his. The moment the door closed on his heels, I promise you he ran like a rabbit, with Geb and Finch right behind."

"So why risk your life to find him?"

"I don't know. Maybe because coward or not, he's all I have." Zara was pleading with him to understand. "If I stop looking, the only alternative is to admit that he didn't care enough to overcome his fear. Or that he simply went looking for more treasure and forgot about me altogether. Somehow… that seems worse."

Yes. It did. False hope was far better than admitting that you never had any hope at all. He ought to know. He'd been limping along on false hope ever since he first learned that Porfiry was still alive.

But now he had to find a way to return Zara to the castle. Her pain had to be bad, or she would never have admitted vulnerability. Not in front of him.

And though he was anxious to get her back to Athven, where Gulver could soothe her burns and help her sleep, Alexei was grateful for the new understanding between them. A part of him could have gone on forever feeling nothing—except perhaps a sense of responsibility towards her—and rejecting any warmer emotions out of the depths of his own disappointment and guilt.

But his fear seemed to have stripped away some of the calluses on his heart, and enabled him to be a little more honest with himself. Ever since meeting her, he had seen Zara as little more than the death of every hope he had never dared admit to himself during the long years of his exile. He

147

had recognized that the fault was not hers, but in his bitterness, he had not been able to feel it. Now, for the first time since meeting her, for the first time since Porfiry re-entered his life, he felt the stirrings of compassion.

He had no right to despise her. No right to continue to treat her as a thief, when it was her own life that had been stolen. The woman who held his people's future in her hands was deeply hurt and deeply human, yet she was also tenacious enough to cling to hope when everything appeared hopeless. It was more than he had managed, and Alexei wondered whether perhaps Beatra herself might not have entirely disapproved of her unlikely successor.

Before he could discuss their return with Zara, the sound of footsteps crashing through the brush brought Alexei's head around with a jerk. More than one set of feet, he realized. Large ones. Not human. He reached out, trying to sense what could be approaching and then he laughed.

"What's so funny?"

"Malichai," he answered her cryptically.

"That's not Malichai." Her words were slurred slightly.

"No," he answered, putting as much cheer into his voice as he could manage. "But it is the love of his life. And she's here just in time to get you back to the castle. I realize as your noble rescuer, I'm supposed to carry you back in my arms, but frankly, that just wouldn't work. I'm out of practice and you're..."

"Too big?" Zara mumbled disgustedly.

"Too uncooperative."

She laughed. "Never doubt it. If I am nothing else, you can always count on me to be uncooperative."

CHAPTER 9

*Z*ara awakened from dreams of fire with the smell of smoke in her nostrils. She jerked out of her blankets, coughing, and wondered dimly why there was no pain. There should have been pain.

"Easy," a soothing voice said just behind her ear, and a hand came to rest gently on her shoulder. "You're all right. You're safe."

Awareness trickled back. The doors had opened. And she had... raced into the night like a woman possessed. Why? She knew she couldn't get away. And she knew her father had left her. Why had she gone looking for him?

A memory of fire flared, along with a thrill of fear. The bear. Or rather, the bear-shaped thing that had appeared in front of her. She had fallen, tried to scramble away, then swiped at it with a branch and it had... it had burned her. She remembered the sickening smell of her charred skin.

Zara held out her left arm and turned it over, twice. There were patches where her skin was too shiny. A place along her wrist where a scar marred the surface. And there was no hair below her elbow. But neither were there any burns.

She twisted her head to stare uncomprehendingly at Silvay. "What happened? Did I dream it all? How did I get here?"

"What do you remember?" Silvay asked in a low voice.

"I remember... I remember feeling suddenly like my father was the only thing in the world that mattered. I ran... I wasn't even thinking. I just ran. Then there was the clearing. And the thing that smelled of smoke. It burned me, and I thought I was going to die. But Alexei came." Her voice faltered. Alexei had come. He had followed her into the night and saved her life with a terrifying display of power. And then he had brought her back. "He set himself on fire and drove away... whatever it was. I didn't know he could do that. Can all of you do that?"

Silvay's laugh was a bright sound in the low-ceilinged kitchen. "Oh no, I'm afraid not. Alexei's gift is far different from mine, or Wilder's."

Different? That wasn't quite the word. There had been something almost other-worldly about him as he stood in the clearing, wreathed in flames, confronting the bear-like creature that had burned her.

"Who is he?" Zara asked in a small voice.

"As to that..." Silvay was clearly hesitant to say, but a new voice interrupted her silence.

"My cousin, Beatra Nar, was the last queen of Erath," Alexei said quietly, standing just inside the kitchen door, looking at his boots. "She had one brother, who is dead. My own brother, Andrei, is in exile in Andar and has chosen to stay. Which means that Porfiry and I may very well be the last of the House of Nar."

Nar? As in Athven Nar? Zara sucked in a horrified breath. "Then... Athven is yours. She was always supposed to be yours." It explained so much. All of his anger and frustration. That strange comment about his house and his birthright. He had been meant to be a king! And it had been stolen from him by a trespassing treasure hunter without any respect for the past.

"No," Alexei said, moving farther into the kitchen and sitting near the fire with a weary slump to his shoulders. "Athven was meant to go to Beatra's brother, who was meant to marry and have children of his own. My cousins and I were meant to go on peacefully using our gifts for the benefit of our people. It was never my plan or my desire to be king."

"But if you're the last..."

"I never wanted it, Zara. Not even when Beatra suggested it could be mine. Not until I came back and saw how things stood, how desolate my land had become. Then I thought perhaps I could do some good. Perhaps I could save some small piece of what was, so that children like Wilder would someday be proud to be Erathi."

"I'm sorry," she whispered, looking into the flames with tears starting in her eyes. "I wish I could give it back."

"I'm no longer certain that I agree," Alexei said.

Both Zara and Silvay turned to stare at him.

"Zara, can you explain why you ran? What you were thinking when you saw the open door?" Strangely, he didn't sound like he was angry or judgmental, just curious.

"I don't know," she said, desperately hoping they would believe her. "It's as though I wasn't thinking at all. I knew he wasn't out there. Silvay already told me you saw no one in the valley. And I know my father. He is quick to begin a new venture, but also quick to admit defeat. He also claims not to believe in magic, so I'm sure he was terrified. I cannot imagine him choosing to stay here, in a place that scared him so badly, with no better motivation than hope."

"So you had no thoughts of leaving before the door opened?" Alexei was looking for something, clearly, but Zara had no idea what it might be.

"I have never stopped wishing that I could leave these walls, even if only long enough to feel the sun and the wind on my face. And I want to believe my father is out there somewhere. I have to. But I also believed you when you said that I would die if I leave. And that if I died too soon,

Athven might not survive the severing of the bond. I wouldn't have done that to anyone, no matter how angry she makes me."

Alexei seemed to stare into the fire for a while, thoughtful and still, before he glanced back at her, his face pensive. "I have been thinking. About my cousin, Beatra. About what I remember of her, and about what happened with you. And I believe that running may not have been your idea at all."

Zara shivered, despite the heat of the fire. A chill enveloped her arms and her chest, and her hands began to shake minutely. "Athven," she whispered.

Alexei nodded. "My cousin was always distant, but there were times, the last few years I knew her, that she seemed to grow less compassionate. Less able to feel. She was never cruel, but she didn't always seem to understand. I assumed it was part of the burden of being queen, but..."

"Alexei, there is no need to frighten her half to death with your theories. You could wait until she's eaten some luncheon, at least." Silvay had risen to her feet and was glaring at Alexei rather fiercely.

"No." Zara pushed back her blankets and rose to her knees. "Silvay, I need to know. How can I make reasonable decisions unless I know the truth? Yes, I am afraid, but I cannot hide from this. It's a part of me now. If I can't go back, I have to go forward." She offered Silvay a placatory smile. "Unless you want to tell us how all of this turns out so I don't have to decide anything."

"Not how it works," Silvay grumbled. Her fierceness seemed to have subsided. "I can't tell you anything that particular, as Alexei very well knows. We are warned to be very cautious about mentioning anything specific until it has already come to pass. But"—she smiled warmly—"you are meant to be here, if that helps. There are no paths forward where you are not a part of the journey."

Strangely, Zara's heart felt lighter. "It does help," she replied. "Thank you."

With a nod of acknowledgement, Silvay glanced at Alexei. "I believe I will go find Wilder," she said, and left the kitchen.

As soon as she was gone, Zara sank back onto her blankets. "Tell me the rest of it," she demanded.

"I think Athven convinced you to run."

Zara nodded. "That does not feel impossible," she allowed. "And it would not have taken much, after all. The impulse was already there, all she had to do was encourage it. And if she is powerful enough to cause me to do that, strong enough to override my conscious decision, what else can she do?"

Alexei's hands clenched on his knees. He clearly didn't want to say the next part. "At her strongest, Athven protected all of Erath. She used the magic of the land and the enchantment of the Rose in order to do so, but she is complex and vast even without them, and I would not care to underestimate her." He glanced at Zara, forehead creased with worry. "It's possible she roused the artenu."

"The what?"

"The creature you faced. The artenu. They are ancient and magical and no one really knows what they are or how they came to be. Erath has always been their home, but they generally reside in deep forest, several days' ride from here."

"It could have just wandered here. Gotten lost."

"Yes," Alexei conceded. "But I don't know if I want to count on that being the case. Athven sent you out there for a reason. She cares nothing for your father, but she does seem to have a single-minded desire to throw us together. What if she was trying to further her cause by forcing me to rescue you?"

Zara felt the flush of embarrassment spread from her face to her neck and down her chest. If it were true... how utterly humiliating.

"Zara, I don't blame you," Alexei said quickly. "In fact, I feel as though I owe you an apology. If I am correct, it was Athven who endangered us and it forces me to question many things I have long held as fact." He fell silent, leaning forward in his chair, no longer meeting Zara's eyes. "I have always believed that Athven existed to protect us. That she could not deviate from the purpose for which she was brought into being. What if that is no longer true? What if the years of pouring our lives and magic into her stones has awakened something new, and she is now pursuing her own agenda, for her own reasons? Does she even have our interests at heart anymore, or her own?"

His voice was bleak. Like a man cast adrift without a rudder.

"Even if she does"—Zara tried to reassure him—"she still needs us. If we weren't here, or if anything happened to me, she would be an empty, dormant shell again, at best. She's not going to risk that."

"But she already has," Alexei argued. "If I am correct, she gambled on me being able to stop the artenu before it killed you. Granted, once, I could have done it as easily as thought, but I am not what I once was. She did not stop to speculate on our human weaknesses, and it could have killed us both."

"So what can I do?" Zara asked, trying not to sound too plaintive. "If she is influencing me without speaking, how can I protect myself? How do I know which thoughts are even my own?"

"My hope," Alexei theorized, "is that now you are aware of her meddling, she will be less able to influence you. And remember, she did not invent the thought, merely hastened the execution." He shook his head and stared at his hands. "I wish I could find a reliable way to speak with her directly. I don't know what she is thinking or planning, but I must convince her that what she has done—what she is doing— to you is wrong. It is a terrible misuse of her power and cannot be allowed to continue."

"Alexei..."

He looked at her and for the first time, Zara did not see the face of an enemy. She could read his concern and it warmed her, as much as the idea of Athven's betrayal had chilled.

"What if..." She heard the tremor in her voice and paused to steady it. "What's to stop her from getting rid of me? I know you don't think she's strong enough to survive that yet, but she's getting stronger every day." Alexei held up a hand as if to interrupt but Zara forged ahead. "She survived your cousin's death, and the death of every guardian before her, so that day will come eventually. What happens when she decides she doesn't want me anymore? I know she'd rather have you. Couldn't she just..."

"No." Alexei's tone was harsh, but it didn't frighten her. "She won't."

"How do you know?" Zara was pleading now, but she didn't care. The thought terrified her.

"Because." He turned his gaze and Zara's followed. Shadow had entered silently and was sitting on the table watching them. "If she does, I will not be a part of it. And if she hurts you in any way again, I will not rest until we find a way to escape. Together."

The cat's tail twitched but she would not meet their eyes.

"We will find a place close enough that the bond will survive, but it will not flourish. It is a weak bond already, so that will not be difficult."

Shadow turned her head to look at the far wall.

"She will not die, but will simply exist forever, unable to speak or see or grow." Alexei focused so intently on the cat that he seemed about to bore holes through Shadow's furry gray body. "And if she kills you, I will walk away. I am too strong for her to bond against my will, and if she tries, I will leave Erath and give up the better part of my magic forever rather than allow her to use me. Even if it means my death."

His expression grew so fierce that his good eye almost seemed to glow. "When you subvert another's will for your purposes, it is not a bond, not a partnership. It is slavery. I know that you were unaware of what you were doing when you bonded Zara, that it was not a conscious choice, but I will not stand by while you continue down that road. You would be committing the same atrocities that destroyed our people, and it would be better for us to go on without you. Better to vanish entirely than to become the thing we hate."

The cat jumped down from the table. She strolled over to the fire, not looking at either of them, and sat, gazing into the flames in silence. Zara shared a brief glance with Alexei, but they both waited without speaking.

When Athven looked up, it was a brief glance at Zara. She stretched, walked over and rubbed briefly against Zara's knees before trotting out of the room.

"And that," Alexei said with a minute twitch of his lips, "may be the closest thing you're going to get to an apology."

"I think she's peeved with you," Zara observed.

"I hope so. And I hope she realizes that I am serious."

"Thank you." He had more or less just threatened to kill himself in order to save her. Zara wasn't sure if that was idiotic or almost romantic. But no one had ever volunteered to suffer so much as a paper cut on her behalf, so the feeling was a bit overwhelming. "I wouldn't want you to actually do any of those things you threatened, but the fact that you offered…"

"We are not enemies, Zara."

"Not anymore, you mean."

Alexei grew still and met her eyes somberly. "I have not given you much reason to believe me, I know. I am sorry. If you feel that you cannot forgive my prejudice, I will understand."

"No," Zara said hesitantly. He had risked his life to save hers, so how could she not forgive him? "It's not that. But if you are not my enemy then what do I call you? You can't exactly introduce someone by saying, 'By the way, this is Alexei, and he is not my enemy.'"

He raised a quizzical brow, but the tiniest beginnings of a smile lifted the unscarred side of his mouth. "You would prefer something else?"

"Well, I'm sure friends is still out. After all, you've only not hated me since yesterday."

"Allies?"

Zara made a face. "I suppose that's the best we can hope for at present. But perhaps eventually we can do better. Maybe tomorrow we can reconsider friendship."

"You never know."

"By the day after that, you may even begin reconsidering whether you want to marry me."

"Is this your third proposal?"

"Why stop now?"

~

Alexei left the kitchen feeling a heavier than usual weight on his shoulders. He had been counting on Athven as an ally, and now he no longer believed she could be trusted. In an ironic twist of fate, he felt more certain of Zara, the usurping treasure hunter, than he did of his own home.

Ahead he spotted the swiftly moving shape of Silvay. She was aiming straight for him and did not look happy.

"Did you See something?"

"Yes," she told him, "but not with my gift. I haven't had a chance to tell you, what with making sure Zara was all right."

"While you were out searching?"

"On the far side of the valley, just before I was about to turn back, I sensed them." She drew her cloak closer, as if to ward off the chill of what she was about to say.

"Porfiry and Rowan?" It was hardly a shock. Alexei had known they wouldn't go far. He was a little surprised they'd held back this long.

"It wasn't one man," Silvay replied, "or even two. It was more like two hundred."

"Are you certain? And they're in the valley?" Alexei didn't know what to think of the news. "Perhaps it's a large group of mercenaries passing through."

"No," Silvay said quietly.

"You've Seen it?"

"I spied on them," she replied dryly. "I do not rely on my gift for everything, and neither should you."

"My apologies," Alexei replied. "I did not mean to imply that you were incapable."

"Yes, I have great hopes for your intelligence." Silvay's smile was weary. "But you'll need more than intelligence to get out of this, I'm afraid. They are not simple mercenaries. They are an orderly unit, and frighteningly efficient. Their gear might not be the best, but they are working together in a way that felt almost eerie."

"Did you get any sense of their goals or destination?"

"I didn't need to," Silvay told him hollowly. "I could feel it. Feel him."

"Porfiry?"

"He was somewhere in the middle of their camp, along with your Andari prince if I read his signature aright."

"And no one saw you?"

"I am more than capable of being difficult to see," she told him sharply. "And if I had been seen I would not have waited until now to tell you. Credit me with some discernment."

"I do, Silvay. I can assure you I do not doubt your discernment, or your courage, or your skills. What I doubt..." Alexei rubbed his face with one hand and grimaced. "I doubt my ability to deal with this entire situation. It is no longer just about Erath, or the future of our people. This could be about the future of kingdoms. And I—we—are ill-equipped to face the problems we already have."

"What," asked Silvay slowly, "if we could use the one to solve the other?"

"I won't ask if it's something you've Seen," Alexei responded, "but if you believe you have a workable solution, by all means tell me."

"How long can Athven hold them off?" she asked instead.

"I don't know. Not without consulting her. Once, she had many means of defense at her disposal. Now, she is clearly able to hold the doors, but I cannot guess whether she could withstand a determined assault. They may be able to break her, with enough force, or they may number gardeners among them, who could undermine her walls."

"But if they have no one with magic?"

"I cannot imagine Porfiry will do them much good, and Prince Rowan's gifts lie in other directions. Persuasion, and the like. I have not seen their equivalent amongst our own people. I assume if none of the mercenaries have a talent for magic, they will be forced to attack with brute strength, and that I believe Athven can withstand for some time."

"Unless they break her walls."

"Yes. And I do not know how difficult that might be."

"So they will be forced to resort to a protracted siege," Silvay continued, tapping her teeth with one fingernail.

"Unless they can gain the Rose without entering the castle."

"But if they could do that, why have they not already? Why lurk on the edge of the valley with an army if you don't need it?"

"Who knows why Prince Rowan does anything?" Alexei responded wearily. "But you can be sure he has his reasons. He is not infallible, but at times he certainly seems like it."

"But we have an advantage. Even if Porfiry has told him of Athven, he cannot be fully prepared for what she can do. If the Betrayer told the truth, and we could tear the castle apart without finding where he hid the Rose, we need him to find it. What if we let him do so?"

"Just let them in and let them have it?" Alexei's brow furrowed with concern. "How would that help us?"

"Let them think the castle is deserted. Let them believe they have the field. And after they have found the Rose, we take it, and Athven throws them out."

"And then we have a protracted siege?" Alexei asked wryly.

"Well, yes," Silvay acknowledged with a sigh. "But it seems better to have a siege and the Rose than to have nothing but the siege."

"True enough. But what if Athven cannot throw them out? If they have the Rose, she may not be able to act against them at all."

"I believe it's worth the risk," Silvay argued. "We are surviving because Athven was able to keep enough of herself in stasis to sustain us. Eventually, her stores will run out, and we cannot count on any outside help."

"You *have* Seen him, haven't you?" Alexei posed it as a question, but one he knew she would not answer. Perhaps she'd had a vision of Rowan standing on the walls of Athven, and perhaps she hadn't. But her plan made a twisted sort of sense and there was no avoiding the fact that an army, even one of only two hundred men, was more than they or Athven could handle at that moment.

"We'll ask the others," he told Silvay. "Malichai may have some thoughts, and as this affects Zara most nearly, we must secure her agreement before moving forward."

Silvay looked at him keenly. "You have changed, and recently. What happened out there?"

"How have I changed?" Alexei countered.

She made a snorting noise. "Zara. From hoping wolves would eat her to deferring to her opinion."

"I don't think I would have let wolves eat her. At least"—he grinned in spite of himself—"not more than a few fingers or toes."

"Don't avoid the question."

Alexei sobered. "I'm avoiding it because I don't know how to answer it. I have accepted that this is not her fault. That we cannot change it, and... perhaps that she is more to be pitied than any of us."

"She wouldn't care to hear that you pity her."

"No," he acknowledged. "She would not. And perhaps pity is the wrong word. But what I feel is more like compassion now than outrage. She has more in common with our people than I realized. She is chained in a foreign land with no hope of escape. Whatever life she is to have from here will not be an easy thing to bear, and it costs me nothing but my own bitterness to smooth her path as I can."

"That's not a cost many are willing to pay," Silvay noted. "And you gain no one's admiration for the sacrifice."

"Perhaps not." He shrugged. "But I gain the ability to look at myself without revulsion. I have seen what my cousin's bitterness has made of him and I have no desire to emulate his example."

Silvay's smile was at once serene and mysterious. "Then we should go and find the others. If Zara is feeling well enough, it is not too early to plan."

～

As Silvay went one direction in search of their companions, Alexei took another, wondering if he had made a mistake agreeing to potentially permit their enemies into the heart of Athven. He had seen Rowan defeated once, but at terrible cost. His own brush with death only a year before had been at the hands of the former prince, who had denied him care for his wounds in order to force Alexei's friends' compliance.

Fingering his scars, Alexei tried to shove the memories away. He had been a fool then, too—rushing to grasp his chance for vengeance instead of waiting and planning. Porfiry had injured him, but it had been Rowan who had used that to his advantage. Or tried to.

What he had told his companions then was still true: he would rather sacrifice his life than see Rowan on the throne of anything. The man was a beautiful, amoral monster. And now, Alexei might be facing another test of his resolve. What would he be willing to sacrifice this time? Was there anything more to fear once he was willing to give his life?

Too deep in his memories to watch where he was going, Alexei tripped over a small, gray obstacle, which glared at him in green-eyed offense.

"You're lucky I didn't land on you," he muttered, still angry over Athven's treatment of Zara. "We're planning a council of war, if you care to join it. Though until you deign to speak with us, I'm not sure what difference it makes."

And then, as before, Alexei fell headlong into the cat's green eyes until he found himself somewhere quite different.

∼

The receiving room. It looked like a cozy sitting room or parlor, but the chair his aunt used to receive visitors could not be mistaken for anything but a throne. Athven sat in it now, scowling at him.

Looking down at himself, Alexei almost chuckled at the appearance of elaborate court clothes. His embroidered, calf-length robes were belted with gold and sapphires, and his boots had golden buckles. There was even a ring on his finger... Alexei ripped it off and threw it into the farthest corner of the room. His cousin's ring of office. The cat had nerve.

"You wanted to speak to me. Here I am."

Alexei matched her stare for stare. Once he would have quailed at the idea of showing such disrespect, either to the queen or to Athven herself, but his experience in the forest had tainted his admiration a trifle.

"Did you bring me here because I asked or because you wanted to prove something?"

"I am Athven Nar. I have nothing to prove." The woman looked far sulkier than Beatra Nar had ever looked in her life.

"Then why did you meddle in Zara's head? Why try to force us to bow to your caprice?"

"It is not caprice!" she hissed. "I have lived far beyond your meager

human lifespans and I know what is needed. I require more power. The future must be secured or I could die."

For the first time, Alexei heard her disdain for what it really was. Fear. He had been right about one thing: Athven had changed. She had learned to fear, an entirely human emotion that had probably rocked her to her foundations. And in her fear and her aloneness, she had forgotten her purpose. Instead of being the thorns to Erath's rose, she had turned inward and chosen to protect herself at all costs.

Just as he had. Twenty years in Andar, pretending to be nothing more than a horseman. At least he'd had his brother. Athven had no one.

"You are not alone now," he insisted. "And your ploy to bring us together could have killed Zara, and then where would you be?"

"I would not have allowed her to die," Athven insisted. "I knew you could save her. It was only an artenu."

"An artenu that burned her badly," Alexei snapped. "Perhaps you have forgotten how fragile our mortal bodies can be. Zara had no defense against that creature. If I had been only a second slower, she could be dead. If you are truly so concerned with your future, perhaps you should safeguard it more carefully."

Athven fell silent. "You have changed," she finally noted, a small smile appearing on her face. "Perhaps you do not hate my new guardian so much after all?"

"I am not going to marry her, Athven. You are going to have to trust my finite mortal reasoning when I say that she and I are extremely ill-suited. We are no longer enemies, but your insistence that we bind ourselves as one is misguided and ill-judged."

"No one ever asked me who I wanted to be bonded to," Athven snapped petulantly. "The heirs were always chosen, and then I had to make do with what I was given. Partnership can be as much choice as inclination, unless you are too much of a child to choose another's well-being over your own."

163

"I have not your immortal existence," Alexei chided. *"And neither does Zara. Yes, partnership is a choice, and you would take ours away from us. We cannot simply wait until next time and hope to choose better. You would have us tied to one another until death. That is a choice we deserve to make for ourselves."*

"Deserve is a strong word, child of Nar. What do you deserve, merely by virtue of being born? Do you deserve your life, when others have been denied it? Do you deserve happiness, when so many others have had theirs ripped away? Do you deserve freedom, when your people have none?"

"No," Alexei whispered, as her words pierced him like nails. *"I do not reserve the right to complain. I only desire to protect my people."*

"And by marrying the woman bonded to me, you would be better able to do that," Athven argued. *"If you do not deserve happiness, then why does it matter whom you marry?"*

"Because Zara deserves better than that," he growled. *"I refuse to tie her forever to a land, a people, and a man she cannot love simply because you bonded with her against her will."*

"Must I tell you again that it was not by choice? Would you rather I have died?"

He could not answer her.

"But if it is free will that you most desire, what if Zara chooses?" the woman continued, her gaze sharp and predatory. *"If she was to choose to add another to our bond willingly, outside of my compulsion, would you still find it necessary to object?"*

Alexei clasped his hands behind his back so she would not see them shaking. How had their conversation even come to this? Athven had trapped him neatly with his own words and he could not deny her point. For many in the world, and especially for those who ruled, who they married was not theirs to decide. Their only choice was whether they would live in harmony or discord.

"No," he answered, sighing deeply. "But she must know the whole truth of what it would be like. What she would be giving up. She already knows about the marriage bond, and I could never lie to her and claim that I love her. She must know that it would be a partnership and not a true marriage, and what woman would be willing to abandon all hope of love for a platonic partnership that can only be dissolved in death?"

Athven shrugged off his concerns. "That is not yours to decide, Son of Nar. Merely remember what you have promised."

"There is something else we must speak of." Alexei was not sorry to change the subject. "The army. Have you felt it?"

"Whispers of it, yes." Athven's eyes darkened. "But they are not Erathi, so I can sense nothing except their feet upon the ground. I feel the two, the Betrayer and the Bright One."

"How long can you withstand them?"

Athven hissed. "It depends. Without magic, they will be forced to break me, and that would not be impossible as I am, merely fiendishly difficult. Without the Rose, without a strong bond partner, I cannot hold them off forever. And when the stores held in stasis run out, I cannot conjure food and water to sustain you. In the end, you may be forced to fight."

"Which is as I feared," he admitted. "We have a different plan, but..."

~

The vision faded abruptly, leaving Alexei standing in the middle of a passage, blinking into Gulver's concerned face.

"Are you well, Alexei?" The shorter man's mustache quivered. "You were so still. I feared you were no longer breathing."

"Damn," Alexei muttered, but put a hand on Gulver's shoulder. "I am well," he assured the healer. "I was speaking with Athven but I did not have the opportunity…"

The cat was already trotting away. He would have to hope she chose to appear at their impromptu council of war. They had little chance of making this work unless Athven herself was on their side.

CHAPTER 10

*T*hey gathered in the kitchen around midafternoon, Wilder rubbing her stomach and making numerous hints about food. Malichai set about preparing some leftover beans with salted meat and a dribble of molasses, much to the girl's delight. As the resulting soup simmered over the fire, everyone sat around the table and looked at Alexei without speaking. Obviously, they expected him to have a brilliant plan.

"Does anyone have any information or ideas they wish to share before we discuss Silvay's news?"

He didn't expect anyone to answer.

"Yes." Zara was sitting on the end of the bench, slightly separate from everyone else. Her white hair was braided and wrapped around her head, and her blue eyes were fixed on her hands. "Though actually, it's more of a question. I want to know what happened to my arm."

Everyone else looked at each other.

"It was burned, and now it's not," she explained. "I know it wasn't a dream. I can see the scars. And I know I wasn't asleep more than a few hours. So what happened?"

"I healed you," Gulver explained, blinking his wide brown eyes repeatedly. "That's my gift, healing."

"You mean, you used magic on it? How bad was it?"

"I've seen worse," Gulver told her, glancing at Alexei, "but it was bad enough. You'd not have kept the arm with mundane healing. Would have gotten infected before you had a chance to grow new skin."

Zara shivered visibly, but still didn't look at anyone. "Have you always been able to do that?"

"Since I was trained, as a boy," Gulver told her. "After my gift was identified, I went to a school that helped me learn how to treat specific wounds and maladies."

"So you weren't the only one?"

Clearly her questions were aimed at something specific, but Alexei could not guess what.

"No, of course not." Gulver closed one eye and screwed up his face. "I believe there were about six of us my age... no, seven. And that was a relatively small group. Some had greater strength, some less."

"Did anyone in Erath ever die of wounds or disease?" Her voice was tight, and her fingers had turned white where they clenched around each other on the tabletop.

"Rarely." Alexei answered before Gulver could. "There were, of course, times where a healer could not arrive quickly enough, but they were stationed as strategically as possible to prevent such tragedies. Please, Zara, what are you asking? Do you have a broader point? Because we do have other matters to discuss."

She lifted her chin, her blue eyes cool and measuring. "I want to know why," she stated. "You've talked about your Rose, and I think I may have an idea what it's supposed to do. Even I know that it was nearly impossible to enter Erath for centuries, and very little was known of your people outside your borders. Until now, I had no idea what Gulver did was even possible. And I want to know why."

"I don't understand." Gulver was clearly puzzled. "Why am I a healer?"

"No," Alexei answered for her. "Why doesn't anyone know. Why have we kept our abilities a secret."

Zara locked eyes with him once more. "I understand that you have little power once you leave your borders. But this is not the same as being able to grow better vegetables, or set things on fire. What Gulver does... It is a miracle. And outside of your little country are people who suffer and die of simple injuries and illnesses, because they have no doctors, no medicine, no idea how to help themselves."

"So you would have us spend our lives and our talents helping those outside our borders instead of caring for our own people?"

"It does not have to be either or," Zara insisted. "Why would you keep such a gift to yourselves without a thought for the suffering of those who do not share your talents?"

"What about the suffering of my people whose magic has been discovered by outsiders with hatred and suspicion in their hearts?" Alexei felt a surge of anger and frustration. "Gulver can probably tell you even better than I how we have suffered at the hands of the ignorant and superstitious. How our attempts to help and to serve have been met with violence and prejudice. Why would we make ourselves vulnerable to those who would as soon betray us as thank us?"

"You cannot claim that everyone has responded to you so," Zara shot back. "And this cannot be the only place in the world where magic is known and not feared. Would a mother refuse an offer of life for her child simply because she does not understand the source?"

"More often than you might think," Alexei growled. "And please tell me how we are to know the difference! Would you have Gulver risk his life on the chance that he will be accepted rather than shunned? Perhaps he could save some. But far more often in our memory, we have been rejected, beaten, even burned on the suspicion of wickedness, simply because those we offered to serve did not understand what they saw."

"I cannot accept that it must be all or nothing," Zara argued, blue eyes blazing. "If you find the Rose, if you restore it, will this once again become a land of isolated wonders? What kind of peace is it that can only be had because you ignore what happens past the end of your nose?"

"A peace that permits our children to live without fear!" Alexei leapt to his feet and leaned forward over the table. "We know too well what happens when we have no way of protecting ourselves. When the barrier fell, my people died."

"You cannot blame an entire world for the actions of one people!" Zara shot back. "What if you had been at peace with your neighbors? What if they had known of what you could do, and been willing to trade their goods for your talents? Perhaps the destruction would never have happened if you had made allies instead of hiding."

"Perhaps we should go back five hundred years and let someone who knows nothing of our people or our history dictate how we ought to live."

"And perhaps we are engaged in an argument that cannot be solved with an enemy at our door," Silvay said tranquilly, her hands folded on the table in front of her. "Alexei did ask for questions, but this one is far beyond what any of us have the power to determine at the present. Zara, your questions are important, but we cannot afford to be divided just now. There is an army approaching who threatens not only us, but the futures of all our peoples. Could this discussion be suspended until after we have determined the best way to face that threat?"

Zara felt the juvenile urge to roll her eyes, but refrained. Silvay was right, but she needn't sound so motherly about it, and Alexei was simply being pigheaded. Why couldn't he see how wrong it was to keep such things hidden from the world? How many people had she known whose lives could have been saved by Gulver's gift?

She didn't think it was her mother's death alone that fueled her anger, but perhaps she would have felt more reasonable had she not been remembering the fever that had finally taken her mother's life. The one that had left her terrified and alone, then following her father on one treasure hunt after another, with no home, no prospects, no hope of a life beyond the road. Not that she had hated it. But she would have liked to have had a choice.

"It isn't as though we won't have plenty of time to argue in the future," she muttered. "By all means, tell us about this army. What army and why are they here?"

"An army gathered and controlled by the former Andari prince, Rowan Tremontaine, with the intent to recover the Rose and use it to fuel their future conquest."

Alexei was at least kind enough not to minimize or dismiss the threat. On the other hand, perhaps he needn't state everything quite so baldly.

"How do we know this?" Zara couldn't help asking. She assumed the answer would be "magic."

"Because I saw the army," Silvay answered unexpectedly. "I also sensed the presence of the one we are assuming is Tremontaine, and that of the Betrayer, Porfiry. We drew the unavoidable conclusions from what I observed."

"They'll have a hard time breaching this place," Malichai offered, combing his beard with his fingers. "She was built to be defensible, even without a wall, and the ground is clear of trees for fifty paces. Not too many windows, and most are high up. Wellspring is protected. We should have no trouble with a siege, if that's what they want." He paused, and wiped an eye surreptitiously. "I'm sure my Loraleen will know to avoid them, if it comes to that."

"She's obviously far smarter than most horses," Zara told him, with what she hoped was a comforting smile. "And you saw for yourself how well she looked only last night."

"Aye, she's eating well enough. And she's battle trained, and loyal to a fault," Malichai agreed. "But I still worry."

"If they attack, can we throw rocks from the towers, or pour boiling pitch on them from above?" Wilder asked, grinning.

"I can't say I'll be much help." Gulver's mustache drooped and quivered a little with his agitation. "Unless it's already too late. I can fix wounds but I'm no fighter."

"Nobody asked you to be," Alexei put in wearily, looking as though he would have liked to pound his head against the table. "I am aware that we are not seasoned warriors, save Malichai, and he is only one man. We have no more chance of fighting them off than we have of changing into birds and flying away."

"Unless you all have been concealing dragons," Zara put in, eyes innocently wide. "Perhaps we could convince them to rescue us."

"Or rain white-hot fire down on our enemies," Alexei responded acerbically. "Alas, I fear to disappoint you, but we have no dragons. Only wyverns, and they do not breathe fire so much as spit venom. Not to mention they would be as likely to hit you as your enemies and they don't care what they eat."

Zara shut her mouth and grimaced. Of course they had wyverns. If giant bears made of smoke were normal, why not flying lizards that spit venom?

"Now, if I may," Alexei continued, "Silvay had a thought of how we might approach this situation that could lead to better than a siege we cannot hope to break." Alexei didn't appear to like whatever Silvay's idea had been any more than he'd liked the wyverns. He was staring at the table, one finger tracing the wood grain. "She suggested we use Athven's strengths and assume that Rowan will not know what those might be or how to counter them."

"We let them in," Silvay said, when Alexei did not immediately continue. "Athven still controls her doors, for now, so we let in only

Rowan and Porfiry. We permit them to find the Rose, and then we take it from them and Athven will throw them out."

"You assume she is strong enough," Zara said, frowning. "She was able to do so with my father, but that effort was literally the last of her reserves. The restoration of her interior has also used considerable power, and she gets little from me. Are you certain she is able to perform what your plan requires?"

"No," Alexei admitted. "I was about to ask her earlier, but lost the opportunity. Do you think she would listen if you asked?"

Zara snorted. "She rarely initiates contact and usually only when she is upset with me. I cannot count on her choosing to invade my dreams."

"What might make her upset enough to choose a face-to-face scolding?" There was a tiny crease at the corner of Alexei's lips that might have been a smile.

"Pushing you down the stairs." Zara didn't need any time to think about that one. "Of course, she would doubtless choose to gloat in person if I kissed you, but I can confidently say that pushing you down the stairs seems far more appealing at the moment."

"At the moment?" Wilder echoed, eyes wide.

Zara felt her face go up in flames. Should have thought that through a little harder before she said it.

Malichai's laugh boomed out from where he stood over the fire, stirring their soup. "I can see that our traditional epics might have glossed over some of the finer details of their heroes' lives." He shook the spoon in their direction. "I will not be making the same mistakes. One wonders whether the great poets of the past ever bothered to go along on any of the adventures they wrote about."

"I can promise you they didn't," Zara retorted. "Those of us who've had adventures know very well there's little of romance or excitement in them."

"Does anyone have any better ideas?" Alexei interrupted, clearing his throat and shooting an enigmatic glance at Zara. "I would much prefer not to permit the Betrayer to enter these walls unbound, and I have no desire to meet the exiled prince again, so if there are any options I would gladly entertain them."

"You speak as though you believe it to be your decision." Zara raised a brow at him. "We all have a stake in this. Me as much or more than any of you."

"You should know," Silvay broke in again, "that it was Alexei who insisted we ask you. He told me that you will be most nearly affected and deserved to have the final word."

Zara could feel her face growing red again. "Well, he could have just said."

"If you will allow that I have done so"—Alexei stared at his interlaced fingers for a moment before lifting his eyes to meet hers—"what is it you would wish to do?"

"Wring Athven's scrawny little neck," she responded instantly. It was true. Right then she was feeling entirely out of charity with the stupid castle that had entwined her in this wretched mess. First she was stuck there forever so the avatar didn't die, and now she was about to be under siege. "But since I'm not sure that would even work, I suppose I would settle for talking to her. It seems like a mistake to plan something with so little margin for error without ensuring the support of one of the major players."

"Agreed." Alexei nodded. "Which stairs would you like to push me down?"

Zara started. She looked closely at his face, but he wasn't smiling this time. "I fancy the ones in the north tower," she replied, when it appeared he wasn't joking. "If I didn't like that room so much I would never go to all the trouble to get up there."

"The north tower?" His face had gone pale and a haunted look appeared in his eyes. "The room at the top?"

"Yes," Zara answered hesitantly. She couldn't imagine what might make him look that way. "I've slept there on occasion. Did someone you know die up there?"

"In a manner of speaking," he answered, "I did."

~

Zara would have let him go alone, but Alexei insisted she accompany him up the endless stairs to the room with the diamond-paned window and the blue-covered bed. When they reached it and Alexei pushed the door open, he let out a sigh that seemed to echo with the weight of years and sorrow and secrets.

"This was your room?" Zara asked softly.

"From the time I was ten," he answered after a pause. "I could have slept below, with the other cousins, but something about this room appealed to me. After training, I often felt like I needed distance, needed quiet in order to re-center myself. And"—he gestured to the window—"I liked being able to see the reason for what I was doing. All the tears and trials, all the pain and sweat and the loss of my childhood—I needed to know it was worth it."

"I thought you said the training was better than play," Zara reminded him.

"And so it was, for a while," he confirmed. "When I was ten, they identified me as one of the strongest enchanters our people had ever seen. I was singled out for great things. I was proud of the distinction, but the responsibility that came with it was a heavy one. There was little time for play, after that. They tested the limits of my gift to the utmost and I had to master every art an enchanter needs to work his craft. Wood, metal, leather, glass, stone—I had to be a master craftsman with them all."

"That sounds like a terrible burden for a child."

"I shouldered it gladly, for the most part," he acknowledged. "Who knows how I would have felt had I grown to adulthood feeling its weight."

Zara thought she heard what he did not say. "I think you did feel it," she said thoughtfully, sitting on the bed and crossing her ankles. "Even in exile, I don't believe that sort of a burden goes away."

"No. But it is easier to ignore. Easier to pretend there is nothing you can do."

"Until Porfiry crossed your path?" she guessed.

Alexei barked an unamused laugh. "Are you sure you are not a seer or a prescient?"

"Just good at puzzles." She shrugged. "It's useful in my line of work."

For once, he neither flinched nor glared at the reminder. "Then yes, until Porfiry crossed my path. I was reminded of my responsibility, and a past I had resolutely set behind me. I thought..."

"You thought if you did that one thing, it might absolve your guilt."

"Yes." He leaned against the wall and folded his arms. "But no one has been content with my quest for expiation. They want more. They want to resurrect the lost crown of a country that no longer exists. They want to see me as the answer to their pleas for salvation."

"And you started to think, maybe you could do it. Maybe this was your destiny. Maybe you really could live up to the expectations of your youth. Until you got here and I was in your way."

Alexei turned and rested a hand on the casement as he peered out through the grimy diamond panes. "I begin to think I'm rather glad you were. No good would have come of me accepting that burden in an attempt to absolve myself. I would have grown to resent it, and my people with it."

"Whereas now all you have to resent is me?" Zara couldn't help her sarcasm. Alexei was congratulating himself for having escaped what she was stuck with. "And when you've found your rose and saved the day you can leave again, because you've done your duty and there's no further need of you?"

"No." He seemed curiously reluctant to elaborate.

"What then? What's going to happen when the threat is gone and you've done what you came for? What of your companions? Will they leave when they find out you're not going to be the king they hoped?"

She hadn't meant to bring it up. Hadn't meant to be so petty in the face of what was coming. But she couldn't help being afraid. She didn't want to be alone again.

"We won't leave you here alone."

How could a man so comprehensively frustrating manage to read her mind so accurately?

"There will be much to be done," he continued. "I'm never going to be the man my instructors hoped I would be, nor the king my companions want me to be. Too much time has passed, and my skills have all but died, just as I have. But I don't have to be that. I'm done hiding from life simply because I cannot fulfill everyone's expectations."

"Is that why you stayed away?"

"Possibly. But I do not intend to leave again." He turned back and put his hands on his hips. "And being irritating will not be enough to change my mind, so don't get any ideas."

"Perish the thought," she replied solemnly. "I'm irritating by nature. It really has nothing to do with you."

There turned out to be no need for pushing anyone down the stairs. Zara went to sleep by the kitchen fire and dreamed of the soaring entry hall, bedecked in splendor, with herself standing over the great seal, wearing yet another elaborate costume.

"You have heard about the army, I believe." Athven was beginning to take on more human mannerisms, and this time she was tapping a toe on the stone floor.

"Yes," Zara answered carefully. "What do you know of them?"

"Little," Athven announced, "but that they are mundane. The only magic in their ranks belongs to the Bright One and the Betrayer."

"We have made a plan..." Zara began, but the avatar interrupted her impatiently.

"I have a better one," she asserted. "The enemy will be allowed to enter. I wish for the Betrayer to bring the Rose to light. And I have decided that you were right about the son of Nar."

"I...what?" Zara did not quite follow. "What do you mean I was right?"

"He will not suffice as a partner for you. Perhaps he is too old. And I do not think he would adapt well to the bond."

Or rather, Athven had realized he wouldn't let her have everything her own way. Zara felt like saying something rude, but she needed Athven's help, so all she said was, "Oh." There was a sensation in her chest that felt like disappointment, but it couldn't have been that. She wasn't disappointed that she would not be forced to marry a man who irritated her beyond all reason. "So you have a new plan, or have you decided that I can meet your needs well enough?"

"No, you most certainly cannot," Athven scolded. "I need to expand the bond if I am to regain even a portion of my former strength. Whether you marry him I have decided to leave up to you. But I have determined that the Bright One will be a far better choice."

"WHAT?" Even in the dream, Zara's shout echoed back from the cavernous ceiling. "You want to bond with an enemy?"

"If he is bonded to me, he can no longer be an enemy," Athven pointed out patiently. "He will be working for us, not against us."

"But... he's a monster. Alexei has met him and almost died for it!

Why would I want to be in the same room with him, let alone share our thoughts and feelings for the rest of our lives?"

"Because he is strong, of course." Athven acted as though Zara were quite dimwitted for asking. "Stronger, younger, and I believe he was described as beautiful, which ought to satisfy you. An altogether more suitable consort, should you choose to make it official."

"Well, I won't," Zara snapped. "And neither you nor anyone else can make me!"

"Perhaps not," Athven almost purred, "but I can certainly put the idea into his head as soon as he crosses my threshold. You are not an unattractive woman, when dressed appropriately, and he would be a fool not to recognize the value of what I could offer."

"Do not presume too far, Athven." Zara glared at the avatar with all the heat she could muster. "I am not yours to be offered."

"And I cannot afford to be as finicky as you," Athven sneered. "You cannot protect me so I must find another way. And this Bright One has more than enough strength to provide what I need."

"I won't marry him," Zara answered fiercely. "And I won't agree to add him to our bond. You will have to do it against my will again, and you won't get all the strength you were hoping for. And anyway, he may not want what you have to offer. What if all he wants is to keep the Rose for himself and leave with it?"

"I am well able to protect the Rose, once it is found," Athven said dryly. "He will not be allowed to steal it."

"It would serve you right if I were to simply walk away and condemn us both," Zara told her, wishing the dream would allow her to stomp or scream, or otherwise give vent to her outrage and frustration. "You think you are so wise and all-seeing, but you don't understand people at all."

"I understand them well enough to know that they cling to life with desperate strength, up until the moment they value something more. The

only thing I have ever seen a human willing to die for is love, or what-ever they mistake for that feeling, and as you are not in love, you are not going to throw your life away to spite me."

Zara wished she could throw the woman's words back into her smugly serene countenance, but what she said was true. Zara did not, had never, loved anyone enough to place her life between them and death. And she had not yet despaired enough of the future to consider throwing herself away as the only possible means of escape.

"True or not, I will not simply agree to be bait," she told the avatar, as calmly as she could manage. She was old enough to have arguments without descending into threats and name calling. Even if those were far more soothing to her feelings. "You did not ask me if I wanted to bond with you, and as I had no part in choosing this fate, I reserve the right to choose whom I share it with."

"I have always permitted my bonded partners a high degree of autonomy," Athven mused. "It seemed natural, given the mutuality of our relationship. But I have had many years to consider whether that was wise, given my age and the scope of my perception. Perhaps I could have prevented what occurred had I acted more as a guide and advisor than simply a protector."

Was that guilt? Or self-preservation? Either way, Zara felt a distinct chill. And a desperate need to escape.

"Then you won't help us?"

"You do yourself no favors when you persist in believing me your enemy, child," Athven scolded. "I have no desires but to preserve the future, and you are my future. What I do, is done to protect your well-being and that of my people. You would do well to remember that and cease your efforts to thwart me."

"Or what?" Zara snapped, and then silently cursed her inability to keep her mouth shut.

"I don't understand." Athven looked genuinely puzzled.

"There's usually a threat after a statement like that. I cease my efforts to undermine you or what? You'll lock me in a tower like a cursed princess and hold a tournament for a brave knight to rescue me? Or you'll arrange for me to have a convenient accident as soon as you're strong enough to survive my death and bond with another?"

"Of all my previous partners, you are the most difficult to reason with," Athven fretted. "I cannot understand you. I will do what I must, yes, but we cannot be enemies."

"If we are not enemies, we must be true partners," Zara insisted. "And we cannot be that when you insist on manipulating me for 'my own good.'"

"I would not need to manipulate you if you would simply listen."

"I am listening! What I hear is that you want to treat me like your possession. Something you can dress up and parade around and bestow at your whim. I will never be that."

"Someday you will understand," Athven said sadly. "I do not wish to be at odds. Only to care for those I was created to serve."

"Look," Zara snapped, "you aren't going to convince me, so why don't you let me sleep in peace while I can? There are enemies approaching and I would rather not be grumpy and sleep-deprived when they arrive."

"Never fear, child. I will ensure that you rest long enough to be refreshed."

"No!" Zara yelled louder than she meant and earned a repressive look from the avatar. "Don't you see how wrong that is? Do not play god with me, Athven. I will sleep as I can and I will wake when I choose. People are not meant to be puppets or playthings."

Clearly frustrated, Athven snapped her a nod. "Very well. For now. But we will speak again soon, after the Betrayer and the Bright One have come. And we will visit my concerns again." Her voice grew cold. "You wish not to be forced into a future not of your choosing, but do not *think you have all the power of choice and refusal in our relationship. As one who is intimately affected by your decisions, I will not permit you to make those that threaten my own existence."*

The avatar seemed to grow taller, and her shadow lengthened until she loomed over Zara nearly to the height of the first windows.

Zara could feel herself begin to panic. The suffocating atmosphere of the vision began to press in on her as Athven's words sank in and the avatar's physical form grew large enough to crush her without even trying. She could sense her physical body respond to the fear, and she begged herself to wake up.

"Calm yourself, child!" the avatar demanded, before her body began to shrink again, then hunch over and sprout fur. Zara's finery faded and her hair tumbled around her shoulders and she screamed as the floor itself seemed to fall out from under her...

～

"Zara?" The voice in her ear was not Athven's. It was raspy with sleep and worry, though the arm that gripped her shoulders was strong. "Zara, please wake up. The walls are shaking again."

Her eyes snapped open, and a gasp of relief escaped her parched lips. The kitchen. The fire. A scarred hand resting on her arm. The vision was over.

To her utter humiliation, tears began to flow down her cheeks. She was stronger than this. She did not cry, especially not in front of provoking men who already thought her weak. But the tears did not ebb and the solid presence behind her did not waver.

He had lifted her, somehow, and her back rested against his chest, with one arm wrapped around her shoulders. It should have felt confining, but Zara was too tired and afraid to feel anything but relief at not being alone.

"I take it Athven deigned to speak with you despite your forbearance in the face of many stairs."

She had not thought Alexei possessed the capacity for sympathetic humor. "Athven chose to instruct me in her wishes," she croaked.

Movement from the corner of her eye became Silvay, holding a cup of water, which Zara accepted gratefully. She became aware, then, of the others settling back into their blankets, and wondered how bad it had been that she had awakened everyone. "Did I scream?" she asked miserably.

"No." Alexei's voice sounded deeper from behind her head. "You cried out, and the castle began to shake again. We wondered at first whether the army was at the gates already, but the shaking quieted as soon as you awoke."

"I made Athven angry," she confessed, reaching up to brush the tears from her cheeks. "But she frightened me... I do not know how to fight her." The pressure of his arm around her shoulders seemed to tighten fractionally in response.

"What did she say to you?" His voice was neutral and calming, so she answered, hesitating only a little.

"She... She has her own plans. She agrees that Porfiry and his prince should be allowed to enter, but..." Zara suddenly found that she couldn't say the next part. Couldn't tell Alexei that Athven had rejected him. Worse, that she had rejected him in favor of another foreigner, and one who had almost killed him. "She has decided that she needs to take a more active role in making decisions. That she is older, wiser, and therefore more qualified. She threatened to force my decisions, to use me as bait." More tears filled her eyes. "I am no more than a thing to her. A means to her ends. I don't know what she can force me to do and it terrifies me."

"I am sorry." The genuine compassion in Alexei's words caught her entirely off guard. "Sorry that you have been forced to endure this. Sorry that you have become the victim of our pride."

"You did not do this." Zara felt an inexplicable need to defend him from his own accusations.

He only sighed, his chest rising and falling beneath her shoulders. "My people did. We thought ourselves strong and we thought ourselves wise and we fed magic into these stones in our desire to create something that would last. We may have created something monstrous instead."

Silvay held a finger to her lips. "Caution," she whispered.

And she was right. If Athven got the impression they had all turned against her, there was no predicting what she might do.

Almost reluctantly, Zara sat up and Alexei released his arm, supporting her weight until she was able to sit upright without wavering. He rose and moved around into her field of vision before kneeling in front of her to look seriously into her eyes. Zara almost couldn't hold his gaze.

"Believe that we are with you," he told her, one scarred hand reaching out to grip hers where it rested on the blankets. "The enemy that is coming will try to divide us and turn us against one another if he can. I believe Athven will protect you from the worst of what he is, but remember, if you remember nothing else, that I am not your enemy. Athven cannot force you to deny your nature or your convictions. I will not willingly leave this place while you are forced to remain, nor will I make a choice that tightens your bonds." He grimaced, his scars pulling at the right side of his face. "I have not always been kind, but I hope I have been honest. I have come to admire your courage and your strength, and while I believe you would be a queen all of Erath would be proud to claim, I will also fight for your freedom if that is what you wish."

More tears? Zara fought to hold them back, but a few escaped in spite of her. "I don't deserve that," she whispered.

"Deserving or undeserving has nothing to do with this, though I disagree with you. I am not free to choose who to treat with honor and dignity based on whether or not I feel they deserve it, though I am guilty of having done so when we met and I owe you an apology for my actions.

Gulver does not choose who to heal based on whether they deserve it. I choose this now because it is right. And whether Athven stands or falls changes nothing. There is no victory in sacrificing so much as a single person to regain what we had."

"Unless that person chooses the sacrifice themselves." Zara was proud that her voice did not shake.

"That person should know what she is choosing and choose it freely," he argued, his lips twisting as though with a particularly unpleasant thought. "But either way, do not commit the error of believing Athven to be all-powerful or infallible. This battle is not lost. We who are here with you are not without our own strengths."

"Yes, as I became aware when you set yourself on fire," she replied dryly.

"If I had known it would impress you so much, perhaps I would have done it sooner," he joked.

Zara's jaw dropped. "That's twice now you have deliberately said something humorous," she accused. "Did Malichai feed us something spoiled for dinner or are you so lacking in sleep?"

"Perhaps I'm making up for a lifetime of being too serious. Or, perhaps you are a bad influence." He shrugged. "If it bothers you that much, I might consider cultivating the skill."

Her lips lifted into a smile, in spite of her dark mood, and his answered. He didn't smile often enough. Possibly his scars made it difficult, but the expression seemed all the more endearing to her for its imperfections.

"So are we going back to sleep or what?" Silvay grumbled. "I don't like to be the curmudgeon, but tomorrow may not be restful and some of us are old."

"Silvay, you like to pretend, but I doubt you are any older than I am," Alexei responded, rising to his feet and shooting her an amused glance.

"I may not be much older in years," she retorted tartly, "but I am infinitely older in wisdom, and don't you forget it."

"I don't think I'll be able to sleep," Zara said honestly. "I might go for a walk." She couldn't suppress a tiny shiver, thinking of walking alone through the dark castle.

"Do you wish to be alone, or would you prefer company?" Alexei asked, startling her again with his perception.

"I... Company would be welcome, thank you," she said in a small voice.

"Young'uns," Silvay muttered, but turned away to her blankets with what looked suspiciously like a smile. "Just don't keep the rest of us awake."

CHAPTER 11

They walked in silence at first, the sounds of their passing echoing against the stones and dying as they moved through the darkness, their way illuminated only by snatches of moonlight. Alexei didn't think Zara cared where they went, so he steered them gradually towards the reception hall, which he had not bothered to explore since his return.

The door creaked open, an eerie wail in the darkness, and he beckoned her inside. Gazing up into the shadows, he stretched out a hand, felt for the enchantment in the stones and pushed some of his own magic into them.

The crystal lanterns flared to life and he heard Zara's gasp of wonder from beside him. His own breath caught at the forgotten beauty of crystal globes, suspended from golden chains, throwing brilliant rays into the far corners of the round chamber.

"We rarely took the time to entertain, either ourselves or outsiders, but when we did, this is where we came," he explained. Zara's mouth was still hanging open as she gazed around the room, and he couldn't blame her.

The floor was seamlessly tiled in quartz, veined with gold, in fanciful swirls of milk, rose, smoke and vermarine. The walls were decorated in scrollwork and blue velvet hangings, while the ceiling boasted painted scenes of sterile ferocity—stylized wyverns, rampant indriks and glittering forests, all surrounded by curling, thorn-bedecked vines. At the center was painted a single enormous rose.

"It's almost a crime that no one got to see this," Zara said softly beside him. "Not that I would want to live in it every day, but it is beautiful. Haunting, really. I can almost feel the ghosts of people who walked here, danced here, lived and believed their dreams under these lights."

"You're remarkably romantic for a treasure hunter," Alexei noted without thinking. When she stepped away from him, he turned to amend his words. "I didn't mean to be harsh. It was merely an observation. I swear that I am done with holding your past over your head. Can you forgive me?"

She didn't say anything. Her arms were folded, almost as if to protect herself, and her eyes darted to his before turning back to the floor.

"Zara, I speak truly." The need he felt, for her to believe him, to forgive him, nearly stole his breath away. "Even if you cannot believe that I am sincere, can you believe that I regret having judged you when I knew so little of your life? That I would know more if you would allow it?"

"Why would you wish to?" she asked quietly, still not looking at him. "There is little to know, and none of it very happy. Not that I was always miserable, but my life has been neither peaceful nor conventional. None of the things that I enjoyed will give you pleasure to hear."

"Tell me anyway?"

When she hesitated, he tried again. "At least tell me of your family. I know that you miss them. If it will help to speak of them I am happy to listen."

"Why are you being so nice?" Zara muttered. "I think I liked it better when you were irritated with me on general principle. At least then our conversations were predictable."

"The fact that I was predictably an ass doesn't seem all that comforting."

"Perhaps you weren't always an ass," she allowed. "But I find it hard to believe you haven't always been a curmudgeon."

"Only since I was five."

Zara made a sound that was almost a laugh, and Alexei marveled at the awakening desire to make her laugh again. To lighten the fear and shadows that seemed to haunt her more each day. Each day... How long had they known one another? Only a handful of sunrises. When had he gone from wishing her to the farthest ends of the continent to wishing she would laugh more?

"My mother died when I was ten, but she left me well before that."

Alexei looked up quickly when he realized she was going to answer his question, but her eyes were tracing the pattern in the quartz at her feet.

"My father was a treasure hunter when they met. He was born Vidori, but the martial lifestyle didn't suit him, and when his father disowned him as a coward, he stole a treasure map that was a family heirloom and set out to make his fortune." Zara let out a breath that sounded like resignation. "Oh he's handsome enough, so I can imagine why my mother fell for him. She was Frenish. They rarely leave their island, but her father was the captain of a trading ship and brought her on one last adventure before she was to submit to an arranged marriage."

"I imagine he regretted it later."

"Probably," Zara allowed, "but I've never met any of my parents' relatives so I can only guess."

"Never?" The idea of such isolation, such aloneness, made Alexei ache with sympathy. True, he'd had only his brother for years, but his early life had been filled with the noisy, boisterous, unrelenting presence of people who loved him. He couldn't really imagine the lack.

"Father was all dash and sparkle, his hands either dripping with riches, or empty of all but promises, but he couldn't exactly go home or ask for help. I could have any number of cousins, I suppose, but they probably wouldn't be willing to acknowledge the connection." Her mouth twisted a little. "My father might be a thief, but he's a proud one. And most likely delusional. He promised my mother the world despite his lack of connections, and because he was young and handsome, she believed him, and he set her up in a little house in an out-of-the-way part of Andar."

"And then he left."

"Well," Zara explained, "he had to make a living somehow, and he had no taste for real work. All his father taught him how to do was fight, and he hated that, so instead he made a profession out of searching for rumors of long-lost treasures and hunting them down. Ancient temples, tombs, forgotten strongholds—he would raid them all and come back boasting of the palace we would live in one day." She glanced at Alexei. "I don't think this is what he had in mind."

"I can imagine not," Alexei murmured. Zara's father didn't sound the sort to appreciate an enchanted castle, unless he could sell tickets for admission. And wouldn't Athven have loved being thoroughly trampled by thrill-seeking tourists.

"I think one day Mother realized it was nothing more than a dream. Whatever he gained, he spent just as quickly and we were lucky to have enough for food, fire, and occasionally new clothes. She stopped speaking, stopped caring, and eventually began to drink. But it was a fever that took her life about a month before Father came home from his latest trip and found me alone."

A silence fell and filled the room with the weight of that memory. She'd been only ten. No wonder she feared being left alone.

"He didn't want to take me," she went on, "but I convinced him I could be useful. I was small enough to fit into tight spaces. I was fast, and I was smart, and I knew how to read, which his henchmen usually didn't. Plus, I ate less." She shrugged. "I only knew that he couldn't leave me behind."

"Did you hate it, living on the road?"

"Strangely, no," she admitted with a sad smile. "I was bored with my quiet life and ready for adventure. We travelled to so many new places and

I saw things most people only dream of. And"—she looked sideways at him —"I was good at what we did. Good at deciphering maps, good at puzzles, and the thrill of it kept me sharp."

"You weren't in it for the treasure." He was sure of it, but he wondered whether she was.

"No. It wasn't the treasure for me. I loved the thrill of solving the mystery, and the awe of walking in places that no one had seen for hundreds of years. Just touching objects that someone long dead had handled and loved made me wonder about their lives, about their hopes and dreams, and whether anything I did or made would survive me for so many centuries."

"And now I imagine you'd give anything to be anonymous and free again."

"Anything?" she echoed. "No. But perhaps I would give much to return to my ignorance. I clung to the belief that my father loved me, in his way. I know that he needed me. Even now, I cannot quite shake the notion that if I could only find him, everything would be all right again."

He could see the defeat in the slump of her shoulders, the absent scraping of one toe over the tiniest smudge on the gleaming floor.

"I am so tired of being afraid," she said finally. "I have walked in a hundred places that would have left others in screaming hysterics, but this place..." She shook her head and wrapped her arms around herself. "It undoes me. I feel isolated and small and powerless. It makes me want to lash out, just to feel less helpless."

She did not mean the stone, he knew. There was no terror for her in a building, no matter how old and dark.

"Are you still afraid of me?" Alexei could not help asking, and dreading the answer.

Zara straightened and turned her head to look at him, and he saw her in that moment not as a usurper, not as a challenge or a mystery, but as a woman. Her white hair fell unbraided around her shoulders, reflecting the many-hued lights of the crystal lanterns, and her blue eyes seemed to glow against her brown skin. She stood like a queen and held his gaze without flinching.

The effect was mesmerizing. Even surrounded by the ancient grandeur of the hall, even dressed in worn leather, her beauty captivated and left him momentarily without breath.

"No," she said, and grinned, a mischievous expression that did nothing to diminish the strange new effect she had on him. "Despite the fact that you can shoot fire from your eyes and turn stones into lanterns, I am not."

"But you were."

She muttered something unintelligible. "Maybe. A little. But I was telling you the truth when I said it has nothing to do with how you look. Your scars are not nearly as terrifying as your air of dismissive majesty."

"My what?!"

"You heard me." She elevated her chin and affected haughty grandeur. "Your outraged righteousness of purpose was enough to intimidate anyone."

He silently mouthed her accusations, eyes narrowed. Outraged righteousness? Dismissive majesty? Had he really been so horrible? "Was it really so bad?" he asked, hoping he didn't sound plaintive. He was too old for whining.

"We are not all honorless thieves," she mimicked in a deep voice, her face drawn into a disdainful frown. "I would never shame the House of Nar so deeply."

True shame flooded him as he recalled the words. "It was bad," he agreed. "Perhaps I was misled, but my reaction was at least as much a matter of wounded pride. It's a wonder you still speak to me."

"Yes," she said, lifting both hands palm up with a puzzled expression. "It really is. I should have Gulver examine my head." She smiled to show she was teasing. "But I have decided to overlook your offenses. Receiving a random marriage proposal from a complete stranger is probably as good an excuse as any for outraged righteousness."

"Many a marriage has begun with little more than that," he said flippantly, hoping to dispel any lingering embarrassment for them both.

He'd miscalculated. Her breath caught and she looked at him like a startled rabbit.

"I could at least have refused politely," he went on hastily. "There was no excuse for trampling on your dignity."

"I wasn't aware that I had any." The startled look faded. "But I thank you for the sentiment." She gazed up, eyes fixed on the rose in the center of the ceiling. "What are we going to do, really?"

"You mean about the army?"

"About any of it. We cannot hope to defeat them, and your vague hints about the man Athven calls 'Bright One' are not reassuring."

How much could he tell her? How much did she have a right to know?

"Vague hints are really all I have, to a point. Rowan Tremontaine is a man of great intelligence and greater ambition. But I do not know whether even he knows what he truly wants. He has enough magic to bend minds to his will, and he possesses no known scruples. The difficulty is not that he is infallible. Rather that he has been defeated, and yet simply rises again as though defeat cannot touch him."

"And you believe he wants to take the Rose for himself and leave?" Skepticism colored her voice.

"It is what I believe, yes. He would not settle for small dreams. Athven is a powerful ally, but she is too contained in her reach. Even if he knows what she is capable of, I doubt he would limit himself by attempting to possess her."

Zara let out a quiet breath and her shoulders seemed less tense, for some reason.

"Perhaps the most important thing I can tell you is that he is never what he seems. You will be tempted to believe he is your friend. That he wants the same thing you want. Even without magic, he is a master of words and misdirection. And"—Alexei tried to keep his voice neutral—"he is astonishingly attractive. There are few women who can withstand his appeal at close range."

"Yes," she replied sweetly, "because looks are all we women care about." She snorted. "Give me some credit, Alexei. I have not been a child in many years, and I hope by now I am old and wise enough not to cozy up to a monster simply because it has a pretty face."

He shrugged. "I would have warned anyone, no matter my estimation of their age or intelligence. I was once blamed for *not* offering sufficient warning and I don't intend to repeat the mistake."

"How long have you known him?" she asked.

"I have known *of* him for years, but it has only been the past few that we have had occasion to be better acquainted," he answered cryptically, hoping she would let the matter rest.

"And?" she prompted.

He sighed. Perhaps it was only fair, as she had shared her story with him.

"I was employed in Andar as a horseman for much of my life after I left Erath," he told her. "There I was as mundane as anyone else, and concerned myself only with hiding who and what I was. But my brother and I grew fond of our employer's daughter and when she fell afoul of one of Rowan's plans, we were marginally involved in the aftermath."

"Did you know about Porfiry then?"

"Not until after Prince Rowan was exiled. When I heard the name, I begged for more information until it became clear he was indeed my cousin. I maneuvered myself into a place on a ship going to Caelan to look for Rowan, and while I was there I made it my goal to find Porfiry and bring him home to face justice."

Zara's brow creased pensively. "What about your brother? Did he not go with you?"

"Andrei never cared much for the concerns of the world at large. He is a gentle man with a gift for animals, and even without magic, he is content working with horses and living in peace."

"And you were not?" Her eyes seemed to look right through him.

"No." He could be honest now, with himself as well as her. "Even when I had no suspicion that Porfiry was still alive, a part of me could not live with the knowledge of what had passed. But I buried it deep, along with the guilt that I felt over running instead of standing to fight."

"You were not much more than a child," Zara scolded. "Why would you not run?"

"Why would I not stay to share in the trials of my people?" he countered. "What right had I to live on in peace when they died in blood and fire and chains?"

"All right," Zara said quietly. "Why didn't you?"

He shut his eyes in spite of himself, and his fists closed so tightly they ached. He remembered it so clearly, the moment burned into his memory by years of anguish and regret. Regret he had never even spoken of to his brother.

"We knew the army was coming. They burned and slaughtered as they came, and we did what we could to hold them off, but they brought silver, which is deadly to magic and painful to magic users. And we were never a martial people." He could feel his hands begin to shake. "As many as possible were evacuated from Athven. We warned everyone we could to leave, but my people were, and are, deeply tied to our land. Many could not leave, many would not. And when the army drew near to Athven herself, my cousin gave orders."

"She could not leave either, could she?" Zara's voice wavered, and her eyes glittered with unshed tears.

"No." His voice grew hoarse with the pain of remembering her courage in those final moments. "She intended to hold here as long as possible. To distract the army to give more people time to escape if they chose. There were not many of us left. Many of my cousins had already fallen, trying to stop the army before it arrived, though she would never allow me to go. She said that my power was not yet strong enough. That as an enchanter, my gifts would be useless on the field of battle."

"She lied." Zara nodded, as though hearing the voices of the past.

"Yes. She sent my fifteen-year-old cousin Yala to build trenches with her gardener's gift. I could have set the enemies tents on fire, if nothing else."

"She wanted to save you."

Alexei felt himself shrug, minutely, and the motion seemed to unleash an anguish he had never dared permit himself to feel. Hot, angry tears crowded into his eyes, but he willed them back. "She sent me away. Told me to leave Erath and not look back. And when I refused..." His teeth clenched on the memory.

"She made Athven throw you out."

"And my brother with me. I think Beatra knew I would never expect him to face what was coming. He was too kind, too gentle to be sent into battle, and he would never have survived being put in chains."

"Did he convince you to run?" Zara's voice was gentle, understanding, and it did nothing to stem the pain.

"No. Andrei is no leader. I think he would have done whatever I asked, even stayed and faced death. But once I was out and the doors held against me, I could see the smoke from the burning that the army left in its wake. I could feel the land's anguish as my people died or were chained in silver and their gifts cut off. And, to my shame, I was so afraid that I did as my cousin asked."

"She needed to know her legacy would survive," Zara told him. "She chose you to restore what was left. She believed that you were the one best able to do so."

"Then she chose badly," Alexei told her bitterly. "She only threw out my brother with me so that I would feel compelled to keep him safe. She knew I would protect him. But I didn't run for him, and it wasn't his safety that mattered at the end. It was mine."

∿

Zara barely held back the impulse to reach out and offer comfort. Alexei would probably not welcome it, but his anguish begged for solace. For absolution. Which she could never grant. But it did give her startling new insight into his response to her.

What had looked like bitterness towards her had probably been at least as much self-loathing. An inescapable conviction that he deserved to be rejected. That he was no better than her father.

"You were sixteen," she scolded gently. "And you had no experience with war or violence. Your cousin knew what she was doing and she gave you no choice."

"There is always a choice," Alexei said fiercely, angrily. "Always."

"Then by all means, continue to hate yourself for your actions," Zara said tartly. "Hate yourself for being safe. Hate yourself for being in a place to help save other lives. Just don't ask me to agree with you."

"You, of all people, should agree with me," he argued. "Your father ran and left you to face this alone. He chose to save his own life over protecting the one person he should have put first. You cannot be angry with him and choose to absolve me."

"Don't tell me what to feel," she shot back. "My father is a grown man who has spent a lifetime being a coward. He is weak and vain and so help me I love him anyway because he's my father."

She tried to soften her voice. "You were a boy and the person you respected the most, the person with the greatest responsibility for your life told you to run and placed you in an impossible position." She walked over to stand in front of him and willed him to look at her. "You did the right thing. There was no value in staying merely to prove your courage. It is not always braver to die than to live. Sometimes, choosing life is both the harder course and the right one."

He did look at her then. "Do you know how hard that is to accept?" he whispered.

"No," she conceded. "I have not yet had to make that choice. But that does not mean I am wrong."

He held her gaze and a sad smile ghosted across his lips. "I have never been more sure that Athven, and indeed all of Erath, is fortunate to have you. And I have never been more sure that I would sacrifice much to see you free of us."

Not really thinking about the consequences, Zara reached out impulsively and grasped his hand. "I am still afraid, but I would not undo what was done. I would not go back to a time before I met you, and Silvay and Malichai and Wilder and Gulver. Better to face this together than to face yet another road, with another empty pile of stones at the end, or to face another day where I have nothing to lose but the hope that my father would ever notice my unhappiness."

Alexei did not pull away, and his hand shifted to tighten around hers for a moment. "You may change your mind, before this is done."

"Maybe," she replied, forcing a light and cheerful tone to disguise the flood of emotions that accompanied his gesture.

She couldn't have explained her feelings in words, anyway. What she felt in that moment was far deeper and more complicated than mere speech could convey. His fingers were warm and rough against hers, and that smallest of touches gave her a sense of belonging that all the words in the world could not have matched. It was such a tiny thing, her hand in his, but it shifted something between them that no reminders of their differences could shift back. Even if she wished it.

She smiled brightly, hoping it would hide the feelings that she was terrified might already be evident in her eyes, feelings she wasn't even sure she could have identified for herself. "Still," she said, pulling her hand from his, "you must not give me more credit than I deserve. I should probably ask you to marry me again, before you start thinking too well of me."

Zara turned resolutely away, determined not to see or wonder what his face would show. She strode towards the window, forgetting that it was night and darkness would prevent her from even pretending an interest in the view.

"Zara..." Alexei's voice sounded odd, but her fear of what he meant to say fell away an instant later.

It was not as dark outside as it should have been. From their position on the second floor of the castle, it was all too easy to make out the line of torches bobbing and waving as they entered the clearing.

"They're here."

Alexei joined her at the window, his shoulder brushing faintly against hers, and let out a sigh that matched his grim expression. "And we have no idea what Athven means to do?"

Zara bit her lip and fixed her eyes resolutely on the distant light of the torches. "She will let them in. After that..."

"We may be on our own." He mistook her silence for ignorance and Zara almost slumped against the window in relief. Perhaps there would never be a need to burden him with the knowledge that Athven had rejected him in favor of his enemy. She would deal with that, and Athven, alone.

"We should wake the others." She turned away from the window and would have simply walked away had Alexei not stopped her.

"I will not let him harm you."

She saw the resolution in his steady gray eye, and answered with the honesty he deserved.

"I do not for a moment imagine that either you or I can control what he might choose to do," she told him. "Whether he harms me or not, I will not let you lay his actions on your own conscience. That is burdened enough. But believe this: you do not stand alone this time. I will use whatever small power I may have to stand in his way if he attempts to hurt any of you again."

His mouth opened and closed, soundless. Satisfied, Zara turned and left the chamber. The silly man *would* try to take everything on himself. It touched her deeply that he would even try to protect her, but she was not going to let him think that he could, or should, do so by himself.

They would wake the others, and await whatever was coming, together.

CHAPTER 12

hey had only moments to prepare. Alexei readied torches of their own, while Zara woke the others. They assembled silently in the entry hall, all except Wilder, whom Silvay had ordered to stay out of sight. Zara had no doubt the irrepressible child was somewhere in the entry hall anyway.

Malichai had somehow found time to don his leather armor and spiked gauntlets, and twirled his staff almost cheerfully in the wavering shadows. Silvay appeared calm, but one hand rested on the hilts of the daggers beneath her cloak. And Gulver? Zara had learned to decipher Gulver's mood by his mustache, and it appeared to be standing straight up like the bristles on a shaving brush.

Or the hair on Shadow's back when she was angry. Zara couldn't imagine Athven wouldn't be observing the proceedings as nearly as possible, but it was too dark to see a gray cat that probably didn't want to be seen.

Zara wondered belatedly if she ought to have thought to provide herself with a weapon. She fully expected to experience the strong desire to stab someone before this was over, so perhaps it was just as well she didn't think to carry any sharp objects on her person.

Alexei, she thought, had no need for sharp objects. Even had he not possessed the ability to set himself on fire, the icy anger in his gray eye was sharp enough to skewer anything or anyone unwise enough to stand in his path. She ought to know. She had been on the receiving end of it often enough. Strangely, the memory held no terror for her now. Instead she found comfort in the crackling intensity of his mood as they stood together and waited for the doors to open.

Through the high windows, Zara could see the ink-dark sky give way to the barest hint of morning. The sounds of voices, barely audible through the solid wood of the door, rose and fell. And when the faint rose of dawn colored the narrow ribbons of light that slashed across the floor, Shadow strolled out of nowhere and sat before the door. She looked at neither Zara nor Alexei, but fixed her green-eyed gaze on the iron-bound beams that swung inward with a groan of neglected hinges.

Zara stifled a chuckle. Either Athven had a bizarre tendency towards the theatrical, or the weather had changed for the worse. The door had not creaked on any of its prior openings.

The voices outside changed. Murmurings of fear and the shuffling of booted feet on stone grew momentarily louder and then died. Into that charged silence intruded the sound of a single set of footsteps. A head appeared, and though the light from outside prevented Zara from seeing it clearly, a chill shot through her chest and clenched her jaw.

"Hello?" said a cheerful male voice. "Is anyone here?"

The only response was a collective raising of their torches. Gulver may have shivered a bit harder.

The visitor stepped all the way inside, his demeanor midway between eager and downright sprightly. He was tall, nearly as tall as Malichai, and as he moved into the brighter light of their torches, Zara could see that his hair was gold and wavy, his eyes as blue and guileless as a babe's.

He stopped before he reached them, and looked down on the scarred gray form of Shadow with a delighted smile before dropping to one knee in a courtly gesture of fealty.

"Athven," he said smoothly, head bowed in respect. "I have so longed to meet you. It is an honor to finally step within your walls."

Zara felt her brows climb up her forehead in dismay. So much for him not knowing who Athven was or what she could do. This ridiculous specimen could only be Rowan, the deposed prince of Andar, and unless she was mightily mistaken, he was presently flirting with a cat. If only Zara could feel certain that the cat wasn't flirting back.

She expected one of her other companions to challenge the intruder, or to at least acknowledge his entry, but no one moved or spoke, and when Shadow likewise made no move, Zara felt as though the awkwardness had gone on long enough.

"How lovely to meet you," she said flatly. "If only you'd waited for a proper invitation, we could have prepared a more appropriate welcome."

"Oh, but I would not have wished you to trouble yourselves." The visitor stood as smoothly as if he bowed his head to feline avatars every day, though Zara doubted he made a habit of owing allegiance to anyone but himself. "My companions and I are well able to see to our own comfort, though Athven did indicate that she intended to apprise you of our coming. She did not seem to approve of my suggestion that it remain a delightful surprise."

Zara couldn't help it. She darted a glance at Shadow, who was staring fixedly in the opposite direction. She had *talked* to him? How? And why had she not said anything?

"Athven is very much her own creature, as you are surely aware," Zara replied acidly. "And she usually enjoys surprises, delightful and otherwise."

"As I see," the prince answered, exuberance pouring from every word. "Would you believe she did not even hint that there was an old friend waiting here to greet me?"

"As if you didn't know already," Zara retorted, resenting the pretense of friendship and familiarity. She would prefer that he stop pretending and announce his dastardly plan. Isn't that what villains were supposed to do? "Didn't your spy tell you everyone's names after you rescued him from their tender care?"

And why didn't Alexei speak up for himself? Why was he standing there as though glued to the floor?

"My former servant has been remarkably reticent," the newcomer admitted, though without much concern. "But there is no need to stand on ceremony now. My name is Rowan. I am acquainted with your warrior friend Cherting, though our history is brief, and with the frozen fellow over there, though I suspect he does not remember me fondly. Might I gain an introduction to the rest of your party?"

"Why look at me?" Zara flipped the end of her braid. "I'm nobody and my name is Zara. If they want you to know their names it's their own affair."

"But are you not the chosen one?" Rowan affected startled confusion. "Athven informed me quite clearly that her latest guardian was a silver-haired woman of remarkable beauty and stature."

A bubble of laughter escaped Zara in spite of her fear. "We both know Athven never said anything so ridiculous. As frustrating as she can be, cat or not, at least she is honest in her assessments. Stone may not be able to feel, but neither does it resort to flattery."

"Perhaps it depends on one's perspective." Rowan's cheerfulness did not abate. "I would not have considered either of those statements to be a lie. But, arguments about your appearance aside, I am certain you are Athven's chosen one, and I believe we will find much to discuss. There is so much I want to learn. So much I am hoping she can teach me."

"About what?" Zara blurted, taken aback by Rowan's enthusiasm. Whatever happened to finding the Rose and leaving?

"About magic, of course." Rowan's eyes brightened with his answer. "I know so little and there are so few willing to teach. I would ask the horseman, but I believe he has too many grievances to consider me as a protégé." He looked over at Alexei at last. "I assure you, I have nothing but the best intentions towards you all. There is no need to be concerned about my influence."

Zara shot a look at Alexei, whose hands flexed minutely. She thought he knew rather too well what Rowan was capable of to relax at the younger man's word.

"Forgive me if I lack confidence in your honor, Tremontaine," Alexei rasped harshly. "Or don't. What you think of me matters less than the contents of the kitchen refuse heap."

"Then it is fortunate for us both that I care even less for your approval than you for mine," Rowan returned, his angelic smile growing wider by the moment. "I think, however, that I have found one point on which we may be able to agree." He turned towards the door. "Come, valet. Come and face your doom, if you have the courage."

A man stepped through the doorway, reluctance weighing every motion and twisting his pinched features till he appeared to be in pain. Zara had never seen him before, but could guess from the foreign taste of fury coursing through her body that this was Porfiry. The Betrayer. Athven was making no effort to hide how she felt and her emotions echoed loudly through their bond.

"What do you mean, face his doom?" On the heels of her fury, Zara felt Athven's satisfaction, as clearly as if it had been her own, but she could not decipher the reason. "What did you bring him for, if not to help you gain what you want?"

"But of course he will help me gain what I want." Rowan's smile faded as he looked at the hunched and terrified form of Porfiry. "In the past, he has proven very useful to me. Loyal, even. But now he has added another to his rather lengthy list of betrayals, and so I have made a bargain. That which is useless to me for that which is priceless."

Zara looked from Rowan, to Alexei and back again. Something was happening, something they had not prepared for and it made no sense. "Just say what you mean," she snapped irritably. "You prattle worse than anyone I ever met. Maybe you think it sounds cunning and mysterious, but honestly you're just tiresome."

A choking sound issued from behind Malichai's beard, but on the outside his stoic demeanor did not waver.

Rowan's smile slipped only for a moment. "Athven did warn me that you are refreshingly blunt. I am looking forward to getting to know you better in the future."

"Look forward all you choose, Andari," she snapped. "You will never know me any better than you do at this moment."

"I hope you're willing to be open minded about that," he answered gently, "but if not there is plenty of time to persuade you otherwise."

"Didn't your mother ever tell you there's nothing worse than a visitor who won't take a hint when it's time to leave?" Zara muttered. "I think I liked you better when I believed you only wanted to steal the Rose and go. Now, are you going to explain yourself or not? I have the strangest feeling that you want to, but you're waiting for the most suitably dramatic moment."

"There is no need for rancor," the former prince remonstrated. "I am happy to explain. Though perhaps that explanation ought to come from someone else. Porfiry? Perhaps you should be more forthcoming with these fine people."

Porfiry shivered and hunched in on himself even further.

"No? Then I suppose it will have to be me." Rowan shrugged. "It was, of course, my original intention to bestow whatever courtesies were required, retrieve the object of power I had heard so much about, and then disappear again. I have gone to the trouble of forming the foundations of my army and had hoped to reintroduce myself to my own people by this time next year. But fate, alas, had other plans. Didn't she, my not-so-loyal subject?"

A whimper escaped the object of his attention.

"You see, Porfiry had been so anxious to gain my favor and approval, when he told me of the wondrous Crystal Rose and how he had so bravely stolen and hidden it, he failed to inform me of the most important fact."

"Oh no," Zara pouted sarcastically. "How could he have been so thoughtless?"

"That question has troubled me also," Rowan said, with evident sincerity. "But once he lied, of course, he had to keep lying, because he valued his own skin. After I had gone to so much trouble to gain and provide for the protection of a valuable magical asset, he could hardly admit that the object I had come so far to find no longer existed."

"What?" The shocked whisper from Alexei echoed through the hall.

But it did exist. It had to. Athven had said she could feel it. And without it, they had no plan. No defense against the army encamped outside.

"Poor Porfiry." Rowan shook his head. "Everything he ever did was a failure. Even his greatest triumph. He stole his people's most wondrous treasure and thought to hide it. Then, when their need was greatest, he would produce it again and claim the title of hero. Protector of Erath."

It made a twisted sort of sense. Which didn't mean it wasn't a lie. But Zara could imagine the man Alexei had described doing just such a thing.

"Don't bother assuming me a liar," Rowan went on, as if he could hear her thoughts. "My gift confirmed the truth of it. He meant to conceal the Rose in a seldom used part of the castle, but fate intervened. Poor clumsy fool. He tripped on the stairs and dropped the most precious item in the world."

A sharp, indrawn breath indicated Alexei's shock.

"Yes." Rowan sighed and his mouth drooped in what looked like genuine pain. "He broke it. The fabled Crystal Rose shattered into a thousand pieces."

~

"Three!" Porfiry's shriek splintered the horrified silence that descended, on the hall and on Alexei's hopes. "It was only three pieces, and I never told you it was whole, only that I knew where it was. That was no lie!"

Then there had never been a future to hope for. Not for Alexei, and not for his people. There was no Rose to be found. And now that Rowan had gained entry to the castle, there would be no means of denying it again unless Athven chose to do so. Considering that the cat had apparently spoken to him mind to mind, and had even now begun to twine herself around the wretch's ankles, Alexei doubted her allegiance could be counted on.

Silver was not an option either, much as Alexei would enjoy seeing Rowan wrapped in silver chains. The Erathi never used silver, and for all Alexei knew, even the presence of the metal within Athven's walls might prove damaging. It would certainly be a threat to her bond with Zara. Alexei was not willing to risk Zara's life, even for the sake of defeating the man who nearly killed him.

"Supposing this is true..." Zara's voice did not waver even once. Alexei found that even without hope, he could appreciate her audacity. She was afraid, but fear only seemed to make Zara bolder. "What does it have to do with us? You can have no purpose here. Athven Nar is the home of Erathi sovereigns, not rejected Andari princelings."

"Oh no?" Rowan said softly, a dangerous glint in his eye. "Then neither is it home to abandoned, homeless treasure hunters, and yet here you are."

A surge of anger threatened Alexei's determination to remain silent. He had never felt such an overwhelming urge to beat a fellow human to a bloody pulp. Not even his cousin. The realization shocked him into remaining still, despite his rage, though his gaze shifted to Zara, willing her to remember that she was not abandoned and homeless anymore.

"If one of us must be labeled abandoned and homeless, I think you will find it is not I," Zara announced coolly. "I have a home, with Athven and I have found her quite hospitable, for a cat. And I have friends, who could have abandoned me if they chose and they have stayed." She stepped forward, chin lifted, until she stood only a short distance in front of the tall, golden prince. "Of the two of us, I am not the one who is forced to resort to compulsion to keep from being alone."

Rowan burst out laughing. "Athven told me I would like you, and she was more right than she knew. I am so looking forward to our partnership."

"I don't think you understand," Zara said softly. "There is no partnership. There will never be a partnership."

"It is you, I fear, who does not fully understand," Rowan said. He spoke slowly and gently, as if to a child. "Perhaps Athven has not explained, but it is necessary. She has been searching for someone who can provide what she needs in order to survive. You have her gratitude, of course, for saving her, but your strength is not enough. She must bond with me as well, so that she can be fully herself once more. And when she has gained the use of my power, in addition to yours, all of us will benefit. Athven has agreed to grant me access to her limitless knowledge and wisdom, while she will be granted her chance at revenge. And you, Zara, will be free to search for your father."

Zara froze. Indecision flitted across her features. "What do you mean 'revenge'?"

"I have promised her the traitor's life," Rowan said simply.

Alexei shot a glance at Porfiry. His cousin's eyes were closed and his lips were moving. Simply being inside Athven's walls once more was probably more strain than his courage could bear.

"How could I be free to search?" Zara asked. "Surely Athven has told you..."

"He is trying to get rid of you, of course." Alexei interrupted, willing her not to say more. There was so much he didn't understand. Why had Athven changed her mind so suddenly? How could she propose to bond with an enemy? Those questions aside, Athven was clearly even more devious than they had given her credit for. She might have talked to the former prince, but clearly she hadn't told him everything. And keeping Rowan in the dark might prove to be the difference between victory and defeat. "You know he will say anything to get you to agree. Once he joins your bond with Athven, he will have no further need of you and no desire for you to be underfoot, meddling in his plans. No matter what they whisper in your ear to try to convince you, they are both more interested in their own power than in you."

"Please remember, I have no need to lie," Rowan pointed out. "Especially once we are bound together, through Athven. She has told me the connection is a deep one, and you will be able to judge my sincerity for yourself."

"What's to stop you from killing me, before or after the bond is made?" Zara asked boldly. "You'd have what you want, so why would you share it?"

Alexei wanted to grin, but suppressed it. Zara had been quick to realize his intentions.

Rowan chuckled merrily. "Because in the first case, Athven would die with you, as you well know. And in the second"—he paused and appeared thoughtful—"I believe she has been honest with me on that point. Depending on the depth of the bond and the strength of Athven's abilities at the time, there is a chance neither Athven nor I would survive its severing."

Or at least so Athven had told him. Alexei wasn't even sure how true it was. With three parts to a bond, the two remaining ought to be able to sustain one another, but it wasn't as though Erathi history had very many examples. It was going to be tricky finding out what Athven had told him and what she hadn't, but Alexei could at least be grateful that she had the foresight to protect Zara's life.

Zara appeared to be lost in thought. Considering. Weighing.

"Zara, you don't have to listen to him." Alexei did not know what that look on her face meant, only that he could not let her agree to what Rowan proposed without knowing the consequences. The closeness of any magical bond, endured with a man like Rowan, would be a horror he could not bear to contemplate.

"Athven once suggested that it might not be up to me..." she said slowly. "She bonded with me the first time without my permission. Can she do this, as well, without my approval?"

"No," Alexei told her firmly. "Not if she wants the benefits of a true partnership." What Athven had apparently suggested was possible, but it was a despicable violation of free will that no Erathi would have agreed to participate in. That Athven had already done such a thing to Zara once— when the avatar was too weak to even be aware of what she was doing— Alexei had been willing to forgive. That she was still considering doing it a second time shook him deeply.

"He is correct, to a point," Rowan agreed. "According to Athven, it is far better if the bond is made willingly. We would require your assent in order for all of us to receive the greatest benefit, but it is not impossible to forge a connection without it. I feel certain, however, that you will decide in our favor."

Zara looked at Shadow, desperation in her eyes, but the cat only twitched her tail.

If you need help deciding," Rowan put in softly, "I am certain I can provide it. Give me a chance. Let me show you that I can be what you need."

"I don't need you," Zara hissed.

"But Athven does," Rowan insisted. "Surely she has told you that you cannot give her what she requires. If Erath is to thrive, she requires power. Power I have. Together we could restore her to her former strength."

"At what cost?" Zara asked, shaking her head. "I cannot imagine you having anything to say that could persuade me to do this."

"What does Athven have to add?" Silvay asked unexpectedly.

"She hasn't said anything," Zara retorted.

But with another tortured groan of hinges, Athven made her wishes known. The door swung closed and sealed itself once again.

"I propose a truce," Rowan announced, apparently undisturbed by the barrier between him and his army.

Had he known what Athven intended to do? Was she so fully committed to her choice that she was actively conspiring with him against them?

"There are far more of you," he continued, truthfully enough, "and you could no doubt threaten my life should you so choose. However, I do have a certain amount of power and could most likely turn you against one another should it become necessary to defend myself. By Athven's suggestion, why should we not agree to a trial? I will refrain from using my magic against you, and you in turn promise that I will go unharmed until a decision is reached." He glanced at his erstwhile valet. "And Porfiry is to be safe as well. If we come to a bargain, his life belongs to Athven, and she might be angry if he is damaged before she has a chance to exact her revenge."

"And what if you don't like our decision? What if we reject your offer?" Alexei scoffed. "On our last meeting, your idea of losing graciously was to murder an old man because he was in your way."

"And by doing so, I cleared a path for a new ruler, who is both fair and just, and who has freed many of your people from their chains. Do you object to the removal of a man who has caused the suffering and death of thousands during his reign?"

"I object to murder," Alexei replied levelly. "It is not my right to decide who is guilty enough to deserve it."

"Perhaps it is simply that you lack the will to do what must be done," Rowan answered, his tone tinged with regret. "There must be those of us who do not shrink from making the difficult decisions, or from acting when the need is great."

"I agree," Zara said suddenly.

"What?" Alexei's jaw dropped.

"To the truce," she snapped, glaring at him before turning her glare on Rowan. "We won't try to kill you in your sleep, and you keep your magic tentacles to yourself. If I catch you meddling with anyone's head, the deal is off and Malichai gets to poison you."

"What a very unromantic way to die." Rowan smiled as though the thought did not trouble him very much. "But I have no plans to break our truce. I hope to spend my time convincing you that I mean no harm, and aiding Athven in showing you the many potential benefits of our partnership."

"I'll give you three days," Zara told him flatly. "I will hear you out. I'll even listen to Athven proselytize on your behalf. But it is my decision, and you're both going to have to accept that."

Rowan beamed as though she had handed him everything he desired. "I accept your challenge, my lady Zara. You will not regret accepting my offer. In three days, you will have seen what wonders could be accomplished if we only work together."

Zara sighed and put her face in her hands. "I'm regretting this already." She suddenly looked up and glanced at Porfiry, who appeared to have slunk farther and farther into the shadows with the hope of disappearing altogether. "What of the Betrayer?"

"As I said, he will belong to Athven after our bargain is complete." Rowan waved a dismissive hand. "Until then, he need only remain undamaged."

"Alexei, would you..." Zara widened her eyes beseechingly. "Take care of him for me? Keep him out of trouble? Make sure he's comfortable?" The performance was entirely unlike her.

"Of course, my lady." Alexei mimicked Rowan's title for her, hoping it conveyed his understanding. "Porfiry will be safe with me."

She had a plan, that much was clear. But unless she could find a private moment to tell him what it was, Alexei had no idea how to help. Neither could he imagine preventing himself from throttling his cousin. Still, he had promised Zara. According to the truce, Porfiry needed to be safe. Fortunately, he hadn't promised anything about Porfiry being happy.

The Betrayer was about to answer questions twenty-six years in the making.

CHAPTER 13

*R*owan's first request under the terms of the truce was that his lady Zara would give him a tour of the castle. She rolled her eyes, but agreed, and Alexei gritted his teeth as the two of them walked off shoulder to shoulder, Rowan's charm in full force. He wished he could trust that Rowan would keep his word and not use his magic to influence Zara's decision. He wished he could trust that Athven would protect her from such an intrusion. But he could trust neither of them. Rowan because he had never earned it, and Athven because she had now more than once betrayed the confidence he had so blithely bestowed.

"He's quite a piece of work, isn't he?" Silvay observed thoughtfully, as soon as Rowan was out of earshot. "Fortunately, Zara's a woman with enough experience to see through him. Smart too." She grinned, and Malichai grinned back.

They both seemed to know something he didn't. "Forgive me for not sharing your excitement," he returned dryly. "Why are you so happy that someone we care about is now alone with the most appalling and dangerous man I have ever had the misfortune to meet?"

"You have it worse than I thought," Malichai noted, still smiling. "If you weren't so worried about your true love, you might have noticed that she arranged for us to be alone with your Betrayer."

"Not my true love," he responded automatically. "And I would be worried about anyone. I have every intention of asking my cousin some very pointed questions, but what makes you think Zara arranged it on purpose?"

Malichai strolled over to stand in front of Porfiry, holding his staff in one hand while casually smacking it into the palm of the other. "Weren't you listening?" he asked. "Your little friend here said he broke the Rose into three pieces. And he still knows where it is."

"What does it matter? It's still broken. Nar is dead and there is no force on earth that can restore it."

"But," Silvay pointed out, "didn't Zara say that Athven could feel the Rose? That she had them both searching for it even before we came?"

"Athven has not been precisely truthful," Alexei retorted. "She could have been mistaken. Or trying to keep us here by giving us false hope."

"But why bother with such a ruse with Zara? She knew nothing of the Rose and she had no hope of escape. I believe Athven was telling the truth."

Despite all his efforts to quell it, a terrible hope rose in Alexei's heart. "You are saying that you believe the enchantment could still be active. That if we can find it, it might be possible to..." He stopped himself. "You cannot be hoping that I can fix it."

Silvay shrugged. "Do we have any other options? Any other ideas? Will it hurt anything to try?"

Alexei's hands began to tremble, and he hastily closed his mind to the voice that begged him to believe in the impossible.

"There is no way for it to be fixed. Once broken, a crystal cannot be truly restored to what it once was."

"But perhaps whatever you can do would be enough," Silvay suggested quietly. "Zara clearly believed it, and I tell you now that I can see no other path."

Alexei's eye jerked to her face in spite of himself.

"No," she admonished. "Even if I had Seen more, I could not say so. I risk much saying even that."

"Very well," Alexei agreed slowly. "I would be a fool to ignore the both of you, and I hope I am old enough to avoid falling into foolishness for the sake of my pride. But I will also not take this road without warning you that it has little chance of success."

"Our chance of success will be much greater if we can keep our endeavors from coming to the attention of our guest," Silvay said, ever practical. "But I believe it can be done, if only because Athven is unlikely to interfere. If our princeling told the truth when he said he wanted the Rose, and Athven herself is only second best in his estimation, she will not want him taking it and leaving."

"And it would also be in her interests to have the Rose whole, so she is unlikely to try to stop us."

A smile drifted across Alexei's face. Fool's errand or no, this was something he could do. Or at least he would try. It would keep his mind off the thought of Zara alone with Rowan.

Even as his own memories of Rowan's cruelty threatened to fill him with dread, Alexei reminded himself that Zara was not as vulnerable as she might seem. She was an intelligent, confident woman who was fully aware of what was at stake. Not only that, but she had given them a chance to fight back without breaking the terms of their truce. It was the only road Athven had left them and Zara had seen it before he had.

She might not be his true love, but she had certainly gained his respect. Brave, beautiful, and devious—he would never have assembled such a list of qualities had he been asked to describe the perfect woman, and yet, he wouldn't wish to change the smallest thing about her.

Not even her impulsiveness, or her thorns, or her ridiculous habit of proposing at awkward moments.

"Let's take him to the kitchen," he said, pointing towards his shivering cousin, "and find out whether my traitorous relative has any sense of self-preservation."

Without much apparent effort, Malichai picked up the squirming, protesting form of Porfiry and hoisted him over one broad shoulder. "Scrawny little thing, isn't he?" Malichai muttered as he trudged off towards the kitchens. "I know you promised Zara you'd keep him safe, but does that mean we can't rearrange him a little? You know, just until he talks?"

Porfiry squirmed harder.

"I really don't think Zara would approve of any rearranging," Alexei reprimanded the warrior firmly. "She's far more compassionate than you are." Actually, he rather thought the opposite was true. "But I doubt she would object to forced labor. Until I can re-enchant a hearthstone or two, there is plenty of wood that will need to be chopped."

If Alexei was any judge, Porfiry would find the idea of chopping wood a greater threat than any nebulous discussion of creative persuasion. And the wretched man knew Alexei too well to believe that his cousin would be party to any form of torture.

~

When Malichai set his burden down in the warmth of the kitchen, Wilder was already there, pretending she had never left.

"Why is he here?" the girl asked innocently. "Is Malichai going to get him to tell where he put the Rose?"

"Don't waste your innocence on me," Silvay reprimanded her sternly. "I know you heard everything. Where were you hiding?"

Wilder just grinned.

"Well I won't chop your wood," Porfiry snapped. "And you won't torture me either. But I'll tell you if you promise to get me out of here."

"Oh?" Alexei sat and spread his hands in front of the fire. "Why would I do that? I believe Athven has earned the right to do with you as she pleases."

"What she pleases is to eviscerate me," the smaller man snarled. "And you'll never find what you want without me."

"The Rose is broken," Alexei replied coolly. "Why should I care if we find it?"

"I heard you talking," Porfiry muttered. "I know you think it could still be active. And it's your only chance to get rid of him."

No need to say who "him" was. "But what makes you think there's anything I can do about your fate?" Alexei asked. "I can't imagine Athven would be very happy with us if we rob her of justice, and it isn't as though we can open the doors without her cooperation."

"There's a chance she'll listen to you," Porfiry said sullenly. "And if I help her get the Rose back, she might decide to let me live."

"I can't stop you from lying to yourself," Alexei told him, "so by all means, cling to that hope with every shred of self-deception you possess. The Rose has nothing to do with this, whether it is restored or no. It is Athven who matters, and how do you propose I go about convincing her that she doesn't want to murder you?"

"Don't know, don't care," Porfiry spat. "But if you want your precious Rose, you'll do it."

"Or, I will wait until a bargain is made between Zara and your master, and then Athven will kill you and I won't care."

"You'll be bowing to the bastard prince forever without it."

"And you'll be dead."

They locked eyes.

Porfiry looked at the floor first. "If it works, the Rose will know who I am. It might throw me out along with my… Tremontaine."

So that was it. "The Rose won't touch you, cousin. You're Erathi. If it was going to throw you out, it would have done so before you had a chance to destroy it."

"Maybe," Porfiry whispered. "But it's the only chance I have. Now that I've betrayed it once, it might make an exception."

"If you tell us where it is," Alexei said slowly, "I will do my best to restore it. If you are correct, it will instantly banish you from the kingdom and you will be safe from Athven forever. If you are not correct, there is nothing I or anyone else can do."

Porfiry studied the toes of his shoes, face pale and pinched with fear.

"You won't get another offer," Alexei reminded him sternly. "Now where did you put it?"

"I threw the pieces down the kitchen cistern," Porfiry answered in a low voice, still looking at the floor.

"The cistern?" Alexei echoed, jumping to his feet and slapping his forehead in frustration. "Why didn't you just smash them to bits while you were at it? The top of the cistern is too narrow for anything to pass! I doubt we can even fit a bucket!"

"Does he mean the well?" Silvay asked.

"No." Alexei dropped back into his chair, rested his elbows on his knees, and groaned. "There is a well, and it has a magic-powered pump that fills various cisterns on the ground floor. The kitchen cistern was dug out fairly broad and deep, but because it is so close to the outside wall, they narrowed the access point behind the scullery so that the bottom couldn't be tunneled into and used to gain entry during an invasion."

"Seems paranoid for people who didn't think much of war," Malichai commented thoughtfully.

"More paranoid than a talisman that prevented anyone who didn't like us from crossing our borders?" Alexei inquired. "I assure you, my early ancestors were often preoccupied with questions of self-defense."

"But can we get the pieces back?" Silvay asked.

"We can try." Alexei rose with a sigh. "But that cistern was designed to be impassable. And we could drag the bottom of it for years and never be able to lift a single piece, let alone three."

"Let's go look!" Wilder jumped up and raced from the room.

"Isn't she a little too excited?" Alexei asked Silvay, eyebrow cocked. "I did just say it's going to be impossible."

She smiled mysteriously. "Don't forget that you are not the only one here, Alexei." Her words were a gentle reprimand. "We all have our part to play. And Wilder is a prescient."

Alexei subsided, shamed by her reminder. He had forgotten. But that had never been his talent, matching gifts with one another to create a sum that was greater than its parts. He had always had to focus too closely on his own, apparently to his detriment.

"You're right," he acknowledged, flexing his fingers and striding towards the scullery. "I should have remembered. But I hope she doesn't get her hopes up too far. Of all our unlikely adventures thus far, this may be the most unlikely of all."

"Then you should feel encouraged," Malichai told him seriously, picking up Porfiry again while ignoring the smaller man's vociferous protests. "In epic adventures such as this one, it is always the most improbable of events that brings about a resolution."

"Yes," Alexei said dryly, "and it is always the handsome prince who wins the lady's hand and carries the day. Let us hope that our adventure strays a little from the well-worn path, shall we?"

"Are there other plans for the lady's hand, then?" Malichai asked innocently.

"Shut up," Alexei replied, "before I decide to practice my enchanting skills on your voice."

~

When they got to the scullery, Wilder had already removed the cover and was leaning much farther over the hole than Alexei was comfortable with. The shaft was as narrow as he had feared, leaving room for little more than the pump that ran down the center. There was perhaps a single hand-span on either side. If they could find a way to remove the pump, they might be able to lower a bucket.

"Are you sure there were only three pieces?" he asked his cousin skeptically. "I can't imagine how they were small enough to fit."

"They fit," Porfiry said shortly, glaring at Malichai and straightening his tunic. "I didn't intend for them to be retrieved."

"I told you I'd be needed," Wilder said cheerfully, removing her shoes and sitting on the edge of the cistern.

"What? No!" Alexei grabbed her arm and pulled her away. "I am not going to let you simply crawl into a well. You'll only get stuck, and if by some miracle you don't, you could drown."

"I won't drown," Wilder protested indignantly. "I can swim, and besides, the water in there probably isn't deep. The pumps haven't been working for ages."

"Then you might suffocate," Alexei insisted.

"No, I won't," Wilder contradicted. She pulled away, swung her legs over the edge and wrapped them around the pipe that housed the hand pump.

"Stop!" Alexei lunged for her, but she was already shimmying down into the dark, so Alexei was forced to grab her shirt collar. "Silvay? Do something!"

"Why?" She folded her arms calmly. "It is Wilder's right to do as her gift bids her."

"So we're just going to let her drop into an unknown hole in the ground?" Alexei couldn't understand why no one else was worried.

"For an enchanter, you're remarkably dense," Silvay remarked. She left the room and came back holding an unmarked crystal. She handed it to Alexei. "You can provide enough light for her to see what she's doing. It'll be easy enough for her to climb back out using the pipe."

"Forgive me if that doesn't make me feel better," Alexei muttered. "Malichai, do we have any rope anywhere handy?"

"I've got a bit with my gear." The bearded man trotted off to fetch it.

"Wilder, wait where you are, if you can," Alexei called down. It didn't look as though stopping her descent should be difficult. The diameter of the cistern was small enough that he still wasn't convinced Wilder would fit, and, at the least, she would be forced to hug the pipe tightly in order to make any progress. "I'm going to make you a light."

Perhaps he should have doubted. It was his first attempt at an enchantment using an unprepared object. His talisman had been second nature, and the crystal lanterns were even simpler, as they were intended to be reused. This crystal could still be anything he chose. But the urgency of the task left him no room to remember that he had ever questioned his own skill. He merely held it in his hand and opened his mind to its natural structure.

Years of painstaking practice came rushing back, and the work seemed easier than it ever had. The lack of depth perception in his physical vision did not seem to hamper his ability to grasp the threads of magic and rearrange them as he willed until they snapped into the form he needed and a soft, golden glow brightened the little room.

A sense of rightness and purpose welled as Alexei looked at the tiny crystal and remembered how it felt to do what he was born to do.

"Here." He reached down to Wilder and waited while she adjusted her grip to allow for the stone. "Be careful, for the love of Erath, and don't try to be stupidly brave. If you feel stuck or grow lightheaded, we're pulling you out."

When Malichai returned with the rope, they made a loop and lowered it so that it rested around the girl's shoulders. Once she wriggled both arms through, bracing against the wall, they pulled it tight, and Wilder was able to continue her descent.

It was not far. The narrowest part of the cistern was only about ceiling height. After that, it widened abruptly and dropped to the floor. A jerk on the rope and a splash was their only warning that Wilder had not only wriggled through, but had let go of the pipe and simply jumped into the water.

"It's c-c-c-old!" Her shriek echoed up to where they waited, and Alexei and Malichai nearly bumped heads trying to make sure she was all right. "But it's not deep. I can touch."

"We'll have to find another way to get drinking water," Alexei muttered.

Malichai laughed. "Trust you to think of dirt at a time like this. The poets always leave out the parts with dirt."

"Well, here's your chance to set the record straight," Alexei said. "There is always dirt. Of one kind or another."

"But nobody who is clean and warm and well-fed wants to hear about that part," Malichai protested.

"Which is the problem with epic poetry," Alexei retorted.

"Going somewhere?" The sound of Silvay's voice brought their heads up with a snap. Silvay had drawn one of her daggers and stood in the doorway, holding it level with Porfiry's heart.

He scowled and muttered imprecations under his breath but backed away, his hands at his shoulders.

"Alexei has sworn to keep you safe, but I doubt Zara will care what we do if you try to escape again."

Porfiry hissed a curse and slumped back against the wall.

"Pull me up!" Wilder called. "But slowly. Or you'll break my head."

They complied. One hand on the rope, one hand over her head, Wilder eased into the shaft. When they had pulled her high enough, she handed them a fist-sized chunk of something hard and dripping wet...

Alexei fell to his knees as the chunk of crystal dropped into his hand and he felt the weight of its years and its magic. It was not much to look at. There was no evident beauty in the uneven edges of its petals, no appeal in its random arrangement. The sharp corners on one side were proof of the veracity of Porfiry's story—it had indeed been broken. But what he held in his hand was evidence that hope was not entirely lost. It was only a piece of the whole, but it still sang. If Alexei focused deeply, he could hear a single note of what had once been a resonant harmony.

"That's it?" Malichai was staring at the crystal with a skeptical twist to his lips. "I know I'm no fit judge, but yon rock doesn't look so valuable as all that."

Alexei glanced at Wilder, who was peering over the lip of the cistern, a wide grin on her face. "All right," he said, smiling. "I'm sorry I ever called you a grubby little boy. I'm sorry I doubted your gift. You were right—you were needed. Do you think you can find the others? I promise never to doubt you again."

"You better not!" Wilder narrowed her eyes at him sternly before lowering herself back down.

It didn't take long. Two more trips to the bottom of the cistern and the complete jagged remains of the Crystal Rose lay dripping on the floor.

"Now what?" Wilder asked, swinging her legs over the edge of the cistern, panting a little with the effort of her climb. "Can you fix it?"

Alexei wished it were so simple. "I don't know," he admitted. "I can hear it, but the notes are fractured. It is doubtful that the original enchantment would survive my efforts to restore the Rose's shape. The pathways, though, might be made whole enough that a new enchantment could take hold."

"Then it will be just like it was?" The faith shining in Wilder's eyes crushed Alexei's enthusiasm.

"No," he told her, holding back the tide of sorrow he felt at the admission. There was no time to mourn. "I am not now nor could I ever have been an enchanter with the skill of Nar. And I am out of practice. All I can do is try."

"What do you need us to do?" Silvay asked.

"Keep Porfiry out of trouble, and try to prevent Rowan from finding out where I've gone," Alexei told them seriously. "I will be in the workshops, testing the pieces, looking for a way to restore them. If Athven tells him what we've done, there's little we can do about it, but I believe she will wait to find out if I can fix it. If she can have Rowan *and* the Rose, that will be her goal."

"What about Zara?" Malichai's face was troubled. "Will he try to change her mind as he did mine? Is there any way we can help her?"

"I don't know." Alexei felt his hands clench at the thought, but he knew what she would want. She had given him this chance and he would not waste it. "Look out for her. If she shows any signs of acting differently than the Zara we know, tell me. Unless we have evidence that Rowan has broken the truce, we are bound by it."

"I'm not bound to be accommodating," Malichai mentioned innocently. "I only said I wouldn't hurt them. The bargain said nothing about making them wish they were dead."

"What do you have in mind?"

"Do you suppose the Andari prince enjoys heroic ballads?"

Zara had to admit that, in spite of his reputation, the former prince could be charming when he chose. She took him on a carefully edited tour of the main areas of the castle as he exclaimed over its beauties, marveling and awestruck by turns. Zara purposefully avoided the towers and did not take her guest into the workroom where she had first felt the beginnings of a connection with the once dour and distant Alexei.

It seemed like ages ago, that moment when he had first unbent sufficiently to share something of his past, and accidentally let slip enough emotion to prove that he was no monster, only as human and hurting as she was.

And now she was depending on him to help her defeat the true monster who walked by her side, golden hair glimmering in the torchlight. Rowan's expression grew ever more animated as he examined the treasures that Athven had held in stasis for twenty-six years.

"Do you not find it awe-inspiring," he exclaimed, "to see the wonders that can be accomplished with magic? That such a being as Athven can exist, that stones can give heat and light, that lives and minds can be changed without the need for blood or pain... this is the final piece of a puzzle I have been seeking to solve all my life."

"And what puzzle is that?" Zara asked, if only because he was expecting it.

"How to wield power without discontent," he answered immediately, the fervor in his gaze suggesting that, for once, he told the truth. "What the Erathi accomplished here—this could change the world."

"Perhaps," she allowed, hearing the echo of her own words in his impassioned declaration. "There is certainly much potential for good. But in the end, it seems a very limited sort of power to me."

"How can it be limited?" he protested. "Magic is only limited by the imagination of the one who uses it. Just as we are only limited by the bounds we choose to put on our actions. It is when we let others bind us by their judgments and doubts that we lose our strength and our ability to change the world."

"So you accept no judgment but your own?" Zara asked, suppressing a shiver.

"Why should I?" Rowan sounded genuinely puzzled. "By what right does any other being judge what I do, even had I not been born to rule?" His expression grew distant. "It is hard to believe there was a time that I was genuinely angry over the theft of that birthright. Now I have realized it was simply a necessary step into a larger world. I was not meant to be confined to one simple kingdom. There is so much more to see and do, so many kinds of power I had never even tasted before I left my homeland."

Zara led him into the reception hall and lifted her torch. "But why chase after power? You are young and gifted. If you have given up your kingdom for good, you have no one to rule, so why not turn your talents to other causes than acquiring power?"

"I never said I had given up my kingdom." Rowan tilted his head back to gaze appreciatively at the ceiling and the crystal lanterns. "Only that I needed to leave for a time in order to see that my dreams were too small. Now that I have begun to gather my army, Erath is only the beginning. Next, I will reclaim my homeland of Andar, then I will turn to Vidor. They are a martial people who study the art of war from their cradle, and my goal will be to bring them peace. Once I control their armies, I will turn to Thalassa, and Fren. Those two kingdoms have been on the brink of war for centuries, always skirmishing and wasting their efforts on petty disagreements. With their ships under my command, I will bring the full might of my will to bear on Caelan once more, and the entire continent will be united under one sovereign." His gaze was far away, as though he spoke of little more than a walk in the country.

"And after that, the world?" Zara asked dryly, hoping she did not betray her dismay. Was he a madman, to believe he could do so much, or merely a born conqueror, driven by an endless lust to possess and destroy?

"Perhaps," he answered, either failing to perceive her sarcasm or simply ignoring it.

"But why tell me your plan?" she asked, gripping the torch tighter to conceal the shaking of her hands. "What if I choose not to join you? What if I choose to walk away? Then I will know all your secrets and you will have to plot some other way to take over the world."

He seemed blissfully unaware that she was unable to leave, which meant that Athven had not told him all the consequences of joining her bond. Rowan's continued ignorance was the one power Zara still had, and she did not intend to enlighten him.

"It does not matter what you know, or where you go," he said softly.

"You cannot stop me. No one can. But even if you could, I am not afraid, because you will choose me in the end."

"How can you be so certain?" Zara scoffed. "I don't even like you, and I most assuredly do not like your goals for the future. And even if I put aside my moral concerns with your apparent thirst for blood and conquest, being bonded to you sounds like an appalling violation of my privacy. It is bad enough sharing my head with Athven, and she is not a man."

"Blood and conquest?" Rowan protested. "Did I not say that my goal was to bring peace? It is not violence I desire, but an end to it." He smiled beatifically. "And I cannot think that a bond between us would be as terrible as you say. I have much to offer, and I would never trouble you, either in body or in mind, without your consent. It isn't as if we would be married, after all, unless you wished it."

"If *I* wished it?" Zara snorted. "You have plans for world domination. I'm sure you have something loftier in mind for an empress than a... what did you call me again? Oh, yes—an abandoned, homeless treasure hunter."

"Zara, Zara..." Rowan sighed, then smiled as though she had given him the world. "You really are the most delightful woman I have ever had occasion to meet. As a prince, I have met many, I assure you, and you make them all seem utterly insipid and colorless."

"I'm sure that's what you tell all the princesses," Zara scoffed, flipping her braid and walking away from him, feeling uncomfortable with his insincerities. How could it be that she would rather hear Alexei call her a thief than listen to Rowan say she was beautiful?

"Not all," Rowan acknowledged slyly, "and I have certainly never offered to marry any of them."

"You didn't offer to marry me," she pointed out acidly, before hastily adding, "and don't. I beg you. Men who offer to marry me for nothing but my enchanted castle make me feel cheap. It will only make me despise you more."

"But Zara," he said, following her across the room, "why should you despise me? I can offer you safety. Wealth. Freedom. The world. Everything you have ever wanted, and more. And I ask so little of you in return. I want only to spend time here, learning what Athven has to teach me. Once I have gained what I desire, I would depart, if you wished, and trouble you no more."

"So you would take what you want and then leave me as you found me?" she queried. "How benevolent."

"I would gain what I need to fulfill my dream," he corrected, "and you would be a part of it. Should you realize that the bond did not chafe overmuch, you could accompany me as we sweep across the continent. You would have your choice of palaces once the battle is won, and servants to heed your every whim."

Zara laughed. What a bizarre picture.

"Or," he continued, "a house of your own, far from the mad bustle of life, and no need to spend one more night on a cold and lonely road, far from home, in search of another treasure that will disappear as soon as you set eyes on it."

Her eyes shot to his. Had he broken the truce? Had he been using his uncomfortable gift to pry her secrets from her mind without her knowledge?

"I had no need to use magic for that, Zara." He made her name sound like a caress. "You clearly despised the vision of riches I spun for your consideration, so it seemed logical to assume that your desires lay elsewhere."

"You know nothing of my desires." She suppressed all of the other words that clamored to be said. Demanded to be said. Because he had come so very close. The dream he proposed would once have tempted her beyond what small sense of dignity she still possessed. But not anymore. Now it was lacking something valuable beyond words.

"Don't I?" He moved closer. "Then tell me. Tell me what you most want. Tell me how I can move you to take pity on me, for I, like you, have been rejected. I have no home. No people. Not even any family. Only what I make for myself. Would you deny me the right to follow the path that my natural-born gifts have set me upon? Deny me the chance to make a home and a family for myself, when, in doing so, I might build something of benefit to all the world?"

"No," she answered, but it was difficult to get the word past her lips. They felt heavy. Slow. "I would deny no one a home. But you do not want a home. You want control. You don't want a family, you want subjects. People who exist only to show you respect and do your bidding."

"Perhaps I do hope to control the fate of kingdoms," he allowed, "but only in order to make them safe. Why can you not see that I wish to set people free from worry so that they might choose the course of their lives? And if I must set myself above them as a benevolent ruler, if that is the only way to preserve the peace that permits those choices, what is there in that to object to?"

"And what if they would choose not to be under your rule?" she asked pointedly. "What if they have no desire to be your subjects at all, but prefer the life that they have?"

"A life under constant threat, petty little kingdoms with their petty little problems always on the brink of disaster? Why should they object to peace? What matters to the average man or woman is that they are safe, not the means by which they were made so."

Zara could only stare at him. Did he genuinely believe what he was saying? "I believe it matters greatly to the ones who pay the price for it," she snapped. "You say you desire to rule for the benefit of everyone, but did you plan to ask them? Did you consider finding out what they wanted? What of the people you send to their deaths in your plans for conquest? What of the innocents who fall because they got in the way of those plans?"

"There are no innocents," Rowan said softly, "but what of them? For the world to change, we must change with it. There is no progress without sacrifice. And someone must make the difficult decisions that lead ulti-mately to peace."

"There are ways to achieve peace that do not begin with bloodshed! Do you care nothing for those you propose to sacrifice?"

"Those of us who would rule cannot afford to be sentimental about those in our charge, or we fail in our responsibilities."

Zara snorted. "How nobly spoken. It seems you have not thought very clearly about your grand ideals. You speak one moment of the well-being of those you would rule, and the next dismiss them as an acceptable sacri-fice. Recall that if you sacrifice too many, you have no one to rule over. Without subjects, you will have no one to grant you the power you crave."

"If I crave power, it is only for the benefit of those who must give it up," Rowan responded, shaking his head. "Power must often be taken, rather than granted, because those who possess it do not understand how to use it effectively. How does it profit anyone if I continue to throw myself into the breach again and again for those who will never thank me, only strip me of everything I have worked for the moment they dislike my actions?"

"And yet you still need them, don't you?" Zara insisted. "You are lying to yourself when you claim it is only for their benefit. You need them, because without people to rule, without minds and lives to bend to your will, what are you but just another man? Can you ever be happy or complete without someone you can control?"

He went silent, his eyes glittering. "Why should I try? If ruling is what I was born to do, why should I not strive to do it? The masses need someone to guide and direct them, so why should it not be me?"

"The masses rejected you once," Zara pointed out. "And you decided for yourself that ruling was what you were meant to do. You need people, because you must have someone beneath you. You may be powerful, and grasp nuances of magic that I will never understand, but I do not envy you. What will happen when this road runs to its end and there is no one for you to command? No one to admire or defer to you? What do you have when you are alone that no one can take from you?"

This time Rowan stared at her as though he saw a stranger. His eyes were on hers, but his thoughts were far away, and his mask changed. If this, at last, was the true face of the former prince of Andar, it was both sad and terrifying.

"I have pain," he said, his voice a rasping growl that bore no resemblance to his former honeyed tones. "I have the agony of being rejected, not for what I had done but for what I am." He tilted his head, blue eyes wide, mouth quivering. "You look at me and you see only a bloodthirsty conqueror, but I did not choose to be this. I did not set out to be a monster. But that is what they named me, and so what choice do I have? If they will have a monster, what am I to do but give them one? When they taught me to use my natural-born gifts for myself, they did not understand that I had the power to be the most terrifying creature this world has ever known." Rowan lifted his hands and turned them over, gazing at his own palms as though he could read his future in their lines. "But I do have that power. And I will use it. Because that is what they wanted. That is what they saw when they looked at me. Never the boy who wanted to be seen and accepted for more than just his face and his title. Never the child who felt he had to earn his father's praise. Just a beast, who could never understand why he was wrong, only that he was hated."

"Are you finished?" Zara asked politely.

Rowan blinked and confusion entered his eyes.

"That was very dramatic, thank you. But I think a great deal of it was a lie."

A smile curved the corner of the prince's mouth. "And why do you think that?"

"Because I am not an idiot, and neither are you." She glared at him. "I don't believe you do any of this out of pain. I'm not even sure you've ever stooped to such a pure emotion as hatred. Perhaps you do feel rejected.

Perhaps you even believe that you are shunned more for who you are than what you've done, or that your choices have been limited by your birth. But those are not your reasons." She took a step closer. "I think you do this because you love it. Because it makes you feel alive. You thrive on testing yourself against the world, aiming for bigger and bigger prizes to find out if you can win. Failing only drives you to try for a greater conquest the next time."

Zara was rewarded by an expression of surprise that vanished so quickly, she felt sure it had been real.

"That's a fascinating theory," Rowan said blandly. "I suppose I should give it more thought, but then, I've never believed that the question of *why* mattered very much. I know what I am capable of. All I need in any given moment is the how."

"So just now you are trying to figure out how you can get what you want from me without giving up anything of yourself."

He laughed, freely and honestly. "Yes, of course. Aren't you?"

"I'm trying to figure out how to get rid of you," she answered, just as honestly.

"But if you get rid of me, eventually, you will only be alone again. Accept my offer and you need never be alone. Not unless you wish it."

"Being alone is no longer the worst thing I can imagine."

"And what is the worst?"

"Having no one to love." Zara felt a strange lightening in her heart as she said the words and knew they were true. "Whether I am alone or not, as long as I have someone to love, there is no reason to despair."

"Love," Rowan repeated mockingly. "A useless emotion, if those you love do not return it."

"No," Zara said firmly. "Love does not have to be returned. My father left me because he is weak and frightened, but I choose to love him anyway. I love my friends, who could have abandoned me and did not. I choose to love Silvay, who is quiet and practical and kind. Wilder, who is an unpredictable ball of energy without judgment or restraint. Gulver, who sees what others don't and gives without expectation of return. Malichai, who has a heart bigger than his body and who lives so enormously that he cannot be overlooked. I love them all. And I would do anything to keep them safe."

Rowan was watching her curiously, rather like he'd discovered a previously unknown sort of bug. "You did not mention Alexei."

Zara felt her face freeze and blessed the torchlight that would not show the color rising in her cheeks.

"Only because I do not know what to say." She shrugged, hoping to appear flippant. "He has saved my life, but he has also belittled and angered and irritated me beyond all reason."

"Then you do not love him."

"I did not say that."

She did not know what she felt for Alexei. Could not have said even in the privacy of her own head. But she did know what she had to do. Dread weighed heavily on her heart at the prospect, but it could not outweigh her determination. For the first time, possibly in her entire life, Zara knew exactly what path to take and what would lie at its end.

It was a heavy burden to bear alone, but she dared not trust anyone with her plan. Her friends would try to stop her if they knew, and unless Rowan was no more than a delusional madman, the fate of the entire world might well depend on her success.

CHAPTER 14

When Zara led Rowan into the kitchen at the end of the day, it felt like a betrayal, admitting him so blithely into the heart of the strange family they had built. But she couldn't leave him anywhere else, and besides, Porfiry was already there, crouched in a corner like a brooding spider.

"Smells delicious," she told Malichai, smiling more cheerfully than her feelings at that moment warranted.

"I've made bread!" he announced proudly, "and after dinner I'll be opening a bottle of something I found in the larder." He frowned. "We'll have to hope it's wine and not some sort of Erathi medicine."

"It couldn't be medicine," Wilder protested, sprawled before the fire, drawing on the floor with charcoal again. "That's what Gulver is for."

"And fortunate we are to have him, too." Zara winked at the healer before reaching down to muss Wilder's shaggy brown mop of hair.

Gulver blushed and smiled at Zara.

"There you are!" Silvay came in and sat next to Gulver on the bench, her face a study in bland curiosity. "I hope you all enjoyed your stroll."

"It was delightful," Rowan announced, "as was the company. I am so looking forward to spending the next three days getting to know you all. But where is my old friend, Alexei?"

"Sulking somewhere, I imagine," Silvay answered. "He did not approve of Athven's choice to trust you. Neither did I, for that matter. But since you don't care what I or anyone else thinks, welcome. May the food give you wind and the wine make you bilious."

Wilder giggled. "Who needs wine? Porfiry's face is sour enough to do that."

"Be nice," Silvay admonished. "He can't help his face. He could probably help his expression, but it's hardly polite to point it out."

Something wasn't quite right. Silvay was behaving entirely unlike herself, and the rest of the group was being too cheerful. They were hiding something.

Well, Zara was hiding something too. If she joined their efforts, perhaps they would overlook her distraction and consider it awkwardness.

"Thank you for keeping him out of trouble." Zara gestured to Porfiry. "I was rather afraid Alexei might throw him down a few flights of stairs while I wasn't looking."

"I could have fixed him afterwards," Gulver offered, his eyes on the table.

Zara blinked. Was Gulver sanctioning violence?

"You never would have known anything happened. I'm quite as good with broken bones as with burns."

"Are you saying you did? Or that you could?" She asked only in the spirit of curiosity. Nothing more.

"Secrets, Miss Zara." Malichai tapped the side of his head. "If you didn't see it, it never happened."

"A crew of hardened reprobates, the lot of you," Zara announced sternly. "We'd better eat before you disillusion me any further."

"Will the horseman be joining us?" Rowan asked politely.

"Not likely so long as you're here," Malichai answered bluntly. "And you know he lived here for years. No finding him if he doesn't want to be found."

"I'm sure Athven would disagree." Rowan's face was bland, but his eyes were sharp.

"You want to go looking for him when he's in a snit? Go ahead." Malichai lifted his hands as if disclaiming responsibility. "But I don't recommend it. Terrible temper that man has, and you've already bad blood between you. Now that you're on his land, I think you'll find he's more to say for himself than before."

"Are you saying he's more powerful on his native soil? Interesting." Rowan appeared to digest that piece of information. "Perhaps I shall have to test that theory."

They ate eventually, but Zara spent the whole evening feeling as though she were dodging arrows. The conversation was filled with hints and pokes and barbs and questions that were never quite asked. It was exhausting, and even when the hour grew late, Alexei did not appear. Was he really sulking as Silvay said? Or had he taken her hint? There was no way and no one to ask. Not without giving themselves away.

They couldn't all sleep comfortably in the kitchen, so after dinner they set about distributing themselves for the night. Malichai, Zara guessed, would be sitting up for most of it, keeping a wary eye on their guests. Gulver volunteered to sleep in the scullery, which at least shared a wall with the largest fireplace and would not be unbearably cold. And Zara herself...

"I'm going for a walk," she announced. "I need some time to think and none of you are invited."

"I beg you to be careful," Rowan said, his face a study in warmth and solicitude. "We all need you, Athven most of all, and it would be a great tragedy if you suffered an entirely preventable accident."

"Stop insinuating and just say it," Zara snapped. "What do you mean?"

"What I mean," he responded carefully, "is that there is another

238

member of your party who may feel they no longer have anything to lose by your demise. I understand that you may feel you owe him your life, but the desire for revenge makes opportunists of the best of men." Sympathy oozed from every insincere word. "Perhaps he did not tell you, but according to Porfiry, your friend Alexei might have been considered the heir to all this, and thwarted ambition is a powerful incentive to violence. Especially given that Athven has already rejected him."

Zara stared at him, feigning confusion to give her time to overcome a surge of rage. What exactly had Athven told the traitor prince? Zara would give every treasure she had ever found to pummel the treacherous avatar within an inch of her existence. But she couldn't pummel a cat, and it would do none of them any favors to let Rowan know just how much she trusted Alexei.

So she throttled her rage and nodded. "I thank you for the warning, but I assure you, it is not necessary. Alexei has been quite open about who he is. He has been frustrating and high-handed, but has never posed any threat to me that Athven herself is not quite able to handle."

"I realize that you are unfamiliar with the machinations of power, so perhaps it has not occurred to you," Rowan said, his eyes not meeting hers, "but despite his disclaiming, he may have been considering the benefits of the forced bond he so loudly rejected."

"A bond he could not possibly accomplish without Athven." Zara waved her hand with a flippancy she did not feel. "He might be able to bond with me, I suppose. I don't claim to have a strong understanding of how these Erathi marriage bonds work. But Athven would have to be involved in order for him to join my bond with her, and, as you say, she has already rejected him."

"True enough." Rowan appeared to subside.

Had he been looking for confirmation? Testing her to find out whether Athven had told him the truth? And if so, could he use his gift to tell when she was lying?

The thought chilled her. The sooner she left the kitchen the better for everyone. "Dinner was delicious, thank you, Malichai. I hope that you all enjoy the wine, but I'm off for a while. Don't worry if I fall asleep somewhere else."

"Sweet dreams," Silvay said, with a significant look, and Zara nodded. "The same to you."

She strode out of the kitchen. Wherever Alexei was, she doubted he wanted to be found, so she would respect his wishes no matter how much she longed to ask him what she should do. The only person she could talk to now was Athven. And pray the accursed cat had the decency to listen.

Zara watched and listened carefully to ensure she was not followed, then set her foot to the stairs at the bottom of the north tower.

≈

The dream was bleak. Zara stood in the entry hall, but she wore her own clothes, and shivered in the wind. The door hung open, and there were gaps in the stones overhead. Moonlight shone through the cracks, illuminating dark stains on the floor.

Athven stood beside her, clothing torn, with bruises and abrasions on her face and arms.

"Very moving," Zara said. "Is there a point to this display?"

"You needed to see," the avatar told her in a hollow voice. "This is what will be if you do not listen to my warnings."

"Are you now a seer as well?" Zara asked. "Can you know the future, or do you but guess out of the heart of your own fears? Worse, do you listen to the treacherous words of others?"

"I know the dangers of power," Athven snapped harshly. "I know what men and women will do to crush those they view as a threat. And I know the subtle poison of hate and fear."

"Who do you fear, Athven?"

"I fear you," the avatar said bluntly. "I fear you will make a decision that could doom us all."

"And how would I do that?" Zara asked her softly.

"By refusing to heed me. By acting for your own selfish reasons and denying my request. I might have bonded you without your consent once, but the son of Nar was correct when he said I cannot do so again. Our first bond will never be as strong as it should because your will did not aid in its making. I cannot risk such a weakness again. You must come to see that your objections will only sacrifice the needs of my people on the altar of your own selfishness!"

"I would say the same of you." Zara lifted her chin and turned to face Athven. "Can you not see the dangers of allowing a man like Rowan into the heart of your power? Can you not hear his thirst for vengeance and conquest? He cares nothing for you or your people, only for what you can give him, and in your fear you risk losing the very things you hope to save."

"Of course I know the dangers," Athven snapped. "I am ancient and have seen many powers rise and fall. You are but a child compared to me."

"That doesn't mean I am wrong," Zara insisted. "Tell me what you see in him. Give me a reason, any reason, to trust that you have judged this rightly."

"The son of Nar is too broken, and there is no one else," Athven said firmly, her anger abated. "I must have a strong guardian. It is in my nature. There are certain compulsions that I cannot ignore, placed there when I first began. You were able to keep me alive, true, but I weaken with my efforts to sustain that life. Without the Bright One, I could die, and hope for my people would die with me."

"Can you see what Alexei is doing now?" Zara asked abruptly.

"I can feel him." The avatar's answer was cautious, and her eyes did not meet Zara's.

"He found it, didn't he?"

"He did."

"Will you try to stop him?"

"Why would I?" Athven snapped. *"If he can mend the enchantment, I will have a means of protecting my lands once more."*

"Then if he can fix it, will you at least consider an alternative to Rowan Tremontaine? I have every reason to believe the Rose would not tolerate his presence."

"If he is bonded to me, the Rose will have no choice." Athven's tone was iron. *"I will have both a powerful guardian and the protection of an enchantment over my lands. Why would I give up either?"*

"Because he would use and oppress your people!" Zara almost shouted.

"Between us, I believe we could prevent him."

"You haven't told him the truth, have you?" Zara asked bluntly. *"He doesn't know what will happen once we are bonded?"*

"No." The avatar whirled to face her. *"And if you think to discourage him by informing him of those facts, remember that I will know. And that I do not forgive treachery!"*

"What can you do to me?" Zara lifted her chin boldly. *"You cannot kill me or you kill yourself."*

"Perhaps. But in any case, it is clear that threats against your person would be ineffective." Athven's eyes were cold. *"It would, however, be a simple matter to snuff out the lives of your companions, one by one, until I gained your attention."*

Zara had guessed it was possible—had almost counted on the threat when she laid her plans—but the declaration still stopped her breath for a moment. *"You can do that?"* she asked, letting her fear and disappointment color her words. They were genuine, and Athven could not mistake them.

"Of course I can. I feel the threads of every life that crosses my threshold. It is no complex matter to remove one or two."

"And if I agree to this... If I do as you ask, they will be safe? You will allow them to leave unharmed?"

"I will have no further need of them," Athven conceded, "so yes, they would be permitted to leave if they chose. Eventually, my walls must be filled once more, but that can wait until my guardians are more prepared to form their own court."

"Then you leave me no choice." Zara bent her head. "I will consider your words. Only give me till the end of the three days."

"And do not think that you can rid yourself of my chosen one merely by telling him of the Rose." Athven had thought of everything. "He must not know until it is fully restored and he is securely bound to me."

"If you believe him to be so fickle, I can only wonder why you would choose to trust him."

"I do not trust him, child. Never think it. I trust no one. But I do understand him, and in that I believe we can find agreement."

"Very well." Zara let her shoulders slump and her eyes fall. "I will do according to your wishes. I only hope we do not both come to regret it."

～

The dream faded, but Zara did not wake. She drifted, formless, through the dark castle, sensing the sleeping forms of her friends and enemies alike, until she saw a light.

She drifted closer, and suddenly found herself embodied again, in a low room filled with the glow of a gargantuan furnace. Alexei was bent over a table, muttering, with a chunk of stone in his hand. He looked up and around, until... could he see her?

"Zara?" No, he heard her. Sensed her. His good eye did not seem to rest where she felt herself to be standing.

"Yes?" She wasn't sure her voice would make any sound in that place.

"You're all right then." There was no mistaking the relief in his voice. "Where are you? What is happening?"

"Isn't this a dream?" she asked.

"Yes and no." A weary smile crossed his lips. "You are asleep, but I am not. I suspect it is similar to the way you speak to Athven. A vision, of sorts."

"Are you not intending to sleep?"

He pushed a filthy hand through his hair. "Not any time soon. Three days is not enough time, but it's all that bastard has given me."

"But you found it?"

"We did." Hope lit a fire behind his gaze. "Thanks to you. And Wilder. I don't know that it will make a difference, but I will not rest until I discover whether there is anything I can do to restore it."

He lifted the stone into the air and Zara wrinkled her nose. "I expected... well, more," she admitted.

"Most people do. I suspect Nar chose this stone for that very reason." He set the piece next to two others on the table. "The enchantment is still alive, but it is faint, and I have not yet made sense of its structure. Restoring it may not be possible, but perhaps remaking it..." He shrugged.

"Do not injure yourself in the trying," Zara admonished him. "There is no enchantment worth your life."

"And yet I would give it," he said simply, "many times over, to keep you from the fate Athven proposes."

Could one blush when one had no face? Zara didn't know but she certainly felt warmer. "I'm not certain there is anything you can do," she said, unable to meet his eyes even when he could not see her. "Even if you restore it, Athven is determined on her course. I tried to tell her of Rowan's greed and ambition, but she believes herself capable of control-

ling him. She either does not see or does not care how he will rage when he finds out that she intends to bind him here forever. He will not take kindly to realizing how badly he has been deceived."

"And I would rejoice to see him so deceived, if you were not also caught in the coils of Athven's snare," Alexei announced, his frustration evident.

Desperate to steer the conversation away from a direction that could prove too revealing, Zara changed the subject. She would not risk Alexei finding out about Athven's threats. "Are you supplied with food and water? Do any of the others know where you are?"

"No." Alexei turned back to the table. "I brought some provisions, and there is a cistern here to provide water for the workshops. I thought it better if no one came looking for me. Better if Tremontaine has no idea what we plan, so that he has no opportunity to steal the Rose before I can finish, or hold you hostage against its completion."

"Can I ask one thing?"

"Anything." He turned back towards her voice, his face set and serious.

"No matter what happens, even if your attempts do not go as you hope, do not offer to trade him the Rose in exchange for his departure. I have spoken with him enough to know that you were right to be afraid of it falling into his hands. My safety is nothing next to the danger he poses, should he gain the power such an object represents."

Alexei was silent.

"Please, Alexei, promise me. I do not know when I will have a chance to speak with you again, and I am begging you for your promise that you will keep it safe."

Still, he remained stubbornly silent.

"Can you not see how vital this is?" Frustration rose and balled her hands into fists. "Why will you not agree?"

"I cannot," he said at length, seeming almost surprised by his own

admission. *"Strange as it seems, I have weighed the risk and I cannot swear that your life and freedom are not of greater value."*

"To whom?" Zara snapped. *"I have no family that has not already mourned me. How can one insignificant life matter more than the future of Erath? Than the plans of a madman to rule an entire continent?"*

"They are just plans," Alexei said softly. *"There is more than one way to bring about an end to his delusions. And your life is of greater value to me."*

Zara swallowed whatever retort she had been about to make. She looked at his weary, familiar face, and saw something new... Something she could not identify, something beautiful and strange...

～

Zara took a single, gasping breath and her eyes opened on the north tower room. The blue coverlet was soft and familiar under her fingers, and the pattern of light through the diamond panes seemed like a friend.

Light. It was morning. She needed to return downstairs. But her dreams... She sat up and blinked hastily. Had they been dreams? Or visions? Athven she was sure of. That conversation had felt like every other time she had spoken to the avatar. But the other...

She crushed the coverlet beneath suddenly shaking fingers. Had it been real? Had Alexei said those things, or was that only the aimless wishing of her lonely heart for something that could never be?

But why would she even have dreamed such a declaration? She didn't want him to have such feelings. Did she?

It was too much. She couldn't even begin to decipher her emotions where Alexei was concerned. But she knew she would be haunted by the tired desperation in his eyes, and by the fires of hope sparked by the uneven lumps of crystal in his hands.

Rowan must never be allowed to touch them.

~

Alexei extricated himself from the complex paths of enchantment woven into the crystal and rubbed his eyes. He had not slept. There was no time for such weakness. But his head—and his eye—ached horribly and if he didn't eat he would collapse. There was no time for that either.

The memory of Zara's voice haunted him, and her plea kept turning over and over in his mind. She was planning something. And as surely as he knew she was planning it, he knew it would be desperate and terrible.

He needed a desperate and terrible plan of his own. There were so many factors he could neither change nor control, beginning with the plots and machinations of the Andari traitor. Athven would do as she willed, and, like the humans who created her, was likely to respond to fear by protecting herself at any cost. He would need to be ready for that as well.

The only thing he could change lay in front of him in pieces, taunting him with tantalizing echoes of power, and with the memories of knowledge he had lost. His gift was as strong as it had ever been, perhaps stronger, but lack of use had left him unprepared for the delicacy of the task he had set himself. Even so, he suspected that had he practiced every moment since the day of his birth, he would still have lacked the skill to rebuild what had been lost. Nar, himself, perhaps, could have mended what he had made, but the complexity of the original work was likely beyond all but a master of equal talent.

Fixing it was out of the question. But altering it—adapting the existing pathways to suit a new purpose—might yet be within his grasp.

He cared but little now for the dream of restoring what had once been. At some point in the last few days, he had acknowledged that Erath would never again be what he remembered. It would never regain its innocence,

247

or be known as an isolated land of enchantment. Once a thing was broken, it did no good to pretend that it could again be whole.

But finding beauty in the jagged edges of what remained—that was a task he could accept. They could build again. Find life in the ashes of destruction. Rowan had reminded him of the enormous task ahead—of finding homes and healing for those of his people who had survived slavery and were now free.

None of them who lived through the destruction of Erath would ever be unbroken. Like the Rose, his own heart had lain in pieces since Erath fell. But that didn't mean there was no hope. Before he could embrace that hope, he would have to move forward, to grieve the loss of his own dreams and accept that he must start anew. His purpose might be different than he had ever imagined, but that was no reason not to grasp it.

And he needed to start with the broken crystal in his hands.

This time, he gathered all three together, fitting the pieces carefully along their broken edges, and delved in, probing the broken pathways, looking for a pattern to emerge. What emerged was not a pattern at all...

～

The workshop faded, and then brightened. It was a different room, a different light, but there was a furnace, a trestle table, and tools. Resting on the bench was the Crystal Rose, whole and unblemished.

"You have found me at last." It was a man's voice, gravelly and amused. "I wonder how long it has been. I wonder if you will remember my name, or simply believe me to be a dream brought on by overwork, or too much wine."

Alexei turned, and was confronted by the slightly blurred form of a man, far older than he, with a lined face and scarred hands much like Alexei's own.

"Nar?" Even his dream voice sounded incredulous.

"Ah, you do remember. That is good. It will make this easier."

"How can you be here?"

"I did not prepare a dissertation on the how. It seemed sufficient to address the why."

"From one enchanter to another, that strikes me as a terrible oversight. But you are dead and I am probably dreaming so I can't see the point of arguing."

"Then you are both wise and foolish. This is not a dream. I prepared for this moment many years before my death."

"You knew the Rose would be broken."

"It was Seen. As were you."

"Then you can tell me how to repair it." It was only a dream, Alexei told himself. He could not afford the hope that it was anything more.

"No. Crystal cannot be repaired."

"Then why leave a vision? Simply to tell me I am wasting my time?"

"No. Not a waste. Not if you understand what was done. When the seer told me what he could of what was coming, I was in the midst of my work. I could not change it entirely, but I could alter it. I built precise flaws into the design of the Rose. Baryte is not as fragile as it looks. The stone was intended to break exactly as it did."

"That is why the enchantment is still active!" Alexei could feel his excitement rising once again.

"Yes. Each individual piece has its own note. Each has its own task. They will never again work in perfect harmony as they once did, but even apart they have a purpose to serve."

"What purpose? How can I find it?"

"That is for you to determine," the old man said gravely. "I could only prepare the way. You are not without skill, or you would never have found me. Use it. And I do not mean only your gift."

"I have no other skills," Alexei protested. "I have hidden for most of my life."

"And is that not a skill? You are more than you permit yourself to believe. Accept what has been. Let yourself be whole, or your life is more a tragedy than a broken piece of rock could ever be."

Nar's words echoed his own resolution, but his doubts would not be stilled. *"And what if I cannot save them? What if I am not good enough?"*

"You were never meant to be enough, alone. Do your part. Embrace what you were born to do and leave the others to their own paths."

Alexei almost laughed. It was too much like a story. Perhaps he shouldn't have tried to survive on so little sleep.

"When I tell Malichai I have had a dream where an old man told me to embrace my path, he is going to insist on adding you to his epic ballad."

The old man brightened. *"I have always wanted to be in a song. Though I admit it chafes my dignity to feature as the wise old hermit who merely advises the hero on his way to victory."*

"Does it help at all to know that you have been revered as a hero for hundreds of years? That the royal seat and ruling family take their name from yours?"

"On second thought"—the old man grimaced—*"perhaps I prefer the hermit."*

Alexei laughed. He almost wished it were not a dream. There was something appealing about knowing that the man he had grown up idolizing had a sense of humor.

"I will not fail you," he promised.

"Of course you will fail," the old man admonished, as he began to fade. *"It is the nature of humanity to fail. And it is also our nature to find our greatest triumphs on the other side of failure."*

"You are not very encouraging," Alexei told him dryly. *"But I suppose that is not part of your path."*

"Exactly right." The old man beamed. *"I can see that I have*

succeeded. My blessings on you, young man, and may you find your purpose at last."

～

Alexei took a sharp breath and found that he was still standing by the table, holding the pieces of the Rose in his trembling hands. He set them down before he could accidentally drop them and took a seat to give himself a chance to recover.

A dream, or a vision?

He did not know which one would be harder to accept. But he would never be able to forgive himself if he ignored the possibility that it might have been real. That Nar had truly foreseen this day and prepared a way forward.

Bending his head over the table again, he picked up a single piece and turned it over, examining the enchantment still resonating within, but not with any intention to fix. This time, he chose to see it for itself, jagged edges, somber notes and all.

Some time later, he set it down and unleashed a yell of unfettered triumph. Nar had been everything he believed and more. The devious old man had not only created the greatest magical artifact ever known, he had prepared a new way to protect his people, hundreds of years after he was dead.

And fate had chosen a scarred, cowardly, half-blind enchanter to finish his work. If there had been anyone else to choose, Alexei would have set down the pieces of crystal and walked away. But his people had no one else. Zara had no one else.

He might not be the best person for the job, but he would be damned before he ran away a second time.

CHAPTER 15

Zara entered the kitchen the next morning to the sound of joyous and enthusiastic singing. A resonant baritone filled the room, and possibly exceeded it, from the pained looks on the faces of everyone except Wilder.

And the singer himself. Malichai appeared flushed and triumphant, his spoon dancing in the air more than in the pot, and his face pouring sweat with the exertion of his dual efforts.

"Good morning, Miss Zara." He paused the song long enough to greet her with a delighted smile. "I was just in the middle of one of my favorite Vidori ballads. No one else can understand a word of it, of course, but there is something about the chorus that goes well with a nice pot of porridge."

Zara put a hand over her mouth to stifle a laugh. She didn't think she had ever appreciated Malichai more than she did at that moment.

Silvay was staring fixedly into a mug and Gulver couldn't meet her eyes, but the expressions on the faces of Rowan and Porfiry appeared to have been carved in stone. Wilder was clearly indulging in evil speculation, which hopefully meant the girl was plotting something devious.

"You're absolutely right. What a lovely compliment to the meal!" Zara perjured herself without hesitation. "And did you know my father was Vidori? I'll bet I can understand at least one word in three."

Malichai opened his mouth, clearly intent upon testing Zara's assertion, when Rowan interrupted, his suave self-assurance vanished beneath a tide of desperation.

"I hope you slept well." He almost stumbled over the words, so hastily were they forced out. "We were considering coming in search of you if you did not appear shortly. However did you manage to sleep, cold and alone in such a place?"

"I am never alone," Zara answered, smiling sweetly. It was so much easier to be generous with her smiles when she knew him to be suffering. "Not here. Athven is always with me."

She turned to Malichai. "Please, continue. I want to hear the rest of your song."

Malichai, ever the gentleman, happily obliged, and managed to complete all eighteen verses before breakfast was ready.

"It would be kinder to kill me now," Porfiry muttered, as Zara handed him a steaming bowl.

"I thought you'd never ask," she replied. "Do you have a preferred method of execution?"

He shot her a nasty glare.

Rowan took advantage of the silence to be insufferable. "I thought today we might begin a search for resources. I am most interested in looking for tools the Erathi might have used in teaching children, books that outline the history of magic, or other artifacts of that sort, unless you have already recovered them."

"It's been twenty-six years, not twenty-six centuries," Silvay answered dryly. "A little soon to be talking of artifacts. And I think you're forgetting that some of us here are Erathi. We have no need of tools. Nor are we very interested in permitting an outsider to misunderstand our history and misuse our knowledge."

"But Athven has accepted me," Rowan reminded her, glancing suspiciously at the bowl of porridge offered by Malichai. "I have magic as you do. Would you condemn me to remain ignorant of my gifts because I was not fortunate enough to be born amongst a people who understood them?" He sampled a cautious bite, but appeared satisfied.

"I condemn you to nothing," Silvay pointed out. "I object to you on the basis of your methods, not your magic. There might be some merit to your claim had you come asking, instead of taking. When you arrive with an army and view our history as your property, I have little sympathy for your plight."

"Then I apologize." Rowan set down his spoon and adopted an air of utmost contrition. "In my eagerness to learn, it appears I have blundered into error and trampled on a topic of some sensitivity. I pray you would forgive me, and help me understand how I might achieve my ends without offending."

"You're still obviously more interested in your ends than you are in learning," Zara interjected. "And that speech might sound more sincere if we didn't know what your ends really are. You desire only to conquer and to subjugate. To use whatever gifts you have in the service of your own elevation. What madness leads you to expect that we would help you do it?"

"The same madness that has demanded I surrender my life to its service," Rowan answered without pause, his face animated by the depth of his enthusiasm. "The madness that declares it is possible for people to live together without questioning one another's differences, or condemning what they do not understand. I desire conquest, yes, but not for the sake of ruling alone, rather for the sake of erasing the barriers that lie between us. The Erathi were forced to isolate themselves for centuries, to protect their kingdom from ignorance and hatred. What if the world no longer relied on borders and otherness to drive us forward? What if we saw otherness as opportunity and chose to learn from it instead?"

"Yes, what if," Zara muttered, but to her surprise it was Gulver who answered.

"It's a good story, isn't it?" he said, looking up from his bowl and smoothing his mustache. "But who is going to make that happen? Who is going to make sure that ignorance and hatred don't win? You? When you've conquered everyone and erased our borders and made us all one family, will you still be there in the night when they come to burn my house because I healed a child's fever?"

"There would be laws, of course," Rowan said smoothly. "And force, to ensure they were followed. No one would go unprotected."

"No?" Gulver asked. "I have lived in a land with laws and a land without, and I can tell you it is not the laws that make people treat their neighbors with respect. The law can make them behave, for a while, but it doesn't make them care."

"And you know this because of your vast experience?" Rowan sounded amused.

"I used to keep an inn," Gulver answered shortly, looking up only briefly. "We got all sorts in there, mostly bad sorts, but they came from all over, and they had one thing in common—a lack of care for their fellows. There was more blood on my doorstep than I care to recall." He shuddered. "They all came here because there are no laws telling them how they have to treat one another. But they didn't learn to be lawless by crossing the border—they brought their lawlessness with them.

"My point is, you can conquer and subdue and trust in your laws to make things right. But it won't, because folks from everywhere are good at hate. And the only thing that stops hate is learning to love, and you don't do that under the sword of a conqueror."

"Love?" Rowan smirked as though he were about to deliver a much-needed lesson. "How would you propose to teach such a thing?"

"It happens one person at a time," Gulver said stoutly, shoulders still hunched over his breakfast. "Miss Zara was right, when she sat here and told us we were wrong to isolate ourselves, wrong to keep our gifts from being used to benefit our neighbors. We should have done something, taken the risk, been willing to give up our safety to save who we could."

"And if they hate you anyway?"

"Then we would have done no wrong. My duty is not different because a man hates me for it."

Rowan laughed. "By your methods, you might change one person's mind, or even two, in your lifetime. And risk your own neck in the process. Why not take the ground and then plow it? You could do your work just as surely after my laws had made you safe."

"And how would they make me safe?"

"By providing swift judgments on any who dared harbor prejudice against magic."

Gulver shook his head, and his mustache drooped. "Young man, you are a fool if you believe that. Laws are good and necessary, but they don't change a person, neither man nor woman. No heart ever softened at the tip of a sword."

"I can see that we are not going to agree." Rowan shrugged, his expression still amiable. "But I must believe that we want the same thing."

They didn't. Even Zara, despite her lack of education and experience, could hear the difference in their visions.

Rowan, despite his innate talent for leadership and his staggering ability to read the minds of others, had somehow completely missed the ability to understand hearts.

And Zara was going to use it because it was the only advantage she had.

"Perhaps Rowan is right," she said, unable to meet anyone's eyes as she said it. She gripped her spoon and took another bite of porridge, chewing slowly while everyone around the table stared. "What if there could be a world where borders were not needed, and those with magic could travel freely without fear of prejudice?"

"The question is not the value of the outcome, but the price of purchase," Silvay said, her tone a cool reprimand. "I would not care to purchase my safety in blood."

"But it need not be much," Zara noted. "If the thing could be done swiftly, without much loss of life, perhaps it would be worth consideration."

"And just how would you accomplish that, Miss Zara?" Malichai joined in, his brows pinched together. "With the magic this fellow claims to command?"

"Why not?" She raised her chin, cringing on the inside. "If there is a way to wage a bloodless war, why not?"

"Why not?" Gulver drew in a breath. "To steal someone's will is a violation. A misuse of power."

"But if it is for their good," Rowan argued, "how can it be wrong?"

Silvay and Malichai exchanged glances.

Zara decided she'd done all the betraying she could stomach for the day. "Come." She stood up. "I, for one, am ready to explore. Athven has revealed even more that was hidden and perhaps we will find new treasures."

Without meaning to, she met Silvay's eyes and withered inside at their expression. But before she could look away, the older woman winked.

Damn all seers anyway. Zara glanced over at Wilder, who had a hand clapped over her mouth, probably trying to hold in a grin.

Gods grant she was wrong and they hadn't both seen through her already. She needed to be able to fool Alexei at the least, and if the others turned against her as well, so much the better.

But if nothing else, her efforts needed to be enough to fool Rowan. Even if her companions guessed at her ruse, there was little chance they would ever suspect the full truth of what she meant to do.

The day passed with glacial slowness. Zara was alone with Rowan for most of it, doing her utmost to keep him away from anything he might actually find useful or interesting. She was forced to exclaim over tapestries, enter countless bedchambers, and endure his poking through the tower she had come to consider her sanctuary.

Shadow trailed them everywhere, pretending she was ignoring them, but watching every move while her tail lashed continually. Her normal feline complaisance was completely absent.

Zara kept one eye on the cat and one eye on Rowan, trying to sound interested while a majority of her mind was elsewhere. Wondering about Alexei. Was he well? Was he making progress? Would he forgive her for what she had to do?

As for Rowan, he seemed to glow ever brighter as the day wore on. He spoke expansively of his plans, and grew increasingly attentive to her moods and opinions. Could he know, Zara wondered, what she was thinking? Did his gift allow him to read her thoughts? Or worse, could he be affecting those thoughts without her even realizing he was in her head?

The effort of seeming unaffected through it all gave Zara a tremendous headache. She insisted they return to the kitchen around nightfall, and just before they arrived, Rowan reached out and grasped her hand.

His skin was warm and smooth, and his hand enveloped hers completely. "Have you thought any more, Zara, about my proposal?"

Her already upset stomach heaved at the thought, but she forced a smile. "Of course I have. A great deal."

"And do you think there is even the slightest chance you might consider me in a more friendly light?"

She let herself hesitate. "A chance, yes." She dropped her eyes. "I am not yet comfortable with all you propose, but I can see the merits of a partnership. I would like to search for my father. I would be happy to know that my new friends need not fear for their lives because of their magic. But..."

"It is enough to know that you are willing to consider me," Rowan said, sounding pleased and stroking the back of her hand with his thumb. "This is only the second day. I have faith that you are wise enough not to reject what I can offer without giving me a chance to show you what we could accomplish."

"Of course." Zara pulled her hand away. She wondered whether he would notice if she went straight to the kitchen and washed it.

~

Bent over his workbench, Alexei scarcely noticed the passage of time. There were no windows, so he could not tell whether it was day or night. It had been night, he thought, when Zara spoke to him, so perhaps it was night again.

There was still so much to do. Nar may have shown him the way, but he couldn't simply snap his fingers and produce a talisman, especially not one of such power as the pieces of the Crystal Rose had potential to be.

He had determined the purpose of the largest piece almost immediately. Its task was near enough to that of the original that the pathways had felt familiar and comfortable, and it had taken only a few small adjustments to stop the breaks and make the stone sing once more. It still looked jagged and broken, lying to one side of the bench, but he could hear the note of its power resonating whenever he dropped the barriers in his mind.

Alexei could understand why Nar had chosen to designate that piece in such a way, but the other two confounded him. One's purpose he knew and did not understand the reason, and the other's he had been unable to decipher. Yet it wasn't as though the phantom enchanter had given him a choice. How much had been seen, those hundreds of years ago, that led his ancestor to sabotage his greatest work in preparation?

Alexei would never know. And in his not knowing, he could only move forward blindly, trusting that what had been seen had been interpreted correctly.

Trust. Oh, how he hated the word. The person he had trusted most in the world had betrayed him most deeply, and even if her motives had proven true, he could not simply wipe away the guilt from a moment that had haunted him for twenty-six years. Porfiry had betrayed him as well, betrayed them all, but it did not sting as Beatra's had. And now Athven. He had not even realized how deeply he had trusted her until she, too, had turned on him.

So why did he now step forward into darkness, with no guide but a vision from the past, and the word of a man so long dead he was more byword than memory?

Alexei had no answer for that. Only the conviction that if his ability to trust was broken beyond repair, if he could find no faith amongst the broken remnants of his soul, he would end up no better than his bitter, shriveled cousin. He had lived for years granting no trust but what had been earned, and so few were capable of earning such a gift. Now he was given a choice between despair and offering his trust blindly, with little in the way of evidence, and without any promise except hope.

Better, he thought, to risk what remained of his optimism, to throw himself wholly into this final gamble to save his people, than to walk away having lost everything and everyone that mattered to him.

His honor. His duty. His self-respect. And her. Because Zara now mattered to him so immensely that his honor and his duty seemed tiny by comparison. Alexei could not explain it, even to himself, but the lack of logic didn't really bother him anymore. If all his efforts, all his striving came down to one chance to keep her safe, he would count his life well spent.

He had hoped, when he began the work, that one of the pieces might be intended to protect her. That if Nar had foreseen this day, he might also have foreseen the need to save Athven's guardian. But that did not seem to be the case.

The second of the two pieces, medium in size, was yet a mystery. The enchantment was so complex, it surpassed anything Alexei had seen or learned and the notes it sang were unfamiliar. And yet, he could feel where it was broken and sense when it was made right. There was some hint of form, of shaping, and of dreams come to life. Whatever its purpose, this piece demanded polishing, a shaving of rough edges, until it sat smoothly in his palms, winking at him in the firelight. Only a few more hours, and he would be finished, even if it chose not to reveal its secrets until the time was right.

Trust, again. Nar must have seen a purpose for the stone that he had not chosen to share.

The third piece still awaited him, bearing a simple enchantment of preservation, but time grew short. The second day could be over already, and the third underway. One more sunrise, and then he would have to face the others and whatever consequences had befallen them while he labored over the Rose.

He almost missed the gentle pressure against his leg, and the rumble of a purr vibrating the surface of the table. Shadow watched him intently from the darkness under the bench, her green eyes reflecting the glow of the furnace.

~

"You have done well, Son of Nar," Athven said, her gaze as sharp as it had ever been. "I was right to trust that you would find and restore the Rose."

"I did not restore it for you," he told her baldly. "And I will never permit it to fall into the hands of an enemy."

"Do you think I don't know that?" Athven responded tartly. "Do not

imagine me a fool. I have seen how you look at him, and I have heard what lies between you. So long as you do not permit your feelings to interfere with your purpose, it matters little what you feel for my chosen one."

"And if he is your chosen one, what about Zara?" Alexei wrapped his arms around his chest and reminded himself this was a vision, nothing more. His rage would accomplish nothing but betraying his feelings and he was not ready for Athven to know that Zara could be used against him.

"She is vital to my survival," Athven answered, *"but she is too weak and fragile to be depended on alone. I will always keep her safe, but it is the Bright One who will restore me fully and make it possible for me to protect my people."*

"That is not his intention, Athven," Alexei reminded her. *"He cares nothing for your people. Only for his own power."*

"Again, do not make the mistake of believing that I am blind!" she snapped. *"I know well what he intends, but he has no concept of the depths to which I will go to achieve my ends. He would use and manipulate me? He will learn once he is bonded that his power and experience are tiny next to mine and think twice before he attempts to use me again."*

"And where do the rest of us fit into this grand plan of yours?" Alexei asked. *"You have decided how to use me and Zara and even Prince Rowan to your benefit, but what then? Have you determined the future once you have achieved your immediate desire? Once you have punished the Betrayer as you see fit? Who will oversee the rebuilding of Erath? Who will care for our people? Do our lives and dreams hold value for you or do you blindly pursue your ends without care for the cost?"*

The avatar reached across the table and slapped him. Real or imagined, the blow stung.

"Respect me or do not speak, Son of Nar," she said coldly. "I represent the collective blood and sacrifice of your ancestors, wrought in stone for the purpose of safeguarding your future. I will do as their sacrifice demands, and not according to the paltry judgments of a boy too sentimental and broken to see what must be done."

"Yes," Alexei said softly. "I can see that you will." Oddly, her accusations did not wound him. With a clarity newly granted, he saw Athven for what she was—frightened, child-like, and entirely out of her depth. "Perhaps then you should permit me to return to my work. I will not be finished within the required time if I am much distracted."

"Tell me this," Athven demanded, eyes narrowed. "Will the Rose be renewed according to its purpose? Will Nar's work be fully restored?"

"Yes," he answered, without hesitation. "The Rose will be exactly as Nar intended it to be."

"Then all will be well." Athven appeared satisfied, and rubbed her hands together. "Only trust me a little longer, and you will see."

"As you say," Alexei agreed. "I will trust a little longer."

～

Wilder's mum had cried when she learned that her daughter shared her prescience. The knowledge had been too heavy for her to bear, and the need to travel a burden she had refused to acknowledge since Wilder was small.

In the end, that denial had killed her, bit by bit, robbing her of energy and life until she could not fight even the mildest fever. Wilder could no more deny the urge to be where she was needed than she could have sprouted wings. Which was why she dangled at the end of a rope at the bottom of a long unused garderobe. At least, she hoped no one had been using it. But it was the only way out of the castle that could not be locked or denied by the watchful avatar, and Wilder had somewhere to be.

Somewhere close, she was sure. She would know when she got there, and when she found the person she needed. It was a strange business, walking perpetually into the dark, trusting the prompting of a gift she did not fully understand. But it was freeing too, a truth her mother had not been able to accept.

Letting go the rope, Wilder dropped to the ground with a grunt. It had been farther than she'd anticipated, but no harm done besides the wind being knocked out of her. No idea how she might get back in now. She wasn't tall enough to shimmy up the walls as she'd done in the well.

But that would come later. Wherever she was meant to be, a way would present itself. Shivering a bit in the damp night air, she turned in a quick circle until the pull of need reasserted itself, then set off in the right direction, back towards the front of the castle, where an army presumably waited. Perhaps she was meant to stop them. From doing what, she couldn't imagine, but imagination was no barrier to her gift.

True to her expectations, the soft glow of banked fires soon came into view. The men of the Bright One's army were encamped on the ruins of the former gardens, their tents spread throughout the cleared space before the front door. A few of the braver souls had even remained on the cobblestones, apparently intending to seize the opportunity should the doors open once more.

Curious as to what might motivate so many men to follow a penniless stranger, Wilder crept closer to one of the fires. A full half-dozen men reclined there, several apparently asleep, but the others conversing in low tones.

"...don't understand why we don't just leave. There's nothing here."

"And where is here, I'd like to know? If we leave, we've got no job and no pay. No notion how far till we find another willing to hire."

"Don't it bother you to be sitting in a forsaken hole next to an empty castle, without any idea how we got here?"

A shrug in the darkness. "We've got orders. What else matters?"

"My life for one, you witless fool. If we don't know how we got here, how do we know what we're here for?"

"We're here to fight, thick-head. What else?"

"Oh, I can imagine a lot else. Being eaten, for one." There was real fear in the voice. "I've heard tales of this land, even if you haven't. My mum said there were creatures that could suck out your soul and eat it in front of you, and dragons that could burn a man to cinders."

Wilder almost laughed. True to Silvay's assumption, the Andari prince had ensorcelled the men into following him. Effective enough, until the enchantment wore off. Perhaps the army would not be much of a danger after all.

The pull of need rose again, stronger, urging her towards the edge of the encampment, where a single tent lay almost touching the edge of the encroaching forest. It seemed quiet, but Wilder watched and waited until she heard a groan from within, not of waking despair, but of a man in the grip of a nightmare.

Her gift eased, satisfied. This, then, was her target. The tent of a mercenary who could slip a dagger between her ribs without so much as a thought. With a brief shrug in the dark, Wilder eased inside the tent flap and sat silently on the end of a pile of blankets. A single man tossed beneath them, caught in the horror of a night's imaginings.

She slipped a hand into her pocket and brought out the crystal she had not bothered to return after climbing out of the cistern. It still gave off a faint glow, enough to see that the sleeping man was bulky, but not strongly muscular. Older than she anticipated.

Ah, well, no putting it off. She picked up the waterskin lying nearby and tossed it onto his chest.

With a gasp, the mercenary sat straight up and threw off the waterskin, looking around rapidly for the source of the threat. He made a brief sound of surprise when he spotted her sitting at the foot of his blankets, but did not immediately reach for a weapon, hardly the reaction of a hardened man of war.

"You're not actually a mercenary, are you?" Wilder asked curiously. She held the crystal higher to show the frightened man that he had little reason to fear. All he would see was a scrawny boy with shaggy hair and dirt on his face.

"Who are you?" the man asked hoarsely, shielding his eyes from the glow. "What do you want? Did the prince send you?"

"No," Wilder answered truthfully. "The prince has no idea I'm here. My name is Wilder. And I'm here because you need me." Now that her eyes had adjusted, she could see that the man was old enough to be her grandfather, gray-haired and weathered but not unhandsome in his way. He was just a bit too clean for a man who supposedly made his living by the sword, and his clothing lacked the utilitarian appearance usually favored by paid soldiers. It was worn, but had been elegant in its day.

"What would I need you for?" the man asked suspiciously. "All I want is to rescue my daughter, and then I can leave. All this business with magic is making my skin crawl."

Wilder's eyes widened. His daughter?

"So that's why you need me!" She clapped a hand over her mouth so none of the men sleeping nearby would be awakened by her laughter. "You're Zara's father."

The man grew still and intent. "How do you know her name?"

"I came from inside," Wilder told him. "She is well, but she can't leave."

"Why not?" he demanded. "You got out. Couldn't you show her the way?"

"It's not that easy," Wilder told him, knowing that an explanation would do no good. "The castle won't let her leave." She half expected the man to call her a liar, but he seemed oddly willing to believe that such a thing was possible.

"Then what can I do?" he begged. "My Dezarae probably believes I've abandoned her. I left the valley, looking for help, until I found this wretched Rowan fellow and his fool army. They're mad, the lot of them, but there was no one else, so I followed them, pretended I was as befuddled as the rest. My daughter is all I have. Can you at least tell her that I came back? That I won't leave until I find a way to free her?"

Was that Wilder's purpose here? To give Zara the gift of knowing that her father loved her?

"No." Wilder shook her head. "That's not it. I think I'm supposed to show you the way in."

"There's a way in?" Zara's father scrambled out of his blankets and grabbed her hand. "Let's go. I don't care where it is."

"No." Wilder pulled her hand out of his grasp. "It isn't time. Tomorrow night, that's when you'll be needed."

"How do you know? Why can't I go now?"

Wilder closed her eyes and tried to remember that it was harder for mundane folk to deal well with the demands of trust.

"Just follow me," she said, not opening her eyes. "I'll show you where to go, and how to get in. But promise you won't try before tomorrow night. It's important."

The man nodded hastily. "Just show me."

Wilder led him back the way she had come. There were no sentries to avoid, so even his heavy tread and occasional swearing did not give them away.

When they reached the garderobe, Wilder peered up at the rope. It appeared to be just the right height. "Lift me up," she said. "I'll climb up and leave the rope here for you tomorrow."

"Why not now?" he begged. "What difference would it make?"

"Trust me," Wilder told him sternly. "Magic might make your skin crawl, but it can also save your life."

After she had secured his agreement, she made her way back up, a harder task than the descent had been. Once at the top, her gift tugged at her again, and she pulled the rope in after her, only to be greeted by a flurry of curses from below.

She sighed. It was never wrong. He had not intended to listen to her warnings.

"I'll drop the rope again tomorrow," she called down. "Go back to your camp."

It wasn't as though he had a choice. After he departed, still muttering, Wilder coiled the rope and laid it beside the wooden bench. Later she would bring back tools to dismantle the seat so Zara's father could fit through—his shoulders were considerably wider than hers.

Her task completed, her gift satisfied, Wilder yawned hugely and crept back to the kitchen to attempt a few hours of sleep before the third day dawned.

CHAPTER 16

On the third day, it rained—torrents and buckets of rain with howling wind and flashes of lightning that flickered briefly through the high windows. Restlessness seemed to consume the party trapped within the castle, and it demanded all of Zara's attention to keep Rowan from wandering too far afield in his search for "artifacts." Wilder disappeared on several occasions, but always reappeared wearing an innocent expression that fooled no one.

Having given up on containing their guest for the moment, Zara was just finishing a meager luncheon alongside Silvay and Gulver when Rowan burst into the kitchen, his face glowing and his eyes bright.

"You must come see this," he told her, holding out his hand as if to take her by force should she not choose to go.

"I'm eating," she said. She scraped the bottom of her bowl with her spoon and licked it clean. "Aren't you hungry?"

"Food does not interest me at the moment, and it will not interest you either after I show you what I have found."

Zara felt Silvay stiffen next to her.

"Well, why don't you tell me about it while I finish?"

"Zara, please." It didn't sound nearly so much like "please" as it sounded like "now."

"Fine." She stood up, every motion slow and deliberate. "But I'm coming back here after you show me whatever it is. I'm cold and it's raining and the fire is warm."

She did not offer Rowan her hand, but he took it anyway and pulled her after him down the corridor. It was not a prisoning grip. Rather he smoothed the back of her hand with his thumb, a lover-like gesture that made Zara's insides churn.

"Where are we going?"

"You'll see."

He led her to the second floor, to a pair of wide doors that Zara had been past several times. The room beyond had always been cavernous and empty with a faint smell of dust. All of the windows were dark and shuttered, and given that it seemed an unlikely hiding place, she had never bothered to explore the deeper shadows to find out whether they concealed anything worthwhile.

"Close your eyes," Rowan demanded, smiling like a child with a secret.

"This is ridiculous." Zara yanked her hand out of his and folded her arms across her chest. "I'm not a little girl anymore, I hate surprises, and I'm not closing my eyes."

"Please?"

The prince was behaving very oddly, even for him. Anything that made him this giddy was likely to be a bad thing for her. But, she needed him to think she was on his side, so she closed her eyes after she rolled them dramatically. "Fine. Just know that if you make me trip or fall I'm telling Malichai not to feed you."

"You are safe with me, Zara." His smooth, golden voice sounded right next to her ear, and she could feel the warmth of his presence at her shoulder. "I would never let you come to harm."

"Easy to say," she muttered. "So where are we going?" She heard the click of the latch, then a puff of air on her face as the doors opened. Rowan's arm around her shoulders drew her forward, and she just barely managed not to flinch at his touch.

"There are no lights here yet, but when there are..."

Zara heard something uncomfortably like awe in Rowan's voice. "We could go back and find torches," she suggested.

"No. Open your eyes."

She complied. For a moment, she blinked, trying to adjust to the gloom, but the curtains had been pulled back and there were no shutters on the windows anymore. The storm still raged outside, so the light was dim and gray, but it was enough to make out what had brought Rowan running to fetch her.

He had found the library.

Shelf after shelf, row after row, from floor to towering ceiling, the room was filled with papers, books, chests and crates. An entire world of knowledge lying unguarded. A treasure beyond compare.

Zara knew her mouth opened and closed, but no sound emerged. Athven had restored her library. For Rowan. The castle knew what he wanted to do with it and she had simply handed it to him.

"This is..." She struggled for words. Fought for composure. "Amazing! I can't believe you found it. The others are going to be so excited when we tell them."

Rowan turned, his head slightly tilted as he regarded her seriously. "I don't think we should tell them just yet," he said softly. "Not until things are settled between us."

Zara's mouth went dry. "What do you mean, settled?"

"Zara, you know what I mean." He smiled coaxingly. "What have you decided? Surely another day can't make that much difference. If we tell the others what Athven has revealed, they may feel that it can only belong to the Erathi themselves. They are not likely to have any wish to share. But if we are together, we can ensure that all this knowledge, all this wisdom—this incredible treasure—will never be locked away again."

His face grew more animated as he warmed to the idea. "It is our burden, our responsibility, to see that this"—he waved a hand to encompass the library—"will be available to anyone who wishes to study, anyone who wishes to know and to learn. We could even"—he darted forward and clasped her hand again—"establish a school, here, where anyone could come to learn magic. It would be a terrible crime if such a treasure as this was to be hidden away, unseen and unused forever, because a few frightened people could not bear to loosen their grasp on the past."

Treasure. There was that word again. This knowledge was treasure. And when she realized what Rowan meant, Zara began to lose her fear of the Andari prince, despite his height, his power, and his words. He was no longer strange and unknowable and terrifying. He was really not that much different than her father.

Rowan Tremontaine was a treasure hunter. But his treasure was not the sort that could be touched or carried away. Oh, you could touch the books, but it wasn't the books he cared about—it was the knowledge that was in them, and what that knowledge could give him. He hunted power. He hunted thrills. He hunted the feeling of exultation that came from exerting his will. From winning.

And he hunted admiration.

"But," she faltered, "that sounds like an enormous task. I thought you said that when this was over, I could look for my father. I'm not an educated woman." She dropped her eyes. "I couldn't possibly run a school. All of this knowledge..." Zara let her shoulders curl in and her breath hitch. "This shouldn't be entrusted to a person like me."

"But Zara!" Rowan shifted his grasp on her hand and moved closer. Moved in for the kill. "You have me. You will always have me, to guide and instruct as we find ways to use what we have found in the service of as many people as possible."

Zara heaved a sigh and let her head droop. "What if I wanted to leave?" she asked, voice quavering. "What if it was too much and I simply wanted to be with my family?"

"Then of course you would be free to go," Rowan said smoothly, reaching up to stroke her cheek with his hand. "Though I am selfish enough to tell you that I would keep you if I could."

Zara looked up, startled, into his shining blue eyes, now so close to her own.

"Zara, you cannot have mistaken that I find you attractive," he told her.

"I'm not," she insisted. "Not at all. And I'm a nobody. You're a prince."

"A former prince," he corrected. "I am now as much a nobody as you. And I find you a beautiful challenge I would spend every day of my life trying to win."

Her face went hot. He wasn't using magic on her, was he? He was leaning closer and she still had no desire to kiss him, or to let him kiss her. But should she, if she wanted him to be convinced?

"Wait!" She stepped backwards. Kissing was simply out of the question. "We haven't decided anything yet."

Rowan did not step with her, but waited patiently, her hand still clasped in his. "I decided days ago what I wanted, Zara. It is only you who need still decide. Will you have me as a bonded partner? I realize it is Athven's wish, but now it is my wish also that you come to this partnership willingly, because you know it is right, both for us and for Athven."

"I... yes." She stumbled over the word. She had known she was going to say it, but it still tasted like wormwood in her mouth. "I will. Tomorrow morning, when the three days are up, we will bring everyone to the entry hall and announce it."

"Oh, but Zara," Rowan coaxed, "why wait? Now that you have agreed, we need no audience to witness. All we need is Athven, and she is already here with us."

"She is?" Zara didn't mean to sound quite so shocked.

"Always." Rowan smiled. "Does she not speak to you as she does to me?"

"We can only speak in my dreams," Zara admitted.

"Then let me assure you that she is here and she is glad that you have chosen well. She is ready to perform the binding today, so that we can move forward as soon as possible."

"I..."

"Come, Zara, why are you afraid? Athven tells me there is no pain, and it will only make us closer, both in mind and spirit once the binding is complete. We will be bound through her, so it will not be as close or as final as the marriage bond, of course, though that may yet be in our future."

Zara's chest felt as though it were surrounded by metal bands. A huge hand squeezed her temples and her stomach knotted itself like rope. She had thought to have another day to prepare. Another day to convince herself that this was the right choice. It was the only choice, she knew, but that didn't mean she wasn't terrified of going through with it.

But there really was no way out of it now. She had already said the words, already agreed, and no objection seemed to weigh with Rowan. If she were a willing participant, as she pretended, what further reason could she give to hesitate?

Perhaps it was for the best. After all, should Alexei actually manage to restore the Rose, her plan required that she act before his task was finished. This was as good a time as any. She had chosen her own plank, and now she was going to have to walk it.

"Yes," she said, her voice firmer. "You are right, of course. This is no time to shrink back. I am only nervous, but that will pass. I am ready when you and Athven say it is time."

Zara staggered backwards as the floor suddenly moved underfoot. A rumbling, like boulders being poured onto the roof, filled the air and brought Zara to her knees with her hands clapped over her ears. Rowan did not move, only smiled as if he knew the sound was a signal of victory.

"Athven believes it is time," he said, as soon as the rumbling died down enough for Zara to hear him. "The only thing she requires is what I have promised her—the traitor's life. She will bring him, and then we can begin."

"Wait." Zara stared at him in horror. "She's going to kill him? Now?"

"I have not asked her plans for him," Rowan said with a casual shrug. "He betrayed me, and Athven is welcome to her revenge."

"But... surely she won't just kill him."

Rowan looked at her strangely. "Athven is a wise and ancient creature. She has seen and suffered much. I am convinced that whatever she decrees will be just."

"But does she have to dispense justice in the library?"

The prince threw his head back and laughed. "Zara, I do love the things you say. Life with you is going to be a beautiful and surprising adventure."

The pang that shot through Zara's heart at that was all too real, unlike the smile she wore. She would have liked to hear those words from someone who meant them. From someone she could say them back to.

Alexei's face flashed into her mind before she could stop it. Even in her imagination, he looked commanding and immovable, but also tired and serious and sad. Zara shoved the image away. She would not think of him now. He would never agree with her decision, neither with what she had chosen to do nor why. He most certainly would not forgive her. But she thought that a life with him in it might have been a beautiful adventure, even if they never left the castle.

The door opened, startling her with its suddenness. She hadn't heard footsteps. Porfiry's head appeared in the doorway, swiveling uneasily until he spotted them.

He sidled in, followed by Shadow, who stalked intently behind him as though she hunted something much closer to her size.

Porfiry shot a sideways glance at Zara and licked his lips nervously. He should have looked a great deal more frightened than nervous.

"It is time." Rowan went down on one knee before Shadow. "Zara has agreed that I might join your bond, my lady. We are prepared."

Perhaps in response to her prompting, he stood and took Zara's hand once more. Zara willed her hand not to shake. The peace of the library seemed anticlimactic as she waited for her unwanted destiny to overtake her.

When it happened, there was not the overwhelming landslide of sensations Zara feared, nor did the new bond overwhelm her mind. Instead, the moment she had been dreading passed without pomp or fanfare or pain. The only difference she could sense was a new awareness, an awakening to the presence of a part of her she had never thought to look for—her magic. She knew it to be hers in part, even as it swelled and grew and changed, before settling back again, though it did not return to invisibility.

Now she could not stop noticing the thing it had become. No longer merely hers, the strange coil wound its way through her consciousness, touching the various parts of her mind lightly yet inescapably.

It itched, was her first thought, when all of the newness had settled into place at last. She looked at Rowan, and determined from his expression that his own experience had been rather different. It must have considerably more than itched. His eyes were huge, and his face was a hue rarely seen on anyone who wasn't dead.

"It..." He gasped for air. "That..." On a second gasp, he fell to his knees. "How do you even breathe?"

And then Zara felt him. Athven was there too, both of them blended with Zara's own magic, both a seemingly inextricable piece of the coil within her mind. It was all Zara could do not to throw up the moment she realized that a portion of that unfamiliar coil was Rowan. His part of the bond seemed less complete, more separate. He was clearly not as deeply intertwined with Zara's magic as Athven was, but even though Zara could not read him, could not yet sense his thoughts or feelings, his signature was

276

unmistakeable. The panic rose in her throat as she wondered what he could feel of her?

"She's in my mind." Rowan clutched at his hair. "She's so vast, so powerful, how do you bear it?"

It must have something to do with the greater strength of his magic, Zara thought clinically, and the fact that he had chosen his fate. She was too relieved at his preoccupation with Athven to care much what it felt like. If Athven was so overwhelming, perhaps he would never even notice she was there.

Her next thought hit her like a plunge into an ice-cold sea.

It was done.

They were bonded.

There was no going back, and Zara had won. A hollow, painful victory, but a victory nonetheless. And the price paid for that victory was small indeed—her own future, sacrificed for Rowan's defeat.

The prince was trapped. Bound forever to an enchanted castle he could never leave. Power he would have, but he would never use that power to conquer and destroy. Athven's own power would be greater still, and she was a possessive creature, who would ensure that his efforts never strayed beyond the boundaries of Erath.

He was going to be decidedly annoyed when he learned the truth of what had been done to him—what Athven had convinced him to do to himself. Zara had nothing to look forward to now but a life spent trapped in a smugly superior castle with a bitter, angry prince. It would be anything but a fairy tale. But her friends would be safe. Now that Athven had what she wanted, she had promised to let them leave, just as soon as Zara could convince them that they should go. That leaving her behind was the best possible future for everyone.

Zara turned towards the door, but a swift motion caught her eye, and she tried to turn back to see it. Something caught painfully at her throat.

She reached up impatiently, and encountered a slender, unfamiliar chain that tightened as she grasped it.

"Did you think I was fool enough to settle meekly for my own death?" Porfiry snarled in her ear. "Your precious Athven cannot save you now. I hope you drown in your own spittle and that the last thing you see as the darkness takes you is my face." Crazed laughter escaped him as the chain tightened. "And after you're gone, I hope it tears my perfect cousin in two when he finds your lifeless body and realizes how helpless he is to fix it."

Zara tried to breathe, and was startled to find that she still could. He was not actually trying to choke her. She ran her finger behind the chain. It was too strong to break, too small to remove.

"What is this?" she gasped out. "What are you trying to do?"

"I'm saving myself," Porfiry snarled. "And gaining the final piece of my revenge! Haven't you ever seen silver before?"

Silver. Zara's vision wavered. The coil resting within her felt strangely heavy. She saw Shadow turn to look at her, crouched low with flattened ears, saw Rowan's face turn sideways, and then she hit the floor as everything within her seemed to unravel at once.

"No, you fool!" she heard Rowan cry, but that was the last she heard before the world slipped away from her.

When Alexei felt the floor shake beneath him, he knew his time was up. Whether his work was finished or not, he would have to chance his hand and pray that it was enough. He had no idea whether it was day or night, nor how many hours had passed since he first entered the workshop. Gathering up the pieces of the Rose, he did not pause to adjust his appearance, only moved hastily toward the door.

On his first try, it slapped him in the face. He shook himself, blinked, and this time, managed to open it before he tried to walk through the doorway. Perhaps he had gone a few too many hours without sleep.

By the time he staggered blearily into the kitchen, he had determined that it was day, perhaps early afternoon, though gray and rainy.

"What day is it?" he asked, provoking a chorus of exclamations from his friends around the table.

"Where in all the hells have you been?" Malichai demanded harshly, crossing the floor to take his arm and lead him to a seat. Ordinarily, Alexei would have scowled at being ordered about, but under the circumstances it was probably wise to permit it. The floor still seemed to be moving.

"Good morning to you too," Silvay said, serene as ever. "It is somewhere in the afternoon of the third day. But we are a bit worried about Zara. Rowan dragged her off somewhere around luncheon, all atwitter about something he'd found, and they've not been back. Also, Shadow took Porfiry."

"The cat." Alexei tried to work out how that might have happened. "The cat took my cousin?"

"She came in here and hissed at us, and then stuck her claws in Porfiry's leg." Gulver shrugged, though his mustache twitched a little at the recollection. "She kept at it until he stopped swearing and started walking, and they went off. Wasn't like we could have done anything."

Alexei collapsed onto the bench and accepted the bowl Silvay handed him. Whatever it was, it was cold, but it smelled like heaven. He took a bite. "So we should find Zara and figure out what has Tremontaine's trousers in a twist."

Silvay eyed him curiously. "You've done it, haven't you?"

"I've done something," he said carefully. "I haven't made the Rose anew, if that's what you're hoping. It's a strange story, and my efforts may all be for nothing, but I have hopes that whatever I've done will prove useful."

"Good enough for me," Silvay said.

Alexei had just lifted the second mouthful to his lips when the world moved. A clamor began inside his head, then the table in front of him simply disappeared. Everyone seated around it fell to the floor when the bench vanished, the bowl vanished—everything but the pieces of the Rose and the clothes they were wearing gone in an instant.

The sound in Alexei's head remained, still deafening, and yet not a sound at all. To his bleary-eyed gaze, the walls and the ceiling seemed to expand and contract, while the floor writhed beneath them. Then the fires went out and everything went still and silent.

A faint glow came from the floor where Wilder had been sitting.

"Lucky thing I kept this." She held up a still-enchanted crystal, which gave just enough light to see that the kitchen was completely empty except for the five of them.

Alexei staggered to his feet. Wilder shoved the crystal into his hand, and he needed neither thought nor effort to renew the enchantment that brought it blazing to life. "Zara," he said. "We have to find her."

They went together, by Alexei's insistence. He did not want to risk losing any of his companions to this strange new mood of Athven's. The floor had stopped moving, but the walls still shifted occasionally, and the ceilings seemed lower than usual. Before he did anything else, he led them all down to the Rose Chamber, where he carefully placed the largest remaining piece of the Rose on the pedestal. He held his breath, but it fit beautifully, and the lines of power graven in the floor began to glow when he nudged the enchantment to life. They were not as bright as they had once been, and the enchantment was quite different, but it was exactly as Nar had intended. It would have to be enough.

"What does it do?" Wilder breathed, eyes bright with curiosity and perhaps with awe. "It's so pretty!"

"It prevents anyone from entering Athven with intent to harm, steal, or destroy," he answered. "I wish we'd had this only a few days sooner, but now at least we can be sure that no army will assault us within these walls."

"And the other pieces? Do they have their tasks as well?" Silvay asked, faint vertical lines creasing her forehead.

"Yes, but don't ask me exactly what they are. I only did as Nar commanded."

"Alexei," she began, the lines growing deeper, "did you say Nar? As in, *the* Nar? He was speaking to you?"

"It was a vision," he clarified. "He left behind a piece of himself in the Rose for me to find."

"For *you?*" Gulver's eyes were wide. "Alexei, how much did you sleep while you were away?"

"I promise I'm not delirious," Alexei insisted. "Or rather, that part wasn't delirium. There was a seer. I swear I'll explain it all after we find Zara."

"I'll hold you to it," Silvay warned, as they filed out of the room, only to stop dead before Wilder cleared the doorway.

Shadow stood in the hall outside. She appeared to have lost half of her fur, but what she did have stood on end as she yowled, a sound of pain and anger that lifted the hair on Alexei's neck.

A word echoed in his mind. *COME.*

"Show me," he said grimly.

Shadow led them up the narrow stair, onto the first level, then up another to the second. Her path ended at the wide doors to the library, now shut. She yowled again, mournfully, before the doors swung open on silent hinges.

The library was dark and empty, except for the new shape that marred the emptiness of the room. A human shape, with long, pale hair that seemed to glow against the dark stone of the floor.

"Zara," Alexei whispered. Before he even registered the impulse, he had crossed the space between them and hit his knees by the side of her still form. She lay on her back, as though posed, her blue eyes closed, and her hands by her sides. Alexei felt frantically for her pulse, listened for her breath, and as his fingers brushed the side of her neck, he felt both the flutter that indicated her heart still beat, and the cold, hard links of a chain.

He yanked his hand back with a curse as his friends reached him and gathered around with cries of dismay.

Gulver dropped to the ground next to him and laid a hand on her shoulder, only to pull it back again with a pained yelp.

"Malichai!" In his terror and anger, Alexei almost yelled the name.

The warrior knelt next to him, tears streaking down his face. "I should never have let her go alone," he wailed.

"Just get this chain off of her," Alexei demanded tersely. "Then we will see if there is any need for tears."

Malichai nodded, too deep in his shock and sorrow to ask why Alexei could not do so for himself. With one twist between his huge fingers, the narrow silver chain parted, and Malichai removed it from her neck. "Is that it?" he asked. "Was it enchanted?"

"Worse," Alexei said shortly. "It's silver."

He had been so sure Rowan would do nothing to endanger her. So certain there was time to change whatever Zara had planned. But while Alexei had labored over the Rose, Rowan had made his move, and the result could be Zara's death.

But why had Rowan risked it? How could he have dared use silver while Zara's life and Athven's were so inextricably intertwined?

Shadow appeared beside him, her ears flat as she watched him feel again for Zara's pulse.

"Are you happy now?" he demanded. "Are you going to tell me what happened? Or how you can still be here, with her neck wrapped in silver and her magic cut off?"

The cat would not look at him.

A faint, slow beat under his fingers told him that Zara had not yet left

282

them entirely, but she showed no signs of improvement now that the silver was removed. There was no movement from her eyes or hands to indicate that she was even aware of their presence.

Gulver laid his hand on her shoulder again and shut his eyes, only to open them again, wide and pained. "It is a survivor's coma," he said bleakly. "I have seen this before, or similar, in marriages, where one partner survives the other. They do not usually survive for long."

"How long do we have?" Alexei asked.

"Hard to say," Gulver told him, his mustache limp and lifeless, shoulders slumped. "But those I have seen do not usually regain consciousness. The severing of the bond is too sudden, too devastating. She may linger for some time, or slip away quickly. I'm sorry, Alexei." He stood and wiped his eyes on his sleeve. "I wish there was something I could do."

Alexei remained on the floor, gazing at the woman who had so recently gained the trust he had once thought himself incapable of feeling. He could not even feel her loss yet, only perceive the beginnings of a yawning and terrible emptiness where his heart had been.

Was this, then, what it felt like to love? Had he succumbed to an emotion he had once sworn did not truly exist? He did not know what else to call the feelings that he cursed himself for only acknowledging now, when there was no longer a chance of their return.

He knew that he admired her. Respected her. Trusted her. Perhaps such feelings were the truest face of love. And if he did love her, it was not for any reason he would have once imagined. He loved her stubbornness, her independence, her defiance and her humor. She would never, ever have quit fighting. Whatever had befallen her, it must have taken her by surprise.

Faster than the beat of a wyvern's wings, he snatched up Shadow by the loose skin on the back of her neck and held her before him. "You," he said, voice colder than winter, sharper than steel. "You swore she would be safe. You proudly proclaimed that you knew what was coming and that you had the Andari bastard right where you wanted him. Now see where your pride has led you!" He held her over Zara's body and shook her. "Look!" he roared. "And unless you want me to toss your worthless carcass off the north tower, tell me how to fix this!"

The cat wriggled in his grasp, but he was not letting go. Not until she looked at him. Not until she acknowledged her part in whatever terrible series of events had left Zara so near to death. But not dead. Not yet. There had to be a way to change it.

His own words punched him in the chest and he turned the cat's face to his. "Gulver has to be wrong," he snarled. "You're alive! You said she didn't have enough power to sustain you, so if the bond had been fully severed, you wouldn't be here. It must still be intact, so tell me what happened!"

But the cat still wouldn't look at him, and if ever a cat bore the look of guilt it was Shadow, hanging from his grip, squirming helplessly, her eyes fixed on the ceiling.

And then he knew.

"You bonded with him, didn't you." It wasn't a question. It was the only way Athven could have maintained any avatar at all, even a half-hairless one. "You let Rowan bond with you and then he killed her, so he could have you all to himself!"

With a frantic twist and a yowl, the cat wrenched out of his grip. The floor lurched under them again as Shadow fell, got to her feet, and disappeared through the open door.

Alexei did not bother to chase her, or even watch her go. Her refusal to speak to him only confirmed her guilt. His eyes returned to Zara's face, and the ever-so-slight movement of her chest that indicated she still lived. For now.

Gulver had not been wrong after all, and Alexei knew what was coming. Bonds such as the one between Zara and Athven were a deep and permanent commitment, an intertwining of souls as miraculous as it could be tragic. Although it was rare amongst a people who could be healed of almost any ailment or injury, early death occasionally struck one half of a bonded pair. When it did, that death inevitably claimed two lives instead of one.

The dissolution of the bond between Zara and Athven had left a gaping hole where their lives had become inextricably entwined. Zara's magic was bleeding out of her now, drop by precious drop, and when it was gone, her heart would inevitably stop.

Deep in his pocket, Alexei felt the shape of the smallest piece of the Rose pressing into his skin, and realized to his sorrow what it was for. He had never dreamed, as he labored over its completion, the pain that would accompany its use. Picking up Zara's hand, he wrapped her limp fingers around the crystal's rough-edged form.

"Is that a talisman?" Gulver asked, through his tears.

"Of sorts," Alexei replied, his voice flat, his emotions buried far off where they could not keep him from acting decisively. "It is a stasis stone. Used to prevent decay. Much like Athven has preserved her contents over time, this should keep Zara alive until we have dealt with the traitor and can say our goodbyes."

"You don't need to worry," Wilder said, as calm and serious as Alexei had ever seen her. "The Rose will protect her."

He looked up. The girl appeared on the surface to be the same, but this time Alexei let himself see the peaceful certainty that lent maturity to her thin face. Even her few short years of surrendering to the strange whims of prescience had given her a resilience few adults could match. She was sure, and her faith gave him hope.

"I believe you," he said. "And yet I would not leave her alone."

"I will bring her," Malichai said, and the jut of his chin dared Alexei to attempt dissuading him from his course. "There's no point in weapons, not the way these bastards fight, so I will protect her instead. No one will harm her while I live."

"Thank you." Alexei nodded. "Now, before we go, you should know—

Athven is now bonded to Rowan. This must have been his doing, though I cannot imagine why he would have risked such a thing, not when it could have killed them all. It proves we should not make the mistake of assuming we know the traitor prince's mind."

"You are certain?" Silvay asked bluntly.

"Yes," Alexei confirmed with a short nod. "I am as certain as I can be. Athven is alive and still able to maintain her avatar, which takes a great deal of her power and focus. She must have a new source, and Rowan would never have risked Zara's death until Athven was his. He and Athven either convinced Zara to allow him to join their bond, or forced it on her before he attempted to cut her out. He did not know..."

Alexei stopped. His eyes shot to the woman on the floor, the beautiful, brave, reckless, impossible woman who had...

"She did it on purpose," he whispered.

"What?" A chorus of denial arose from all sides, but Alexei had never been more certain.

"The last time we spoke, she made me promise not to give the Rose to Rowan. She wanted to be certain he would have no reason to leave. She planned this."

"But why?" Gulver wailed. "I thought she was faking when she pretended to be on his side."

"She was," Silvay interjected, nodding slowly. "She wanted him to believe she would accept him eventually, but she needed to hold his interest by making him work for what he wanted. She drew him in, then pushed him back, and then gave in at the last." She looked up at Alexei. "But why?"

"To save us. To save Erath. To keep Rowan from winning."

"She gave him more power in order to save us?" Malichai snorted. "Now I know you're delirious."

"Athven never told Rowan the whole truth," Alexei reminded them. "Rowan still believes he can leave whenever he wants. Only Zara knew that if she left, the bond would break, and both she and Athven would die. Now that Rowan has usurped the bond, that limitation applies to him."

"She's tied him here forever," Silvay breathed. "He's trapped, along with his diabolical dreams for the future."

"Yes," Alexei agreed, stunned anew by Zara's sacrifice. She had clearly made her decision days ago, and carried the weight of it alone. "And she knew she would have to share his exile as long as she lived."

Gulver's mustache bristled like Shadow's back when she was angry, and his cheeks grew red. "I am no warrior," he said. "And I am forbidden to use my gift to harm. But I would. For Zara I would. Even if it meant losing my magic forever, I would find him and I would make his heart explode and his brain bleed out his ears and…"

Alexei felt the need to say something, do something, laugh, cry or rage to somehow acknowledge the depth of courage and loyalty that Zara had both shown and inspired. Even placid, timid Gulver was moved to violence.

Silvay rubbed her face briskly with her hands, then scrubbed them on her cloak. "But we need you, Gulver, so as moving as I find that description of Rowan's demise, I beg you not to put it into practice," she said tartly. "There are other ways. And I'm guessing the third piece of the Rose has its own task to fulfill."

"We need to follow Shadow," Alexei told them. "She and Rowan will have a lot to talk about, and they will both be angry. I don't believe Athven meant for Zara to be harmed, or she would never have sought us out, or led us here. She is suffering from guilt, perhaps for the first time in her existence. We may still have an opportunity to learn what she, or he, plans to do, or even find a way to escape."

"Escape?" Malichai exclaimed fiercely.

"Yes. Now that Zara…" Alexei stumbled over her name. "None of us is tied here any longer." He refused to acknowledge what that meant for the future. For him or for Erath. "I would not choose to leave Tremontaine as master of this place, now or ever, but I do not see what choice we have. And yet, I would know Athven's mind before we leave, to know whether he has turned her against him. If not, he is a great danger even trapped here with no escape. He may find a way to persuade Athven to act against her nature. But," he added, "if she has turned against him, perhaps we can risk leaving her to deal with him as she wills. We cannot kill him without harming her, so I can only hope to find a way to contain him, and then get as far away as we can."

"Wisely spoken," Silvay said briskly. "We should move quickly, and be ready to abandon our possessions if needed. Wilder, I would tell you to stay in the rear with Malichai and Zara, but I suspect you wouldn't listen."

"No, probably not," the girl acknowledged. "I'm needed elsewhere."

"And I should just stop trying to protect you, whether you look like you need it or not," Silvay admitted wryly. "I know very well you can take care of yourself, it's just…"

"I know," Wilder said, with a smile that added years to her face. "And I don't mind."

Gulver sobbed quietly as he moved towards the door, followed by Silvay, her arm around Wilder's thin shoulders. Malichai prepared to lift Zara, his own face still wet, but set in a fierce expression that would have sent anyone who didn't know him scrambling for cover.

Alexei stopped him for a moment, and bent one last time over the still body of the woman he loved. He doubted she could ever have loved him back. Not after he'd been such a beast to her when they met. And when she proposed. Both times. It was a miracle she had ever forgiven him enough to speak to him.

"We won't leave you," he told her. "You won't die alone. And I won't let you die here. I'll try to get you home, no matter what it takes. And I'll make sure your family knows what happened." He knelt and grasped her hand in his. "I know what you did, and I know why. If you were here for me to yell at I would be…" He swallowed a rising surge of pain. "Angry, probably. I would have yelled at you for days, for doing this to yourself, and for feeling like you had to bear the weight of this choice alone. Or maybe I would have told you that I loved you and begged you to love me back. Now, all I can do is promise that we will honor your sacrifice, and make sure that the task you began is finished. Rowan Tremontaine will not leave this place alive, I swear it."

Bending down, he blinked back tears and pressed his lips to her brow. Then he stepped away and allowed Malichai to lift her into his arms. Slowly and carefully, they followed their companions out of the library and shut the door behind them.

CHAPTER 17

They did not have to go far. Their quarry stood in the entry hall, engaged in a stare-down that appeared likely to last for all eternity. Rowan's face was pale, his blue eyes blazing with indignation, while Shadow sat sternly upright, her scarred ears pointed forward, her green eyes fixed on the man she had chosen to be her champion. Alexei hoped she was questioning her decision.

Porfiry was nowhere to be seen.

Rowan shifted his gaze to Alexei, sardonic smile fixed on his handsome face. "How fortuitous. You will, of course, have hoped to arrive in time to witness my triumph. But I must deny you the pleasure for a short while longer. Athven and I have some unfinished business to attend to. Excuse us while I explain why we must all have the ability to come and go as we please. No man was meant to be confined in such a space forever."

Alexei folded his arms and willed himself to a state of outward calm. "Actually, I had no hopes beyond watching your face when you learn what Zara did to you. Or rather, what she convinced you to do to yourself in your quest for power."

Rowan laughed. "You mean when she allowed me to gain control over an unfathomable source of power and knowledge? When she handed me the means to see my vision come to fruition? Or when she signed her own death warrant by foolishly choosing to believe that I willingly share with anyone?"

Only the thought of what was coming allowed Alexei to face Rowan's taunts without dissolving into rage. That and his conviction that the prince was lying. "I don't think you intended for anything to happen to her," Alexei mused. "You might claim to have done it, in order to cause me pain, but I can't imagine you endangering the source of your power. No"—he shook his head—"you knew the risk. And I doubt you respected Zara enough to see her as a threat." The look on Rowan's face told him his conjecture had hit the mark.

"It was Porfiry," Alexei said, the realization hitting him like a physical blow. "He waited until you were bonded and then made his move, hoping you would all die when Zara did. But her bond with Athven wasn't strong enough, so she was the only one affected."

Rowan wore a cruel smile. "You are more perceptive than I gave you credit for. It seems your cousin has a remarkable talent for failure, and his treachery only succeeded in handing me an even greater victory. But take heart. If it quenches your thirst for revenge, be assured that Athven took great exception to Porfiry's actions and responded accordingly."

"I doubt there is any punishment Athven could have devised that would have been enough," Alexei replied harshly.

"You underestimate her," Rowan assured him.

"And you underestimate how much I cared for Zara." Alexei felt cold and grim, and capable of anything had Porfiry been within his reach. "What, exactly, did she do?"

"She ate him." Rowan pronounced the words with a faint tinge of horror, though he did not permit his face to show it.

"She..." Alexei felt faintly shocked, and yet still a little curious. "However did she..."

He was interrupted by a shifting in the floor under his feet. In the expanse between Shadow and Rowan, the stone flowed and swirled. A man-like shape emerged, slowly rising through the rock, until the rock itself parted and ran downward to reveal Porfiry. At least his top half. The bottom half remained mired in stone, and even as Alexei took in the stomach-turning sight, Porfiry began to scream, a hair-raising sound of soul-crushing terror.

"PLEASE!" he howled.

The sound seemed certain to remain etched in Alexei's memory forever.

"For the love of Nar, HELP ME!" Almost before the last syllable of Porfiry's plea left his lips, the stone swallowed him up again, closing over his head with a soft slap before it once more turned flat and solid.

"Ate him," Rowan said, and shrugged.

Alexei managed to drag his horrified gaze from the spot where Porfiry had disappeared. He'd spent years imagining his cousin's demise, but this... "That was... instructive," he managed. He'd not realized Athven had the capacity for such flexibility. Or such cruelty. Whatever end he might have desired for the man who had betrayed him yet again, he would have wished such a fate on no one. "I certainly hope you are planning to take this warning to heart."

"Whyever would I need such a warning?" Rowan mocked. "Unlike Porfiry, I am my lady Athven's staunchest ally. Despite our misunderstandings, we have the same goals and desires, the same interests at heart."

"Really?" Alexei had no need to feign disbelief. "Then you have no desire greater than to see the Erathi people restored to their former status? To see Athven herself flourish, and the land grow rich with power once more?"

"That is part of my vision, of course," Rowan replied smoothly. "If I indulge in dreams beyond that, I have no doubt that Athven will come to share them in time."

Alexei nodded. "Then I'm sure it won't bother you at all to learn that your entire life from this point forward is tied to hers. That your bond with her is both deep and true, and should she die, you will follow her into death."

"Athven is mortar and stone and magic, my friend." Rowan smiled patronizingly. "She cannot die, not with me to sustain her."

"Very true," Alexei agreed. "As long as you remain within the boundaries set by her magic."

"Boundaries?" Rowan echoed. "What boundaries? How can there be boundaries to such power?"

"Athven Nar is tied to the land," Alexei said softly. "At her heart is Erath itself, and her power comes from her people. She protects her land as a thorn protects a rose, and she cares nothing for what lies beyond. She was not made to do so."

"I have no doubt that I can change her mind in time." Rowan's confidence remained unabated.

"You cannot change her mind, because she has none," Alexei reminded him. "Mortar and stone, remember? She is a created thing, composed of blood and magic and sacrifice. As such, she has rules. Limitations."

"And what has that to do with me?" Rowan asked, still wearing an easy smile of utmost certainty.

"You are bound to her, and therefore her limitations apply to you." Alexei smiled back. "Should you step beyond the edges of this valley at any time for the remainder of your life, you will break the tie that binds you to Athven and your bond will be severed. As you did to Zara, so it would be done to you, and you would wither and die before you took another breath."

Rowan's smile faded. A faint question appeared in his eyes, which darted to Shadow, then back. "An unlikely story," he announced, "though I admit you nearly had me convinced for a moment. I cannot imagine anyone creating a source of power that tied them so tightly to a single location."

"That is because you did not bother to understand the Erathi before you attempted to steal their power for your own," Alexei said sternly. "You came to take and to destroy, but not to learn. If you had asked, if you had paused for even a moment to seek the true nature of Erath and her people, you would have known that we are tied to our land. Our hearts, our lives, our very blood sings with the love of our home. When we leave her, we are but a shadow of ourselves, and cannot be at rest until we feel her stones underfoot once more. It is no mystery that my ancestors tied their power to this place. It was the very beat of their hearts, and they would have died to protect it."

The exiled prince grew still, and his gaze fixed on the cat. "Is this true, my lady?" he asked in a deadly soft voice. "Have you deceived me so deeply, and tied me here in the service of your own interests?"

"I have." Beatra Nar had never looked more commanding, or more regal. She wore a midnight-blue dress, and a golden circlet rested lightly on her brow. "As you would have done to me. Do not forget, Andari, that I can now see your heart and read your purposes like the pages of a loathsome book. You cannot hide your darkness from me, any more than I can hide mine from you."

Alexei looked around him. His companions stood wide-eyed, gaping at the vision of the restored hall. Athven had enough power now to include them all. All but Malichai and Zara.

"You have cheated me." The former prince's voice sounded almost plaintive, a little boy who could not understand why his dessert had been taken away. "You swore to partner with me, to give me access to your power and knowledge. You said I was your hope for the future."

"I did," Athven acknowledged. "I believed you were the only one with the necessary power, and the will to use it, and so I did what was needed to gain that power. All that I said was true, but you chose an interpretation that suited your inflated sense of self."

"My inflated sense of self?" Rowan's voice rose. "What of you? You believe it is acceptable to enslave me to your own needs and deny me my freedom without my consent!"

"As you would have done to others, given half a chance," Athven declared. "We both entered this partnership seeking our own ends. Do not blame me if I proved better at the game than you. I have had hundreds more years to become skilled at manipulation."

Rowan, for the first time since Alexei met him, appeared genuinely stunned. At a loss.

"You have gambled, my lady," he said at length. "Gambled that I would prefer a life of servitude to the freedom that comes with death."

"It seems that I have," she acknowledged. "I did not foresee Zara's death, but even had she lived, this would have been a risk. I gambled that you lusted too fiercely after power and control, that you desired life and adulation too strongly to choose annihilation. And now that I can see into the unplumbed depths of your soul, I know that I was right. You will fight me. You will ever seek to turn me to your side. To win the advantage and take my power for your own. And to my shame, there was a time when I might have allowed you to succeed. A short while where your lies sounded tempting and sweet."

"And now?" Rowan watched her intently, his face shadowed, unable or unwilling to admit defeat.

"I have seen what you are, my champion. I know what you desire, and how far you are willing to go to get it. There is much I am willing to overlook, but Zara belonged to me, and now she is dead."

"That was not my choice!" he protested. "That was Porfiry's doing. You heard him!"

"Porfiry was the one who acted, yes." Athven did not appear to doubt. "I heard his words, but I hear your heart and your thoughts. You intended to do exactly as he did, after your power was secure and you were certain you would survive the attempt. And while I understand, I cannot forgive."

"Then what?" Rowan appeared confused. "We remain locked in contention, battling for control until one or both of us is dead?"

"I believe there is still a chance for something better," Athven replied, unperturbed by his ire. "But I swear, now, in front of these witnesses, that I will redeem my mistakes."

She turned to Alexei. "You were wrong, Son of Nar. I can change. I can learn. But I cannot take back what was done. What I can promise, what I pledge on my own future existence, is that Rowan Tremontaine will never leave these walls. Until he has learned to love another more than himself, he will remain imprisoned here, safe, where he cannot touch or harm the world beyond. This I do swear."

"And how will you stop me?" Rowan's whisper was soft and danger-ous. "Your physical form is a cat. You might have been able to swallow up Porfiry, but he had no way to resist you. You and I are bound, and as you have access to me, so I have access to you. To your power, to your knowledge, to your memories of magic. There are a thousand ways I can cheat your vow and you would never know until it was too late. Given time, I will find the way out."

"There is possible truth in what you say," Athven acknowledged, "but I have sworn what I have sworn and I will not yield. As you can come to know me, so I can come to understand you. I choose to believe that we will have the opportunity to grow, to become better than we are through our years with one another."

"And how many years will that be?" Rowan sneered. "It will not be long before I run mad, imprisoned alone here with no one for company but myself and a cat. How can I be expected to change for the better under such conditions?"

And then Alexei knew what the third piece was for. "Athven, if I may," he interjected, "perhaps I can offer you a gift, wrought by Nar himself, to make those years less tiresome."

Rowan's handsome face twisted with hatred, all veneer of imperturbability vanished. "Offer me nothing, Erathi. I will accept no gifts or platitudes from a man who was foolish enough to lose everything he ever cared about."

"I do offer you nothing," Alexei assured him, smiling faintly. "Athven, in light of your promise, to hold Rowan Tremontaine without possibility of release until he might learn to love and be loved, I offer you this." He held out the final piece of the Crystal Rose.

"I thought you said it was restored. What am I to do with a broken talisman, Son of Nar?"

"Take it," he urged. "It is not as broken as you might think. When Nar created the Rose, he knew of our need. He intended that it be broken, just so, and I believe this piece is for you. Even broken things can have beauty and purpose, if you are willing to see it."

Athven reached out, then drew back. "That is a physical object," she protested. "I cannot hold it, not once this vision is done."

"Trust me," Alexei said.

She put out her hand and he placed the final piece of the Rose on her palm. It was bigger than her hand, but Athven gripped it tightly and held it closer to her face. After only a moment, her eyes began to glow *with wonder. "It sings!" she exclaimed, and before anyone could think to stop her, she thrust the piece of crystal directly into her own heart...*

❧

The vision faded, but to the wonder of all, Athven did not. Instead she remained before them, a perfect replica of the last queen of Erath, staring at her own hands as though they represented an unimaginable miracle.

"What have you done?" She sounded as stunned as anyone.

Alexei blinked back lingering memories at the sight of her. She might look like his cousin, but her intonations were entirely her own.

"I merely carried out the wishes of Nar himself," he answered. "While you carry that piece of crystal, you will retain the ability to live as a human does."

"I have often wished to have the power to sustain such a life," she admitted shakily. "To walk amongst my people and speak to them at will, but it has always seemed impossible. My power was used for other things. But this..." She gazed at Alexei in awe. "It uses so little. I will be able to sustain this avatar as long as I choose!"

"*This* is your miracle? Your gift?" Rowan exclaimed in derision. "Instead of being imprisoned alone, I am now to be left with an ancient harridan who has no idea how to be human. Your magnanimity knows no bounds."

"No, I really think you're right," Alexei replied coolly. "I have made no attempt to kill you for taking the life of someone I care for deeply. Be thankful, Andari, that I have sworn to shed no blood within Athven's walls."

Rowan's lip curled. "But I have made no such vow."

The attack, when it came, took all of them by surprise. Gulver, meek and peaceful healer, snatched the dagger from Malichai's belt and tried to plunge it into Zara's heart.

But Malichai had been too long a warrior to succumb to a sneak attack. He twisted at the last second and took the dagger in his arm with a bellow of pain. Bleeding, and unable to draw a weapon to defend himself, Malichai was still far from helpless. His booted foot lashed out and caught Gulver's ribs hard enough to knock the smaller man backwards across the floor.

His head cracked against the stone, but the blow did not knock him out. Undeterred, Gulver scrambled to his feet, drew back and prepared for another stab.

"Stop!" Silvay held one of her own knives poised to throw, but Alexei thrust himself between her and Gulver.

"It's not him, it's Rowan," he gasped out, just as Gulver changed his target, snarled in hatred and embedded the dagger in the back of Alexei's shoulder instead.

A searing pain shot through Alexei's torso and threatened to rob him of consciousness, but he fought to remain upright. He could not fall. They needed him. He reached for Gulver with his magic, but his strength faltered.

"I can't fight this!" Silvay cried desperately as she looked for a target.

"Get Rowan." The words came out weak and rasping, but Silvay heard them, and turned. She was a fraction of a moment too late. Rowan had used the confusion created by Gulver's attack to slip behind Malichai, who was setting Zara down as gently as possibly while his arm bled rivers of crimson. The prince snaked an arm around Malichai's neck and tightened his hold, cutting off a howl of rage from the bearded giant.

Zara fell to the floor as the two men struggled, her limp form twisted at an odd angle. Silvay rushed to catch her, only to be tackled to the floor by Gulver, whose dagger remained embedded in Alexei's shoulder.

And through it all, Athven simply watched, with a perplexed expression, as though she did not believe any of it was real. Perhaps she didn't, Alexei realized, his thoughts fuzzy and indistinct. She had not had a human body before. Even during his aunt's reign, she would have considered it a waste of power to maintain such a complex avatar. She had never needed one. Hands might still be an illusion to her.

Wilder had disappeared, perhaps some time ago. How long had she been gone? Alexei hit his knees and crawled, one handed, to where Zara lay. He had promised she wouldn't die alone and he meant to keep that promise, even if it meant dying beside her.

Malichai appeared to be losing, both his blood and the battle, but the effort to wrestle him to the floor seemed to have distracted Rowan enough that he could no longer direct Gulver. The healer's grappling match with Silvay ended when he suddenly went limp, placed his hands over his eyes and began to wail, an incredibly high-pitched sound of denial and despair.

"Stop!" Silvay slapped him full across the face and the sound cut off abruptly.

Into the silence, as Rowan and Malichai continued their struggle for dominance, a new voice, low and harsh, intruded with an imperious demand:

"What have you done with my daughter?"

All struggle ceased. Even Rowan and Malichai froze, still locked together, as Alexei lifted bleary and pain-dimmed eyes to consider the newcomer. Who really ought not be there. However did he get in? He hadn't come through the front door.

"Zara," the man gasped and dashed to her side. "My Dezarae! Am I too late?"

He was gray and worn, but he had been handsome once. The ravages of time and dissipation had taken their toll, but in his proud bone structure, Alexei could see an echo of Zara's own. She had believed her father cared for nothing but treasure, but once Alexei restored the Rose, he could not have entered the castle with avarice in his heart.

He loved her. And he was too late to save her.

"Who has done this?" Tears ran down the man's cheeks, soaking his short gray beard.

Wilder, who had appeared as if by magic behind Zara's father announced, "He did," and pointed to Rowan.

The older man rose, pulled the short sword from his belt, and started forward. "Then he'll pay with his life."

"Be careful, old man," Rowan said softly. "I know you. You're one of my army, though I'm not certain why. Now you're out of your depth, and meddling with powers you don't understand. I wouldn't wish to send you to join your daughter."

But Zara's father laughed and a hint of iron entered his voice. "You ridiculous young puppy." He held up the sword to the light. "This hilt is silver-chased. I know well enough why your men follow you like sheep without half a brain between them, and it's no fault of mine that you never questioned my loyalty."

Even in the midst of pain, Alexei found that he could smile. Zara had more of her stubbornness from her father than she realized.

"Silver or no," Rowan said dangerously. "You would surely not challenge me while I remain unarmed, and you stand no chance against me with a sword in my hand."

The stone swirled again near Athven's feet, and to everyone's surprise, spat a sword into her hand. She tossed it to Rowan. "Say on, my champion."

Alexei would have protested, but he did not have the strength. He hoped Athven knew what she was doing.

Rowan lifted the blade and shook his head. "I am gracious enough to give you a chance to rescind your threats, old man."

The old man stood loose, sword point angled down, seemingly at ease with the taller, more muscular opponent who threatened him. There was a pride in his bearing that had not been there before, as if his daughter's death had awakened a dormant fire in his heart. Or perhaps stripped away something he had chosen to hide behind.

"I realize you have no way of knowing what this is"—he waved the sword again—"but it seems only fair to tell you. This is a Vidori ceremonial blade."

Rowan looked puzzled. "And why should that affect my intention to run you through?"

"Because these are only granted to young warriors who have drawn first blood in combat with a Master of the Blade," Zara's father stated flatly. "You might not think it to see me now, but I was born and raised a warrior. No one hands you one of these for playing at swords. They are a rite of passage and a sign of strength."

Alexei had heard of some of the more violent Vidori customs and rather thought Zara's father was downplaying the truth. A man who carried a ceremonial blade had to have proven himself in their brutal school of war. A man who carried one with a silver-chased hilt and rubies in the pommel...

Was either a prince of Vidor or had robbed a prince of Vidor's tomb. Considering who he was dealing with... The only chance Zara's father had was for Rowan to believe his bluff.

But it seemed the Andari prince had been thwarted too many times that day. He did not pause to verbally take up the challenge, but lifted his sword and, with a vicious shout, thrust straight for the old man's heart.

Alexei's own heart nearly stopped. He could not bear to see Zara lose her father, even if she would never know what had happened.

But the old man moved, faster than anyone would have thought possible. He did not shift his feet, or duck, or even try to guard, merely brought his sword up and slapped Rowan's aside.

The former prince stumbled, then recovered, and whirled to face his adversary. His immaculate golden hair appeared a trifle awry. "You were lucky. I won't be granting any last requests, so if you have anything you want to say before you die, say it now."

"You're a lousy swordsman?" Zara's father quipped. "You should have paid more attention to your instructor? Or, better yet: your footwork stinks. A Vidori child with a wooden blade could have executed that thrust better than you."

A hand on his shoulder interrupted Alexei's appreciation of the man's nerve. Swordsman or not, he knew how to put on a show.

"Gulver is going to heal your wound," Silvay whispered in his ear. "Quick, while they are distracted."

Alexei turned, and saw Gulver hovering three strides away, quivering and hiding his face in his hands.

"I can't," he said softly. "I have broken my vow, and I can no longer be a healer."

A clang of metal drew Alexei's attention back to the fight. Swords crossed, the two men stood eye to eye and toe to toe, but neither would give ground.

"You can, and you will!" Silvay snapped quietly. "You were under Rowan's control, and if you think we don't know that, you're a bigger fool than... than him!" She flung a hand out to point at Rowan. "Now get over here and do what you are called to do!"

Gulver lacked both the conviction and the strength of will to resist her. He stumbled over, and laid his hands on Alexei's shoulder, wincing as he drew out the dagger he had placed there himself. "I am so sorry," he babbled. "I never meant to hurt anyone..."

The heat of his magic seared through skin and muscle and bone, and Alexei hissed as it knit his flesh back together.

There was a shout as the swordsmen broke apart. Zara's father still stood in the exact spot he had begun, sword point low, not even breathing hard.

"I grow tired of your posturing," he complained. "Are you going to kill me or not? Because I am certainly going to kill you if you don't."

Rowan struck for a third time, and it was over almost before it began. A blur of the older man's weapon, and Rowan's sword went flying out of his hand to spin across the floor until it hit the bottom of the stairs with a clunk. Rowan himself was abruptly leveled by an ankle sweep, which snapped his head hard enough onto the stone floor that he fell instantly unconscious. The ceremonial sword, the one Zara's father had most emphatically *not* stolen from anyone, rested at the defeated prince's throat.

Wilder clapped enthusiastically. "Could you do it again?" she begged.

"Not after he's dead," the older man growled, shifting forward as if to lean into the hilt of his weapon.

"No," Alexei gasped hoarsely, scrambling to his feet, holding his newly healed arm. "You deserve your revenge, but please do not kill him."

"Did he or did he not kill my daughter?" Zara's father demanded.

"No," Alexei was forced to admit. "She is not yet dead."

Her father threw his sword aside and dropped to the ground by Zara's head. "Then why is she lying here? Why has no one helped her? I saw what that man just did to your shoulder. Can he not do the same for her?"

"I am sorry." Athven interjected, moving at last to place herself across Zara's body from her questioner. "Her fate must be laid to my account. When I ejected you from my halls, I thought only to preserve my life, and in doing so have sacrificed hers. It was never my intention that she be harmed. She should have lived a long and peaceful life, and her loss is my greatest regret."

"You? Eject me? Who are you?" Zara's father demanded.

"I am Athven," she replied serenely. "These are my walls, and even this floor is a part of me. What you see is my human form, but I am ancient and powerful and the castle is my true self."

The old treasure hunter went ashen. "That was you?" He turned slightly red, no doubt with the memory of why he had first entered that valley. "And even you can do nothing? How was she harmed?"

"She entered into a magical bond with me. Or rather, a magical bond that I forced upon her," the avatar confessed. "That bond was severed, and its severing created a tear, of sorts, in Zara's magic, which is bleeding out. When it is gone…" She lowered her head.

Silence reigned, broken only by a ragged sigh from Zara's father. "I did not know…" he began, pausing to brush a lock of white hair from his daughter's forehead. "She must have had her magic from her mother," he admitted, to Alexei's surprise. "We never spoke of it. Leandra chose to lay it aside along with her past, so I had no idea Zara had it too."

Alexei looked down at Zara's face, still peaceful and undisturbed by the violence that had played itself out around her. Somehow, though the rest of her body was limp, she still held the piece of crystal, her fingers curled around it as though she would never let go.

Never let go.

"Athven." Alexei whirled to face the avatar. "If there is a… a gap, where your bond used to be, what if it could be filled with something? Could she use a talisman, as you have, to block that hole and give her magic back?"

"She is human, Son of Nar," Athven said sadly. "She cannot absorb the crystal as I did. She can only absorb another's magic, and it would simply bleed out as her own has…" Athven broke off and looked thoughtful.

"There is one thing."

"What?" Alexei almost screamed in his frustration at her hesitance. "Athven, if there is any way to save her, you must tell us. We cannot simply let her die if there is a chance."

Zara's father fixed him with a burning, still-wet gaze. "And what is my daughter to you?" he demanded.

Alexei drew in a breath to answer and held it. What was she? "Everything," he said.

"Then take her hand," Athven said.

"Why?" he asked, even as he did so. Her cool fingers rested lightly in his.

"Do you love her?" Athven asked shrewdly.

"Yes." He did not even hesitate.

"Then marry her."

"What!?" Shock struck him. "Athven, that is not a thing to be done without her consent. And you are asking me to..."

"Yes," Athven acknowledged with a solemn nod. "I am asking you to risk your life to save hers. I believe there is a chance that if you bond with her, it may heal the place where our bond was torn. If I am wrong, and she dies, you will very likely die with her."

"Alexei, wait." Silvay appeared pale and shaken as she rose to her feet after knotting a cord securely around Rowan's wrists and ankles. "You must be sure. I, too, wish to save Zara if it can be done, but Erath needs you as well. How will we rebuild without a Nar to lead the way?" She took his arm and looked deeply into his eyes. "I have not been able to See past this moment. Athven is lost to us now, and if we lose you as well, we lose hope. Do not do this unless you are fully convinced it can work."

Malichai struggled to his feet, shaking off Gulver who had just finished healing the deep gash in his arm. "And I say, it is the right thing to do." The big man was crying again. "I knew this would be a tale for the ages, and I was right. You can save her. The story couldn't end any other way."

Wilder appeared by Zara's father's shoulder. "It is for you to choose," she said.

"I want to be worthy of her," Alexei said softly. "She was willing to sacrifice everything to save a people she had never met. I would do no less to give her a chance at the one thing she wanted most." He looked at her father. "But this is not a thing that can be undone. I fear that even if she lives, she will be angry to find that I have tied her to me forever. I cannot imagine that she cares for me. I was..." He grimaced. "Arrogant. Unbearably so."

"She followed me on countless roads when all she wanted was a home," Zara's father acknowledged. "And she still loved me. I can't imagine why. But her heart is big, and I believe she will forgive you."

"She has a crown," Wilder added. "In her aura. And it looks just like yours."

A crown? Alexei didn't care about crowns. He cared about Zara. About setting her free and seeing her scowl at him one more time. Was it selfish of him to want this? Or did he owe her every possible chance at life?

"If you're quite finished being noble," Athven said dryly, "I shared her mind for some time and I have reason to believe that your attempt to save her life would not be unwelcome."

Alexei's eyes locked with hers. "You mean..."

"I mean only that you should get on with it," she snapped. "How many times does a girl have to propose for you to say yes?"

He caught himself midway between a laugh and a sob. "I wish it had been once more," he said. "But perhaps I will still be able to say it."

He heard a brief gasp from Gulver, but it disappeared into the background as he took Zara's hand between both of his and focused intently on his gift. He knew, in theory, how the marriage bond should work. It was a braid, of sorts, composed of her magic and his, tied together with the strand of their unique history together, composed of trust, respect, and mutual affection. He would have to supply the memories, and manipulate the three strands without her help.

Perhaps, had he been anyone else, the task would have been over before it began. But Alexei had spent years in the punishing school of his craft, and he was driven by a desperate desire to save the woman he loved.

Strand by strand, he grasped at the delicate lavender tendrils of her magic and plaited them together with the shimmering bronze of his own. And between them he placed the cord of his memories of her—her strength, her determination, her courage, her sharp-edged humor and her refusal to give up. He wove them with his love and his admiration and his determination to see her well and happy once more. And when the strands tried to slip away, he bound them by sheer will.

Bit by bit, the bond formed and gained in strength. Strand by strand, it began to glow with the love and magic he poured into it as he worked. And when at last he reached the end and knotted the cord, sealing his work in place, it shone with an inner fire that filled him with awe even as he released it and pulled back.

He had done it. But there was no way yet to know whether his desperate attempt would save Zara's life or doom his own.

CHAPTER 18

Zara could feel nothing but her own breathing. The air in her lungs seemed to have a life of its own, and it was loud as it rasped and rushed, in and out. She could hear voices, but those were as distant as a dream, and almost as unlikely. She heard Alexei say that he loved her, and Athven say she was sorry, and she even heard her father threatening to kill someone. Those might happen in her dreams, but never when she was awake.

Then she felt something new, a warmth and life that filled the cold darkness at her core and spread, from her heart to the very tips of her fingers. She flexed them experimentally and opened her eyes.

She was lying on the floor. It was cold and hard and her head hurt. There were faces above her, but they were blurry and no one spoke.

"Am I dead?" she asked.

"No, love," her father said. "I came back for you."

Her father? She must be dead. He wasn't at the castle. But that would mean he was dead too, and that would make her sad. She blinked a few times to clear her eyes and the faces grew more distinct.

It certainly looked like her father. And Athven. But Athven was gone.

"You aren't there anymore," Zara said to the avatar, a bit plaintively. "That means I died. You said when you were gone, I would die."

"You nearly did," Athven said, and though the avatars of enchanted castles probably did not stoop to tears, neither did she sound entirely unmoved.

Zara's gaze shifted once more and landed on... Alexei. He looked as if a wind could have knocked him over, even though the wind outside had ceased to buffet the walls and the rain no longer fell and you could have heard a whisper from across the hall.

He looked terrified.

"Alexei," she said, "will you tell me the truth?" He would, she knew. He always had.

"You're alive," he said softly, one tear trailing slowly down his cheek, and Zara realized the warm pressure against her fingers was him. His thumb stroked the back of her hand slowly, gently, as though it were precious and fragile, and the caress felt nothing like Rowan's.

"Well there's no need to look so upset about it," she told him, trying to smile. What could he be terrified of, if she wasn't dead?

"How do you feel?" Her father's face appeared once again on the other side of her.

Zara considered the question. There was a spot on the back of her head that felt as if it were bruised, and a matching spot on her hip. She wiggled her fingers and toes and then sat up. A collective gasp surrounded her, as though she actually had been dead and risen again. Silvay, Gulver, Wilder and Malichai stood around, gazing at her with wary excitement.

"It's never been done before," Gulver said in an awed whisper. "We didn't even know it was possible."

Malichai burst into happy tears. "I hope you'll forgive me, Miss Zara, for dropping you. I swore you'd come to no harm, but yon bastard attacked me and I couldn't keep hold."

What bastard? Zara followed the motion of his arm and saw the supine body of Rowan, limp and bound, lying a few paces away.

She shot a glance at Athven.

"He did not have permission to hurt you," Athven said sternly. "He will learn."

Zara thought about that. "Wait, if I'm not dead, and not dreaming, how are you..."

Athven smiled, the first genuinely happy smile Zara had ever seen on her. "I have been given a gift, by Nar himself, and by his descendent—the ability to remain embodied as I choose, without draining myself of power. I am looking forward to learning how to live as humans do."

"At least until she has to use the privy in the middle of winter," Malichai muttered under his breath.

Everyone laughed, breaking the tension that had gripped the room since Zara opened her eyes. Everyone except Athven, who looked puzzled by the sound.

"Perhaps," Silvay suggested, "we might move to the kitchens. Malichai could prepare us something to eat while we discuss the future?"

A chorus of agreement went up and there was a general movement in that direction. Malichai paused to sling Rowan over his shoulder, then strode off whistling cheerfully.

In a matter of moments, the entry hall was empty but for Zara and Alexei, and, considering the looks on her friends' faces as they left, Zara suspected it was by design.

"All right," she said, resting her elbows on her knees and raising an eyebrow suspiciously. "What's the bad news they left you here to tell me?"

He did not meet her eyes. "Do you think you could walk?"

She groaned, but accepted his hand and rose ungracefully from the floor. "Where are we going?"

"The tower."

"So it's to be death by stairs?"

Alexei let go her hand. "We could try my workshop instead."

Zara was curious about the place where he worked his magic, but the tower still felt like the safest part of the castle. "I'll manage," she said. "Lead on."

Curiously, she felt more energetic than usual, and was not in the least bit tired when they reached the room at the top. "Apparently being unconscious is healthy for me," she noted. "I feel amazing. Lighter, even."

Alexei still would not look at her, even to comment on her recovery, and Zara knew the news must be even worse than she'd anticipated.

"You might as well just tell me. I know no one else has died, because I saw everyone downstairs. Did Porfiry get away? Is that it?"

"No." Alexei's expression grew haunted. "He certainly did not. Athven... took care of him."

"How?"

"Trust me"—Alexei actually shuddered—"you're better off not knowing."

"So if that isn't it, what are you so terrified of me finding out? You've looked ill ever since I woke up."

"Zara," he began hesitantly, "Athven didn't lie to you. When Porfiry put that silver chain around your neck, it cut off your magic. Your bond to Athven was broken."

"But she was already bonded to Rowan, so she survived," Zara said, then snapped her mouth shut and flushed as she realized what she'd admitted to.

"I know what you did," Alexei told her. "I even know why. But that's not what we need to talk about."

"It's not?" Zara thought he seemed to be taking it rather calmly. "I surrendered your home into the hands of your greatest enemy. I thought you'd be furious!"

"Furious that it nearly killed you," he said with a scowl. "But as I said, I know why you did it. And when you nearly died, Athven finally allowed that perhaps she'd made a mistake. She's promised to keep Rowan imprisoned here until he no longer cares for conquest."

"That could be forever," Zara pointed out.

"Forever is likely to be a lot longer for her than for Rowan."

"But your castle!" Zara protested. "That means you won't be able to live here, and you'll have no way to rebuild Erath."

"There is more to rebuilding my land than that," Alexei reassured her. "So Athven is lost to us. Perhaps it is for the best. In the past, we leaned so heavily on her, and on the protection she provided, that we forgot about the world. You were right, you know. We turned inward, and our ignorance was not to our credit."

"So where will you go?" Zara felt a quick pang, that their parting was nearly at hand. Her father had come. She was no longer tied to Athven, or to Erath, and would be free to leave. She should be ecstatic that she would not be compelled to remain, but the thought of departure gave her no pleasure. Not when she knew that he was staying.

"Zara, when I said Athven didn't lie, I meant it. She told you if the bond was cut, you would die."

"I feel like you're working your way up to something when you should just state it plainly," she insisted. "So I died. Am I some sort of horrible undead thing now?"

"No!" He scrubbed a hand across his forehead. "I... Zara, look inside. I'm too much of a coward to even say it."

Perhaps those last few days—working on the Rose without food or sleep—had unhinged him. But there was no harm in humoring him, so Zara shut her eyes and felt for the place where her bond with Athven had been. That dark, heavy coil was gone, as she expected, but its place was not empty. An intricate braid of power rested there instead, winding through the darkest places of her being, glowing with an inner fire and warmth that begged to be embraced. Where the other bond had been strange and unknowable, this one seemed somehow familiar. Zara could see the strands that composed it, strands of glowing bronze and ethereal lavender, mixed with something else that felt, somehow, like music.

She opened her eyes. "What is it?" she breathed. "It's beautiful. Did Gulver heal me?"

"No." His voice shook. "Zara, it was me. I did it. And I didn't ask for your permission, which I should have, but there was no time. You were dying, and Athven said it might save your life."

"And you think I will be angry with you for saving my life?" Zara asked incredulously. "How could you think I would be so ungrateful?"

"Because I didn't just save your life," Alexei said desperately, meeting her eyes at last. "The bond you lost had to be replaced. Look again."

Utterly confused, Zara did as he asked. But this time, she gave in to temptation and reached out with her mind to touch a glowing bronze strand. The moment she did so, a torrent of thoughts and memories hit her, sights and sounds and feelings that were not hers, and yet now they were. An emotion blazed through her, something fierce and wild, unyielding and strong. It did not come from her, but it wrapped itself around her and Zara felt that somehow she'd come home as it settled deeply into her bones. She brushed against it with her mind once more, and then she saw him.

It wasn't his face or his form. Zara saw Alexei not as a physical being, but as everything he'd poured into the bond, everything he'd given, everything he'd risked to save her. His determination, his honesty, his self-sacrifice, and his loyalty. She felt his respect and his admiration, and his despair.

He had saved her, believing she would never forgive him. But Zara knew a thing or two about saving someone she wasn't sure wanted to be saved.

She opened her eyes. Alexei stood by the window, head bowed, waiting for her.

"Marry me?" she asked softly.

He straightened, the terror on his face melting suddenly into hope. "I've been a beast," he said.

"Maybe." She shrugged. "But I love you."

"Technically," he hedged, "I already married you. Without asking."

Zara walked towards him, smiling. "Idiot man," she said fondly. "I already asked you three times. How many times does it take to get you to say yes?"

Alexei wrapped his arms around her waist and rested his forehead against hers with a sigh that echoed deeply through them both. "Apparently, this many," he said, and kissed her at last. His arms were strong and gentle, his lips warm and soft, and Zara knew that no matter where she went, it would always be home as long as he was with her.

"You still haven't answered me," she said, a little breathlessly, as soon as they broke the kiss.

"Still angling for a yes?" he said into her hair.

"A girl likes to know her proposal has been accepted," she muttered. "Can't go around kissing just anyone."

"Before I say it"—Alexei pulled back, took her hand, and turned to face the window—"you should know what you're getting with me. I'm afraid you may find it a poor bargain."

"Oh yes, it's always been a great fear that I might end up marrying a man I loved."

"And I love you," he said seriously. "If you could not already tell from our bond, I love you so much more than I could even begin to tell you. But I have other burdens we should discuss."

He pointed out the window, at the land sprawled beneath them. Rivers, forests, mountains—the tapestry of Erath lay beyond the glass. "My people will be coming home. There is so much to rebuild. Mercenaries and thieves to drive out. Homes to re-establish. Governance to consider."

"Alexei," Zara admonished, "I know that Erath is your heart. It is not something I would wish to change about you."

"No," he corrected. He threaded his fingers through her hair and leaned in to kiss her deeply. "You are my heart now. More truly than you know. We are tied too deeply to be parted, and while that brings me joy, I also regret that you must feel my burden for my people. Wherever we go, whatever we do, that will always be a part of me."

"What do you mean, wherever we go?" Zara scoffed. "Where else would we go? Can you honestly think that I would deny you the chance to restore your land? I may be your heart, but this place is your blood and bone. You've been away too long and I can see the joy it gives you to be here and use your gifts freely. What kind of beast would I be if I condemned you to lose that again?"

"But Zara, you did not choose this of your own will," he insisted. "I would never tie you to such a difficult, uncertain future when you had no say in it. All you ever wanted was a home, and while this may be my home, it is nothing but a foreign land to you. I swore before I bonded with you that I would follow wherever you chose to go, and I will not break that promise."

Zara grasped the front of his shirt and yanked him closer. "Stop trying to be noble," she snapped. "How many times must I remind you, *I* proposed to *you*. And while I have your attention, you should know this: *you* are my home. No matter where we go, no matter what we choose to do, or where we choose to live. As long as you are with me, I am content." And this time, she wrapped her fingers in *his* hair and pulled him in for a kiss.

"Then it won't bother you if they try to make me king," Alexei said, when she let him breathe again.

"Ugh. Sounds ghastly. But I'm willing to suffer through it under one condition."

"Anything, my love. Except cats. I won't have a cat, even for you."

Zara shuddered. "Fair enough. I was going to say no enchanted castles."

"That, I think, goes without saying."

$\mathcal{A}$lexei set down the book and looked sternly at the three children in front of him. "I have examined your work," he said solemnly, "and I find that your memory for detail is lacking." The two girls' eyes widened, but the boy remained stoic. "Did I not explicitly tell you that after you finished the assignment, you were to have playtime *at once?*"

A chorus of giggles answered his admonishment, followed by a noisy exodus, with multiple whoops and a minor amount of shoving. Alexei grinned, and followed them out of the low wooden building into the warm summer afternoon.

The town had changed in the past year, almost past recognition. Thirty-seven houses had sprung up, along with the school, an inn, and a few fledgling businesses. Several gifts were now offered in trade: gardeners, artisans, even a stonemason. Gulver was no longer their only healer, which was fortunate, as he spent better than half his time helping to run the inn and courting its owner, Dalmar.

Stepping into the street, Alexei began the walk back to his home, waving goodbye to his students as he went. The three would be skilled enchanters one day, if they chose. There were twenty-two children that called this town home, and seventeen of them were now able to be instructed in their gifts. It was a blessing Alexei had not dared imagine when he first saw what Erath had become in his absence.

A roar behind him, together with the thunder of giant hooves pounding the earth, announced the arrival of Malichai, who pulled Loraleen back to a walk as they drew even with Alexei.

"And how are things in the valley?"

"Fair and getting better," Malichai said cheerfully. "The gardeners are working in shifts, and I don't doubt the task will be complete within the year."

"Good," Alexei muttered. "It can't be too soon." His first priority, after gathering a small group of refugees, had been sealing off Athven from the world. Three gardeners had volunteered to encourage the forest around the castle until it formed an impenetrable warren of thickets and thorns. Alexei hoped to deter the curious from exploring the valley until Athven's very existence faded into memory.

He had no desire for a passing traveller to discover Rowan Tremontaine's prison. When they left the castle at the last, the former prince of Andar had been promising to haunt their children's children's children, while Athven held his feet captive in the stone floor to prevent him from doing himself or anyone else an injury. His army had already fled in terror of the trembling earth underfoot, so he was utterly alone but for Athven herself as the door sealed itself behind Alexei and his friends, hopefully ensuring that Rowan would never again be free to do magic or murder until his heart had changed.

Perhaps it made him a monster, but Alexei rather thought that day would never come.

"Have you heard anything from Silvay, then?" Malichai asked with studied nonchalance, swinging out of the saddle to walk alongside his mare.

"She's in the north now, I believe," Alexei told him, suppressing a smile.

"Wilder said they were needed up there. Apparently there's a steady stream of refugees coming across the border and they're considering a settlement for the purpose of helping them."

"Aye," Malichai rumbled. "It would be a fine thing if someone familiar was there to greet them. Someone who can help find their homes, if they still exist. Feed them up and give them hope."

"We've a ways to go yet, but yes. That's the idea." Alexei shot a sideways glance at his friend. "Now that you've established the border patrol, are you getting anxious to be off home?" he asked innocently. "I'd be sorry to see you go, but King Hollin has got to be wondering what we've done with you."

"Oh, as to that," Malichai muttered, "I sent him a letter."

"A letter?" Alexei echoed in mock surprise.

"Telling him I wasn't coming back just yet. And to tell the truth I'm sure he was just as glad to be rid of me. I don't much fit in with the king's men, and I can be of more use here."

"Here, or in the north?" Alexei asked, and Malichai blushed.

"Oh, here and there," the warrior answered. "But I was thinking, perhaps, if you didn't need me for a few weeks, I might ride north, see if anyone is in need of a cook. There will be a lot of refugees to feed and Silvay has enough troubles without needing to worry about food."

"And you're sure that's the only reason? It wouldn't have anything to do with the twilight rides you two went on together before you left?"

"I don't know what you mean," Malichai mumbled into his beard. "And anyway, I wouldn't be gone for long. Just to check on things."

"Stay as long as you need," Alexei urged him, grinning now.

Malichai grunted and patted Loraleen. "I can't stay away forever," he protested weakly. "How am I to write the last verse of my epic if I don't know how it ends?"

"It ends," Zara said from just behind them, "when we go home to a warm fire, warm food, and good friends to share it with."

"That is the best kind of adventure," Alexei agreed, pausing to wrap his arm around his wife's waist and kiss her forehead. "I missed you. Did your father seem happy to be off on his travels again?"

"Happy enough, I suppose," she said with a sigh. "He said he's looking forward to settling down soon, but I'm not fool enough to expect it until he's too old to ride." She smiled fondly. "He'll be back though. Someday."

Alexei could feel her contentment as she thought of her father. Perhaps the lure of the road was too much for him, but she was right—he would be back. Zara no longer had to wonder whether her father loved her.

"How far did you get?" he asked curiously. "I could feel the bond stretch, but it didn't seem painful."

Zara shuddered. "It was awful. Only about half a day's ride, and I never want to do it again. It felt like being pulled in half."

"Sorry, my love." Alexei pulled her closer. "I'll go with you next time. I thought you might want a few hours alone with your father before he left."

"What I want," Zara grumbled, "is a few hours alone with my husband. Now that everyone is off on their separate pursuits, perhaps we could have a quiet evening at home?"

"And that's your idea of a happily ever after, is it?" Alexei asked, as their thatched stone cottage came into view.

"It can't be," Malichai argued, tugging at his beard. "What about daring deeds and lost crowns and claiming kingdoms? What of heroic battles and legendary journeys? The story can't end here."

"Yes," Zara said firmly, "I think it can," and shot him a pointed look.

Malichai chuckled. "Aye, very well. I'll be off. But I'll be back. I feel like the poem needs another verse or two. Perhaps I'll set it to music while I'm on the road..."

He walked away, deep in earnest conversation with Loraleen, who at least swiveled her ears politely so that she appeared to care. Perhaps she did.

"Sometimes it seems like we already have children," Zara muttered.

"It's only going to get worse," Alexei warned her, "once the voices demanding a coronation become more organized."

"Then we'll run away," she announced dramatically. "Maybe to Vidor. I hear I have relatives there."

"Yes," Alexei pointed out, tugging gently on the end of her braid, "but I don't think the coronation problem would go away in that case."

"Drat. So you're saying we might as well stay."

"I'm saying that this *is* a happy ending, epic poems, clamoring subjects and all."

"You're right," Zara admitted. She sighed and pulled him even closer, resting her head on his shoulder. "I am happy. Even if they decide to make you a king. Just promise me one thing."

"Anything, love."

"Promise me you won't let Malichai sing at your coronation."

"Done. In fact, I might lock him in the dungeon for the duration."

"We don't have a dungeon."

"Every king has a dungeon."

"You can't lock him up for singing."

"I can lock him up for threatening his sovereign's modesty."

"He's not Erathi, so he doesn't have to do what you say."

"He's on diplomatic loan. I can threaten him with exile. Sort of."

"Loraleen might eat you."

"Do you have any idea how much I love you?"

"Why don't you tell me again in case I've forgotten?"

Hand in hand, they stepped through the door of their home and closed it firmly behind them.

~

THANK YOU

Thank you for reading! I have loved writing this series and getting to know its characters and I hope you have enjoyed going on this journey with them. For more of their adventures, check out the rest of the series, or sign up for my newsletter to be the first to find out about new releases.

http://kenleydavidson.com

If you loved Shadow & Thorn and want to share it with other readers, please consider leaving an honest review on Amazon or Goodreads. Not only do I love getting to hear how my stories are impacting readers, but reviews are one of the best ways for you to help other book lovers discover the stories you enjoy. Taking even a moment to share a few words about your favorite books makes a huge difference to indie authors like me!

THE ANDARI CHRONICLES

The Andari Chronicles is a series of interconnected fairy tale retellings that evoke the glittering romance of the originals, while infusing them with grit, humor, and a cast of captivating new characters. *If you enjoyed the world of Andar, be sure to check out the other books in the series:*

Recommended Reading Order:

- *Traitor's Masque*
- *Goldheart*
- *Pirouette*
- *Shadow and Thorn*

http://kenleydavidson.com/books

ABOUT THE AUTHOR

Kenley Davidson is a story-lover, word-nerd and incurable introvert who is most likely to be found either writing or hiding somewhere with a book. A native Oregonian, Kenley now resides in Oklahoma, where she persists in remaining a devoted pluviophile. Addictions include coffee, roller coasters, more coffee, researching random facts, and reading the dictionary (which is way more fun than it sounds). A majority of her time is spent being mom to two kids and two dogs while inventing reasons not to do laundry (most of which seem to involve books).

kenleydavidson.com
kenley@kenleydavidson.com

ACKNOWLEDGMENTS

I set out on this journey with Alexei without actually knowing where he was going or how the journey might end. As I wrote the first few words, I wasn't sure I was all that excited about the book, but then I met Malichai, and Silvay, and Wilder and the rest of the cast and loved them all so much that I couldn't wait to see what was going to happen.

I definitely didn't know when I started Shadow and Thorn that it was going to be the last of the Andari Chronicles for a while. But somehow, as the story wrapped up, I realized that I was happy with where things ended and felt ready to move on and write in some of the other story worlds I've been dreaming about.

As I close this chapter of my journey as a writer, I can't possibly overemphasize how much I owe to the people who have been with me since the beginning.

Janie, you started as my beta reader and editor and somehow became that friend who reads my mind and knows the right answers to even my absurdest questions. I'm not sure how I survived the first thirty-odd years of my life without being able to text you about everything from writerly angst to plumbing disasters.

Chandra, you have helped my stories find their voice and helped me grow as a storyteller through your deep and thoughtful editing process and I am grateful for the dimension you have added to each book that has passed through your hands.

Tiffany, you are one of the biggest reasons I ever wrote more than one book. Even if you were the only reader I ever had, I would have written them for you.

Jeff, I could never, ever, have done any of this without you. These books are more yours than mine, from the chaos you endured while I was writing, to the incredible amounts of time and energy you put into publishing and marketing. Your talent and creativity are only slightly less amazing than your patience.

And to my readers, I would like to express my deepest gratitude. You have made it possible for me to pursue my dream of being a writer, and every day I am amazed that my stories are being read and enjoyed by so many people that I have never met. Your time and your encouragement are a gift, and I am continuously thankful that out of the all the books out there, you have chosen to read mine. Thank you so much for going on this journey with me!

Made in the USA
Monee, IL
15 January 2021